W9-CDK-670

The Unlocked Path

A Novel

JANIS ROBINSON DALY

Black Rose Writing | Texas

The author grants the final approval for this literary material.

First printing

This is a work of fiction. Names, characters, businesses, places, events, and incidents are either the products of the author's imagination or used in a fictitious manner. Any resemblance to actual persons, living or dead, or actual events is purely coincidental.

ISBN: 978-1-68513-014-5
PUBLISHED BY BLACK ROSE WRITING
www.blackrosewriting.com

Printed in the United States of America
Suggested Retail Price (SRP) $21.95

The Unlocked Path is printed in Sabon

*As a planet-friendly publisher, Black Rose Writing does its best to eliminate unnecessary waste to reduce paper usage and energy costs, while never compromising the reading experience. As a result, the final word count vs. page count may not meet common expectations.

Cover design by Author Bytes
Cover photo: Marj Warnick Photography
Author photo: Jessie Cassie

For my grandmother, Elizabeth Peirce Elliott Robinson.
I never knew your full story, so I created one.

PRAISE FOR *THE UNLOCKED PATH*

"Daly's careful crafting of each character, and her detailed, old-fashioned setting of each scene, encourages readers to root themselves in the moment, and as a result, they'll feel emotionally invested in the protagonist's every sadness and joy. Daly also develops Eliza's family ties and shows her passion for social change through her career choices and her opinions, which have a strong feminist element. It results in a work that effectively showcases the power of love, friendship, and faith—both in one's calling and in oneself—to create change in the world. An often riveting fictional testament of a doctor's life at the turn of the 20th century." – *Kirkus Reviews*

"A story of resilience, empowerment, and coming of age. Eliza's journey and discovery of "the why" echoes a story that we all carry in our hearts. Great historical fiction is timeless." - Eliza Lo Chin, MD, MPH, Executive Director, American Medical Women's Association and editor, *This Side of Doctoring: Reflections from Women in Medicine*

"It's a story of the ties of family, and friends and colleagues who become family. It's about love and loss, and the eternal struggle to live one's best life. Fans of literary medical historical fiction such as Abraham Verghese's *Cutting For Stone* or *The Girl In His Shadow* by Audrey Blake will enjoy the rich period detail and emotional impact of *The Unlocked Path*." - Tracey Enerson Wood, Author of International Best Seller, *The Engineer's Wife*

"In *The Unlocked Path*, Janis Robinson Daly movingly depicts the monumental struggles early women physicians faced, and the much-needed niche they filled." - Sally Cabot Gunning, Author of *The Widow's War* and *Painting the Light*.

"Eliza's personal and professional journey is both unique and yet consistent with the tenor of the times. Daly's care in telling a story bursting with historical detail is evident in every page." - Juliette Fay, *USA Today* best-selling author of *The Tumbling Turner Sisters*

"Eliza Edwards chooses an unconventional path by possessing an unwavering belief in herself. She decides that to succeed, she must change the system. Eliza will win you over with her quiet strength and kind heart." - Kerry Chaput, Amazon Best-Selling Author of *Daughter of the King*

The
Unlocked
Path

PART ONE

"[The] determination which has brought me to your country against the combined opposition of my friends and caste ought to go a long way towards helping me to carry out the purpose for which I came, i.e., is to render to my poor suffering countrywomen the true medical aid they so sadly stand in need of and which they would rather die than accept at the hands of a male physician. The voice of humanity is with me, and I must not fail. My soul is moved to help the many who cannot help themselves."

–Anandibai Gopal Joshi,
Graduate of the Woman's Medical College of Pennsylvania.

CHAPTER ONE

May 1897

Blackened toast crumbs clung to the soft yellow egg curds. Four white plates dissolved into the white tablecloth, a blur of sameness. Eliza Edwards reached for the plate next to her spot at the end of the table, always to her mother's left.

"Miss Eliza!!!"

She turned toward the hallway, the call of her name piercing her ears with an urgency not often heard from Molly. Dropping the plate, a crust bounced onto the carpet. As she stooped to retrieve the nibbled toast edge, again, this time a screech.

"It's Mrs. Maria. Please, hurry."

Eliza flew up the staircase, her auburn hair streaming behind her. As she sprinted down the hallway, a lump of briny gruel traveled up her throat. Preoccupied with her own concerns over the past few weeks, she had disregarded traces of Aunt Maria's increasing distress. Now, with Molly sounding an alarm, how could Eliza help?

Curtains drawn tight blocked fresh air from circulating life into the bedroom. Eliza bent over her aunt's listless figure; rank odors of an unbathed body seeped through the sheets. On the nightstand, a bottle of digitalis tablets lay empty. Two ovals remained on the table, white with their false innocence, disguising their potency. Maria, translucent like a crescent moon, curled on her side, clutching a pillow to her chest. Shallow, intermittent breaths rattled with a faint rasp. Eliza picked up a pale, wilted wrist. Maria's stream of life pulsed feeble and slow while Eliza's throbbed in her ears and across her temple. "Aunt Maria, what have you done?"

Maria lifted her arm in a ballet dancer's flowing arc to Eliza's face. With the back of her hand, she brushed Eliza's cheek before the weightless arm fell to the bed. Molly tapped Eliza's shoulder, "She was singing to William when I came for her tray. Fifteen years since he went to Our Lord. This is the first time she's said his name. Gone upstairs, she is."

Eliza pushed Molly away, hissing, "You are never to talk like that. Aunt Maria has her troubles, but we always take care of her. Fetch Dr. Wilcox. Tell him it's an emergency."

"No," Maria said, her voice faltering. "Those men don't understand."

Eliza placed the heels of her hands on the windowpanes and thrust the window up with a bang. Turning to the bureau, she moved Maria's journals aside to reach the ewer. A torn page fluttered to the floor.

Sweet William,
Your stem never rooted.
Your cheeks never bloomed rosy petals,
Your time too short in my garden.

A mother's anguish spilled over the paper. Eliza slid the poetic lines into the bureau drawer before picking up the ewer. She poured perfumed water over a flannel. Twisting the cloth above the ripples, she shook the excess droplets and returned to her aunt's side. First, she wiped Maria's forehead, pushing away the gray strands which crept across Maria's head too early. From wrist to underarm, she wiped Maria's bony limb while Maria remained motionless. Did she view another scene? Perhaps Mary Cassatt's latest painting? A mother caressing her child with cleansing love.

A sudden gasp, then quiet. Eliza's fingers encircled Maria's wrist again. Tears welled and flowed onto her aunt's limp body.

The gap between life and death narrowed. In an instant, Maria slipped away while Eliza stood holding a lavender-scented cloth. A moist flannel held no curative powers. Eliza possessed none either.

•　　•　　•

The white marble obelisk, with PEARSON etched into the footed base, marked the family plot in Laurel Hill Cemetery in Philadelphia's northern corner. Eliza's grandfather chose it high on the hill facing Race Street. When her grandmother strolled to the end of their street, she could look to the graves of her three infants, their names listed forevermore on the gravestone, Lindsay, Adeline, and Daniel. Other Pearsons' and Edwards' names headed the obelisk's four sides. Soon, a stonecutter would engrave the marker with Maria Pearson Edwards, Wife and Mother with the years 1852-1897. Eliza suggested they add an inscription, Your time in our garden was too short.

The undertakers and Eliza's brothers, Albie and Freddy, lowered Maria's casket into the deep opening. Its oak edges scraped against the one which held her husband below and the smaller one at her feet. The emptiness of Maria's life vanished. You're whole again, Aunt Maria, thought Eliza.

Amidst the dark dresses and suits surrounding the gravesite, a glint of gold shone at the throat of Eliza's mother. An ivory cameo, edged in filigree, refracted the sun's rays. The sheen from the brooch followed the attendants' gazes into the hole. Stem by stem, Eliza, her mother, aunts, and Molly released bouquets of lilies into the grave. The darkness of farewell clumps of soil and sod slowly covered the light of the petals.

• • •

Eliza's home returned to its quiet routine. After the excitement of her graduation from the Agnes Irwin School for Girls two weeks ago, and then the desolation of Aunt Maria's funeral, her days melded into endless boredom. As she did most afternoons, she wandered into her grandfather's library, searching for a different book to fill the hours until dinner. Pausing in front of one shelf, she espied a thick volume. High above the reach of her five-feet-two-inches, the tome stood beyond her line of sight. As she stretched on her tiptoes and grabbed the spine of the book, Molly poked her head through the library's doorway.

"Miss Eliza, there's a letter for you. I left it on the sideboard."

Startled by Molly's announcement–Eliza rarely received mail–she dropped the thousand-page book, wincing as the volume crushed her stockinged big toe. Not bothering to put on her shoes, she hop-limped to the foyer. A pile of letters lay on a gleaming mahogany sideboard. Separate from the stack, a square linen envelope waited, propped against a crystal vase. Uppercase curling E's and a P were centered above the address. In her eighteen years, the only mail for Eliza came from her Aunt Florence. This envelope didn't show Boston in the upper left corner, nor her aunt's familiar flowing script.

Eliza pulled open the sideboard's drawer to retrieve an oak letter opener steeped in family history. Over time, it freed many messages from their envelopes, but none that could be as life-defining as this one.

Eliza Pearson Edwards.

Her name stared up at her. Black ink bled into the creamy linen. An imprint. A meaning of the Pearson and Edwards names intertwined into a future.

The opener slipped from her moist hand, delaying a few more seconds until she could read the words. Did she need to? She knew what they would say. She pressed her palms down on her skirt, its cotton absorbing their sweat like Molly's dish towel. A scroll border peeked out of the envelope as she slit it open. She pulled out a card.

Philadelphia Assembly, 1897
The Favor of Miss Edwards'
Company is requested for the Season.

Three lines. Nothing else. Everyone who was anyone in Philadelphia knew what this invitation meant. Eliza Pearson Edwards would make her debut in November at Philadelphia's Charity Ball. The city's elite had not forgotten, nor dismissed, Eliza's family. Most of the selected women hailed from notable families whose lineage dominated Philadelphia's Blue Book. Their parents engaged in civic, societal, and professional endeavors. Fathers who led banks, business establishments, courts, and government. Mothers who attended teas, lectures, and luncheons.

She had neither.

But now, in her palm, she held proof of acceptance, a key to unlock her future. Yet questions surfaced. Once Eliza inserted and turned that key, would she feel the decisive mesh of metal cogs aligning with certainty and direction? Or would the key jam, stranding her at an entranceway of unknown possibilities?

CHAPTER TWO

Eliza returned to the library with the invitation tucked into her yellow print cotton skirt pocket. She lowered herself into a wingback chair and placed her afflicted foot upon her knee. With slow, rhythmic pressure, she kneaded the aching toe back to life. Next to her, the book she dropped splayed across the Persian rug, revealing pages of dense text in English and Latin, interrupted with illustrations in shades of gray, red, and blue. Eliza gazed down at the drawings. Rivers marked boundaries and roads crisscrossed a primitive country. Each picture detailed landscapes begging for bold, inquisitive pioneers to study and conquer them.

Despite hovering on the upper shelf for years, she never opened *Gray's Anatomy*. Eliza read three times and more the other abandoned choices strewn across her grandfather's desk: Dumas, Dickens, Twain, Brontë. One of her favorite authors, Jules Verne, carried her to far-away destinations. She sank twenty-thousand leagues into the sea, bored deep into the center of the earth, and flew high into the skies for an around-the-world-trip. During those rousing voyages, she traveled to alternative worlds. She reveled in these remarkable tales, so much more than the Brothers Grimm stories her mother read aloud to her as a child. Eliza later learned she re-cast the tales in her own words to ensure Eliza heard the preferred endings scripted for heroines in fairy tales, and in Philadelphian homes: love, marriage, and happily ever-after.

From the front parlor, Eliza's mother called out, "Is that the mail? Can you bring it in, please?"

On a worn, green, velvet divan, Laura Pearson Edwards sat erect, holding a thin bamboo reed paintbrush in her right hand. The bristles glistened with a drop of gold. She was applying the final brushstroke to a fine bone china tea saucer. Her eyes focused on the saucer's rim, deepening the crow's feet at their corners.

Eliza passed the other mail pieces over to her mother.

"Is that all of it?" Laura asked. For the past month, Eliza watched her rifle through the piles on the sideboard, searching for square linen envelopes like the one buried in the folds of Eliza's skirt. Eliza considered keeping it hidden. Producing the evidence would all but seal her fate.

The wrinkles at her mother's eyes matched the creases around her lips as they settled into a frown of disappointment and worry. She knew when those lines first crept onto her mother's face: eighteen years earlier when she carried Eliza in her womb. A pregnancy, however, was not the source of her mother's dismay. Pregnancies carried joy and hope, especially for a woman like Laura, mother to two sons and at thirty-two-years old, possibly the last chance to bear a daughter. The sadness and despair arrived with a telegram: *Albert has died. Sincere condolences. More to follow.* An ogre entered the Edwards' family, cloaked in black and carrying a scythe to slice their hearts and rend their souls.

As a young child, Eliza would steal into her mother's room and shift the brittle envelope, yellowed and water stained with drops of grief, from its spot in front of a silver frame. She stroked the glass over the photo. Her fingertip traced a balding head and ran down a cheek, over bushy whiskers and a mustache which tried to distract from thinning strands on top. She moved to the man's nose, running one finger down his and another along her own. Each finger trail sloped along a similar route, straight to a button end. The photo's sepia tone denied the color of his eyes. Eliza imagined they stared at her own blue ones in a mirror image. Being careful not to disturb the frame, she spoke to the man she had never known. The husband who succumbed to a weak heart when his wife was five months pregnant with their daughter. In a whisper as soft as rose petals beginning to wilt, Eliza lamented, *Papa. Why didn't you want to be my Papa?*

Eliza handed her mother the linen envelope.

"This came for me," she said

Laura beamed as a light sigh escaped from her lips.

Eliza watched the sparkle of radiance return to her mother's countenance. The card turned hope into possibilities. Laura rose from her seat. She reached for her daughter and pushed aside Eliza's auburn wisps, fallen from her haphazard bun.

"Wonderful news!" Laura exclaimed. "I'm thrilled for you. There's so much to plan. How exciting!"

"I guess," Eliza replied.

Laura took a step back, "You guess? This invitation is an honor. Girls across Philadelphia dream of receiving this envelope. You must write your acceptance right away. You can use your grandfather's pen and my stationery. But practice your reply first. Your penmanship must be perfect and your wording precise."

Breathless in her excitement, she paused. "We'll have a special dinner. Would you like a strawberry meringue? I'll speak to Molly. Shall we have a glass of sherry with dessert? We've much to celebrate."

Unfolded from Laura's embrace, Eliza reflected a moment on her mother's traditional path, which she expected Eliza would follow. A debut followed by marriage to a gentleman from a prominent Philadelphia family. A union based on equal values of becoming a couple and sharing their love with little souls, tiny dependent, and ready to return unfailing love. Laura and Albert Edwards' story began with dreams of their happily ever after. Eliza masked her hesitation. An alternative, if there was any, would require time, consideration, and advice to ensure a triumph over defying her mother.

• • •

Before posting her reply, Eliza circled back to the library. She picked up *Gray's Anatomy*, pulled over the footstool, and returned it to the empty spot on the shelf. From a wooden box on the desk, she pulled a sheet of plain notepaper. One person would understand her dilemma: Fearless Florence.

Florence Pearson shared her bedroom with Eliza until she was thirty-two, treating her more like a younger sister than a niece. Together, they knit a closeness despite the twenty years between them, and which remained strong after Florence's move to Boston.

> *Dear Aunt Florence,*
>
> *Believe it or not, I have news. I will be Presented in November. As I've written before, I've longed for a sign of what my future may hold. This invitation could be the key. Mother can quit fretting they would forget me. She's excited to start the planning. From what I've heard, a lot goes into the preparations: selecting and fitting my dress, shoes, and gloves; considering whom may be the best choice as my escort; the guest list and menu for the pre-ball tea. There's more: practicing for the receiving line; determining my hairstyle and jewelry. It seems like a big bother for one party.*

Eliza lifted the pen from the paper. She looked out to the surrounding shelves. Her eyes and mind wandered up the walls and along the book spines.

> *As I write from the library desk, I see rows of leather bindings and handmade volumes you bound from the clippings about Elizabeth Cady Stanton, Lucy Stone, and Susan B. Anthony.*

(They're getting thicker as I continue to add to your columns.) From Grandfather's legal references, to his collections of the classics, to the beautiful artwork of James Audubon, and his copy of Gray's Anatomy, I am inspired by this array of characters, places, and ideas! Do you remember those cozy nights when we would gather around his feet to hear the adventures and trials of Ali Baba, Huckleberry Finn, and my favorite, Captain Nemo? A multitude of paths connect and diverge across those pages. The immensity of it all makes me wonder.

I can ask you these questions. While Aunt Josephine and Aunt Estelle seem to enjoy their work, I think if their circumstances were different, they would have followed Mother and Aunt Maria into matrimony and family life. They want the same for me.

Oh, poor Aunt Maria! I'm so sad she's gone. Yet, at the same time, I'm happy for her. Is that disrespectful? She's finally with Uncle Andrew and baby William. She's fulfilled. And that makes me sad again. To think without her husband and son, she felt she had nothing else in her life.

While I thought I wanted the same, perhaps what I want is something strange, yet familiar, something more than losing my name and becoming someone's wife. Yet, Mother and Aunt Maria lost their husbands. That could happen to any of us. Mother, however, has me and Albie and Freddy. But Maria didn't, so what else was there for her?

I yearn thinking shouldn't there be more in a woman's life?
And how will I ever tell my mother?
Your loving niece,
Eliza

• • •

The raised windows pulled in the spring air, light and dry before the humidity at the height of a Philadelphia summer descended. Fragrant lilac blossoms beckoned Eliza outside where an explosion of conical lavender and white clusters framed a courtyard circle. The gentle breeze loosened a few of the miniature petals, snowing their hint of spring's waning freshness onto the flagstone patio.

She tucked the latest issue of *Harper's Bazaar* into the crook of her arm and took it outside to read. Ten tiers of lace-edged flounce with three more above the waist on a Paris midsummer gown graced the cover. More bows and frills covered the model's neck and hat. Whipped white ruffles from head to toe. All Eliza could envision was a tiered wedding cake, frosted innocence waiting to be served. She pulled the Assembly's invitation from her pocket and inserted it in between the magazine's pages. *Please write back soon, Aunt Florence.*

CHAPTER THREE

Snatches of her mother's voice floated out the window. Facing away from the house, Eliza kept her head lowered, pretending the short story in *Harper's* about a schoolmarm in Wyoming held her interest. She forced her eyes wide open in case it helped clear her ears to catch the conversation between her mother and Molly from inside the kitchen.

"You'll need to double up on your batches of gingersnaps," said Laura. "No doubt our calendar will fill up quickly with gentleman callers for afternoon tea after Eliza's debut."

"Yes, ma'am. She is a beauty. That hair of hers is the envy of any Irish lass who missed the red-gold touch when the Good Lord blessed her head."

Eliza shut her ears. She knew the line of other remarks which would fall from her mother's lips. Comments about suitors and marriage. A means for Eliza to escape a household of maiden aunts and their subtle suggestions Eliza follow them into a career. Eliza deserved happier days, her mother would say.

By six o'clock, Estelle, who was always later than Josephine to arrive home, swept into the dining room, dropping her battered leather satchel next to her empty chair.

"Good, you aren't too late. We've been waiting the entire afternoon," said Laura.

"Goodness, what for?"

"Eliza received mail," Laura said.

Her mother, Aunt Estelle, and Aunt Josephine crept forward in their chairs. An ice cube shed another layer as it sank further into a cut-crystal glass and clinked against the side. Eliza placed her spoon across the bowl of creamy asparagus soup and withdrew the envelope from her pocket. Once spoken aloud, Eliza couldn't capture the words on the invitation and stuff them back in.

She tugged at her dress cuffs, pulling the lace edges down tight to her wrist. Standing up, she locked her arms ramrod straight out from the puffed caps of her shoulders. She focused her eyes on her quivering fingers, commanding them to still. Drawing upon school elocution lessons, she read the card. "From the Philadelphia Assembly. The Favor of Miss Edwards' Company is requested for the Season."

Josephine clapped her hands into a tight squeeze. Estelle grinned, her usual solemn face lightened. Eliza's aunts knew how her empty days languished since graduation.

"Our Eliza. To be presented. This is a great honor," said Josephine, drawing both hands to her heart.

"The Judge and your grandmother would be pleased, dear," Estelle added.

"Have you sent your response?" asked Josephine.

Her mother answered for her. "Yes, in this afternoon's post. I checked her handwriting and made sure she used the formal reply protocol. But there's much planning needed before November."

Josephine held her palms up and out to her sister. "We're here to help. Most of the Trustee members' wives are well versed and practiced in the preparations. Marion Lippincott made her presentation last year. I'd be happy to speak with her mother."

Josephine, the eldest Pearson daughter, served as the sole woman on the Board of Trustees for the Naval Asylum and Woman's Medical College of Pennsylvania. Both institutions offered her a chance to socialize with the Trustees' wives to keep abreast of current news and happenings of Philadelphia's inner circles. As Secretary for the College's Board, Josephine assumed the position vacated by her father, Judge William Pearson, one of the school's founders.

"How clever to think of Mrs. Lippincott," Laura said. "We'll appreciate her advice."

"That's fine. But I'll manage the appointments to keep us on schedule," announced Estelle. Estelle, a stenographer in the Philadelphia courts, honed her organization skills every day. She thrived on maintaining schedules and details, at work and at home.

"You're both so kind." Laura turned to Eliza, "Few girls have aunts to help them. I think we should say grace again."

Laura, Josephine, and Estelle. Three Pearson women, impatient to see Eliza dressed like the model from *Harper's Bazaar*, ready to be served.

• • •

Ten days later, Eliza answered a rap at the front door. The telegraph delivery boy stood on the stoop asking for Miss Eliza Edwards. Two pieces of correspondence within two weeks and one with the importance worthy of a telegram. She signed the boy's pad and pulled the letter opener from its safe spot in the sideboard drawer. She rubbed her thumb over the etching in the oak handle, recalling her grandfather's deep voice as he recounted the opener's history.

William Pearson presided at Philadelphia's Court of Common Pleas for forty years. Before his judgeship, the Anti-Slavery Society of Philadelphia requested his defense services in nearly every fugitive-slave case brought to trial before the War Between the States. Despite criticism of his work from citizens and fellow lawyers alike, he accepted the cases and secured Not Guilty verdicts for most.

Eliza looked through the double-French doors into the library. Years ago, she, her brothers, Albie and Freddy, and Aunt Florence begged the Judge to re-tell the story of his most high-profile case, that of Daniel Dangerfield, a runaway slave. Harkening back to his days before the bench, his baritone voice began the tale with Dangerfield's escape, running north from Virginia through woods in the night and hiding in bushes during daytime.

The machinations of the laws and their grandfather's defense tactics fascinated her brother, Albie. Eliza and Freddy preferred the high adventure of Dangerfield on the run. They would jump from sitting on the floor and race through the library, ducking behind chairs and the desk. Florence would settle them down and guide her father's tale back to other details to make sure eight-year-old Eliza also heard about Lucretia Mott, the quiet woman from the Female Anti-Slavery Society. Over the three days of the trial, Mrs. Mott attended every hour, including the night William Pearson's arguments ran into the early morning hours. She sat stoic in the gallery, listening for the words of justice. Her commitment, Florence told Eliza, marked the depths of her belief in decency and equality for all citizens of their grand country, Negroes and women included.

To close the story, the Judge would rise from his wingback chair and cross to his desk. Raising the glass plate which covered the desktop, he picked up a scrap of brown paper preserved beneath the glass. Despite winning a Not Guilty verdict, rumors of white kidnappers planning to grab Dangerfield reached his protectors. They sent him north to Canada through the Underground Railroad. Several months later, a brown-paper parcel arrived at Judge Pearson's office containing a hand-carved oak letter opener. Etched deep into the wood handle, triangular marks spread outward in each direction with one longer point extending downward on to the blade. Inside the wrapping paper, scrawled in childish lettering, a note read:

May Our Lord always help you guide others to freedom—D

With that, the Judge ushered the children off to bed with a message that embedded itself in Eliza's heart. Six years after the last time she heard her grandfather tell the Dangerfield story, Eliza could recite his words, *Those that have, and can, must care for the defenseless and the powerless, for they have no one else. Find the way to guide yourself and others toward a self-defined freedom.*

With the weight of its history in her hand, Eliza slid the opener's blade under the flap of the telegram envelope and sliced it open. Pulling the sheath out, she scanned down to the FROM line. Florence Pearson.

Received your letter. Home in three weeks. There is more.

CHAPTER FOUR

June 1897

There is more.

Those three words waged a continual debate in Eliza's mind over the next two weeks. More choices? What choices? How to choose? She did not raise those questions to her mother. Laura's answer would be a simple one, "There's nothing to think about."

The heavy front door swung open with a bang. No clang of the polished lion's head against the dense metal knocker. No polite rap on the teak panels. The interior glass knob fit snug into a slight indent in the wall.

Eliza heard the commotion in the foyer. She jumped from the kitchen stool, upsetting the bowl in her lap. Spirals of pear parings dropped to the floor. Florence was early! *How wonderful*, she thought, glad she'd skipped accompanying her mother to the market. She may have the chance to speak with Florence in private before dinner.

Instead, sonorous voices in unison announced, "Ladies of 1710 Race Street. Your men are home."

Eliza's brothers descended on the house a few times each year like a boisterous gang of street urchins. Pushing through the swinging door, Eliza quick-stepped down the hallway, calling out, "I thought you were Florence. Why didn't you tell us you'd be home? How long are you staying?"

Albie stretched above his head and opened his arms to welcome his sister. "Lizzy, please. Do you always have to launch your bevy of questions the minute we step over the threshold?"

Eliza punched his upper arm, feeling the flex of his toned muscles from hours of smashing rubber balls across nets to claim trophies and ribbons for the University of Pennsylvania.

"Sorry. I'll scale down my assault," she said with a sly wink, never intending to cease her teasing.

Stepping back from Albie, she assessed her other brother. "Look at you, Fred! When did you start with the mustache? Just like the picture of father. So handsome."

Eliza missed her brothers. For the past three years, they attended the University across the Schuylkill River. To Eliza, the river seemed wider than the Atlantic Ocean to the east, a chasm keeping her from the men in her life. She loved the air of levity which accompanied them home. They brought carpet bags packed with stories and told them with a twinkle in their eyes. Many of the tales carried enough absurdity to make her question their truth. Eliza didn't care. She hung on their words, enthused to hear about their classes, their friends, and the antics at Sigma Chi—or at least the ones they would share with her.

Soon they would finish Penn. Albie would no doubt pass the bar exam this summer. He would enter the Edwards Wool Company as junior counsel and bring an Edwards back into the executive offices after eighteen years. Freddy had one more year left, with expectations to join his brother at the company. Once again, Edwards men would reign in Philadelphia's business circles.

Molly emerged from the kitchen, brushing flour from her hands, snowflake motes falling onto her black skirt. "Boys! Do you always have to crash in like the devil's spawn? Save me, Mary, Mother of God. One of these days that knob is gonna bust through the wall!"

"But you won't tell Mother it was us. Right, Molly girl?" Freddy said.

They dropped their bags to the worn runner with a soft thud and swooped Molly into a bear hug. Both at five-feet-nine-inches, they exchanged a matched set of grins in the space above the flames of red curls which escaped from her white cap.

Molly squirmed from their embrace to continue her scolding, "And no warning."

Freddy rolled his head, looking to the ceiling. "Ah…right. Albie, I thought you sent word around last week?"

"I've been up to my eyeballs in review study. When would I have contacted Mother? It's the least you could have done. You finished your exams days ago," said Albie.

"Oh never mind, you two. You're here now," Molly interjected to settle the usual protracted blame and counter-blame between the brothers.

"What brings Aunt Florence home again so soon?" asked Freddy. "Did we miss a birthday? Mother will skin us if we forgot one. Damnit, is it Mother's fiftieth?"

"Language." Molly shook her finger in Albie's face. "I've still got the bar of soap. Don't think you're too old."

Albie held his hands up, surrendering to the small, yet mighty maid.

"No birthdays this month," continued Molly. "But it wouldn't hurt if you would write them down. The good Lord did not put me on this earth to be your personal secretary. Can't say why Florence is back. She replied to Eliza's news and mentioned she'd be home."

Albie straightened and cocked his head to the right. "Eliza, why's Florence coming?"

"Molly, the pears are ready for your pastry, and I think the apples are stewed. Shouldn't you go check on them?" Eliza said.

Molly left them, muttering loud enough for Eliza and her brothers to hear.

"I know when my apples are stewed. Jaysus, now I've got to see to the rooms. We'll be full up again. Eliza will have to sleep with Mrs. Edwards. Florence in with Josephine. I haven't cleaned out Missus Maria's room. These feckin' eejits never plan or consider the extra work."

Eliza smirked, catching the last utterance as Molly pushed through to the kitchen. When Molly muttered, her brogue became thicker, signaling to steer clear.

"Let's go sit. I'll tell you my news before Mother gets back from the market."

They headed to the front parlor. Their mother's paints and china pieces occupied the circular pedestal table, the yellowed lace tablecloth draped over them kept the dust at bay. Vases on every surface held bouquets of irises and final blooms of the lilacs. Their fragrances overpowered the otherwise stuffy room.

Freddy unlatched their grandfather's liquor cabinet. A lonely bottle of sherry stood on the top shelf like a solitary sentry. Seeing him shake his head, Eliza feared her brothers' visit would be another short one. How many times had they described the allure of their Sigma Chi fraternity house? Hand-rolled cigars which had sailed north from the mystery island of Cuba sent acrid smoke floating above their heads and settled into crew sweaters. A pour of whiskey at any hour. Evenings of lively debates on economics, law, literature, and sports. Time spent with a younger sister, mother, and maiden aunts was a doomed competition. Eliza would never win their complete attention.

Albie rolled his blood-shot eyes, looking at the velveteen divan obscured by a mass of flora and feathers latched onto multiple hats. Long slim gloves and beaded reticules of varying sizes covered the single full-length spot to nap. "Geez, it looks like you all cleaned out Wanamaker's again. Why do you need all these trappings?"

He gathered the heap of femininity into piles and deposited them on the floor, nudging them with his toe toward a darkened corner beneath the divan. With a cleared landing, Albie collapsed and pulled a crocheted afghan over his slight frame. Their grandmother's favorite parlor armchair covered in a dusty rose damask with matching footstool would suffice for Freddy. He settled in, slouched down, his lanky limbs askew, and rested his feet on the stool.

"All right, go ahead, Eliza. Spill it before Albie passes out," said Freddy.

Perched on the sliver of space Albie left for her on the divan, Eliza glanced over to ensure all four eyelids remained open. "I received my debut invitation," she said.

Albie attempted a low whistle from his dry mouth, "Whew," he sputtered. "Maybe Mother can relax now."

"Yes. Well, perhaps not. I'm not sure I want to." Eliza nibbled on a hangnail which had irked her all day. She stopped. Her hesitation came from an adult decision to consider her future. No need to sound like a petulant child, stamping her foot and exclaiming, *I don't want to!*

"I mean, I need to discuss some ideas with Florence. Wearing a fancy gown, waltzing through a ballroom in front of suitors, a dance card dangling from my wrist, feels..."

The right word escaped her. Pointless? Empty? Phony? Like a horse auction, gussied up with her mane braided with ribbons, being paraded around a ring? She didn't know how to fill in the blank, nor did she have an alternative. She lived in limbo, waiting for Florence to pull her out of a world of quandary.

"Look, sis. You're pretty smart for a girl," Freddy winked. "If you want to go to one of those girl colleges or something, you'd do fine."

"For a girl?" She glowered at him. "My grades were always two or three spots earlier than yours in the alphabet chain, Fredrick."

Freddy slunk deeper into the damask.

"The problem is, I don't think Mother will pay for more years of reading Dickinson and writing Revolutionary War essays when the intent of those colleges is to help women find a husband. The debut accomplishes the same goal in less time. I need a stronger reason to continue my schooling. I want to learn. I want to learn more, but I've no idea what it might be."

Albie lifted his head from the puddle of drool which wet the velveteen beneath his cheek. "Florence is your best choice to counsel. Can we talk later, after you've spoken with her? I've got to sober up before Mother gets home."

Men. They knew how to argue and win legal cases and balance asset sheets. But ask them to consider hard questions about a woman's desires, and you might as well talk to a statue in Monument Square. Albie and Freddy's snores came quick, leaving Eliza lost in a reverie of the discussion she should present to Florence.

Molly poked her head into the parlor, "Shall we set the table with your mother's china?"

"Yes, absolutely. We'll need the extra place settings," said Eliza, pleased to have a diversion from her meandering thoughts and her brothers' useless comments.

Laura's dinnerware was a novelty in Philadelphia, a port city, yet with few trappings of the sea. Her father had commissioned an intricate shell pattern. Hand-painted, spring green porcelain pieces swirled in a design of pink coral, trimmed with gold scalloped edges. The handles of cups and bowls curved into arched fishes. Twenty-four place settings with matching serving ware, imported from Coalport pottery in England, graced the shelves of two china cabinets. Eliza stood back to survey the setting as Molly laid the last bread and butter plate on the white linen. A marvelous treat. Albie, Freddy, and Florence home on the same night without the pall of Maria's funeral hanging over them.

Fearless Florence, as Eliza and her brothers called her in private, inspired Eliza to dream beyond a life at Race Street, Philadelphia. With gumption and a valise packed with paint brushes, Florence headed to Boston to take an art teacher position at Boston's settlement houses. There, the world came to Florence.

In her letters to Eliza, she revealed the thrill of working with children from Lebanon, Syria, Hungary, and Romania. With every stroke across a canvas, they learned from her, and she from them.

"It's beautiful, don't you think?" said Eliza.

Molly nodded, "Yes, 'tis lovely."

"I'll cut roses for the centerpiece. I lack Florence's artistic flair for arranging, but I'll try. Which vase shall we use?"

"The Rose Medallion is her favorite. A fine, grand dinner table. And it will all be yours someday soon."

"Don't start packing it up yet, Molly."

• • •

Over the clank of tableware, Albie recounted another dramatic night at Sigma Chi with their fraternity brother, Tom Wright. "The common area flickered from a few candles. Before Tom started the next chapter, he ran back to his room and returned with an old black cape. I swear he stole it from his granny's closet. Anyway, he tied it around his neck and pulled the sides close. His eyes glowed a wolfish red. He picked up the book and snarled, 'No man knows till he experiences it, what it is like to feel...'"

"'...his own lifeblood drawn away into the woman he loves.' I love that passage from Mr. Stoker's fiendish new novel," Florence said in her own matching low tone.

The clinking of silverware stopped as everyone turned to the petite figure framed in the doorway. Dressed in a smart navy suit, splashes of paint dotted her skirt. Train soot clung in the folds of its pleats. Her long dark blonde braid hung halfway down her back, fraying at the edges. Her lips parted into a gentle grin, colored with a soft tinge of red. Fearless Florence wore lipstick. Her hazel-green eyes matched the mirth of her smile. Eliza jumped from her chair, "Aunt Florence! I thought Count Dracula was coming for us!"

"Albie's a fine storyteller, but it's just a story."

Eliza fell into her aunt's waiting arms. Her mother and aunts arose to receive their sister with a kiss on her cheek. Josephine pushed her youngest sister back two steps for a full critique. "You are a sight. Did you come straight from work? Look at your skirt. Did those urchins use it as a canvas? You couldn't have worn clean clothes for traveling?"

"The splotches brighten it up. Adds character," Eliza piped up. "Those moppets must adore painting with you."

Who wouldn't love classes with Miss Pearson? A free-spirited woman willing to sit cross-legged amongst her pupils and splatter paint across canvases. Eliza envied those children and the time they spent with her aunt.

Laura gestured to her sons, "Albert. Fred. A kiss for your aunt?"

"Aunt Florence, you stole my thunder. But I forgive you. Isn't that a brilliant line? Stoker is a genius. We've read from *Dracula* every night since Tom bought it a few weeks ago," Albie said as he picked up his aunt's hand for a formal peck. Freddy copied his brother.

"Yes, my roommates and I at the boarding house have done the same. A chapter or two before bedtime leads to some harrowing nightmares!" said Florence, a twitch in her eye.

Estelle carried a steaming plate in from the kitchen. "Molly kept your dinner warm. And, yes, we saved the crispy end piece of the pork roast for you. All right. Everyone sit-down. Enough with your storytelling, Albert. Now that Florence is here, we should turn to more important matters. Eliza needs an escort for her Presentation."

Aunt Estelle, always down to business, thought Eliza. Her brothers turned to her. Albie arched an eyebrow. Freddy kicked her shin under the table. Eliza shook her head. Not yet.

For the next half hour, Albie and Freddy presented pros and cons of their classmates as potential escorts. One by one, Josephine, Estelle, and Laura overruled each choice.

"Too dense."

"That paunch isn't from inactivity at his age, must be a drinker."

"Weren't there rumors his father had shady financial deals?"

"Too short."

"I pass the O'Mearas every Sunday going to St. Paul's. The Papists never miss a Mass."

"His sister was in the family way too soon after her hasty wedding."

Florence reserved comment. Eliza dared not add any reaction. What could she put forth? Her mind swam with unformed reasons and answers, unprepared for tonight's discussion. There was no escape from the inevitable, trapped like a mouse in a cat's claws. Why wasn't Fearless Florence speaking up? She must have some thoughts. She always had an opinion. Eliza hoped Florence would intervene soon.

After another fifteen minutes of endless point, counterpoint, Albie stood from his chair. "This is absurd. This isn't the Queen's coronation, it's a debut. I've been to enough of them. Everyone forgets them within days."

"Albie's right. We need not decide tonight, and if not..." Eliza said.

"If not?" Laura's voice rose with the color in her cheeks. "If not, what Eliza? You need an escort, or you cannot attend. You must attend. Your future to escape from life with a bunch of old maids depends on it."

The room quieted. Josephine, the oldest old maid, banged the dishes into a stack and left for the kitchen. Freddy cleared his throat. "I agree with Albie and Eliza. We should table this discussion for now. I've got news of my own."

"Dear Lord, Fred. Please. I'm in no condition to hear you failed your exams." Laura sank into her chair. She splayed her napkin, fanning her reddened face.

"No, Mother. I passed them all."

"Barely," snickered Albie.

Freddy shot his brother a deadly stare. "What I wanted to share is, I'll be joining Tom and two other fellows for a trip. We leave next week."

Laura straightened. "An astute decision. London is an excellent idea before you graduate. You can meet with our brokers there."

"I didn't say London. We're going to Alaska."

Eliza stifled a scream mixed with a laugh as she clapped her hand over her mouth. Freddy off into the wilds of Alaska? Her debut paled in comparison. Freddy should have spoken up sooner to save them from the tedious discussion about her escort.

Laura pushed herself up from her chair. Her thickened waistline had added weight in recent years. She pressed her palms upon the linen tablecloth like the hot iron Molly had used to smooth it earlier in the day. Laura's hazel eyes deepened to gray. She fixed the steel on Fred. From a dark spot in her throat, as deep and evil as the monster in Bram Stoker's novel, Laura spat, "What kind of a feckin' eejit are you?"

CHAPTER FIVE

Silence engulfed the room, frozen stiff as a blanket on a winter clothesline. Never, ever, had Laura Pearson Edwards spoken the words of an Irish housemaid. Eliza gaped as Josephine moved to Laura's side, placing her arm around her waist. "There, there," Josephine urged in a soothing cadence. "You're not feeling well. An early evening is best. We've had a long day. Molly will bring a cold compress."

Eliza paled. Freddy's announcement amazed her, but her mother's response frightened her. Now she uttered the thoughts running through the minds of the others. She leaned into Florence, "Is Mother all right?"

Albie stared straight ahead. Freddy hung his head, hiding the teardrop rolling down his cheek. Eliza felt his shame and remorse, grateful she wasn't the cause of their mother's outburst.

Florence patted Eliza's trembling arm, "Don't worry, my Lizzy. She'll be fine. Josephine is right, it's best we turn in early. Boys bring my bags upstairs. Lizzy, I'll stay with you like we used to, it'll be fun."

Eliza grabbed for her aunt's steady grasp. Florence gave it a light squeeze. "I didn't want to speak in front of your brothers. There's nothing to worry about. Let's get upstairs. I'll tell you a story about the grandmother of one of my most advanced and talented students."

The past five years Eliza had spent many lonely nights remembering the stories and secrets Florence would whisper over the narrow space between their beds. Whether it was news about the next meeting of her suffrage group or details of a painting which hung in the Pennsylvania Museum, Florence embellished the tales to teach as much as to entertain young Eliza. With the bedroom door shut tight, Eliza turned to her aunt, eager for another story. "What's an old lady got to do with my mother?"

"Mrs. Gibran is a dear woman from Lebanon, a country in the Middle East. Two months ago, we celebrated her grandson Kahlil's six-month mark. She joined us to review his charcoal drawings. Suddenly, she fanned her face with heavy puffs like a fireplace bellows. Next thing I knew, she let loose a stream of Lebanese obscenities. Kahlil's mother rushed from the kitchen to calm and usher her mother-in-law out of the room. When Kahlil's mother returned, she apologized, explaining the outburst. The elder Mrs. Gibran had begun her mother-gone stage. You know, these foreigners are so free with their discussion of private matters."

Eliza furrowed her brow. "Mother-gone?"

Florence stepped out of her skirt. "It sounds odd, but it's an appropriate and clever way to describe the change as women age. Our monthly visits stop. The ability to become a mother ends. I suspect Josephine has passed through it and Laura's starting hers. Facing the fact you'll never bear a child, or another child, creates great distress, along with physical discomforts. She's gained some weight, don't you think?"

Eliza nodded. Since becoming a woman herself and finally being able to fill the bodice, Eliza often borrowed an article from her mother's wardrobe. Tying a sash tight at her waist, she had admired her mother's ability after three pregnancies to share a dress size with her teenage daughter. More recently, however,

Eliza had noticed her mother sharing a dress with Josephine and new arrivals from Wanamaker's.

"And tonight, did you notice the flush in your mother's face? When a stressful situation causes internal heat to rise, it boils over, spewing forth all kinds of emotions."

Eliza had learned about her menstrual cycle when she turned thirteen. Her mother told her how, like closed buds on springtime azaleas, Eliza would soon bloom with an explosive step into womanhood. Who knew the monthly visitor would someday wither and die, unlike the bushes pruned at the end of season, yet returned every year with their vibrancy and vitality? The mysteries and wonders of the human body were as vast and fantastical as the Alaskan wilderness.

Eliza paced across the small bedroom.

"I feel terrible, causing more anguish when I suggested we reconsider my Presentation. I suppose proceeding as planned will keep her on an even keel."

Florence stroked the quilted coverlet. "Come, sit."

"When I wrote," said Florence, "I told you there's more. You needn't trouble yourself about your mother, it's a natural progression for women. Whether you make your Presentation, or not, won't change its course. Yes, with your debut you'll meet suitable men. You can marry, have children, and lead a comfortable life. But a woman should discover other ways to fulfill her life, with a husband, or without. You should investigate and form your own decision."

A knot in the floral quilt's seam had pulled loose, its white threads unraveled. One quick tug and it would fall apart. Eliza picked up the strings to re-tie them.

"But how? I have no idea what else I may do," Eliza said.

Florence continued, "Despite your mother's comment about old maids, I think Josephine and Estelle have found their definitions of fulfillment. We need to remind your mother of that fact. You can start next week. Accompany them to the Asylum, the courthouse, and the library. Ask them questions. Then ask yourself hard questions. You'll come to your own conclusion."

Burrowing under her covers, Eliza considered Florence's suggestion. She had sat in the gallery of Estelle's courtroom, but she had never joined Josephine for her days at the Asylum or College. Old veterans and women medical students. What could they teach her?

At her bedside, Florence bowed her head, closed her eyes, and knotted her hands together for a minute. Before crawling under the cotton coverlet, she tapped her finger to Eliza's nose. "Good night, sweetie. Remember, changes mean life goes on."

Eliza curled onto her side in the matching twin bed. "Good night, Aunt Florence. There's so much to think about. Thank you for coming home."

She interlaced her fingers, imitating Florence's silent prayer, *Grandpapa. Papa. I love you and miss you both. What would you want for me? Dear God, please keep Mother in your care. Maybe the doctors at Aunt Josephine's College can help her. Amen.*

Moonbeams sliced through the night sky, projecting shadows on the walls. What inquiries would she ask of her aunts? Eliza opened her eyes to notice amorphous shapes above the outline of her aunt's body, a vagueness mirrored in her thoughts. What questions would she ask herself, and what answers might she find?

CHAPTER SIX

A week later, Eliza again scanned the crowded library shelves. Shoulder to shoulder, the books on each shelf resembled a Grade One class, the tops of heads forming a ragged line, the insides as unique as each student. *There you are, you cursed toe-crusher.* She pulled the bulging *Gray's Anatomy* off the shelf and opened it to the frontispiece. Inked on the vellum, Eliza read the dedication:

Until the day's dawn, and the shadows flee away.
Song of Solomon, 2:17
For the Honorable William S. Pearson on your retirement
from the Board of Trustees.
We are forever indebted to you for your commitment
to the founding of the Female Medical College.
Your vision and support allow us to banish the shadows in the
study of medicine and bring forth
the light of a woman's intellect, ability, and empathy.
Our world will benefit from their bold strides forward.
A new day has dawned. God Bless You.
Dean Edwin Fussell, M.D. Female Medical College of Pennsylvania
May 20, 1860

Eliza hadn't considered her grandfather's involvement with the Woman's Medical College of Pennsylvania. None of his five daughters had felt the call to medicine. If not Pearson women, who were the bold ones who strode forward endowed with intellect, ability, and empathy?

The table of contents covered six pages. Eliza recognized a few chapter titles from her science and Latin classes. Others seemed like a foreign language. She slid her finger down each page, then turned to the back Index. She stopped at *F, Female, page 1317*.

Chapter 17, Urogenital System. She skimmed the details of the male system, blushing at a few of the illustrations and noting the page number, until she reached the female section. Starting on page 1317, she read the fifteen pages devoted to organs and their functions. Each detail pulled her deeper into the story of womanhood. Facts documented a woman's maturation beginning with menstruation and referenced back to Embryology. The last pages of the section provided the information she sought regarding her mother's condition, the end stages of the reproductive cycle.

In old age the uterus becomes atrophied, and paler and denser in texture; a more distinct constriction separates the body and cervix. The isthmus is frequently, and the ostium occasionally, obliterated, while the lips almost entirely disappear.

Eliza re-read the medical description of mother-gone. Mrs. Gibran's phrase was gentler than the harsh words chosen by Dr. Henry Gray: atrophied, obliterated. She closed *Gray's Anatomy* and re-shelved it. She had answers for when and why a mother-gone stage occurs. But the pages lacked any reference to actions needed to cure and ease a woman's pain.

She returned to the more immediate task ahead of her. Crumpled balls of scrap papers littered the desktop like clenched fists of frustration. One sheet lay flat amidst the heaps. Centered and underlined in Eliza's script, she wrote a single word at the top: *Questions*. Down the sheet's left-hand side ran numbers one through five: What, Why, When, Who, and How. She had spent the morning considering how to prompt her aunts to elicit answers. She reviewed the list again as she recalled many evenings in this same library with Albie and Freddy reading aloud from *The Adventures of Sherlock Holmes*. Eliza prepared her investigation, drawing upon Holmes' example of intent listening and logical reasoning. She left a note for her mother: *Going to Asylum with Aunt J.*

Twice a week, Aunt Josephine read to the residents of the Naval Asylum, a home for the brave men of Philadelphia and Germantown who had marched west and south during the Rebellion. Many of them had arrived at the Asylum over thirty years ago, carried by train directly from the bloodied battlefields of Gettysburg and Chambersburg. Most would be forgotten men if not for women like Josephine Pearson.

Eliza trudged along the last three blocks with her aunt. The heat outside burned as hot as the bundles of nervous energy coursing through her body. The high white lace collar of her plain beige dress scratched her chin. Josephine must be wilting in her heavy black dress. The purple sash at her waist expressed her grief. No one would mistake Josephine as anything but a widow. A title she had clung to since the Battle at Gettysburg.

Eliza wiped her brow with the back of her wrist. A dampness chafed under her arms. She lowered her head and sniffed, remembering she had forgotten her vial of rosewater. "Do you think they'll enjoy the letter?" she asked.

"Yes," Josephine replied. "These poor men, they devour any news. There are few relatives left to visit or read to them. Freddy's account of his travels will top yesterday's dismal showing by the Phillies with a nine-inning loss to the Boston Beaneaters."

A lengthy letter from Freddy had arrived, heralding his safe arrival in San Francisco. Eliza's mother approved his trip after she extracted promises he'd be back in time for the fall semester, regardless if he made it to Alaska, and to write once a week. This first note home detailed Chapter One of his adventure.

At the foot of the massive granite building's front stairs, Eliza braced herself for her entry into the Asylum. She had limited experience with elderly gentlemen. Her grandfather, a portly man with a quick wit and full physical abilities at seventy-four, had spared them a dramatic, long-suffering exit from their lives. His wife found him in the early hours of a November morning, slumped in his wingback chair. His pince-nez glasses pinched on his nose. In his hands, he held a legal brief for the next day's trial, preparing to live another day.

Eliza and Josephine stepped through the entryway bordered by Ionic columns. Inside, Josephine escorted Eliza into Philadelphia's own Greek tragedy. White strands of hair hung from balding domes, veined and splotched, which framed the pallor of blank, pock-marked faces. Pant legs and sleeves cut ragged at shortened lengths and pinned up accented missing limbs. Eliza averted her eyes from the vacant stares of the remaining 150th Pennsylvania Volunteers who hailed from the Germantown neighborhood of Philadelphia. The Bucktails had sent over seven hundred men into battle.

These survivors deserved reverence, thought Eliza. They had saved the Union and helped free the slaves her grandfather had defended. Every May, Eliza and her family walked to Monument Square to place a wreath at the remembrance monument. The Judge always removed his hat and bowed his head. They stood in silent prayer with him for 197 seconds, one second for each Bucktail name engraved into the monument.

"Well, now, hello, Miss Josephine. And who is this fine young lady?"

A man supported by worn wooden crutches balanced in a doorway as Eliza and Josephine passed. His navy jacket dangled to his knees. A single gold button struggled to stay within the buttonhole and keep the coat in order on the man's feeble frame.

"Corporal Boisbrun! Wonderful to see you up today. Allow me to introduce my niece, Eliza. Come join us, Eliza is reading today."

Eliza said, "Good afternoon, Sir."

The Corporal planted his crutches on the scuffed planked floor and swung his way alongside the women, edging ahead before they reached the common room. Drawing forth a voice which had disappeared thirty years ago, he barked to the collection of veterans. "Men of the 150th–a special treat today. A hardy hello please for Miss Josephine's niece, Miss Eliza."

With his introduction, five men arose from their chairs and broke into song.

"From there we went to Gettysburg, our march it being so far..."

Eliza stood rapt, watching their maimed faces and bodies come alive. From the corner of her eye, she noticed Josephine swallow hard as she fought back the blink of a tear.

"Our First Lieutenant, he fell there, we are sorry for the same,
He was a noble young man; Chancellor was his name.
He was a loyal young man, generous, kind and free;
He was a credit to his country and the pride of Company B."

First Lieutenant Henry Chancellor, Josephine's betrothed, had marched off from Germantown with the 150th. Eliza whispered to Josephine, "I am honored to read for these men. Thank you for letting me come."

Enlivened by their song, the men stirred with more energy, sending their ghosts to far corners of the room. Eliza squared her shoulders and cleared her throat. A smile spread across her face as sun rays entered through a double window. "I can't recall Emily Dickinson's poems I learned last fall in school. But you remember this wonderful tribute from thirty-four years ago? How marvelous! I'm thrilled to be here today with you. I hear the Phillies are struggling these days. How about more exciting news? My brother is on his way to Alaska!"

Eliza unfolded Freddy's letter and began, "Buffaloes! There must have been thousands, nay maybe millions, right outside our windows. Great, hulking beasts who snorted wildfire and shook the ground with their thunderous hooves. Their grunts, louder than the clack of the train's wheels along the rails..."

The men hooted and hollered as if they rode noble steeds, galloping across the dusty plains in pursuit of the mighty buffalo. Eliza laughed and let out a "Yeehaw!" with them. Who knew the simple act of an enthusiastic letter reading could elicit life? Eliza would not divert her eyes again from gaunt and scarred bodies.

•   •   •

The William Penn bronze statue stood atop City Hall. Eliza had joined her brothers three years earlier to witness the engineering feat. While Albie and Freddy discussed the mechanics of the assembly, Eliza focused her interest on the workers. How did those men dare to climb five hundred and forty-eight feet into the air? Had there been any accidents or injuries? she asked.

Two days after her visit to the Asylum, Eliza and Estelle approached City Hall on a hazy Thursday morning. Eliza craned her neck skyward. The Penn statue stood secure in its position, lording over the city of his founding. The low-hanging clouds obscured the statue's hat. A right arm extended out, waist high, with the palm facing downward. In the haze, the hand pulsed against the air, gesturing to those below to slow their pace. Eliza wished Aunt Estelle would take heed. Estelle's purposeful stride, even in her narrow skirt, made it difficult to keep up during their half-mile walk to the Court of Common Pleas.

The women turned the corner to use a side entrance reserved for law clerks and court reporters. Estelle pushed Eliza forward through the swarm of suit jackets and pant legs. Their skirts blended into the mass. Estelle had instructed Eliza to wear her most conservative dark gray dress, no jewelry, and to pull her hair into a tight, neat bun. A coolness accompanied them into the building, an air of indifference. Eliza slowed to watch the men enter the building. Each man carried a leather satchel under his arm, speaking in low tones to the gentleman to his right or left. No one acknowledged her aunt. There were no cheery greetings like the ones the veterans had for Aunt Josephine.

Estelle pushed her gold-wire-rimmed glasses up her nose, "Stop your dawdling and gawking. Trial proceedings begin at nine o'clock. You need to get settled while I review my transcription from yesterday and check my machine."

Eliza had heard her grandfather remark several times of Estelle's passion for his legal work. When Estelle's schooling ended, she visited his courtroom to watch trials. In his final years, they marveled together at the invention of a stenography machine designed to provide more accuracy in reviewing transcripts and to shorten trial proceedings. A court stenographer position applied her intellect and attention to detail.

"We're hoping the Wiltbank case concludes this morning. You need to listen to the closing arguments and Judge Green's decision."

"Yes, Aunt Estelle. I will."

•   •   •

The hot and darkened courtroom fought to pull Eliza into an apathetic stupor. She railed against its tug, entranced by the scene unfolding before her and the myriad of words and phrases used by the opposing legal counsels. On past visits, her interest had been cursory. Today, the Wiltbank case featured intrigue and conflicted characters. Affidavits, contracts of suretyship promissory notes, endorsements, litigants, plaintiffs, defendants, hearsay, the Act of 1893. Eliza sorted them through her head and made notes to ask her aunt for clarification when they broke for a recess.

The plaintiff, Thomas Wiltbank, sat next to his counsel. Wiltbank slouched in his chair, legs stretched long, and crossed at his ankles. Every few minutes, he drummed his index and middle fingers against the table's edge. His lawyer poked him with his elbow. The drum solo finished.

At the defendant's table, Cornelia Tobler, a plump woman in her early sixties, appeared much like anyone's grandmother, with kind eyes framed by creases from smiles and worries. Her ample bosom probably held grandchildren in close hugs. Despite the summer heat, she wore a fringed, black shawl over her widow's dress. Tucked into the sleeve she kept a handkerchief, dulled to mustard yellow with age. Each time the plaintiff's lawyer spoke of repayment, Mrs. Tobler sniffed into the handkerchief. A bespectacled junior news reporter seated next to Eliza scratched down Mrs. Tobler's every movement, including the sniffs and dabs. Eliza wondered if Mrs. Tobler play-acted her way through her defense, sinking to pitiful levels of exploiting the image the men held of her, a helpless, elderly female.

Why had Aunt Estelle suggested this case? Eliza deciphered the debate centered on Mrs. Tobler's signature on a $3,000 promissory note with her husband with a demand for the loan's payment to Mr. Wiltbank. Eliza understood enough about the simple mechanics of banking to know loans needed repayment. From the raised platform, Judge Green presided. After three and a half hours of presentation, he announced his adjudication, "Not guilty. Case dismissed."

At the declaration, Wiltbank leapt to his feet, overturned his chair, and slammed his fist onto the table. A chorus of shouts broke out from the gallery.

"Preposterous!"

"A dangerous precedent."

"Wiltbank must appeal."

Estelle continued her work, never looking down at her fingers flying across the stenograph machine's keys. Mrs. Tobler grinned as she shook her attorney's hand. On her way to the exit, she stopped by Eliza's aisle seat and snickered, "Sometimes it pays to be a woman."

Under the spread of maple trees clustered in the courtyard's center, Eliza and Estelle unwrapped rolls, sausage chunks, and cheese wedges Molly had packed in Estelle's lunch tote. Estelle chose the benches for her noon meal, where she sat alone away from the men. They preferred to crowd the nearby taverns where they praised each other's victories, maintained their debates, laughed over questionable verdicts, and kept a man's world intact.

Eliza, happy to be outside after the long morning of eye-opening testimony, welcomed the solitary spot so she could ask Estelle to translate the Tobler decision.

"I don't understand. Mrs. Tobler co-signed the promissory note with her husband. Shouldn't she pay the note?"

"Yes, it would have been a straightforward case if Mr. Tobler had not passed away. There are so many laws, Eliza, which deny a woman her rights and standing in a court. The most blatant denies us the right to vote. Perhaps if we could vote, we would push to repeal other outrageous ones."

Estelle bit into the hard sausage. "In the most basic terms, the law came back to mock them. Laws prohibit women from acting as a surety, or cosigner, on any promissory notes. Mrs. Tolber's signature is worthless. Which means Mrs. Tobler has the last laugh."

•   •   •

Estelle left Eliza on the bench, hurrying inside for afternoon sessions. Eliza had learned from past visits Estelle rarely spent over fifteen minutes at lunch, preferring to prepare for the next trial and make herself available should an attorney request her transcriptions. Overhead, the sky darkened. The heavy air of the morning gathered into thunderclouds. Eliza rolled the napkins into a ball and stuffed them in the tote.

As she rushed to beat the rain home, her observations from her time spent with Josephine and Estelle swirled like the summer storm clouds, each one clamoring to burst forth and clear the air and refresh the ground. Charity work and legal work. Aunt Josephine and Aunt Estelle found immense satisfaction at the Asylum and courthouse. The "why did they enjoy their positions" question on her sheet was obvious.

Josephine reveled in the company of the Bucktails. She reminisced with men who knew and honored her beloved. Time froze when she entered the Asylum. She avoided the finality of Henry's death when his memory lived on through his comrades. Eliza, however, did not mourn a lost betrothed. She did not want to live in the past, someone else's past. She needed to define and claim her own future.

Estelle thrived in a courtroom's logical order and demand for precision. As a woman, she couldn't present cases and argue for plaintiffs and defendants, but she helped to ensure each side would have accurate notes at day's end. Yet, Eliza pondered the words which swam through her head as she recalled Mrs. Tolber's case, and others she'd listened to on other visits. What worth did they hold when they resulted in as many losses as wins?

She doubted a visit to Josephine's library would yield any fresh ideas. She loved to read. But the thought of cataloguing textbooks and the quiet for hours on end seemed as solemn and boring as a Sunday sermon. Her mother had been suggesting they schedule her dress preview appointment at Wanamaker's.

She needed more time. There remained too many blanks on her sheet. And in her mind.

CHAPTER SEVEN

July 1897

A burnished brass chandelier hung from the reading room's ceiling. Serpentine arms like a Hindu goddess radiated electrical light needed for long hours of evening study. On the walls, framed enlarged visuals from *Gray's Anatomy* captivated Eliza's attention as she and Josephine entered the room. Women who stayed on in Philadelphia for the summer sat at two large leather-inlaid tables. They were the students of Woman's Med., as Aunt Josephine told Eliza they affectionately dubbed their college. *What dedication, sitting in a stuffy library over their vacation,* thought Eliza.

The scratch of pencils on notebook pages transcribed symptoms, procedures, and chemical compounds, ready for future readings and exam preparation. Despite Eliza's and Josephine's soft footfalls on the floral-patterned carpet, heads rose from the depths of their study. Foreheads relaxed and lips smiled. Josephine stopped at one of the rush-bottom chairs and placed a mothering touch on a student's shoulder, "Anandi, how's your thesis coming?"

Eliza scrutinized the petite woman hunched over a splay of notes and texts. A warm honey colored face turned up to them. Thick dark brows arched over deep brown almond eyes. A strand of jet-black hair fell over her forehead, visible beneath a white cotton scarf draped over her head and wrapped under her chin, trailing down the nape of her neck. Her headscarf wasn't the usual bandana kerchief or turban worn by a Negress. *Such an exotic looking woman*, thought Eliza.

The woman marked her page with a strip of blue ribbon and rose to answer.

"Not as well as I hoped. My lab notes are more confusing than I thought. But Dr. Koch's bacteriology research is helpful. Thank you for finding it for me," Anandi said, her words rising and falling in a breathy, sing-song voice.

"That's what I'm here for, dear. If you require anything else, please let me know. And, if you need a break, join us for lunch. We'll be in the courtyard."

Eliza nudged her aunt. "Aunt Josephine."

"Oh goodness, where are my manners? Anandi, my niece, Eliza Edwards. Eliza, meet Anandi Gopal Joshi."

Anandi held out her right hand, clasped her left on top of Eliza's, and raised her face. Anandi at full height reached below Eliza's chin. "So nice to meet you. Your aunt speaks of you often."

"Nice to meet you, too," said Eliza.

As Eliza and Josephine headed toward the exit, Eliza's head whirled again with more questions punctuated by words from her brief introduction to Anandi. *Dr. Koch? Bacteriology? Thesis?*

• • •

Behind the Italianate-style building, benches, tables, and chairs dotted a fenced square of green. The spot greeted toiling students who sought respite from days locked inside. Breaks of fifteen minutes seemed like an hour with a schedule packed with six hours spread across laboratory sessions, lectures, and dissection procedures.

Eliza launched her onslaught as they neared a table. "Where is Anandi from? I've never seen anyone like her. How long has she been in America? She's well-spoken in English. What does bac-te-ri-ol-ogy mean? Who is Dr. Koch?"

Josephine pulled out the paper bag of mixed berries they purchased on their walk to the college. She offered Eliza a handful. Their softened skins bled drops of blue and red into her palm, swirling into a palette of purples like one of Florence's painted canvases. She inched her chair closer and commenced the story of Anandi.

"Everyone loves Anandi. Her full name is Anandibai. Not only is she brilliant and dedicated to her studies, but what she's overcome inspires our students and staff."

"What do you mean, what she's overcome?" Eliza asked.

"Quite a remarkable journey she's had. Among India's upper castes, it's customary for parents to arrange their children's marriages. Anandi married a man twenty years older than her when she was nine years old..."

Eliza's eyes widened. "Nine! She was a child. Shouldn't that be illegal? Or at least immoral?"

"In this country, yes. But who are we to question another culture's customs? Fortunate for Anandi, her husband is well-educated and open-minded. He supported her decision to study medicine."

"That's progressive for someone who wed a nine-year-old," said Eliza.

"He's also a kind man who loves his wife. When Anandi was fourteen, she bore their child. She barely recovered from the birth when the baby died from typhoid. With limited medical care available for her son and herself, grief and distress overwhelmed her. Those feelings turned to anger. It was then she heeded a calling to care for others in her situation. With her husband, they researched how and where she could enroll to study medicine. Their search took three years until they discovered our Woman's Medical College and sent an application. At the time, I sat on the

Admissions Committee. Her words moved me like none other I'd read before. I've kept a copy."

Josephine produced a folded sheet from her tote.

"I've got to get back to the library. I never know when a student might need my help. Read Anandi's letter, then come find me."

Eliza unfolded the sheet and read the scripted words:

The determination which has brought me to your country against the combined opposition of my friends and caste ought to go a long way towards helping me to carry out the purpose for which I came, which is to render to my poor suffering countrywomen the true medical aid they so sadly stand in need of and which they would rather die than accept at the hands of a male physician. The voice of humanity is with me and I must not fail. My soul is moved to help the many who cannot help themselves. With sincerest regards, Anandibai Gopal Joshi, Kolkata, India.

Eliza dropped the letter into her lap, folding her hands on top to safeguard it from flapping away in the breeze. Dearest Anandi. How brave. How strong. Her loss so similar to Aunt Maria. Yet, Anandi's resolve gave her life and purpose. She channeled her grief and observations into an application letter for an institution which shone a light on women's intellect, ability, and empathy. Anandi strode forward; Maria shrunk backward.

Behind Eliza's shoulder, inside the brick building, women's able hands dissected bodies. Their wearied eyes peered through microscope lenses. Keen minds listened to globally renowned professors. Knowledge in words awaited translation to experience in practice. The myriad of questions which plagued Eliza's thoughts these last weeks faded into shadows. She stowed the pure words of a bereft mother from India in her side pocket and headed to the doorway, leaving the remains of the berry stems in the courtyard.

"Excuse me, Anandi. I'm sorry to interrupt," Eliza asked as she approached the cloth-covered bent head.

Anandi patted the empty chair next to her. "Please, do not apologize. I'm at a perfect spot to stop."

"If you have a few minutes, I'd love to hear more about your thesis. You said it's on bac-te-i-ol-ogy?"

"Yes, bacteriology is the study and origins of bacteria. Some are helpful in our bodies to aid with digestion, but they also cause many diseases, including typhoid. Through laboratory analysis using agar gels, we isolate different microbes and classify them."

Foreign words clogged in Eliza's ears. *Microbes, agar gels.* "I'm sorry. I guess what I'm really asking is, what's involved with medical school?"

Anandi chirped a chortle. "How much time do you have? Explaining bacteriology may be quicker!"

Over the next forty minutes, Anandi revealed the trials and triumphs of studying medicine. Each day ended in exhaustion. Brains felt like they crashed into stone walls. Loosened rocks buried bodies too weak to lift their limbs from the suffocating crush. Stressful and scary days filled four years.

But there were also times when treating actual people, not dissected pieces or skeletal specimens, which lifted the students above their doubts and fears. Those moments magnified their success to push aside despair. How watching a patient under their care recover from an illness meant the patient would hold her beloved's hand again. Or, how pulling a newborn from its mother's womb and witnessing a first breath of life, could turn a birthing room into a space of uncomplicated joy.

"Medical school is not for the faint-of-heart, nor frail-of-mind."

Eliza deduced that an hour ago, but sat transfixed, listening to Anandi.

"Through it all here at Woman's Med., you have the most wonderful circle of support. You have sisters who walk with you. We fret and cry. But also laugh and sing. These women are your professors and your classmates, your teachers, and your friends. Some have attended other colleges. Others enter straight after high school. Some, like me, come from other countries. Others hail from Philadelphia. It doesn't matter how old we are or where we come from, we have the same goal: to become doctors who can relate to women and their health issues. We want to give a voice and care to those who suffer in silence, rather than seek help from male physicians."

"Thank you, Anandi. I'm sorry I took you away from your work for so long," said Eliza. A stirring of wanting more information from this petite medical student opened and crowded Eliza's mind. "You have no idea how grateful I am."

Anandi re-wound the headscarf, which had fallen loose around her face. "I needed a break and speaking with you is most satisfying. Perhaps we can chat again?"

"That would be wonderful," said Eliza.

Eliza smiled at Anandi, an Indian woman who could deliver more verdicts than found in a courtroom and touch more hearts than wounded war veterans.

• • •

As she walked to the trolley stop, Eliza gathered Anandi's inspirational words, written and spoken, along with other examples of guidance she gleaned over the past few weeks.

Whether a volunteer at a veterans' home, a professional in the legal system, a librarian at a college, a settlement house worker, a medical student, or a mother, the women in her life devoted themselves to following their hearts and helping others. Her grandfather also taught the rewards of defending the powerless among them.

A Pearson granddaughter summoned to assume her rightful place on the society pages of Philadelphia's Blue Book would decline the invitation. Other plans awaited Eliza Pearson Edwards. Her name, destined for other pages.

CHAPTER EIGHT

A heavy rain pelted the windows. The pounding woke Eliza. She stirred in her bed, the smell of Molly's coffee creeping under her bedroom door. A strong cup would suffice this morning. With her stomach somersaulting throughout the night, she couldn't hold down anything else. Tremors of excitement and nervous apprehension wove like wicker into a basket. She imagined Anandi's words at its center.

"Miss Eliza, ya comin' down?"

"Yes, coming."

Eliza gripped the banister, seeking strength from its solid and straight-line descent down the staircase. At the bottom, she inhaled deep into her lungs and stepped onto the foyer's floor. Six paces away, on the other side of the closed parlor door, low tones of a conversation buzzed.

By the front door, Josephine held a folded umbrella. Rubber galoshes covered her ankle-high shoes.

"Are you positive, Lizzy?" she asked in a halting, soft voice.

With Florence in Boston, Eliza needed another ally who knew her mother and how to form a discussion with her. Someone who every week attested to the personal triumphs of the Woman's Med. students. When Eliza confided in her, Josephine gushed with pride and excitement, but she had also wanted to ensure Eliza's decision was firm and true.

Eliza went to her aunt for a quick embrace. "I think so. No. I am. I mean, I must be to speak with Mother."

"You'll be fine, Dr. Edwards."

Josephine crossed the threshold to the stoop so as not to open her umbrella in the house.

Eliza chuckled to herself, welcoming the levity of the moment. Josephine clung to superstitions as tightly as she kept her memories of Henry Chancellor. Eliza, too, would grasp at any means to avoid bad luck. She lifted her eyes to the streaks of sunbeams filtering through the morning sky as they broke through the gloomy rain clouds.

• • •

The fifteenth of July marked Laura Edwards' monthly appointment to review the family's financial accounts. Neat rows of figures lined pale green ledger sheets with the headers, "Income" and "Expenses," aligned along the top. Each month the right-hand column grew while the left column remained unchanged: *Estelle's Wages, Josephine's Wages, Net Income from the Edwards Wool Import Company.*

Eighteen years after his death, the company established by Albert Edwards continued to provide for his family. Shipments of the finest English and Scottish wool traversed the Atlantic into the bustling port of Philadelphia. After inspection, it traveled up the coast to their mills north of Boston. Laura's father, Judge Pearson, had written the incorporation documents. He included safeguard clauses to protect his daughter's interests should anything happen to Albert. His foresight was also fortuitous when he selected a successor whom he knew would be capable, fair, and reliable. Every month, Laura sent a prayer of thanks to her father for choosing Charles Putnam. Sustaining a household on a dwindling inheritance and her two sisters' wages would be difficult. Albie and Freddy's education would have been unimaginable, and funding Eliza's debut and a wedding, impossible, without some additional form of income.

Eliza paused outside the parlor and pressed her ear closer to the door. A man's voice mingled with her mother's.

"I wish the report were more positive. You should consider the Boston expansion. The cost savings would be considerable, and Nathan is keen on the plan. He believes Harvard men will make excellent business managers."

Charles Putnam. Charles Putnam, father to Nathan Putnam, the youngest son who had attended school sandwiched between Albie and Freddy in grades. He surprised his family, and his friends, when he headed north to Harvard. Eliza's brothers never forgave him for his traitorous act. Or so they joked.

As Eliza reached for the glass doorknob, the door swung open bringing her face to face with Mr. Putnam. He startled back to give proper space between himself and Eliza. His whiskers tapered down his cheeks into a trim beard. A light gray suit, fashioned from the finest blend of Edwards Wool, fit his solid frame. The chain of his watch draped across his midsection and disappeared into a vest pocket where he often hooked his thumb in a casual stance.

"Miss Edwards. Nice to see you. I've been hearing about your Presentation. My daughter, Jenny, had a marvelous debut. With proper planning, yours will be grand, too."

Eliza caught her breath.

"Yes, I'm busy with many plans," Eliza said. She wasn't lying.

Eliza watched him proceed down the front steps, then wrapped her arms around her stomach to calm the rumbling tremors and walked into the parlor.

Her mother closed the ledger as Eliza entered the room. "Good morning, honey. A late rising? Are you feeling ill? I hear there's a touch of summer ague circulating. I hope you didn't pick something up at the courtroom with Estelle last week. All those people. You never know what type of diseases they may be carrying."

Sometimes it pays to be a woman. From the moment Mrs. Tolber snickered those words to her, Eliza had taken them, redefined them, and molded them into a more meaningful context. Women could be of value in distinct ways. She could comfort the aged and advise the young. She could support a family with respectable wages. Like her mother and Florence, she could guide children, whether they were her own or students at a settlement house. Eliza's worth would be defined as a medical professional.

"No, I'm fine. In fact, the verdict was interesting. I haven't told you about it, or my visits with Aunt Josephine to the Asylum and Medical College. Do you have time now?"

"Yes, I'd like to hear about your little excursions. The rain stopped. Let's sit outside, it'll be much cooler. I'll see if Molly has any lemon tea and a plate of fruit for you. Will you grab a towel to dry off the bench?"

A curved reed-thatched bench stood at the courtyard's edge. An ancient elm centered the brick circle, its trunk and root tops ringed by a low black wrought iron coping. Eliza tilted her neck up to the maze of the elm's limbs. The branches stretched outward and upward in every direction searching for the sun, the energy source needed to exist. A child could climb this tree, but which gnarled and forked branch would support the heaviest weight? Which would lead the highest? Many of its leaves had succumbed to disease or age. Most, however, were vibrant and lush green, open wide at the apex of their existence. The time was ripe.

Eliza recounted first her visit to the court. She shook her head and asked, "Can we claim it as a victory if Mrs. Tolber felt compelled to play the distressed damsel, right down to teary eyes?"

"Of course," said her mother. "Instances when women are taken seriously are rare. If she thought she needed an edge, why not use it?"

Eliza continued with her visit to the Asylum. "It was amazing. Most of the men have terrible infirmities. But when they sang the ballad about Henry, they came alive. They hooted and hollered when I read the section from Freddy's letter about the buffaloes."

"How sweet of you. I'm sure they loved that. I expect, though, you must have found the College library bored you to no end. I don't know how Josephine finds any pleasure in scouring medical texts hour after hour and recommending purchases. However, it sounds like you enjoyed going to the Asylum. Josephine has mentioned they always need volunteers. She can schedule you in for a rotation spot. That would be a fine idea."

A squirrel chattered as it sprang to a lower branch, releasing a leaf with its claws. The frond fluttered, alighting onto Eliza's shoulder. She picked it off, rubbing it between her thumb and index finger, her eyes glued to the leaf's veins, the minute anatomy of a majestic tree's life in her hand.

"I have another idea," said Eliza.

Her fingers trembled. Her tongue thickened and her planned speech froze. She needed to give air to the foreign words, unsure if her mother would comprehend their full meaning.

"I want to help, but in a different way. I'd like to apply to the Medical College."

The bend in Laura's back straightened as a string pulled taut to tie a parcel. She turned her head in a slow arc toward her daughter. Eliza watched as a mask of disbelief descended across her mother's strained face.

"Medical college?" she sputtered. "What a noble thought. But the studying is so arduous. The nasty guts and blood those students endure. There's plenty of gore at the Asylum. I'll speak to Josephine about the volunteer reading position."

Eliza inhaled to cool the fire building in her gut, "No, I'd prefer you not. I've been thinking more about the Presentation. My visit to the Medical College was eye-opening."

She swallowed the liquid which pooled beneath her tongue as the flood of her words surged on.

"Aunt Josephine introduced me to a student from India who hasn't seen her family in four years. She lives in a boarding house. I can live here at home and take the trolley over to North College Avenue. Josephine has already discussed my credentials with Dean Marshall. She said my grades are in line with the aptitude their students need for admittance."

Not daring to give her mother an opening to comment, Eliza refueled with a quick intake of air.

"Even if I'm book ready, the student I met, Anandi, cautioned me about the work. But she also shared her hopes for a rewarding career. The students at Woman's Med. have forged their own paths. I wish to do the same."

Laura sat silently. Eliza groped for what else she might say to make it known she hadn't arrived here without hours of contemplation. That her decision wasn't a burst of enthusiasm which would melt away like an icicle in March.

"Eliza," Laura tsked rather than spoke. "It's impossible to start studies at Woman's Medical during your debut season. I've spoken with Mr. Putnam. He's agreed to write to Nathan and request he escorts you. Nathan's a fine choice."

Did her mother not hear any of her words? Was all the time she spent rehearsing each night in her bedroom for naught? Eliza's heart beat as if it might smash through her arterial wall. "I don't think…"

Before she could finish, Laura raised her palm facing outward to Eliza's remarks. Her middle fingers went to her temples. She rubbed the spot in circles, "Enough of this foolishness. I need to lie down." She swayed as she rose, the pain in head overtaking her body. With her hand shielding her eyes from the light, she headed toward the door.

Eliza watched her leave, knowing she couldn't help, afraid her mother wouldn't want any from her. She hoped her mother's headache was a debilitating symptom of menopause as Florence had suggested. She abhorred the idea her announcement caused undue distress. This first discussion had not proceeded as she had hoped. Yet, waiting for her mother to finish a mother-gone stage was unimaginable. That might take years. She had rushed headlong into the conversation. She should slow down, become more methodical and present her case like the lawyers in Estelle's courtroom. One by one, she would address objections until her mother heard the truth.

• • •

Over the next two weeks, Laura remained unconvinced of Eliza's declaration. Eliza persisted with pleading her cause. From marriage to finances, Eliza's answers rolled off her tongue like a waterfall, giving life to her choice.

Laura: "By the time you graduate, you'll be twenty-two. Do you have no desire to marry?"

Eliza: "Unlike teachers, there are no laws prohibiting women doctors from marrying."

Laura: "Wherever would you find a suitable husband holed up in libraries and laboratories?"

Eliza: "In a library or laboratory. They have co-ed lectures with Jefferson by the Fourth Year, so who knows? I could even meet him on the trolley on his way to his work."

Laura: "Women in professional positions threaten most men. Look at Estelle."

Eliza: "The right man, the man I would marry, will respect my decision as much as I would support his choice of a profession."

Laura: "Your name, our Edwards name, will become known in public. Not in the Blue Book, but as a woman employed in a male profession."

Eliza: "Won't that be wonderful? I can see it now, a carved sign with my name and the initials, M.D. swaying from a post outside an office door."

A deep sigh escaped from her mother's mouth. The exhale hung in the air, deflating like a slow leak in a bicycle tire. Their conversation stalled until Laura picked up Eliza's hand. She pulled it to her breast.

Laura: "How could you be a doctor and a mother?"

Eliza: "Why not? Dean Marshall mentioned many graduates are mothers and find fulfillment in both roles."

Eliza refrained from sharing Dean Marshall's opinion that a woman doctor's intellect and training in hygiene and physiology made her a more capable mother. "And, since I have no intention of leaving Philadelphia, I hope my children will spend many hours with you. You'll be a wonderful granny."

Laura: "Albie's law school has overextended our finances and we've seen a downturn in the Company's most recent financial reports. I've saved for your debut and a wedding, not for further education."

Eliza: "We can put the monies for the Presentation toward my first year. Whatever we would have spent on my gown, a muff and coat, shoes, silk stockings, gloves, a corset, a corsage, a hired carriage plus the catered tea, must come close to the $135 expense."

Laura: "There are three more years of costs. I refuse to deplete your wedding account. You may need it someday."

Eliza: "Josephine says there are limited rooms at Briton Hall. I'd be happy to share my room, just like I did with Aunt Florence. We'd have to feed a boarder, but she won't eat as much as Albie or Freddy's friends. There must be a few women with five dollars a week, looking for a room before the fall term starts. And, with

Molly's cleaning talents, we'll pass the required sanitary inspection."

On a steamy evening two days later, they strolled the banks of the Schuylkill River, searching for a stir of air off the water. Laura voiced another concern in her long litany of hesitations, "Josephine mentioned the Entrance Exam is more difficult than the one for Jefferson or the University."

Now her mother questioned her academic abilities? Eliza had always been a serious student and secured the highest marks through her years at Agnes Irwin.

"Yes, I know," Eliza said. "I must study every day before the exam the first week of October if I'm to pass. Josephine has offered to show me how to organize my note-taking, and Estelle insists she prepare my Latin exercises. Maybe you'll help me with the arithmetic section?"

"At least you know it's better to ask me, and not your brothers, for that type of help," said Laura.

CHAPTER NINE

Eliza forged ahead with studying. In ten weeks, prospective students would sit for the Entrance Exam for Woman's Med. Eliza intended to occupy one of those seats, whether she had secured her mother's approval by then or not.

English, Arithmetic, Algebra, Physics, and Latin. Like the five points of a star, each subject area would challenge test-takers to shine with aptitude. The English and Latin sections posed no concern. Eliza mastered writing contemplative essays and compositions in earlier schooling. The basics of fractions, percentages, and the use of the metric system should be straightforward. Algebra and Physics, however, loomed like a starless night over Eliza's head, an unguided darkness ready to wreak havoc with her scores. For these parts, she needed help. Whom better to advise her than a student who had taken the Exam, passed, and excelled in every subject Woman's Med. required?

• • •

In a quick reply to Eliza's request to visit, Anandi suggested the next Sunday afternoon, *Sundays are best. Please come for tea.*

Eliza stood at the entrance of Briton Hall, which housed students, like Anandi, unable to travel home for recess. Upon Eliza's rap on the door, it swung open with a flourish. Eliza caught her breath. A peony-pink, silk sari draped over Anandi's shoulder, wrapped around her chest and waist, and fell to the tops of embroidered red slipper shoes. A red dot centered on her forehead.

Anandi shook Eliza's hand and waved her into the visiting parlor, "Come in, come in. I'm so delighted you came."

"Are you sure I'm not taking you away from your studies, or an outing?" asked Eliza, following her.

"Not at all. Sundays are my day of reflection. My mind is clearer. And, my third eye, here," she lightly fingered the dot on her forehead, "my bindi, wakens my spiritual sight to guide you."

A soft smile spread across Anandi's face, putting Eliza at ease as she remembered Anandi's application letter. *My soul is moved to help.* Anandi acted upon her words in so many ways.

"Do you have a notebook?" asked Anandi.

Eliza opened her tote and pulled out a blank journal she'd taken from the stack on Maria's bureau. She paused, wondering what Aunt Maria would think. Eliza was eager to fill the pages with facts, not poetic prose, which may be of more help to other women like her aunt.

"You're already ahead of the game, Eliza," Anandi winked. "Prepared and excited. Let's get started, shall we?"

Eliza flipped to a blank page and poised her pen.

"First step: Obtain copies of *Avery's Elements of Natural Philosophy* and *Gray's Anatomy*. Both are indispensable reference texts. *Avery's* will help with the Physics section. *Gray's* reinforces your Latin and exposes you to anatomical terms and descriptions. If you can find someone to read passages aloud, that would be perfect for you to practice transcription."

"We have a copy of *Gray's*. A gift to my grandfather. I'll ask Josephine to dictate."

"Wonderful! Second, if you can't answer a question after your first reading, skip it and come back rather than waste time worrying about it. As far as Algebra goes..." Anandi continued.

When the wall clock chimed five, Eliza paused from her furious scribbling to flex her fingers. Crumbs from a blueberry scone littered her lap. A teacup, drained twice, rested on its saucer on the pedestal table next to her. She needed a trip to the water closet before heading home.

"Whew," Eliza exhaled, fanning eight pages of notes. "I feel so much better now. I've got plenty of ideas to organize my study. Thank you!"

She rose from the divan and crossed to where Anandi sat in a side chair. Another handshake or a hug for the woman who ceded her reflection time to speak with her? Eliza spread her arms wide. Anandi arose and stepped into the sisterly embrace.

"You're welcome," she said. "But, if you have a couple more minutes, I have one more tip before you leave."

Eliza shifted her weight from left leg to right leg. She couldn't say no to Anandi. The water closet visit would have to wait. Her eyes followed Anandi's hands to the lid of a three-foot, rectangular, wooden pine box at her feet. In black paint, someone had painted in block letters, GOPAL JOSHI. Eliza had noticed the mysterious box when she entered. She hadn't wanted to appear rude and inquire about it in case it was part of Anandi's Hindu rituals.

"May I present," Anandi announced as she lifted the lid, "Miss Annabel Lee."

Eliza dropped her notebook, sending her hand to her mouth to stifle a snort-squeak. Anandi cradled Miss Annabel Lee in her hands, an alabaster white human skull complete with empty eye sockets and a full mouth of teeth.

"I hope that's a laugh, not a shriek. You won't make it past the first week if you're afraid of a few bones rattling around."

Eliza examined Annabel Lee's well-sculpted cheekbones. "I imagine she was beautiful. What a perfect name," she said.

Anandi picked up another item from the box. "And this is her femur. The College requires you to secure a bone box to reference throughout each term. We each receive a skull and five other bones. Amongst the class, there's enough to make two full skeletons. We share the bones we don't have with each other to make sure we're familiar with all of them. There's a five-dollar deposit made at the start of the year. You receive eighty percent back when you return it with a full inventory of pieces."

More expenses. Eliza added the fee to the running calculation in her head.

"And here's my last tip," said Anandi. "The demands are intense but try to enjoy yourself when you can. Savor the precious moments when the students gather for a bit of fun, too. Everyone chooses creative names for their study partner, as we call them. Like His Nibs the Rib or Padraig Skullivan. Some girls even bring them as their dates for the annual Halloween party the sophomore class hosts. You're clever, Eliza. I expect you'll come up with a fun name, too."

CHAPTER TEN

Eliza moved her index finger down Page 530, pausing at the paragraph titled, *Size*. She traced the words: *The heart continues increasing, and also in length, breadth, and thickness, up to an advanced period of life: this increase is more marked in men than in women.*

Humph, thought Eliza, *the esteemed Henry Gray has made a mistake.* There was no question a woman's heart is larger than a man's, works harder, and grows until it bursts from beats of joys and sorrows.

Her mother touched the lace collar at Eliza's neck where tendrils strayed from its bun. Startled, Eliza jerked her head up from the book. She had holed up the entire afternoon with Chapter Seven, *The Blood-Vascular System*, while Laura called on a few friends, overdue in thanking them for their support after Maria's passing.

"You're home early," said Eliza.

Losing Maria had taken its toll. Eliza noticed her mother's late morning risings, earlier evenings, and a hollowness in her eyes which never faded despite the extra hours in bed. She hadn't dared to broach the subject of Woman's Med. over the last three weeks, nor had she relaxed her study schedule.

Laura dropped her reticule and black shawl to the wingback chair and sighed. "Mrs. Lippincott means well, but I couldn't listen to another minute of rambling about Presentation protocol and tips about gloves and hairstyles."

A sliver of hope? Was her mother warming to Eliza's decision?

Standing over Eliza's shoulder, Laura tapped the open page. "That heart illustration is amazing. Who knew it was so intricate? What is an *aur-i-cle*? Is that how you pronounce it? Most of the text looks like a foreign language. I don't think my French will help."

Eliza's intent gaze softened. "No, I've come across little use for French, although my Latin is helpful. *Auricle* comes from the Latin word, *auricula*, with the root, *auri*, pertaining to the ear. The shape of the right auricle resembles an ear. When a test asks me to identify the parts of the heart, I'll recognize the ear and know it's either the right or left auricle."

Eliza hesitated, saying more at this moment may fall on deaf, stubborn ears. Yet, this was the first sign her mother showed any interest in her commitment to study. Time flew by as rapid as the beat of a hummingbird's wings. Days were getting fewer. She took a breath, steadying her thoughts and words, "The Entrance Exam is October 2nd. I need to pass it and be ready for the first term. Anandi suggested reading *Gray's*."

She lowered her eyes as if expecting a sharp retort. When none came, she went on, "Also, I hoped to uncover some clues to Aunt Maria's condition. I started this chapter on the blood-vascular system yesterday. There must be some relation between circulation and the heart's function. Oh, I wish I could have helped her!" Eliza lifted her chin, her eyes hopeful. "The only way I could help anyone else like Aunt Maria and other women is to attend Woman's Med."

Outside, the clang of the trolley moving down Cherry Street two blocks away ding-dinged into the silence hanging between Eliza and her mother.

"I understand," Laura said. "I just hope you know what this decision involves. The commitment is greater than anything you've ever faced."

Eliza fingered the scrap of paper which had taken up residence in her pocket. She needed to bring it forth from the hidden folds of her skirt. Her mother must hear Anandi's words. She must accept Eliza's desires. It was time. "Anandi's letter says what I'm feeling," she said.

As Eliza read aloud, she grasped Laura's hand. Looking up from the page, she recited the words she'd adopted as her own. "The voice of humanity is with me, and I must not fail. Mother, Anandi articulated my desire. It's as if a light within me has waited for someone to find its wick and place a match to it. I want to be a doctor."

Eliza spoke a woman's words. She was no longer a child boasting of schoolroom achievements, but an adult asserting her choice and who would not be deterred.

Laura nodded toward the notes and books strewn across the library desk. "My French may be useless, but my arithmetic skills are sharp. What can I do to help you prepare for this exam?"

Eliza's heart skipped a beat. She'd passed her first test and would mark the night with A's for assertion, affirmation, and acceptance, signed by a mother willing to guide and support her.

• • •

"Sic transit Gloria mundi?" Estelle expected Eliza's Latin to extend beyond the basics found in the elementary level of Harkness' Latin Reader.

"So passes the glory of the world," Eliza replied.

"Correct. Did you translate, or do you recall this phrase?"

Eliza remembered. Her grandfather had often repeated it to her and her brothers, translating it to, "Cherish the memory of those who have gone before us."

As she gathered her books at the end of the evening's session, Eliza recollected those who had gone before her, the women and men worthy of remembrance.

Lucretia Mott as Florence had told her. From sitting in the courtroom of Eliza's grandfather to bear witness for the rights of a Negro man, to helping to pen the Declaration of Sentiments at Seneca Falls, stating, "all men and women are created equal," Lucretia deserved recognition. Her championing of women's rights included the right to become a doctor.

Josephine, Estelle, and Florence Pearson. Eliza's cherished aunts encouraged her to discover, form, and strive for an alternative path and passion, as they had found theirs.

Anandi Gopal Joshi. The brave woman from faraway India, who within minutes moved Eliza to consider medicine as her road forward.

Judge William Pearson. The abolitionist lawyer and father to five daughters who in 1850, with other progressive men, served as a Founder and Trustee of the Female Medical College of Pennsylvania, now known as the Woman's Medical College of Pennsylvania.

Daniel Dangerfield, the man who never forgot her grandfather's defense and reminded them through a scrap of paper that everyone needed to find their freedom.

Laura Pearson Edwards. A widow and mother who headed a family with as much decisiveness, success, acumen, and devotion as any man.

These women and men laid the routes for Eliza to follow. Inspired by their examples, she would step into their large and formidable footprints. God willing, and with her own hard work and dedication, the doors to Woman's Medical would open for her, too.

• • •

By the second week of September when Eliza started *Gray's* Chapter 18, the musty scent had faded, replaced by the freshness of her rosewater. Fixated on the illustrations of *The Skeleton*, Eliza missed the first ring of the bell as she examined her hand. *This is my carpus, the wrist-bone.* She twisted her wrist. *These are my phalanges.* She wiggled her fingers. *These are my metacarpals.* With her fingertip, she skimmed over the deep-set grooves of her palm, drawing it closer to inspect the faint, split ends of the uneven lines beneath her pinky finger. Maybe someday she would treat herself and Josephine to a visit with a gypsy by the docks for a palm reading. Josephine would love that type of outing.

The second chime broke her inspection.

"I've got it, Molly."

One letter showed the hand-scrawled return address from Molly's cousins in Queenstown, a port city on Ireland's southern coast. The other envelope bore an imprint in the upper left corner, Woman's Medical College, North College Avenue, Philadelphia, with ELIZA P. EDWARDS typed in the center.

Picking up the letter opener, she reflected on the day three months ago when her anticipation focused on the contents of a different envelope. The blade carved with the North Star's longest point sliced through the flap. Eliza pulled the linen card from its confines, her hands trembling.

Eliza P. Edwards is invited to join the Class of 1901
at the Woman's Medical College of Pennsylvania.
Matriculation is contingent upon passing marks
in all subjects of the Entrance Exam.
Introductory Address:
Wednesday, September 29, 1897
at four o'clock in the afternoon.
Entrance Examination:
Saturday, October 2, 1897
at ten o'clock in the morning.

The words couldn't be more different from those on her Presentation invitation. How she styled her hair, and which gloves she wore, would be the least of her worries.

•   •   •

Eliza curled her fingers around the pen's black lacquered barrel. One evening, in the middle of drafting her English essay, her mother joined her in the parlor. In her hands she held a narrow box. Opening the box's cover, Laura presented her with the Judge's pen. "Your brothers commissioned and re-tooled it with an ink reservoir inside. You won't need to carry a well like your grandfather."

The weight of the instrument the Judge had used to forge the rightful paths for others passed into her fingers. If she succeeded, she would write the next chapter of history, the first Pearson to become a doctor. Now Eliza sat with the pen in her grip. She needed to make the afternoon post.

Dear Aunt Florence,

There is more. I will sit for the Entrance Exam on October 2nd. My review study is progressing well with many thanks to Josephine, Estelle, and my mother. To the best of my abilities, I pray I'll pass the Exam and begin my journey toward Eliza Pearson Edwards, M.D. I never would have gotten here without you. Great changes lie ahead. I can hardly wait.

Your loving niece,
Lizzy

CHAPTER ELEVEN

September 1897

Eliza tapped her boot in a hurried beat against the floor. Her knee bounced as the electricity from her foot traveled up her shin. The skirt covering her legs swayed with the bobbing as if wind rustled the fabric's tan-leaf imprint on a blue-gray light wool sky. She stood from the parlor chair and called toward the staircase, "Aunt Josephine, please. It's almost two-thirty."

Maybe she should change. The high collar of the ivory cotton chafed her neck. It may cause her to fidget. She had no intention of attending the Introductory Address at Woman's Med. this afternoon with a bothersome collar distracting her. Her fingertips pressed the muslin downward, commanding it to stay in place. She untied the matching cream-colored sash at her waist and retied the ends, pulling the knot taut with a snap.

"Aunt Josephine..." Eliza stepped up a stair riser, calling again.

"Please calm down, I'm coming," said Josephine, descending the stairs. "There's plenty of time. The Address starts at four o'clock and they never open the doors before three-thirty. Last I checked, it didn't take me an hour to walk a mile and a half. These bones may be old, but they're not retired yet."

"Sorry. Nerves, I guess," said Eliza.

Eliza's mother emerged from the kitchen. "I thought so. Here." She offered Eliza a tumbler of a cloudy liquid. Eliza hesitated, unwilling to fill her bladder.

"Your first college level chemistry class. Bicarbonate of soda settles butterflies."

"Thank you," Eliza accepted the glass and sipped the fizzy liquid. "Blech. I trust you're right. If it works, it may be a good idea to have Molly stock up on a four-year supply," joked Eliza.

• • •

Josephine left Eliza at the lecture hall's door to join the other early arrivals of faculty and staff. She steered Eliza to a cordoned off section in the middle of the room. Three rows in the first tier awaited with reserved spots for prospective students. Front and center and on display. Eliza felt the scrutiny of five women upon her. If each of them passed the exam, they would be classmates along with the others filing in behind Eliza and choosing seats. Eliza gathered her skirt into a clutch, eased into a spot, and glued her attention on the doorway.

Anandi arrived with a group of Fourth Years. With heads held high, self-assured and steeped with knowledge, they engaged in conversations, happy to reconnect after the summer recess. Eliza wished she could sit next to Anandi to draw upon her confidence, pull it in, and possess it as her own. Her hopes soared when Anandi looked toward her. But only a light wave of recognition must suffice. The start of medical school meant following instructions, even if it required sitting in an assigned seat.

A stocky woman took the podium at the room's center. Her aura of authority loomed as large as her frame. Clara Marshall, M.D., in her eleventh year as Dean, and a graduate herself, opened the 1897-1898 term of Woman's Medical with an Introductory Address.

"On behalf of our esteemed faculty and our valued staff, welcome, one and all, to the forty-eighth year of Woman's Medical," Dean Marshall spread her arms wide as to envelop the hall.

"I am pleased to see nearly all our upperclassmen are here with us for another term. As students, you have learned your burden is a two-fold responsibility: devotion to the interests of our noble medical profession and fidelity to a glorious cause of advancing women into careers still dominated by men. While we currently comprise less than five percent of all doctors, we're making progress. Thank you for your dedication."

A round of applause circulated through the auditorium. Eliza watched as the current students beamed at being acknowledged by their revered Dean. She closed her eyes, trying to envision sitting in their seats, congratulating herself and her expected classmates. Success was so close. She could feel it in the vibrating hands clapping up and down the surrounding rows. Saturday's exam loomed less than seventy hours away.

Dean Marshall proceeded with other remarks. This fall, the College would publish a book to commemorate the advances of its graduates. National medical societies now admitted them, with many holding official positions. A large number reported annual incomes up to $20,000, considerably higher than other traditional female professions, like teaching. Of the 832 alumnae who responded, over five hundred had published papers in their respective fields, covering topics from the use of anesthesia in surgery to proper care of destitute pregnant women to popular fallacies in vegetarianism. The news encouraged Eliza, further proof that becoming a doctor would lead to a rewarding career.

Re-adjusting her stance to face the center where Eliza sat, Dean Marshall continued, "Members of our expected Class of 1901. Those of you who took the Exam earlier under supervision in your home state or country–congratulations. For those who will sit on

Saturday, we reviewed your application, assessed your abilities, and invited you here with no doubt each of you will pass, too."

Eliza considered the women seated around her who would learn on Sunday if they would matriculate into the oldest medical college for women. Which ones had already taken the test? The woman with the blonde braid next to her? The one in the row below, with the tight bun who looked the same age as Aunt Florence? Who had gone to another college and would move directly into Second Year? Did others suffer from a nagging, nauseous stomach like Eliza?

"When you walk through our doors on Monday morning, we implore you to take advantage of opportunities. Too often women are a slave to society. You are wise and shrewd enough to make society serve you. Learn to reach out to your patients and cure them by a scientific application of your sympathy. Know that every woman is born a doctor. Men have to study to become one."

With Dean Marshall's statements, combined with Anandi's tips and months of studying, Eliza's conviction soared. She chased away the fears which hung heavy on her shoulders and sat taller in her chair.

CHAPTER TWELVE

October 1897: First Year, Fall Semester

The opening-day rush to classes swept Eliza up into the frenzy. The Second-, Third- and Fourth-Year students paraded the hallways, their sure steps locked in unison. With linked arms and encircled waists, they paired into sets like cups and saucers, ready for knowledge to fill them before hours of study drained them dry. Their exuberant voices called out to friends. The First Years wove tentatively among them, scanning bronze plaques and referring to a sheet of paper in their hands, holding their initiation into medical school. Forty-two pairs of eyes searched for Room 204.

2-0-4. Here I am. Visions of mysterious worlds spread ahead of her. Unbidden but deeply comforting, a memory of Aunt Florence's steady voice reassured Eliza. Snuggled together on the parlor divan, Florence would read from her worn copy of *Alice in Wonderland*. They laughed at Alice's misadventures, agreed they did not care for the Queen of Hearts, and wondered what amazing creatures would walk across the next page. At bedtime, when Florence tucked seven-year-old Eliza in, she would feign a proper English accent and recite, *"'I know who I WAS when I got up this morning, but I think I must have been changed several times since then.'* How about you, Lizzy? How did you change today?" Then she would tap her index finger against the tip of Eliza's nose. Their secret good night.

Eliza's fingertips went to her neck. Its vein, *jugular arterial,* throbbed deep and primal. Behind her, another student with a blonde braid twisted into a snug bun brushed past, her maroon skirt swishing. Eliza waited for the woman to pass before she too crossed the threshold.

Inside, Eliza tapped her finger to her nose and let it linger. Seven rows of desks with their ladder-backed chairs formed six columns, filling the windowless classroom. Students choosing their seats spanned three decades. Young, fresh faces like Eliza at eighteen, and older ones lined with maturity; each called to find an outlet for their ambitions to heal and give purpose to their lives.

Eliza gathered her green muslin skirt to the side to take the empty seat next to the woman in the maroon skirt and white blouse. She was the same woman Eliza sat beside at the Introductory Address. Were they fated to pair up? As Eliza bent to open her satchel and retrieve her notebook, she turned to her right with a bright smile and said, "Hi. I'm Lizzy, er, Eliza Edwards."

The woman kept her eyes downcast, transfixed by the pencil in front of her. She had positioned her matriculation ticket on top of her notebook, centered and visible. Eliza retrieved her card from her satchel and positioned it on her desk.

"Isn't this exciting? Sometimes I have to pinch myself to be sure I'm really here."

Eliza's seat mate remained motionless.

This girl wants nothing to do with me. Maybe it's not fate at all.

When the door banged shut, the woman raised her head. Eliza followed the turn of the woman's attention. A broad-shouldered man with tousled black hair and piercing blue eyes strode into the classroom. His angled nose crooked to one side, broken at some point, and reset by an amateur. Low conversations echoing around the room ceased. Placing his armful of books atop the oak-paneled podium, he cleared his throat.

"Good morning, ladies. I'm Doctor Callaghan."

While not as harsh as Molly's, his brogue was thick enough for Eliza to notice. Silence lingered as the class locked their full attention on Dr. Patrick Callaghan. The 1897 fall semester at the Woman's Medical College of Pennsylvania was underway.

"Allow me to start by saying congratulations," Dr. Callaghan said. "You have passed your most difficult exam. I'm not referring to our arduous Entrance Exam. It's no secret many have said it's more challenging than the test for Jefferson and Penn. You should know Dean Marshall wishes to give no further fuel to our opponents that Woman's Med. students are in any way inferior to male medical students, beginning with the quality and intellect of the student we admit. Your attendance here is a testament to your abilities."

Four of the older women clapped. The others followed their lead, applauding their first victory.

"Yes, yes, well done. But the toughest part of your next four years is already behind you. Not the test, but your decision to dedicate yourself to the selflessness of our profession. We look to you, our next generation of doctors, for a fresh approach in healing. We ask you to combine the science of medicine with the art of sympathy, to become empathetic experts in your craft."

Turning back to the podium, he lifted the thick text to hold before him, "Class of 1901. Let's begin at the beginning. Chapter 1 from *Gray's Anatomy*, Embryology, from the Greek, *embryon* meaning the unborn."

Eliza released her tensed shoulders. As if the King of Hearts had spoken, Dr. Callaghan invited them to *begin at the beginning, and go on till you come to the end: then stop*. With the recollection of other sentences read by Aunt Florence, Eliza was ready to begin.

•   •   •

Eliza flipped back through seven pages of notes. Throughout the past two hours, she filled her pages, her transcription skills flawless, the words neat and primed for later review. The woman next to her uttered her first words, in a halting, clipped voice, "I'm Olga. Olga Povitzky from Marijampole, Russia."

Eliza guessed she might be foreign-born. What a marvel! In less than five months' time, Eliza had met a woman from India and now had a classmate from Russia. Women from unfamiliar parts of the world, yet all with a shared goal: to learn from the best teachers and become doctors.

Olga spread open her notebook. Singular words scattered across the page. "I will need more practice with note-taking. His accent threw me off the track. I studied with an English tutor from India. This Dr. Callaghan, he is from Ireland, no?"

"Yes, he sounds similar to our maid, Molly, from Ireland. You've got a good ear for accents."

"You give me much credit," said Olga with a light laugh. "It's the black hair, blue eyes and nose from a barroom brawl that makes me think Irish. Oh, I shouldn't have said that? I'm filled with the nerves."

"Me too," Eliza admitted. "I thought I might faint or vomit in the hallway before I came in." She raised her arm to her forehead and swayed, then brought her hand to her mouth to motion a gagging gesture.

Olga smiled, "Me as well."

As the students gathered their books to exit, Dr. Callaghan issued one more directive. "I trust you have secured your Bone Box? Bring it to our next class. Osteology is the backbone of the study of Anatomy. Ha! You see? Backbone?"

Chuckles slipped from the students' lips. Medical school needn't be grim and serious every minute of the day.

• • •

When Eliza learned from Anandi of the five-dollar fee required for the "Bone Box", another dilemma arose. Besides the Bone Box deposit, she also needed to purchase dissecting materials and pay a reading-room fee. If she were careful, those would be the only other expenses, unless she broke any slides or other equipment in the Bacteriological laboratory.

The outstanding fees, plus her $135 tuition, loomed in her mother's Expense ledger column. Over a section of algebra problems with Estelle one evening, Eliza chewed her pencil, "There's one equation I can't solve. How will I find twenty-two dollars for my additional fees?"

Estelle reached for the gnawed pencil, "We wanted to wait for Sunday. But I can see you're distracted, so best to tell you now."

Eliza's pale cheeks pinked as Estelle revealed the surprise. Florence would loan her money for her Bone Box. She could repay Florence at the end of the term when she received her deposit back. Estelle would contribute the sixteen dollars for the dissecting materials. Josephine gained permission from Dean Marshall to have her salary cut by fifty cents, equivalent to the reading room fee.

"There's one more," Estelle said.

She moved to the library desk and opened a side drawer, pulling from its depth four empty leather-bound journals. "I know you have one of them, but I'm sure Maria would have wanted you to have the rest."

"I-I-I- don't know what to say! You're the best aunts a girl could ever have."

From her literature class at Agnes Irwin, one of Eliza's favorite poems by Christina Rossetti surfaced from a tucked away spot in her heart.

For there is no friend like a sister in calm or stormy weather;
To cheer one on the tedious way,
To fetch one if one goes astry,
To lift one if one totters down,
To strengthen whilst one stands.

More than her mothers' sisters, her aunts were her sisters and friends, too. *And from what Anandi has told me, I may find more sisters at Woman's Med.,* Eliza thought.

• • •

Eliza and Olga walked together in search of the chemistry lab.

"Have you picked up your Bone Box?" asked Eliza.

"Yes, but my hotel room is cramped. I did not want the housekeeper looking inside, so I stowed it under my bed. It is giving me the night scaring dreams."

Olga is staying in a hotel? Eliza calculated the cost in her head. The expense must be astronomical. Yet, from the looks of Olga's Italian leather boots and the diamond hoops in her ears, Eliza expected cost was not an issue. A thick bankroll, however, could not buy other particulars a woman alone and in a foreign country may need. Wouldn't Olga prefer to live surrounded by the comfort of a family and share a room with a classmate who could help her with note-taking?

Eliza's mother had agreed to use the savings planned for Eliza's debut to cover her first-year tuition. But for her next three years, they would need rental monies from a boarder. The young Russian woman with the uninhibited laugh and money in her pocket would be a perfect solution.

CHAPTER THIRTEEN

December 1897: First Year, First Exams

A sharp elbow jab woke Eliza from her stupor. She started with a shake and lifted her chin to see Reverend Abrams at the lectern. He opened the book to the marked page and adjusted his glasses. Eliza's eyes sagged again, dreading the Reverend's droning voice for the Scriptures.

"From Romans. Chapter 15, Verses 4–13."

Another jab, followed by a hiss, "Eliza, sit up and look alive."

Eliza's mother sat next to her in the pew of St. Clement's Episcopal Church. Fir boughs hung from the pews' edges, tied with streams of purple and white ribbons. A wreath of more greenery occupied a pedestal beside the lectern. Around the wreath stood one pink and three purple candles with a single white one in the center. Two purple candles glowed with flickering flames to mark the second Sunday of Advent.

"For everything that was written, the past was written to teach us," intoned Reverend Abrams, "so that through the endurance taught in the Scriptures and the encouragement they provide, we might have hope. May the God who gives endurance and encouragement give you the same attitude of mind..."

Today's reading fostered the ideals of prophecy, endurance, and hope before the Savior's birth. Would it be blasphemous if Eliza thought the ideals should apply to term exams?

Dear God, please give me the endurance and encouragement to make it through next week. My mind is addled. My hopes are dim. These examinations may kill me. If the College uses my body for dissection, I doubt they'll find the cause of my death buried in tissues and organs. Mental exhaustion hides itself deep in the brain where neurons send tired tentacles out to every muscle until they cannot move.

Under leaden eyelids, Eliza's thoughts wandered far from the pew of St. Clement's back to the hallways of Woman's Med. Thanks to the hours she spent over the summer poring through *Gray's Anatomy,* she breezed through her Anatomy and Physiology classes. The cause and effects explained in the Materia Medica lectures captured her interest and fed her desire to understand the applications of different medicines for healing. She smiled to herself, recalling the eight rolls of gauze from Bandaging class which found their way into Olga's satchel. A charming Russian mummy attended the sophomores' annual Halloween party with her date, Countess Cassandra, Olga's Bone Box study partner.

Eliza's exhaustion stemmed from the bane of her existence: Chemistry. How many times in the last week had she checked the library's mantle clock thinking three hours had passed and seen the minute hand had advanced twenty minutes? She had five more hours of study ahead of her. When she returned to the pages of skeletal structures of compounds, the letters and numbers danced across the sheet like notes of a discordant symphony, jumbled and out of tune.

• • •

"Eliza, did you see Sally Cummings? I mean, Sally Devon?" asked her mother as they descended the church steps to the brisk December morning. "Looks like she may miss Christmas services.

She shouldn't be out much longer in her condition, although she looks marvelous. You should pay her a visit."

There were not enough hours in her day to bathe, eat, or sleep, yet her mother wanted her to visit pregnant Sally? Once Eliza started medical school, her former classmates, like Sally, disappeared into matrimony or preparing for their debut. The Presentation Ball had taken place five weeks prior with fanfare, well documented in the newspapers and over tea in homes like Eliza's across Philadelphia. Conversations around its success entered their parlor, too, when Laura's friends came to call. More than once, Eliza overheard her mother's pat response when asked about Eliza's plans. "Josephine says many of the female professors marry. Eliza can always teach after she graduates. A husband will consider a teaching position more amenable than hospital work."

"Sally's expectant glow is lovely, but honestly Mother, I can't think of anything else before my exams. I should have skipped church. I've lost two study hours I don't have."

"Nonsense. Church refreshes the soul and the mind, and it gets you out of that dreary library. The altar was exquisite today. The Guild outdid themselves with the decorations. Remind me to compliment Mrs. Lippincott."

Eliza smirked. There must be another filing cabinet somewhere in her brain to tuck in a note to compliment Mrs. Lippincott about wreaths, bows, and candles. *I'll just toss aside the notes about hydrocarbons, or maybe I won't miss my pages on ketones.*

As Eliza fit her hand into the crook of her mother's arm to walk home, she felt a presence behind them. A stutter stalled their steps.

"Excuse me. Mrs. Edwards. Miss Edwards."

Eliza peeked over her shoulder. Nathan Putnam stood behind them, turning his bowler hat round and round in his hands. Square shoulders filled out his brown tweed suit to complement his sandy hair and pencil mustache. The crimson-colored cashmere muffler at his neck matched the redness building in his cheeks as he looked at Eliza with his wide-set, velvet brown eyes.

Laura replied first to his interruption, "Nathan Putnam! Aren't you a pleasant sight? You're home for Christmas break?"

"Yes, ma'am. Arrived yesterday. Finished on Friday. I was wondering...um, I'd like to...may I walk you home, Miss Edwards?"

Gray narrowed eyes stared at Eliza. Eliza caught the stare, knowing full well the answer her mother wanted to hear her say. She considered for a moment the implication of accepting his offer. Placing her hand on Nathan's arm posed no danger. Albie and Freddy considered him a friend. A walk was a walk, and nothing more. Moreover, here, at her feet, was a chance to escape from twenty more minutes listening to ceaseless rambling about expectant friends, floral arrangements, and subtle hints about working too hard.

"Thank you, Mr. Putnam, I would enjoy your company."

• • •

Once back in their home library, failure awaited Eliza in the guise of Organic Chemistry. The amber arc from the glass lamp glowed warm and low against white pages scattered over the desktop. Eliza loosened her hair; it spread over the desk in rivulets as she rested her head upon her folded arms. She opened her red-rimmed eyes and propped her chin on the back of her hands. The textbooks before her became a mountain range. Their ragged, steep walls closed in on her.

Defeated, she closed her eyes again to return to a half-dream state, walking on the arm of Nathan Putnam. With his tongue tied, Eliza launched into a conversation about a sensational story covered by Philadelphia newspapers.

"Did you read the story about the incident in the Italian tenements?" she asked.

"Who hasn't? My father read the entire story from the *Inquirer* aloud over breakfast yesterday. It sounds like a Shakespearean play."

Jerry Timboni evicted one of his boarders, Antonio Tucci, a "Love-Crazed Italian," after learning Tucci attempted to kiss his fifteen-year-old daughter, Teresa, on her lips. Enraged by the eviction, Tucci shot Mr. Timboni six times, threw a lamp at Timboni's son, and held a match to the oil-saturated boy before police descended on the scene.

"I hope they rushed Mr. Timboni to a hospital. The report sounded dire. If any of the bullets hit his internal organs, terrible infections can develop if they're not cleaned well immediately."

"I haven't heard any more, but we should commend him for his heroic act, taking not one, but six bullets in the name of his daughter's honor," Nathan said. "Many men could learn from his actions."

"And from Teresa," added Eliza. "The paper didn't need to lead with describing her as 'a pretty girl with large black eyes and long, coal-black tresses.' The reporter should have led with the fact she hit Tucci on the head with a fireplace poker before telling her father of his advances."

Their conversation had been genial and easy. When they reached Race Street, Nathan paused. Lest he imagine there was anything more between them than a mile stroll, Eliza wished him a Merry Christmas, stepped across the threshold, and back to her fortress of solitude.

How much simpler it would be to continue her stroll with Nathan. How much simpler it would be to walk away from the rigor and demands of her studies, and into a comfortable home where a man admired the honorable acts of another. Nathan Putnam might be such a man, someone like Mr. Timboni to protect and provide. Eliza would file her stack of textbooks on her grandfather's shelves next to *Gray's Anatomy* and pick up her mother's version of *Grimms' Fairy Tales*. Attending medical school would never have occurred to Cinderella.

Yet how could she abandon her studies now? The chemistry class was demanding, but she had done well in her other classes. Lost in her thought, she kicked off her shoes. *I don't need a glass slipper. I'll pull through this nightmare somehow and awaken to my happy ending.*

· · ·

Olga tiptoed into the library, her dressing gown tied loosely at her waist, her long blonde hair hanging down her back.

"Napping Beauty," she shook Eliza awake. "You'll hear from your mother, keeping those expensive Edison bulbs burning at this hour."

Olga dubbed Eliza the Napping Beauty after finding her night after night asleep before her opened textbook, usually the Chemistry one. "I'm resting my eyes," Eliza argued to no avail.

Eliza stirred, interlaced her fingers, and stretched her arms up. "What time is it?" She squinted at the mantle clock's Roman numerals. Twenty after two. Two hours ticked by since she last noticed the time. Time wasted in her combat against the pile of notes. "Drat. I have four more chapters. This is hopeless."

Eliza envied Olga's innate ability to decipher the maze of Organic Chemistry. One evening, Eliza discovered Olga squirreled away in their bedroom, reading the new dramatic play and love story, *Cyrano de Bergerac*, instead of studying.

Olga gathered Eliza's hair into a loose knot and soothed, "As Cyrano shared his gift of poetic eloquence with his friend, Christian, I shall share my gift of knowledge in Organic Chemistry. I won't listen to you speak of hopelessness. I will be your Cyrano."

How could Olga suggest such an idea? Above the fireplace mantle hung a gilded-framed painting of Judge William S.

Pearson. Eliza felt him peer over his frameless eyeglasses at her. He was a stout man with thinning hair, neither gray nor white except at his temples in the manner of distinction. Thick muttonchop whiskers sloped down his cheeks. Organizers for the Centennial Exhibition in 1876 commissioned the portrait to commemorate notable gentlemen of Philadelphia. Years after the Exhibition, Harvard University wrote several times to Josephine, requesting it for the Hollis Library at their Law School. Each request received a prompt and courteous reply: No.

"Surely, you won't whisper answers to me during the exam!" said Eliza, her hand flying to her chest. "I could never cheat! That's worse than failing."

"Don't be absurd. You're exhausted. There's a light at the end of the tunnel. It may be dim, but I'll lead you to it. We'll get through this together. Give me your notes, I'll quiz you," Olga said.

"You're amazing. You always make me smile." Eliza handed her notes over and encircled her friend.

"You know what makes me smile?" asked Olga. "The seventh cranial nerve!"

CHAPTER FOURTEEN

April 1899: Second Year, Spring Semester

Eliza stood beneath a white arbor arched over a walkway in Logan Circle. She lifted her chin and inhaled a deep breath through her nose. One, two, three, four…

Neat rows of grape hyacinths popped their heads up from brown earth. Dew drops moistened the purple clusters, giving them a fresh glint of life. She pulled the fruity, warm scent further into her being.

…twenty-one, twenty-two, twenty-three. Specks of silver flickered before her eyes. Her body wavered.

"For heaven's sake. What are you doing?" Olga grabbed Eliza's arm and shook her. Eliza's lips opened with a gushing exhale, "Breathe it in."

"Breathe what in?"

Eliza dropped her satchel of notebooks and pencils. Eight months' worth of work thumped onto the park path, sending up puffs of gravel dust to settle on the toe of her boots. Her arms stretched high. The tips of her fingers wiggled, reaching for the mass of free-flowing loops of golden honeysuckle dangling from the arbor's lattice work. Yellow and white petals, pistols, and stamens floated above her fingertips. Their sticky scents lingered on her lips and tongue.

"The air. The delicious smells."

Olga rolled her eyes, "We weren't told to act out the chapter about the insane, just read it."

"Don't be a bore. I'm not mad. Or maybe I am. Starting Monday mornings with Chemistry is bad enough, but at least it's out of the way. But two hours in the pathology lab? Locked inside that prison? That could drive anyone loony."

Woman's Medical championed the opinion that its students must remain at the forefront of evolutions in medicine. To stay true to its mission, recent expansion included a separate laboratory. Students immersed themselves in preparing cultures, learning plating techniques, staining slides, and identifying microbes. Dr. Lydia Rabinowitsch of the Berlin Institute, already a preeminent infectious disease expert at the age of twenty-four, chaired the Pathology department. Eliza and her classmates dubbed her Rabid Rabi, for her ardent approach to teaching. She turned the mundane into the marvelous with her passion and intellect.

Most students found the squirming bacilli swimming through agar solutions captured their curiosities as they investigated diseases and treatments. But not Eliza. She would rather cradle a wrist, touch a forehead, and to the best of her abilities, know how to care for a patient, not the impersonal laboratory work of developing cures.

Olga picked up Eliza's satchel and urged it back into her fingers. "You've made it this far, what's three more weeks? And you have to appreciate Rabid Rabi's contagious flair. How could you not love lab time?"

"I'm thankful for Rabi. But it's the smells. I can't breathe those hideous fumes one second longer. They make me gag every day. Blood, pus, intestines, brain matter. Those I can take. The cultures' rancid odors are the worst. Worse than the foulest stink of Albie's and Freddy's sweaty tennis shirts rolled into balls and left in their athletic bags for months. They reek to high heavens and the depths of hell."

"That's saying something! I had no idea they bothered you so much." Olga reached into her skirt pocket. "As your friend, I'll let you in on a secret. Why do I grab the station in the corner every class?"

Eliza never paid attention to where everyone sat. What difference did it make? Each spot had a chair pulled in tight, sitting inches away from odorous villains on slides clamped beneath microscope lenses. She shrugged at Olga's pointless question.

"In the corner, no one sees my secret."

A secret? Olga shared everything with Eliza.

Olga produced a slender wooden clothespin from her pocket and clipped it on her nose, "Use it and take my spot today. I'll suffer through somehow," she said, her words pinched as tight as her nasal passages.

•   •   •

As Eliza walked to the corner station, she stroked Olga's secret weapon. Thinking only of the savior at her fingertips, she bumped into a side table holding the day's supply of petri dishes. Three fell to the floor. All but one dish was closed tight. The loose lid rolled and twirled in time with a centrifugal force, coming to rest against Eliza's boot. Splinters of glass mingled with an amber gel of a culture.

Forty-two pairs of eyes shifted from lenses to the clatter.

"Oh drat!" Eliza reached for the shattered pieces of the dish labeled *Salmonella typhi* by her foot.

A sheath of light gray muslin intercepted her hand. A worn handkerchief dropped over the open dish.

"Don't touch it," said Edith Haskins. "It may not have been heated yet."

Dr. Rabinowitsch moved forward while the rest of the women shrank back to the safety of the room's perimeter.

"Very good, Miss Haskins," she said. "Precaution and prevention are often the most effective medicine. Miss Edwards. Place your name on the sheet. Everyone else, take a seat. I'll see to the clean-up."

For two years, Eliza avoided signing 'the sheet'. Every other time in class when she scripted her "E's" and "P," her signature heralded accomplishments. Rabi's sheet marked failure. She broke a valuable piece of equipment and ruined the culture. Next to E. Edwards, on the sheet of shame, she entered the assigned amount. She would have to tell her mother she needed an extra two dollars by the end of the term to pay for the breakage.

• • •

A couple more hours remained on her schedule before Eliza could hurry home to the comfort of dinnertime. Molly's savory lamb stew awaited, a favorite to finish the remains from Easter dinner. Dr. Frances White's call for responses circled the physiology class, drawing Eliza out of her daydream of rounds of carrot atop a bowl of steaming stew, with a fresh baked snowflake roll, and a pat of creamy yellow butter on the side.

Dr. White: "Dell–Cytosol."
Caroline Dell: "Intracellular fluid."
Dr. White: "Edwards–Ribosomes."
Eliza Edwards: "The site of protein synthesis."
Dr. White: "Fairbanks–Stratum lucidum."
Charlotte Fairbanks: "Clear layers of dead skin cells in the epidermis."
Dr. White: "Haskins–Centrosome."
Edith Haskins: "The organelles needed to form the cilia and flagella which serve as the main microtubule organizing center."

Dr. White finished with Katherine Ulrich and dismissed the class. Eliza pushed back from her desk, pleased with her answers during recitations. They weren't as expansive as Charlotte's and Edith's, but they were correct.

The last of the students exited the classroom, ready for their two-hour dinner break. Despite her weariness, Eliza scurried to catch up with the woman ahead of her with a tight bun of mousy brown hair. A few gray strands loosened from hair pins disappeared into the shoulders of a drab brown suit jacket.

"Edith!"

Edith's purposeful gait halted. Eliza came to her side.

"I haven't thanked you for your quick thinking and helping me this morning in pathology," said Eliza.

"Don't mention it, dear."

Dear? Aunt Estelle used old-fashioned terms like that. Eliza studied Edith's face a moment longer than what would be polite. She never noticed the fragile lines creased at the corners of her dull, brown eyes, nor the set of her quiet lips, used for recitations, not light conversation. She also had never seen Edith at any of their get-togethers like the occasional tennis match, or a rare Sunday afternoon hoop-rolling or bicycling along the Schuylkill.

As Edith moved to continue out of the classroom, Eliza touched her arm, "Would you care to join us for supper? A delicious lamb stew's been simmering all day. I find I need extra fuel to get me through Monday night's dissection class."

• • •

Over a fresh blueberry crumble and coffee, Estelle asked what led to Edith's decision to study medicine.

"I lost my mother three years ago to an unfortunate medical error. My work at my father's practice became meaningless. I felt capable of more than accounting tasks, something where I could help other women avoid my mother's fate simply because she was going through the Change. Medical school made sense," answered Edith.

The Change. Could Eliza's mother have died during her most afflicted menopause days? Eliza cringed at the thought. An Ovariin prescription eased her mother's discomfort. Yet did the powdered substance contain fatal side effects? Eliza scrutinized her mother's face. A shadow of concern lurked in Laura's eyes.

Eager to put her mother at ease, Eliza interjected with her own question, "I don't mean to be so forward, but can you tell us about the error? Was your mother taking anything?"

"I wanted her to try Ovariin when her emotions flared, but my father ignored my suggestion. He would only listen to the general practitioner who visited once and claimed a hysterectomy would cure what he called, a woman's hysterics," said Edith.

A seething crimson blush crept across her face. She lowered her eyes and her voice. "The doctor botched the operation. My mother never woke from the ether."

No wonder, thought Eliza. Between the loss of her mother and decisions made by her father and the doctor, Edith has good reason for her subdued, stern demeanor. At least the world would gain a dedicated professional of high intellect when Edith Haskins earned her degree.

"I'm so sorry for your loss," murmured Eliza. She glanced around the table at the Pearson women gathered there, her mother, Estelle, Josephine. "We lost my Aunt Maria two years ago and miss her every day." She hesitated a moment before whispering, "Her last words were 'no male doctors.'"

The Pearson women lowered their eyes for a moment of remembrance. Estelle lifted her eyes first, looking directly at Edith. "I'm sure your mother would be proud of the choice you made, Edith, and how you're honoring her," she said.

"Thank you. You're very kind."

"You'll return to Harrisburg to open a women's practice after you graduate?" asked Olga.

"Eventually, yes. But first, it will be China or the Philippines. Father refused to pay my tuition and board, so I had to secure the funds. I sold the few pieces of jewelry and sterling I inherited from my mother and have some savings. My father paid me a small salary to manage his office handling appointments, correspondence, recording and filing transactions. I hoped to find a similar part-time position in Philadelphia but haven't found anything. Dean Marshall directed me to the Ladies' Missionary Society. They're paying my tuition for the next two years in exchange for my service after I graduate."

"I'm surprised the Bible-thumpers would approve of an unmarried woman doctor," Estelle said.

"They must be desperate for medical staff. And I'm not too keen on living with them for three years in a foreign country either, with their fire and brimstone judgments, but I don't have any other choice to finish my degree."

Across the table, Eliza exchanged a knowing smile with Olga. With Olga's rent monies put toward Eliza's tuition, she needn't fear shipping off to the wilds of the South Pacific. Instead, she stayed home at Race Street in the warm embrace of family and friends.

• • •

Soon after her visit, Estelle referred Edith to Isaac Baldwin, a junior lawyer who would consider hiring an assistant with no inclination for flirtations and who wore loose fitting dark suits. Six hours a week at Baldwin's office would help Edith cover her last two years' tuition.

After Embryology class one Thursday early in May, Eliza inquired of Edith how she was managing between classes, study, and Mr. Baldwin's office. At no surprise, Edith replied she was sufficiently handling the demands on her time. Yet, her boarding expenses remained a drain on her income, she told Eliza. "I may join the Bible-thumpers after all," she said.

Eliza came home that night with an idea. Before readying for another night's battle of the books, she found her mother and Estelle in the kitchen discussing tomorrow's market list. Eliza poured herself a cup of coffee from the blue speckled enamelware pot Molly learned to keep on a low flame every evening.

"I caught up with Edith today. I invited her to come over on Saturday and study with Olga and me before exams start next week. She's a whiz in physiology, I'd love her help. You don't mind, do you, Mother?" she asked.

"Not in the least. She seems very pleasant."

"And, smart and hard-working. Mr. Baldwin thanked me again just yesterday for referring her. He's quite impressed with her aptitude," said Estelle.

"Yes, she asked me to thank you, too. She said the wages are a tremendous help." Eliza swirled the black coffee around in the cup. She focused on the eddy. "But she's worried she'll run short for next term's tuition. Her rooming house raised its rent to six dollars."

A dribble of the hot coffee spilled out onto her lap. With her other hand, she brushed the drips away.

"Maybe we could rent Maria's room to Edith for four dollars? At that rate, she should be able to decline the missionary service."

Estelle immediately remarked, "That's a fine idea, Eliza."

"Mother?" asked Eliza, hopeful for an echo of Estelle's approval. "Sixteen dollars a month can go a long way toward the layette Albie and Mamie will need soon."

"Playing on a grandmother-to-be's desires? You're a smart one, too," said Laura.

"Is that a yes?"

"Yes, we'll tell her together on Saturday."

Eliza drained her coffee, rose, and crossed the room to squeeze a thank you into her mother's hand. As she turned to head upstairs, her mother summoned her back. "I hope Edith knows how to wash a coffee cup." She picked up the dirty cup Eliza left in the sink and handed it to her along with the dish cloth and soap.

CHAPTER FIFTEEN

December 1899: Third Year, Fall Semester

Eliza lifted Mamma Mia, as she named the skull, from her Bone Box, preparing for today's lecture on the cranial cavity. She and the rest of the class looked up from their boxes when they heard a sharp rap. Without waiting for an invitation to enter, the door opened. Dean Marshall walked to the lecture hall's prime speaking spot in the middle of the room. Eliza sat up straighter in her chair. Dean Marshall rarely attended lectures.

After dismissing Dr. Stevens, she addressed the class, "Ladies, a serious gastrointestinal outbreak has affected many students and faculty members, including Dr. Parish and Dr. Rodman, and many Jefferson Medical faculty. You will stay on schedule by completing Dr. Parish's Advanced Physiology and Dr. Rodman's clinical surgery classes by attending lectures and observations at Pennsylvania Hospital with students from Jefferson. We are combining classes and sharing instructors until the illness passes. This allows you to finish the semester on time and keep to your plans if you're traveling home for the holidays."

The silence which entered the room with Dean Marshall faltered. Eliza bent to whisper to Olga just as every other student did the same with her seatmate. "A co-ed lecture? Those are reserved for Fourth-Years."

Olga tugged on Eliza's upper sleeve to pull her closer. "A nice early Christmas surprise. If they wear bow ties, they'll look as tempting as gifts under a tree."

Eliza shook her head, imploring Olga not to make her laugh. Their naivete glowed as bright as the Bunsen burners in the chemistry laboratory. Dean Marshall picked up Dr. Stevens' textbook and dropped it to the podium. The heavy thump quieted the whispers churning among the rows.

"Report to the lobby tomorrow morning by ten o'clock. Dr. Callaghan will accompany you on the streetcar. Many of you attended Agnes Irwin's School, or other similar institutions, and this may be the first time in years you've attended a class with members of the opposite sex. Likewise, many of the men attended all-male secondary schools and are unaccustomed to having women present."

The dean leveled her eyes behind her bifocals. With a cursory scan of the women, she pointed to one and then another.

"Miss Haskins. Miss Fairbanks. Will you please stand? Ladies, make note of their dress choices when you consider your attire for tomorrow. Neat, plain brown or gray woolen or tweed suits are best. No lace trimmings or other adornments. Jackets should remain buttoned. No jewelry, cosmetics, or rosewater. You are students of medicine, not debutantes."

No, we aren't! Eliza thought with a triumphant toss of her head. *We belong to a far more important society.*

"Thank you. Miss Fairbanks, Miss Haskins, you may sit," directed Dean Marshall. "I have one more piece of news which will be posted tomorrow in our bulletin. Since I know a few of you"—she searched the rows—"knew Anandi Gopal Joshi, our first graduate from India, I thought it might be best to inform you in person. We've received devastating news."

Eliza's hand flew to her chest. Did her heart still beat? Was there air in her lungs? Her body silenced into dread.

Olga grabbed Eliza's hand and pulled it to her lap. She entwined her fingers to still the tremble coursing through Eliza's body.

A hint of moisture sneaked into the Dean's eyes. She blinked.

"On November 26th, Anandi succumbed to the ravages of tuberculosis. Please join me in a moment of silence to honor Dr. Joshi. We will plan a larger remembrance in the spring. She asked that her ashes be sent to America for burial."

Eliza melted into Olga. Only moments before, she and Olga chuckled about men in bow ties. Now, the truth of life and death banished trivial thoughts. Her eyes closed tight. She willed her throat to follow suit and trap the sobs surging up from her heart. Her tremors turned to convulsions. Powerless, against the ferocity of her anguish, her tears burst forth as she wailed into Olga's shoulder.

With a gentle nudge, Olga pushed her upright. Taking her by the elbow, she guided Eliza out of the room. Eliza sank onto the bench in the hallway, her head sagging toward her lap, hands covering her face, shaking uncontrollably. The storm of her grief engulfed her. In between gulps of air, Eliza sputtered, "Anandi. How could this happen? So unfair. Why?"

"I don't know," said Olga as she rubbed Eliza's back in maternal circles. Eliza's sobs slowed. Her heaving calmed for her mind to voice other thoughts. "Where is the humanity?" she asked Olga. "How does this reflect a God who loves his people?"

A voice behind them interrupted her questions of injustice. "The revered William Shakespeare wrote in Macbeth, '*Give sorrow words. The grief that does not speak whispers the o-er wrought heart and bids it break.*'"

Eliza hadn't heard the door next to them open and close again. She lifted her head to see Dean Marshall standing before them.

Dean Marshall addressed her directly, "Miss Edwards, there will always be questions and a hole in our hearts that Dr. Joshi was denied fulfilling her dreams to become the doctor she so desperately desired to be. Throughout my years in medicine, I've witnessed many losses and much grief. As such, I have amended Mr. Shakespeare's lines. Rather than give sorrow words, to raise you above your grief, give it actions to fortify your breaking heart."

Eliza wiped the back of her hand across her cheeks. "Dean Marshall. Forgive me for my outburst. I..."

"There is no need to apologize. With this sad news, I'm glad I can speak with you. While Dr. Joshi's death is a tragedy, you must look beyond the questions. You can sit and wallow in sorrow, or you can stride forward. Which choice would Dr. Joshi expect?"

A simple answer.

"I would be honored for Anandi to know I became Dr. Eliza Edwards," said Eliza.

Olga's arm encircled Eliza's shoulders. "With Anandi watching over us, you will become Dr. Edwards. She will unwind her headscarf and drape it over us as she smiles upon us on our graduation day."

• • •

Eliza bristled as a group of Jefferson men brushed past her and her classmates in the hallway at Pennsylvania Hospital. With feet stomping and snickers spreading through the corridor, the men headed in the same direction toward the oversized classroom. Arriving first made no difference. The students who listened, learned, and queried would be the victors.

Behind them, Dr. Callaghan stopped and waved off the noise. "Your attention belongs to Dr. Parish and Advanced Physiology. You are here to learn and form questions for our discussion afterward. I expect you will be thorough. In fact, perhaps more so than the Jefferson students. Your intellect and passion equal theirs. I daresay, you exceed most of them who lack a calling to heal and the many who are here at the behest of a father who may be a physician."

The women followed him, single file, into the classroom and took their seats. Drab skirts blended into one as Eliza sat on the aisle next to Edith and behind Olga. Across from her, Eliza heard two men exchange comments.

"Ah, will you look there? A red rose amidst a dandelion and horse chestnut."

"You think the flames below are as fiery as those on top?"

Eliza steamed. She occasionally overheard her brothers talk about women, but their comments never veered into uncomfortable innuendos.

The man on the aisle, two feet away from Eliza, with his back turned, tilted his chin toward his friend's lap, "Down, boy. She's out of your league."

Olga snapped her head around and quipped loud enough for three rows to hear, "You bet she is."

•   •   •

"Well done, Eliza. Your question about pancreatic enzymes' inactive forms turned those Jefferson men on their heads," said Olga as she sidled up to Eliza and draped her arm around Eliza's shoulders.

Eliza beamed. "Well, you know far too well chemical reactions aren't my strong suit. I spent an extra hour studying last night; it seemed like a logical question. I'm surprised no one else thought to ask."

Most medical students could shape questions about chemical reactions. But for Eliza, it was a major victory in her battle against the trials of chemistry. Each night she fell asleep lying on her side staring at the Periodic Table of Elements tacked to the wall next to her bed. Mysterious markings populated the symmetrical squares, a jumble of puzzle pieces. Metals and non-metals. Noble gases. Atomic structure. Positive and negative charges. Actions and reactions. Glass beakers in the chemistry lab terrified her. One wrong pour or one inaccurate measurement could be disastrous, sending out toxic vapors–or worse–an explosion to level the lab and maim or kill her classmates. She pinned her singular hope on mustering a passing grade and moving on to the next required course.

Their next class entailed observing a rare and challenging surgery. A patient from Pittsburgh sought the expertise of Pennsylvania Hospital's surgeons. A cancer ravaged his face. To ease his pain, he pleaded with the surgeons to attempt a delicate procedure and remove the tumor.

"Let's move along ladies," said Charlotte Fairbanks to Eliza and Olga as they lingered after the lecture.

Charlotte Fairbanks, from St. Johnsbury, Vermont, declared her intent to become a surgeon when she arrived at Woman's Med. as a Second-Year, after obtaining degrees in chemistry from Smith College and Yale University. Eliza dreaded being paired with the much more adept Charlotte during dissection class. Her hands shook, while Charlotte's commanded confidence and competence, further emphasizing Eliza's lesser abilities. Eliza instructed Olga, "If I ever go under a knife, please make sure it's in Charlotte's hand."

"That figures," said Olga. "Charlotte hurrying us along to watch a surgery. Have you ever seen her at a dinner table? She carves a roast beef like it's a cadaver."

"I think she sleeps with a scalpel in her hand," Eliza said.

"She probably does," said Edith, joining the women outside the door. "I know she's looking forward to this surgery, but I for one, am not. I've heard facial surgeries are dreadful. We need to watch each other, too. If you see anyone wavering, pinch her or something. We can't give these Jefferson blockheads any fodder to think we don't belong in the operating room as much as they do."

Eliza nodded to Edith, "Wonderful idea. Pass it along to everyone else."

"A facial surgery may be gruesome, but do you think they chose it for us to observe on purpose?" Olga asked.

"On purpose?" Edith said.

"Can you imagine if men and women students, together, witnessed the exposure of any other body part? A patient in the nude? At least his body will be wrapped in sheets as tight as a chastity belt." Olga winked, her long lashes lingering over her eye.

"Honestly, Olga, you come up with the zaniest thoughts," said Eliza.

"Go ahead, laugh, but I bet I'm right."

A wooden table occupied the center of the theater, a white surgical sheet pulled taut over the surface. A miracle or doomed fate would transpire there. Overhead, a bare lamp flickered off and on until its stream of light shone steadily. Two stepped platforms encircled the room like choir risers around a church altar. The Woman's Med. students entered, walking down the center aisle, solemn, with heads bowed in reverence. This patient will need our prayers, thought Eliza.

Sensing the operation's serious nature, the Jefferson students followed them, with prior banter and jabs quieted.

The surgeon preceded the patient, orderlies, and nurses. As the orderlies arranged the anesthetized man on the table, Dr. Palmer addressed the students, "The patient presented himself to his local practitioner four months ago with a tumor on the left side of his face the size of a quarter. Since then, it's doubled in size, extending into his mouth area, and diagnosed as malignant. Our Medical Jurisprudence team advised him there is no hope removal will restore his health. Our evaluation board certified his sanity to ensure he understands the ramifications. This operation is proceeding under the pretense of experimental and demonstrative purposes of a living organism."

Eliza reached for Edith's hand on one side and Olga's on the other. The height of the risers' front panels screened their clasped hands from sight. Down the line in domino fashion, every Woman's Med. student took up the woman's hand on either side of her. They trained their eyes forward to the table, following the lamp's lightened path.

The first incision started below the inner edge of the patient's eye and continued along the nose line to his lip. Two slits from each corner extended outward to the jawbone. A wave of nausea enveloped Eliza. She gritted her teeth as she felt her body sway. Averting her eyes from the table, she watched a Jefferson man slump to the floor. She turned back to the surgery unfolding before her. With a pair of clamps in each hand, one of the surgical residents peeled the flap of skin as Dr. Palmer snipped the tendons. Eliza gripped Edith's and Olga's hands tighter. They returned the pressure. Another Jefferson student dropped. Out of the corner of her eye, she glimpsed an ashen pallor creep across Olga's face as her grip weakened.

Heeding Edith's warning to remain steadfast, Eliza pinched the fleshy underpart of Olga's forearm.

"Owww," Olga exclaimed.

Eliza ignored the cry. The blood returned to Olga's face.

By the end of the surgery, beneath their jacket sleeves, bruises and welts from pinches and crescent moon shaped imprints from fingernails appeared as medals of valor.

• • •

A cluster of dead leaves tumbled along the sidewalk and blended into the trio of matched skirts. The gusty, mid-December air brought cooler temperatures with snow forecast for the evening. The women leaned into each other, drawing upon the warmth of sisterly friendship and strength.

As their fifth semester concluded, courage and determination braced them. In sixteen days, a new year, a new decade, and a new century would dawn. 1900 promised possibilities. Eliza and her classmates would define a new woman. Independent women who strove for more and achieved more. They would become doctors. An enlightened century of medicine would emerge. The time had arrived.

Olga tightened her arms to squeeze Eliza's and Edith's hands linked into the crook of her elbows. "I've never seen such a horrific scene. Dr. Palmer carved up the poor man's face like a Christmas goose. But we did it! Not one of us old medic hens hit the ground. Hurrahs for us! A new day is coming, ladies. 1900 best be aware."

Tone deaf and off-pitch, Eliza never sang outside of church. But in this moment, after this quiet triumph, she added a musical rhythm, stressing the lesser-known words of Tennyson as the women marched down the sidewalk.

Ring out the old,
ring in the new.
Ring, happy bells,
across the snow.
The year is going,
let him go;
Ring out the false,
ring in the true.

CHAPTER SIXTEEN

May 1901: Fourth Year, Final Exams

The watch's second hand ticked away the last moments of the exam. Eliza set her grandfather's pocket watch at the top of her desk, nearby to track her remaining minutes. Around her, six sets of desks formed clusters of the Class of 1901. Eliza raised her head from her composition notebook and glimpsed her classmates writing their final Obstetrics reports with fervor. Over four years, their study had been intense, their commitments unwavering, their support of each other undeniable.

"Time. Pencils down," called Dr. Callaghan from his chair in the rear corner.

Eliza dropped her pencil. Her shoulders slumped. "Oh, dang it."

Across from her, other exhausted hands dropped pencils into the grooves at the edge of desktops. Eliza felt sure the other students documented their patients' cases with complete information from an initial mother-to-be assessment down to the exact hour of births, infants' measurements, and responsiveness levels. Her notes strayed. She spent too much time chatting with the mothers, wanting to better assess the home life they would bring a child into, their hopes, and their fears. Perhaps she erred too far on the side of sympathy over science.

"Eliza, it's fine. You've already passed Hygiene, Pediatrics, Practical, and Clinical," said Olga.

"Passed? Yes, by the skin of my teeth. But I still have thirty more slides for histology. I bet it was evil Professor Stevens who insisted on 200 rather than let us stop at 150. Any of you girls need to go to the lab?"

"Off to the reading room for me," said Charlotte, pushing her round wire spectacles back up her long narrow nose. "My horrid thesis, the bête noire of my existence, beckons. I need to wrap it up tonight to get out to County tomorrow. One of my patients is not recovering as well as I'd like. I followed proper procedures for an antiseptic ovariotomy, so it shouldn't be an infection. Then again, she could be play-acting to avoid her cell in General Population. Her history as an actress is well-documented in the report of her attempted suicide."

Charlotte's grit to stare down the goriest specimens, from frogs and turtles to unidentified cadavers from the city morgue, fueled her interest in surgery. After reviewing her abilities, the College's Corporators encouraged her to apply for the residency at the Philadelphia County Prison in the Female Department. On paper, the warden argued a woman surgeon could attend to minor surgeries. Unspoken, but equally as important, she had the potential to monitor and reduce the common occurrence of abuse by male staff on female inmates.

Eliza pitied those women, the ones who lost their way and replaced their dreams with never-ending nightmares and self-loathing. They required a doctor like Charlotte, not Eliza. More likely, she would find her future in the tenements of South Philadelphia. Throughout the spring of this, her fourth year, Eliza learned to look beyond the sparse furnishings and dirtied floors to see the souls who lived inside those sordid walls. Even in the sparsest and dirtiest buildings, Eliza witnessed the overflowing adoration mothers shared with their children. These women clung to the same hopes and longings as Eliza: the chance to live freely, nurture their children with a clear love, hold them close, and guide them toward a future of brighter possibilities.

With Charlotte off to the prison, Eliza turned next to Edith.

"Edith, how about you?"

"I've got to complete my ventilation system analysis, then my afternoon hours for Mr. Baldwin. Two birds—one stone. See you later."

Besides exams, clinical and lab work, another graduation requirement involved inspections of public buildings to analyze ventilation, heating, lighting, and drainage systems. Their analyses emphasized bacteriology principles and the demand for tighter sanitation measures to combat the spread of germs and disease. Edith chose the Philadelphia City Hall, making it convenient to visit from Mr. Baldwin's office around the corner.

"Olga, you'll come with me?"

"'*Out, damned spot! out, I say!*' My horrors continue," said Olga. "I cannot bear looking at another slide. I think I'll re-energize with a game of tennis, followed by the promise of Molly's gingersnaps and lemon tea at home, and the fluff of the puff on my bed for a nap."

Eliza's tightened jaw slacked, and her eyes twinkled when Olga referred to Race Street as her home. From the moment Olga unpacked her valises, she became more than a lucrative rent check. She joined the family as another daughter, another niece, a sister. Most of all, Olga's amiable nature, inclination to comedic remarks, and ready laugh captivated their hearts. Whenever a new face joined them for dinner, Olga heartily retold a favorite story from their first year.

"Our physiology professor droned on and on about Darwin's theory of evolution. At the end, Eliza asked how I liked the lecture. I replied, deadpan and without the slightest knowledge of my pun, 'I did not understand it very well, but there seemed to be a lot of monkey business.'"

"Besides," Olga continued, "I cannot risk breaking any more slides. My name on the sheet of shame extends onto the second side. I dread handing the tally for my breakage to Father when he arrives next week."

At the mention of Olga's father, Eliza's gleam dulled. Mr. Povitzky's arrival signaled Olga's departure. She would return to her family in Russia. Eliza tried to banish the image of a severed limb sawed from a torso during a dissection procedure from her mind. At least the cadaver felt no pain, the rending of its limb, the break of its bones. Its soul had departed, its heart had stopped beating. Eliza's had not. Her severed limb, her Olga, her sister, would sail away to the other side of the world.

• • •

The women deposited their notebooks on the podium and headed to exit. Dr. Callaghan interrupted the group, "Miss Edwards, may I have a word, please?"

Eliza froze. "Go ahead. I'll be just a minute," she said to Olga and Edith. *Oh, Lord, I hope it's just a minute. What does he want?* Perhaps her inspection report on the Naval Asylum lacked details? What if she failed an exam—a grading error? Years of dedication, months of tears, days upon days of stress flew through her mind's eye.

"Yes, Dr. Callaghan?" Eliza edged toward his seat. The stack of notes she held fluttered.

A black leather-bound journal rested atop other books in a weathered, tan canvas satchel at Dr. Callaghan's feet. He withdrew it from the bag and opened to a page marked by a red ribbon.

At the doorway, Olga called over her shoulder, "Excuse me, Dr. Callaghan?"

He looked up from the desk toward the exiting students, "Yes, Miss Povitzky?"

"May we expect that our scores will be ready by tomorrow?"

"Yes, I'm sure you're all anxious. I'll post them by noon tomorrow. I'm certain you all put your best efforts forward," said Dr. Callaghan.

With his attention diverted, Eliza peered over his shoulder at the open journal. Along the left-hand side, in neat block lettering, ran last names listed in alphabetical order. Subject courses of their Fourth Year headed the top columns: Practice of Medicine, Hygiene, Pediatrics, Obstetrics, Clinical Surgery. Each line contained squares with scores. The column for Obstetrics awaited today's results. Eliza couldn't help noticing the entries for Fairbanks, Charlotte and Haskins, Edith beneath her name. Their rows included a string of two-numbered figures which began with nines. Further down, Olga's row displayed a mix of numbers in the eighties. Her eyes raced across the row of figures next to Edwards, Eliza searching for the culprit of her angst. 86, 78, 82, blank, 72.

Turning back to Eliza, Dr. Callaghan cleared his throat, "Miss Edwards, Dean Marshall asked me to speak with you concerning your final grades."

The sides of her cheeks quivered. Should she wait for him to continue, or could she save herself by cutting him off before he outlined her deficiencies? Self-preservation prevailed.

"My apologies for the tardiness. I'm heading to the histology lab now for my last batch of slides. I'll complete them by four o'clock."

"Thank you for alerting me about your slide work. I'm sure that's acceptable if you finish by the end of the day. Dean Marshall's concern, however, is your scores. They are," he chewed a corner of his lip and lifted his eyes to hers, "what shall I say? Less than stellar?"

Eliza clamped her teeth, forcing the tightness to close her tear ducts. Despite her clench, her line of sight to the exit wavered.

"I'm sorry. I don't mean to upset you. You needn't panic. I've seen your work in the Obstetrics ward, I expect your reports will be more than satisfactory. You'll graduate."

The breath she held in her constricted chest escaped, more audible than she intended. He ignored her sigh, "After graduation you'll sit for the state medical boards. As you know, the Board of Corporators hold our students to a superior standard for a reason. We need Woman's Med. to succeed, if not exceed."

An embarrassment. Dean Marshall and the Board feared Eliza would embarrass Woman's Med. Dr. Callaghan's chastisement surpassed her misgivings. It scorched her like a branding iron, as if an F for Failure burned into the breast of her cotton shirtwaist. Hester Prynne's scarlet A paled in comparison. The heat rushed to her cheeks and out to her hands. She, Eliza Edwards, granddaughter of an original founder of the school, singled out. She might disappoint the Board and disgrace her grandfather's memory and his work. Her papers fell to the desk as she grasped the nearest chair back to steady herself, fearing her burning palms may char the wooden slat.

"Yes, Dr. Callaghan. I plan to review with Charlotte Fairbanks and Edith Haskins, who intend to stay in Philadelphia. We start the day after Graduation. My Aunt Josephine, Miss Pearson, secured the reading room for us."

"Miss Fairbanks and Miss Haskins are excellent choices as study partners, you should be fine. I'll share your plans with Dean Marshall."

Eliza released her hold of the chair back. As she bent to retrieve her notes, she followed the angle of his crooked nose up into his blue eyes. In four years of focusing her attention on him instructing from a lectern, she saw Dr. Patrick Callaghan for the first time. A man whose eyes revealed the stormy seas of a soul.

He was worried. Yet, he showed faith in her, too. He would reassure Dean Marshall as her ally.

"I want you to know, Miss Edwards, grades are but one measure of success. I've spoken with your supervisors at the hospital. Each commented on your abilities in patient care, the way you listen and your willingness to recognize the patient's state of mind instead of an immediate drug prescription. A few patients have been asking about your plans. Will you stay in Philadelphia after graduation?"

"I would prefer to, but I know there are limited options for maternity hospitals which will accept women into their residencies. My brothers have moved to Boston, so I may also look into the New England Hospital for Women."

"West Philadelphia accepts three graduates from Woman's Medical each year," Dr. Callaghan said. "I am supervising there for the coming year. Might you consider applying? I believe they would accept you immediately given your senior rotations at the College's Maternity Hospital."

Helping others, the immigrant women of West and South Philadelphia. The prophetic words from Daniel Dangerfield's note to her grandfather and Anandi's letter floated back to Eliza.

As Mr. Dangerfield asked, with our Lord's help, I must help guide others to their freedom–freedom from pain. Dearest Anandi, I want to become the doctor you were meant to be. I will pass my exams, graduate with my friends, and succeed on the state boards.

"Thank you, Dr. Callaghan. I would be honored to work with you."

CHAPTER SEVENTEEN

May 1901: Graduation

The activities before graduation muddled in Eliza's exhausted mind. Final preparations packed each day and sparked different emotions. She breathed relief when learning she passed Obstetrics with her highest mark, a 94! Dread of five more hours in the Physiology lab persisted. Disgust overwhelmed her when identifying another sampling of medicines by taste and smell. Revulsion surged as she handled filthy vials filled with urine, feces, and spoiled foods for toxicology analysis. She basked in pleasure when visiting Wanamaker's with her mother and Olga to select their white dresses. Her heart bubbled with the thrill of checking on her last patients and finding them settled after a difficult delivery. Jubilation united the women during the prior evening when she and her classmates danced around a pyre built of outdated texts from their first years as they chanted,

> *"Where, oh where, are the lectures that vexed us,*
> *Where, oh where, are the books that perplexed us,*
> *Where, oh where, are the fears that oppressed us,*
> *On May-day so lately now flown?*
> *Where, oh where, are the loving memories*
> *Of all that has gladdened us here?*
> *Laid away in our heart's deepest niches*
> *To blossom for many a year."*

Eliza leaned her head on Olga's shoulder. Her skirt, drawn up to her knees, exposed her pale, bare legs stretched out on the narrow bed in Edith's room. A cool spring breeze from the open window tickled her toes. She wiggled them in reply to the breeze's hello. The mattress beneath her shifted with her salutation, stirring Olga from a drowsy stupor.

"Isn't this divine?" asked Eliza. "Absolutely nothing to do but relax with dearest friends."

The precious minutes gave Eliza time to collect her memories like a bouquet of fragrant, fresh blossoms, bundle them together, and tie them up with her heartstrings.

Edith sat at the student desk tucked into the corner of the attic room where she studied her way through their final courses. Through long and tedious nights, she composed reports, essays, and opinion pieces on treatments. The pages before her today, however, presented her toughest assignment. She glared at the two women lounging on the bed. "Did you hear me?"

"Sorry," Eliza sighed, "I'm dog-tired from last night. Skip the introduction. Pick it up where you mentioned something about monuments."

Edith shuffled her notes, returning to the start of her Toastmistress speech. She stood from the desk chair, tucked it inside the kneehole, and faced her audience.

"Fellow graduates, will there ever be a monument to us, the women physicians of the new century? Over the previous fifty years, our sisters before us were never celebrated. Will we receive any recognition? For we are the leaders, the pioneers of a movement who have the energy, determination, and talent to free ourselves from the bondage of prejudice and the misguided notion we are lower beings when compared to men."

"Ouch!" Eliza cringed, "You realize those superior beings you condemn will attend the Luncheon? Our professors, Olga's father, Freddy. What if your father makes the trip? I agree with your intent, but it's too harsh. Let's put our heads together and think of a softer opening."

"How's this?" Olga rose from the bed and unfolded her arms, palms up, "Allow me to introduce you to the Class of nineteen-oh-one. I'll start with Olga P."

She brought her thumb to her chest. "Who with so much spunk, always exclaimed, 'I'm going to flunk!'"

She bowed to her audience and fell back laughing at her own self-deprecation. Eliza leaned over to tickle Olga's ear.

"Ever our court jester!" she said. "But Edith needs something a tad more serious. My grandfather's evening discussions often included a quote. I'm thinking something Dean Marshall shared at our Introductory Address might be a more prudent choice: 'Every woman is born a doctor. Men have to study to become one.'"

"Much better than Olga's suggestion. I'll take it under advisement. Thanks for the help. Go on now, you two. I can manage from here."

•   •   •

The next morning, Eliza fingered the fine silk, bringing a swath of the soft cloth to her cheek. White pleats descended in tiers; its last layer brushed the bedroom floor. The inanimate dress form readied to cede the dress to the vibrant young woman. Leg o'mutton sleeves puffed at the shoulders and tapered at the elbow. A flare of lace cuffed the wrist. The bodice inset covered the chest area with a semblance of modesty.

Eliza rejoiced at shedding four years' worth of drab shirtwaists, loose fitting suit jackets and ribbon string ties at her throat. This afternoon, she would don a dress similar to the one her mother hoped she would wear for a Presentation Ball. When she held a stethoscope in her hands instead of a bouquet of roses, would Laura see a doctor? Because after the graduation ceremony, Eliza would enter a larger society; in her opinion, a more purposeful society. They would be women who gave lectures, not attended them. They would be women who treated charitable cases, not raised funds for them.

A gentle knock rapped at the door. Eliza's mother nudged it open with the toe of her boot. "I'm glad I caught you," said Laura. "You've been so busy with studies and exams, I feared I wouldn't find a chance to speak with you alone before we left."

From behind her back, she brought forth a rectangle covered by floral paper and tied with a white grosgrain bow. "This is for you."

With a hand as steady as when she now held a scalpel, Eliza ripped the paper edges to reveal an Oriental jewelry box. The inlaid black walnut pictured tiny figures in a rickshaw and cherry trees made from mother-of-pearl. The pearly flakes reflected the bureau lamp's light.

"Oh, my goodness!" Eliza ran her fingertips over the polished wood, imaging the mysteries of the Orient and what treasures it may hold inside.

Eliza placed the box on her bureau and raised the lid. A string of pearls, matching earrings, and a cameo brooch nestled into the folds of blush pink satin. She lifted the string from its pillow and caressed the smooth beads with her fingers.

"Mother, they're beautiful!"

"They are magnificent," Laura said, "just like you."

Her hand went to Eliza's cheek.

"I spent an hour at Wanamaker's jewelry counter discussing options. The saleswoman said pearls symbolize wisdom gained through experience. And pure white ones signify new beginnings. I think they're the perfect choice for the doctor who stands before me. A woman driven to gain great wisdom and who is ready for her next beginning. I couldn't be prouder of you."

This afternoon, Dean Marshall would place a diploma in her hand. Now, here, in her bedroom, her mother spoke of her accomplishments and saw her daughter, the doctor. Eliza wasn't sure which moment would mean more.

Laura lifted the strand from Eliza's palm and draped it over her head. The beads fell against Eliza's neck and hung to her bosom in a U-shape.

"They're perfect, Mother," Eliza said. "Thank you so much. I'll cherish them forever. While medical school was not your plan for me, I hoped you would see it was something I needed to do."

"I know it hasn't been easy for you and, Lord knows, I've had my reservations each time another semester started. But here you are. Dr. Edwards. There's the brooch, too."

Laura picked up the glistening ivory cameo; its oval shape edged with gold filigree.

"Really? But it's so precious to you," said Eliza.

The brooch bore an etched profile of a woman resembling Aunt Maria. A thick ribbon band covered with peonies held sweeps of hair back in waves. Long lashes covered downcast eyes. A dainty hand drew another peony to the rosebud nose. Maria commissioned the cameo as a gift. She presented it to Laura on Maria and Andrew's wedding day, forever binding the women as sisters and sisters-in-law. Laura wore the piece close to her heart; the last time at Maria's funeral.

"I would like you to give it to Olga. Maria would have insisted. Olga is as much your sister as Maria was mine."

Eliza slumped to the bed, tears sliding down the side of her nose. Her mother's beautiful gesture made her recognize that Olga's friendship plugged a hole in her mother's heart. A mother's joy came from her child's happiness.

Eliza brushed the drops away. She stood to wrap her arms around her mother's shoulders. "This is the greatest gift."

She wrapped the cameo in her lace handkerchief and asked, "Is Olga back yet?"

"I believe she's downstairs with Josephine."

Eliza called toward the parlor as she and her mother descended the staircase, "Olga, are you there?"

"Been here for a while, Napping Beauty!" Olga chuckled.

Eliza grinned. The friendly tease. Oh, she would miss her friend! Olga finished a twirl to model her graduation dress.

Josephine cooed, "It's lovely. Too bad you need to cover these gorgeous dresses with those dreadful black gowns and silly caps, but no one argues with Dean Marshall. I guess they lend more formality to the ceremony, like other colleges. We'll be thankful you don't have to wear them for the luncheon. All right, I have got to skedaddle. I'll see you there."

Josephine gave each woman a quick kiss and hurried off to supervise set-up, completing the seating plans, and directing the proper placement of tables.

"I love your dress. An empire waist flatters your figure," Eliza said.

She turned to her mother, "But I think it's missing something. Don't you agree, Mother?" Eliza returned the lace handkerchief to her mother's hand.

"Olga," said Laura as she unwrapped the brooch, "My sister, Maria, gave this to me. I am forever grateful Eliza brought you home to us. You've become her sister. I hope whenever you wear it, you'll think of us."

With trembling fingers, Eliza pinned the brooch over Olga's left breast.

"Oh no." Olga blinked to pause the tears welling in her eyes. "I don't need anything as precious as this to remember you. I already feel like an Edwards."

Eliza swallowed her tears, "You're my sister, too. We all love you. Take it."

"Well," said Olga as she fingered the edges of the brooch, "I suppose if you wish for this piece of the Pearson Edwards family to travel to Russia, it shall embark on an extraordinary journey."

After the luncheon, Olga would board a steamship docked in Philadelphia's port. Her brother waited for her, hoping she would bring new treatment ideas for his hemophilia. She would return to her country and the privileged life her family enjoyed under the rule of her father's second cousin, Tsar Nicholas Romanov.

"Keep it safe with you on your travels. Maybe one day, she'll help you find your way back to us."

Florence walked into the parlor where Eliza and Olga stood in an embrace. She arrived the day before to celebrate Eliza's triumphant day and to witness first-hand the more Eliza had discovered.

"Let's go, ladies," Florence said, "we can't have the guests of honor late to the party."

• • •

The Woman's Med. Class of 1901 marched single file into the Association Hall's banquet room. Festivity exploded with streamers and buntings hung over the doorway and draped across the stage. Green ferns and white roses, commemorating the class colors, stuffed crystal vases at the center of each table. The Pearson Edwards party commanded Table Four with places reserved for the graduate, her mother, her aunts, and her brother, Freddy. Business in Boston detained Albie. Edith Haskins joined their table alone, her father unable, or unwilling, to make the trip.

Eliza expected Olga and Mr. Povitzky would sit at their table, too. At first, she was disappointed to learn Dean Marshall requested Olga and her father join the head table to sit with the Board. But Josephine explained the status Mr. Povitzky brought with him, and the expected donation in honor of his daughter's graduation. The College's hunt for funding never ended.

At the eighth place, above the gold-rimmed dinner plate, Eliza noticed an ivory tented place card for Dr. Patrick Callaghan. *Why would Josephine put Dr. Callaghan with us?* thought Eliza. *He should be with the academic staff. And where is his wife? Shouldn't she be in attendance like the other spouses?*

Two hours of polite conversation may lie ahead. She wanted to celebrate with her family, who supported her through the long toil, and applaud Edith's Toastmistress speech, polished into a respectable address with Eliza's and Olga's help. There were goodbyes to impart before her classmates scattered to other states and across the seas, many of whom she might never see again.

Instead, she would feel Dr. Callaghan apprise her every move. She imagined he would see every spoonful she took of her consommé. *Fill your spoon by pushing it away from you and then drawing it to your lips.* The way she cut into the filet mignon. *Fork in the left hand, fingers pressed down toward the tines, not grabbed around the handle like a heathen.* The flaky crust of a berry tart on her fork. *Don't let crumbs fall upon your bodice.* Every sip of champagne she drank. *One glass; for heaven sakes, don't get tipsy.*

She moved to take her seat next to Josephine, when a large, blue-veined hand reached for the chair back and pulled it out from the table. "Congratulations Dr. Edwards, allow me."

Behind her, Dr. Callaghan gestured for her to sit. He wore a charcoal gray suit with faint pinstripes, the crease in the leg as sharp as a surgical knife. A crisp white shirt stretched tight across his broad chest, covered by a matching vest. A dark green necktie, its knot a perfect square, was fastened by a gold tie pin. He slicked his hair into order with heavy dabs of pompadour cream; its musky scent drifted toward Eliza.

"Thank you, Dr. Callaghan," Eliza pulled the flounce of her dress tiers into a skirt clutch. The purity of the white silk brushed against his gray wool. She turned to her right and raised her eyebrows with an inquiry to Aunt Josephine.

Josephine motioned her into a secretive whisper, "He told me last week he'd be solo and asked if there was room at our table. When Edith's father sent word he wouldn't be coming, I had to fill the eighth spot."

Remaining with her back to Dr. Callaghan, she surveyed the room. Fifty years ago, her grandfather would have sat at the head table bearing witness to the brave and pioneering women who took the initial steps into a man's profession which needed a woman's intellect, ability, and empathy. Her grandfather's commitment to the school's mission guided Eliza. *Are you here, Grandpapa? Do you see me? I'm holding a diploma from your College. I'm a doctor.*

• • •

Dean Marshall opened the luncheon with a moment of reflection for Anandi. Eliza closed her eyes and lowered her head in prayer to honor the woman who inspired her. *Dearest Anandi, you spoke with me when I started this journey. Today, I ask for your help again. Please step with me into this calling and I promise to remember your determination and dedication every day of my practice.*

Next, Reverend Abrams from St. Clement's took the podium for a droning benediction. Eliza didn't need to listen to him expound with platitudes of their God-given abilities and success. She may have prayed to God in the wee hours of a night before an exam, *Heavenly Father, give me the strength to defeat the study of organic compounds.* Or, in the amphitheater observing their first surgical dissection of a cadaver, *please God don't let me faint.* Or, at the delivery of her first maternity case for the well-being of the mother and child, *bless this child, dear Lord.*

As much as God may have helped her, Eliza knew it was sheer will, persistence, and self-sacrifice which guided the Class of 1901 to this moment. Today, they would raise their glasses to each other and to the professors and administrators who stood by them as they earned their degrees. Eliza and her classmates would enter a medical society unnoticed with footfalls as soft as the fifty classes before them. From receiving a diploma, to delivering a baby, to performing a life-saving surgery, their endeavors would always be marked as quiet triumphs. Not as lady physicians. Not as a doctress. Doctors. For a teacher is a teacher. A bookkeeper is a bookkeeper. A clerk is a clerk. A doctor is a doctor.

"...and may Our Father and Lord continue to guide you in your calling to heal. Amen."

Opening her eyes, Eliza looked out to her classmates seated around the other tables. Today they celebrated their futures. They would not be bound by constraints of tradition but directed forward with joy in their hearts and the bonds of sisterhood. Forevermore, they would champion each other with a sense of connectedness and commitment. The success of one was the success of all.

As Eliza lifted her chin, she watched Dr. Callaghan's right hand move from his forehead to his chest and across from his left shoulder to his right before bringing a dull pewter object in his fist to his pressed lips. She had seen the ritualistic motion while tending Italian immigrant women. The sign of the cross. The Irish brogue. Dr. Patrick Callaghan practiced Catholicism, a foreign, papist faith according to Eliza's mother, the devout Episcopalian.

Dr. Callaghan raised the crystal champagne flute teeming with iridescent bubbles.

"I'd like to make a toast from an old Irish prayer," he announced. "May God give you for every storm, a rainbow. For every tear, a smile. For every care, a promise, and a blessing in each trial. For every problem life sends, a faithful friend to share."

His eyes locked on Eliza.

"For every sigh, a sweet song, and an answer for each prayer. Sláinte."

CHAPTER EIGHTEEN

November 1901

With each step forward from the trolley stop, Eliza tightened the hold of her cape, pulling it closer under her chin. A nip sneaked into the air as the November day darkened early. A single star shone on the fabric of the fading blue-gray northern sky. Her doctor's bag, new and still gleaming, swayed from the crook of her elbow, bumping her hip.

The primary tools of her trade knocked about inside the kit: stethoscope, thermometer, and forceps. Over the past four months, Eliza used the stethoscope and thermometer daily, diligently wiping the thermometer with alcohol to disinfect after each use. The forceps, with its steel blades and ebony-handle, lay wrapped in flannel. Her obstetric cases so far progressed without resorting to using the cold, metal tongs. Three cases required chloroform. Eliza thanked Queen Victoria in those instances. In 1853, the Queen set a precedent by accepting chloroform to quell the suffering during the birth of her eighth child. She forged a path for all but the most pious. Those women claimed God's judgement demanded they atone for Eve's sin. During one arduous delivery, Eliza suggested chloroform to an Irish woman, who responded between her labored breaths with Genesis 3:16, 'To the woman he said, I will surely multiply your pain in childbearing; in pain you shall bring forth children.'

Like other evenings, Eliza looked forward to her shift. Appointments, deliveries, case write-ups, clinics, and lectures occupied her day shifts at the hospital. Nights offered extra time to meet mothers in their early stages of labor who may have checked in during the afternoon. Sitting by their bedsides, she answered their questions, held their chafed hands, reassured them their delivery would proceed without complications, and a healthy child would soon nestle in their arms. Often, she read from the dog-eared copy of *Alice in Wonderland* or recited poetry from Dickinson and Rossetti, to distract them from their contractions and the screams of other patients.

One of her favorite duties was rounds to check on the newest arrivals. She relished in each tiny face peeking out of swaddled wraps, resting at a breast, the mother staring at the wonder as love spilled forth from her heart, lungs, every pore of her body. The infant might be her first, or her fifth, or her eighth. A mother's countenance remained unchanged. Complete devotion.

• • •

Passing through the maternity hallway, Eliza smiled. The sound of women's agonies and pleas from behind the hallway's doors didn't concern her.

"Please. Please."

"Mary, mother of God, pray for me."

"No more, I can't."

They were pleasing noises signaling labors progressed according to nature's schedules. The miracle of birth she witnessed through the first months of her residency heightened Eliza's desires. Someday, somehow, she would hold her own beloved babe.

At the nurses' station, Harriet Mitchell acknowledged Eliza with an abrupt urgency in her voice, "Mrs. Silvestri is in Room 8. She's struggling and refused chloroform. You would think after

six children she could deliver this one herself. And the husband…"
She glanced toward the man pacing in the corridor, a nurse
speaking to him in hushed, even tones, striving to calm him. The
staff made valiant efforts, but they didn't drown out the cries of
the man's wife behind the closed door.

"Screaming in Italian, gesturing at us like he's herding goats in
the old country. He is such a nuisance." *If you can't sympathize
with an expectant father, it's time to retire*, thought Eliza, not
daring to utter the words to the more experienced Nurse Mitchell.

"He's agitating her with his yelling and kicking the
baseboards. I have a mind to send him the bill for the damages.
Although I doubt he'd pay, what with a stonemason wages and
eight mouths to feed at home. From what I can gather, he didn't
want a hospital birth and suggested the janitor's wife help. But the
Mrs. said she felt this pregnancy was different."

Eliza turned toward the distraught husband. The man ran his
gnarled fingers through his thinning, graying hair. The frayed cuff
of his navy wool pea jacket stopped short of his wrist, ill-fitting
on muscular arms.

"Insist that he go home or behave civilly," instructed Eliza.
"Clearly, Mrs. Silvestri has a reason she wanted to be here."

This wasn't the first time Eliza learned of the tussle between
husband and wife over hospital births. Women preferred a
doctor's care. Their husbands argued it was unnatural to have a
doctor tend to a woman's birthing, too intimate for another man
to attend, midwives were more than fine. However, as more
doctors like Eliza joined the staff, wives maintained that a woman
doctor could deliver them, not a man. As women won more
arguments, the maternity ward expanded.

Nurse Mitchell fluttered through the pages held securely on the
clipboard to find the case record on Antonina "Nina" Silvestri.
She pressed hard on the clip with the heel of her calloused palm
to pull the form out and handed it to Eliza. The top left corner
bore the name of the attending physician, Callaghan.

"Where's Dr. Callaghan?" asked Eliza. "I'll want to confer with him, and he needs to be present when I see Mrs. Silvestri."

"On his dinner break. He left instructions for you to manage without him, but I expect he'll be back before Mrs. Silvestri delivers."

A resident alone to deliver any patient may be negligent. Although negligence would be charged only if any difficulties ensued. Dr. Callaghan must be confident in Eliza's abilities to attend to Mrs. Silvestri with the help of a nurse. This thought calmed the nagging pinpricks running up and down Eliza's arms. As she scanned Nina Silvestri's intake sheet, she familiarized herself with the woman's vitals before she entered Room 8.

Admittance Date: November 19, 1901
Name: ANTONINA "NINA" SILVESTRI
Age: 43
Marital Status: Married
Height: 5'0"
Weight: 130 pounds
Residence: 18B Walton Avenue, Philadelphia
Speaks: Italian, limited English
Religion: Roman Catholic
Number of Live Births: 6
Number of Pregnancies: 8–possibly more, unsure
Multiple Births: 0
Last Birth: 1895
Estimated Gestation Period: 41 weeks
Existing Conditions: presence of tapeworm, persistent heartburn
Temperature: 98.8
Blood Pressure: 110/60
Pulse: 92
Fetal Position: Vertex down
Fetal Heart Rate: 130
Chloroform: Refused.

The information showed no reason for Mrs. Silvestri's struggles. On paper, she presented like most other immigrant patients. Multiple children, limited English. Vitals within normal ranges. No evidence of syphilis, a rare blessing. Two miscarriages were expected of a woman her age. Age. Eliza ran her finger up the sheet. At forty-three, women became grandmothers, not starting again with newborns.

This little one is a tad stubborn, that's all. At school, Eliza attended eight maternity cases, following them from initial assessments through postpartum check-ups. Since beginning her residency, her experience list grew. She and Nina would coax out this seventh Silvestri babe and make sure the family was home for Thanksgiving. While she preferred the help of almost any other nurse on staff, Nurse Mitchell was reliable and capable. Eliza smiled as she unbuttoned her cuff to roll up her sleeve and entered the room. Her glowing radiance comforted many mothers lost in the darkness of labor.

"Good evening, Mrs. Silvestri. I'm Doctor Edwards. It appears we have a little one far too comfortable right where he is. Let's convince him it's time for his birthday. November 19th will be a fine date for a celebration, don't you think?"

Nina sat on the edge of the metal framed white hospital bed, her bare, small feet dangling above the cold, tiled floor. The sheets behind her tangled into heaps like snowbanks, balled and moist from her sweating body. Her cloudy green eyes peeked out from her long, undone black hair; a streak of white invaded the black like a stripe along a skunk's back. She pushed aside the strands matted against her cheeks and plastered to her forehead. Pointing to her overextended belly, she grunted. "It is slow. My others, so fast."

"Yes, well, 'Slow and steady wins the race.' Look at *The Tortoise and The Hare.*"

A blank stare. Eliza tucked an idea into the file cabinet of her mind. Books. She would send her immigrant patients home with a children's book to commemorate their birthday.

"Aaaaiiiiiii," Nina wailed and grabbed her belly.

"It's time, Nina. We need clean sheets. I'll call for the nurse. Please lie back."

Moments later, with the baby's head crowning, Nurse Mitchell called out drops in Nina's heartbeat and pulse. Eliza's heart raced as if urging Nina's to match her pace. *Where are you Dr. Callaghan?*

The nurse pushed her aside. Ripping open Eliza's doctor's bag, she grabbed the forceps. Eliza stood frozen in her thoughts. Eighty-two. She assisted with eighty-two successful deliveries. She watched a few breech births and two cord tangles. But each one resulted with a baby latched to a mother's breast, guided by the skillful hands of someone like Dr. Callaghan. Not hands four months out of medical school.

The glint from the overhead light hit the steel curve of the blade and refracted into Eliza's eye. She took them from the nurse's hands and ordered her to blindfold Nina and hold her down at the shoulders. Eliza eased the blades into the birth canal. Nina wailed louder.

"I'm sorry Mrs. Silvestri, I know it's dreadful. Soon, soon, it'll be over."

The infant's head emerged. Eliza tugged gently, holding the handles firm. Shoulders, then the rest of the body slipped out to the starched sheet beneath its mother.

Eliza's fears quieted. She snatched up the swaddling cloth, wiped his face, wrapped him, and turned to Nina, "A son, Mrs. Silvestri."

Nina Silvestri's eyes rolled back as Nurse Mitchell removed the blindfold and checked Nina's pulse. "Tis, all right. She fainted. Poor dear. Exhausted, as she should be. She needs to rest."

Eliza stroked the cheek of the placid form and dismissed Nurse Mitchell, "I'll tend to him."

She stayed with the baby while his mother slept. Eliza rocked the baby in the blue flannel. His small skull was not in proportion to his body. She held him in a firm grasp as if he needed her arm muscles toned from tennis. No cries. No sounds. Eliza gazed upon him. A new life awed her with promises of tomorrow. This child's sallow, flat face told a different truth. His eyelids remained closed, hiding the faint white spots in the iris. With her index fingertip, she traced ovals around his eyes, following the upward slant of each one. His cheeks puffed, and a saliva bubble blew from his soft pink lips. Eliza brought her finger to his lips and wiped it away. A drop from her eye replaced the burst bubble. His features identified a diagnosis.

New fears jabbed at her heart. Her job not finished. She needed to tell the parents about their son. How would a father react? Would he accept the challenges which lay ahead? Would he acknowledge the added responsibilities of caring for this precious gift? This babe would never run and play with his siblings, go to school, or help his father as he grew into a young man. How, in fact, he may not live beyond his tenth birthday; the odds he saw his first birthday were unlikely. Helping to bring life into a family was one of the greatest privileges for a doctor, losing a patient, the worst. Yet even death had a finality. This situation, this sense of limbo, of no hope was worse.

•   •   •

Eliza stirred from her half-sleep to the escalating noise of jovial laughter and clomping of boots approaching from the hallway. Hopeful the pair of footsteps belonged to Dr. Callaghan and Mr. Silvestri, she gazed down at the child, quiet in her lap and unaware of soon meeting his father.

The laughter carried the familiar lilt she heard many times after Albie and Freddy spent evenings in a local pub, arriving home with twinkles in their eyes and cheery banter on their tongues. Dr. Callaghan's voice rang over the sound of a hearty back slap. "A lucky man you are, Mr. Silvestri. A seventh child. They must keep a man young, yes?"

"Ha, you may be right. Could be the last one, for even Our Lord God rested on the seventh. I suppose Nina's due a rest from this old pecker."

Dr. Callaghan, with his long-legged, youthful stride out-paced Domenic Silvestri and entered the room, calling out, "Well now, it appears there's a new Silvestri in our world. Pray tell, is it a strapping chap or a fair beauty for Mr. Silvestri?"

Eliza roused and stood. A steely glare bore into Dr. Callaghan. She motioned him to the corner, "A word please, Dr. Callaghan?"

Out of Mr. Silvestri's earshot, she informed Dr. Callaghan of her immediate diagnosis. The twinkle in his eyes dulled, his brow furrowed.

Dr. Callaghan faced Domenic, forcing a smile.

"What is it, Doctor? Ay, no, my Nina. She's gone?" Domenic's face reddened with a fiery rage and his hands clenched into fists, as hard as the stones he lifted every day.

"Shhh, please, Mr. Silvestri. Your wife is fine. She had a tough go, but she's sleeping comfortably now. The baby..."

"It nearly killed her, did it? If it died, it's a blessing. I'm not sure I could forgive it for nearly taking my Nina."

Hurrying to his wife's bedside, he brushed past Eliza, nary a glance at his son. He leaned over Nina and stroked her hair. He held her limp hand and crooned soft Italian words to her.

"Mr. Silvestri, your son." Eliza extended the bundle of blue toward him. She pulled back the hooded cover to expose the child's head. Innocence bathed his face. His lips curled into a crescent as if he wished to greet his father with a cheerful smile.

Mr. Silvestri surveyed the baby from the bald pate to the dimpled chin. Eliza followed his inspection. If not for the marks above his ears and the slanted eyes, the boy resembled a miniature version of his father. The indentations heralded his arrival. Pink scars announced he could not make his way into the world without help. A foretelling of his future.

Mr. Silvestri boomed at Eliza, "Nurse, where's the doctor? I want to speak with the doctor who did this."

She wouldn't look at Mr. Silvestri. She focused on the child she clutched to her chest. Dr. Callaghan placed a hand on her shoulder, urging her to stay still. She twisted away from his sleeve, repulsed by a stale and acrid scent of spoiled grains mixed into ales and whiskey, and splashed across the cuff, disgusted by his presence.

"I'm the doctor, Mr. Silvestri. I delivered your son," Eliza said. "He's a beautiful child. But there will be some challenges…"

"You?" Domenic leveled his eyes at her, the veins in his neck strained with a pulsing throb beating as fast as Eliza's heart. "You did this? You call yourself a doctor? Using that thing. You ruined him. What challenges? Did you damage him? What doctor would hurt a baby? We should not have come here. A midwife would have been fine. Midwives don't use such medical equipment. A woman doctor. Bah, you know nothing."

We must hold steadfast to our duty and bring forth the light of a woman's intellect, ability, and empathy so they may progress with strength and respect. How wise, the message inscribed in her grandfather's Gray's Anatomy. Bolstered by those words, she shrugged Callaghan's hand from her shoulder.

"Mr. Silvestri. This was a difficult delivery. The forceps saved your wife's life and possibly your son's, too. They did not cause his condition. We don't know the causes of these mental deficiencies," said Eliza.

"Mio Dio! Un imbecille? Take it away," Domenic spat. "Nina is to never see it. 'Tis better to tell her it died."

The singular window in the room faced north. A star's streak glinted through the caked grime of the glass pane and flickered onto the baby's chest. Anandi's determination crept in with the starlight. Sweet Baby William. Aunt Maria.

No. Eliza would not be an accomplice to heartbreak. A mother's love slays any difficulties a child may have, if she could hold him, love him, keep him near, to keep herself alive. Without giving the enraged father or the silent Dr. Callaghan time to reply, Eliza stood from the chair, "I won't lie to your wife. This child will need extra care. The Sheltering Arms will take him, and there's the Elwyn Training School when he gets older. But for now, his mother needs to know he lives."

CHAPTER NINETEEN

Eliza rushed down the hallway looking for Nurse Mitchell, finding her at the nurses' station. She thrust the baby into the nurse's arms. Her voice faltered. "Hold him. Keep him here. Safe from the father."

A curdled cream taste rose from her stomach. She slammed the bolt lock across the ladies' room door. At the cold porcelain sink, she seized the rim. Her shoulders heaved with each retch from the bottom of her gut. As she laid her forehead on the icy edge, she let her knees find the solid concrete floor. Who deserved the larger share of her rage? Mr. Silvestri for assuming she was a nurse, for spurning his son, and conceiving a diabolical lie? Or Dr. Callaghan for abandoning her? Not only did he leave for a dinner break, but he had washed his meal down with several pints at a pub. And what of his silence during Mr. Silvestri's tirade?

A light knock rapped on the door, a single knuckle, not four.

"Dr. Edwards, are you all right? Can I help?"

A male voice. Low, soft, hesitant.

Water spurted from the faucet. Eliza cupped her hands to bring the metallic-tainted liquid to her lips and splash upon her face. She swished a mouthful of the cool water over her teeth and under and around her tongue, urging it to form the words she lacked.

"I'm fine," Eliza replied in a curt tone.

She opened the door and stamped past Dr. Callaghan. The morning staff bustled through the hallways. After imparting strict instructions to the day nurse, she strode down the corridor, through the main entrance doors, and descended the front steps of the West Philadelphia Hospital for Women and Children, all children, even those like Baby Boy Silvestri.

Pink clouds streaked the sky. After a night shift, the hope of a day's dawn calmed Eliza. This morning, the pinks intensified to reds and oranges. Fiery colors spread across the horizon, ready to rage and suffocate.

Eliza walked the three miles home, ignoring the neighs and clops of horse-drawn carriages mixed with the clang and whir of trolley cars. She needed time to clear her mind of hospital sounds. Mrs. Silvestri's laboring wails, Nurse Mitchell's stern instructions, the baby's weak cries, Mr. Silvestri's harsh accusations, Dr. Callaghan's imploring plea. The voice she needed most was an ocean away. Olga's.

Since graduation, Eliza received one letter from Olga announcing her safe arrival in Russia and a joyous reunion with her family. She secured a research laboratory position, the hospital administration conceding it was better to have a woman locked away in a lab room than in the public eye as a staff doctor. She forged on with her study of hematology, determined to discover treatment options for her brother and other hemophiliacs.

Eliza responded promptly with news of her hectic summer.

June 28, 1901
My dear friend,
How wonderful to hear from you! I'm relieved your trip was safe and uneventful. Your lab position sounds perfect. Congratulations! I admit we all chuckled at your expense thinking of you surrounded by glass slides every day, after bumbling and breaking your way through four years of histology...

Eliza imagined Olga laughed out loud too, at the irony of her position. The rest of Eliza's letter noted her success with the State Boards, securing the residency at West Philadelphia, Molly marrying, and Edith staying on with them after accepting a job with the Board of Health. Eliza promised to write again soon, affixed the six-cents stamp, and sent her best wishes off to Russia.

This morning, by the time Eliza made it home, the grandfather clock read quarter past eight. Her aunts and Edith had left for work. Her mother was in Boston visiting Albie and his wife Mamie while they awaited their second baby. There was no mention of Eliza joining them. She could not afford to miss even two days away from her new position. Now, after the Silvestri delivery, she feared she would be of no help to her sister-in-law.

The quiet house welcomed Eliza, and she welcomed it back.

"Oh Olga," she said out loud, looking into the gold filigree mirror. Deep circles beneath her eyes accented her drawn face. "What a horrible night. Why did I let Mr. Silvestri bother me so much? I thought I chose the right procedure, but now I'm not sure. Will Mrs. Silvestri confront her husband and demand the best care for her son? The sweet dear. He will need his mother. I'm afraid the situation is out of my control. What would you have done, Olga?"

Eliza turned from the haunted woman in the mirror and plodded to the kitchen, hoping to find a slice of Josephine's brown bread in the ice box. A thick slab with a smear of peach preserves and a mug of coffee should tide her over until lunch, when she would share the Silvestri case with Josephine. She would tut-tut and pat Eliza's hand, but she could never know the depths of Eliza's anguish.

Wearily, she pushed up from her chair. At the sink she washed her dishes and knife and left them on the wooden rack to dry. She lathered her hands and scrubbed them over and over while the scalding water cooled. As she headed to her bedroom, she unbuttoned her blouse and shimmied it to her waist. Halfway up the stairs, she heard the brass door knocker clang. She grappled with the blouse edges to peek through the long vertical lace window sheers. A hulk of brown tweed blocked her sight line of the stoop.

"Dr. Callaghan?"

"Yes. Dr. Edwards? May I come in?"

Heavens. Half-dressed and no one home. She couldn't allow a man into the house.

"No," she said.

"No?"

"I mean, I can't accept visitors at the moment, I'm…" *Not dressed? Exhausted? Angry with you?*

She fumbled with the buttons. The pearly balls refused to meet the slits. She dropped her arms to her sides, defeated in the battle of buttons versus buttonholes. From her side of the door, she spoke into the dense wood.

"Do you require me at the hospital? If I go back, I fear I'll make mistakes. There have been enough today, I don't need to make any more."

Outside, the November wind whirled. Eliza peeked through the sheers again. Dr. Callaghan rubbed his gloveless, chafed hands together.

"Everything is fine. Mrs. Silvestri is awake, and her husband has gone to the Sheltering Arms to inquire if they'll take the child as soon as he's released. You handled a difficult situation admirably. You did not make any mistakes. I did."

Affirmation. She acted correctly. Confirmation he was the one who erred. Eliza backed against the door, bracing herself as she slid into a heap on the floor. With her blouse open and her skirt tangled around her ankles, she leaned her elbows on her bent knees and her forehead in the heels of her palms.

"I'd like to explain myself," he said. "Will you join me for breakfast if you won't let me in?"

I've eaten, I'm not hungry, thought Eliza. But the mournful tone of his pleading voice moved her. His nearness entered her and quickened the beat of her heart. A brief breakfast would be harmless.

"I need to change. You may let yourself in and wait in the parlor."

She unlocked the door.

• • •

"Ach, Doctor Callaghan. Come in and close that door behind ya. The wind's a-blowing again."

Catherine "Ma" McGillin ushered Eliza and Dr. Callaghan in and seated them at a rear corner table of McGillin's Ale House. The dark paneled walls rose a short distance to meet the low-hanging stucco ceiling, crisscrossed by thick timber beams, yellowed from years of smoke. Sparse windows allowed the mid-morning sun to enter for a brief appearance before being shadowed by the nearby courthouse and other taller buildings. Three men on barstools bantered with the barkeep, who kept their tumblers full of whiskey and rye.

A dim lamp in the center of the table where Eliza and Dr. Callaghan sat offered enough light for Eliza to note the nicks, blemishes, and water spots on the tin eating utensils. Dr. Callaghan suggested McGillin's, which appeared to be the only dining spot he knew in Philadelphia.

Ma McGillin sized Eliza up. The pale brown and white striped dress with lace cap sleeves covered by a cashmere wrap and a string of pearls at her neck with matching ear bobs did not belong to an Irish lass from the dockyard neighborhoods.

"And, who's the fine young lady here?"

"Dr. Edwards. Dr. Edwards, Mrs. McGillin."

Eliza added, "I work with Dr. Callaghan at West Philadelphia." She wouldn't have any speculation there was anything but a professional relationship between them.

With a cocked head, Ma McGillin ordered for them.

"Two full Irish breakfasts for our doctors. Need to fill you up with some bangers and eggs before you tend to the young 'uns and their mas."

"Thank you, Mrs. McGillin, but tea is fine for me," said Eliza. Her stomach churned during their walk to the pub. She did not want any distractions while she listened to Dr. Callaghan's explanation for his behavior. She silently thanked Ma for seating them in the quiet corner.

"Nonsense. You're skin and bones, Miss—'tis no trouble."

Ma bustled past them and disappeared into the kitchen. Eliza folded her hands in her lap. She had no inclination to start a conversation. The silence between them was his to break. Dr. Callaghan turned his head toward the long bar as if he hoped the regulars would saunter over and pull up a chair to join them. None of the men acknowledged his presence.

His left hand disappeared into his jacket pocket. Eliza heard a rustle as he fumbled with an item, a slight clink of metal against metal. A chain of some sort? Finally, he splayed his hands on the table in front of them. His right ring finger moved to caress a barren left one.

"Dr. Edwards," he began, "I neglected my duties last evening. My actions are inexcusable. What's more..."

Ma McGillin returned with a tray of two earthenware plates and cups of tea. She set them down and pivoted to the demand for another bottle of whiskey from the bar stools.

Eliza stared at the plate before her. What a strange combination. Despite Molly's Irish roots, a meal like this had never seen the light of day in the Pearson-Edwards, English-bred household. A dense circle of a black substance made from grain and ground meat of an unknown ilk. The thick sausage link, what

Mrs. McGillin called a "banger," waded into the broken, runny egg yolk. She pushed the plate forward an inch away, praying Dr. Callaghan wouldn't notice. She didn't want to appear rude as he fought to form an apology.

"You showed incredible strength and presence of mind," he continued. "I should have told Mr. Silvestri we wouldn't lie to his wife about the baby. I should have also demanded he apologize for the way he spoke to you. You didn't allow his insults to interfere with your work."

Eliza sipped the tea, keeping her eyes on the bits of leaves crumbled at the base of the cup and welcoming the burn of the liquid in her throat.

"Before I came to your door, I ducked into Saints Peter and Paul. You must find comfort living so close to that magnificent Basilica. I asked for God's forgiveness, but I feel I must also confess to you."

Confession? Eliza surmised he had visited a bar last night, most likely here at McGillin's. When he arrived at Mrs. Silvestri's room, his hand on her shoulder steadied his own sway, but he didn't appear to be falling-down drunk or belligerent. Was there more to it than that?

"Dr. Callaghan, thank you for your words about Mr. Silvestri, but confessions are between a man and his God," she said.

Eliza wished to end this conversation, duck out of the pub, and get home to bed before Estelle saw her when she'd be out for her noontime walk around the courthouse. His imploring eyes told her to wait, to hear him.

"As Nurse Mitchell must have told you, I left the hospital for my dinner. I visited a favorite spot in the neighborhood I lived in ten years ago. Hanging behind the bar, I noticed a wall calendar with today's block circled and a notation of 'M's Birthday'. I don't know who M is, and it's irrelevant. Except, today, November 20th, is the date my daughter, Moira, would have turned ten."

A chill ran down the hollow of Eliza's spine.

"My wife, Aileen died giving birth to her. The midwife gave me Moira to hold while she tended to Aileen. She lived for twenty minutes. She was beautiful. The lightest wisps of ginger hair, just like my Ma's. If the baby was a girl, Aileen and I had chosen Moira after my Ma, Mary. Aileen insisted. She knew how happy I'd be to write my next letter home with joyous news that we would name our child after my mother."

Married, a widower, lost fatherhood...Eliza leaned in closer.

"Instead, I disappointed everyone. I couldn't save Aileen or Moira. I failed to plant the Callaghan name in America for my parents. They sent me here twenty-two years ago with my brother, Eoin, hoping we'd escape a second blight hitting Ireland. They lived through the first one but feared another famine was coming."

Eliza couldn't imagine the agonizing depths of Dr. Callaghan's life. His parents sending him away when he was but a boy, traveling to a foreign land, marrying a kindred woman, only to lose her and their child. Eliza's world revolved around a five-mile square of Philadelphia where she returned home every day to her mother and aunts. Comfort, love, and familiarity greeted her at the end of each day. Dr. Callaghan was alone in his hearth and his heart.

"I don't think you failed them," said Eliza, her voice soft, searching for a way to console him. "You became a doctor and a teacher. You've helped so many, including me."

"I didn't last evening. When I saw that calendar, memories ripped open the wounds scarred into my heart. I lost sight of the reason I entered medicine was to help women like Aileen, those like Mrs. Silvestri. I betrayed my oath to heal and allowed weakness to control my actions. I drank my dinner to drown the ghosts of Aileen's screams and Moira's whimpers at her first and final breaths."

Eliza blinked her tired, downcast eyes. How did one respond to a man who bared his soul to a woman he knew within the confines of a student–professor relationship? She recalled the day of her final exam when she stared into his blue eyes and found the silent storm behind them. A torment as deep as the sea bubbled below the surface until a circle on a calendar caused it to roil into a tempest. She reached across the table. His hands bracketed his plate, flat against the table's rough homespun cloth. Her hand came to rest on top of his.

"For ten years I've indulged my losses, letting them direct my life," he said. "The way you handled the Silvestri situation. Your self-confidence, it helped me admit a truth to myself."

Slowly, he turned his cold and clammy palm open and closed his fingers around hers.

"I've grown fond of you. You're a woman whom I'd like to get to know better. If you'll allow me."

In that moment, Patrick Callaghan's admission awoke a stirring buried in Eliza's heart. He understood and supported her vocation and dedication. From the playful way he could present the most boring Anatomy lecture to the vulnerability he laid upon the stained tablecloth between them, he was a man ready to think of another woman again.

"I would like that, Dr. Callaghan."

"Please, when we're not at the hospital, call me Patrick."

Eliza lifted her eyes to meet his. "I will, Patrick, if you will call me Eliza."

CHAPTER TWENTY

April 1902

Eliza stooped to position her shoulder under the patient's armpit. Her slight frame failed to offer much support, but the girl still leaned hard. Dr. Callaghan grabbed around the girl's shoulders. He looked at Eliza and mouthed, One, two...they hoisted her onto the exam table on three. A grimace spread across the young face on the bed while Eliza attempted to pull the voluminous folds of the plain cotton skirt down over her swollen legs.

"These are the worst," the girl cried as she pressed against her midriff. "What did I do to deserve these? Never had 'em this bad."

Two hours into Eliza's Wednesday morning shift, the girl waddled into the clinic complaining of debilitating menstrual cramps. With her name next on the patient rotation list, Eliza shepherded her into an exam room with Patrick following to supervise. They conferred in the room's corner. She appeared to be in her teens. Eliza supposed fifteen or sixteen from the outbreak of acne vulgaris on her shiny forehead. The blackheads, however, were not the parts of her body ready to pop.

Eliza patted the girl's legs as she scanned the intake form on the bedside table. "It's Adrienne, yes? Looks like you didn't answer all the nurse's questions when you came in. We need a few more details so we can help you."

Adrienne inclined into the pillow at the headboard, propping herself up on her elbows. "Make it quick, these darn cramps are killing me."

"When was your last doctor's appointment? Did they give you an estimated due date?" asked Eliza.

"Appointment? I haven't seen a doctor since they admitted Ma for the consumption three years ago."

"You've had no medical monitoring of your pregnancy?"

"No. Why would I? Doctors cost a lot," she said, giving Eliza the once-over. "Ma never used one, just the midwife for delivering me and the other kids."

As Eliza placed her hands over Adrienne's extended belly, Patrick shifted to the other side of the bed. He palpated Adrienne's mid-section and gestured for Eliza to replicate his motions. He covered Eliza's hands. A quiver fluttered inside her, as delicate as the way expectant mothers described the first movements of a fetus announcing its presence. She felt more than a teacher's touch. He soothed as much as he taught. In these fleeting instances, knowing glances marked the extent of her personal contact with Dr. Patrick Callaghan within the hospital's walls. Eliza insisted on professional interaction. She didn't need distractions at work. She would not provide fuel for gossip from other residents or barbs from nurses like Harriet Mitchell. Nor did she want to free her feelings: foreign, unsure, forbidden. Sorting them out would take extra efforts of energy and reflection, impossible luxuries during a residency. If he abided by her terms and waited, Eliza's respect for him would grow. Until then, their relationship would stay hidden, constructed from hushed whispers and slight touches.

Together, they felt a contraction knot hard and stretched taut as Adrienne released another scream, "Dear Mother of God!"

"All right, Adrienne. I think we know your due date. Your baby is on its way. These pains are not cramps, they're contractions. You'll need a quick examination before we send you to the labor and delivery room." Eliza pulled on the rubber gloves at the ready on the tray next to the bed.

Adrienne turned at the snap of the glove against Eliza's wrist. "What kinda exam? Whadda those for?"

"I'll check the dilation, the width, of the birth canal to determine how far along you are into your labor."

"Wait, what? You wanna spread my legs," Adrienne panicked, looking at Patrick standing silently as he allowed Eliza command of the evaluation, "and let him see all my glory!?" She shook her head, her hair whipping back and forth like the mane of a bucking bronco. "No ma'am. My Ma would have a fit! Ain't no man seen me down there, not even Johnny. He just looked at the wall behind me when he took care of his business."

"Adrienne, Dr. Callaghan is a fine doctor, and he's my supervisor," Eliza said. "He must watch and make sure I examine you correctly." Eliza pushed the skirt up Adrienne's legs.

Adrienne pushed it down. With the next contraction, her fight ceased, and her knees fell open in agony.

"Dr. Callaghan, perhaps you could turn away for a moment? I'll narrate my process, if that's sufficient?" During the first months of her residency, Eliza learned patient comfort went far beyond the physical.

• • •

Less than forty-five minutes after the exam, Eliza announced a healthy baby girl. As she completed her shift, satisfied with her performance and Patrick's praise, Eliza wished she thought only of the successful results. She performed her obstetrics duty with skill and empathy and delivered a squawking infant into a young mother's hesitant arms. Yet, other thoughts crowded her mind and vied for life. Could Adrienne, at sixteen and unmarried, provide for her daughter? Would her family accept another child, or would they close the door on both of them? What about Johnny, would he step in and become a responsible parent?

Eliza's musings spilled over into the afternoon when she joined Edith and Charlotte at The Century Club. Formed in 1879, the Club offered professional women a meeting place for discussions promoting science, literature, and art. At the core of many meetings, the suffrage question took center stage. Today, Susan B. Anthony, at eighty-two years old, the revered champion and leader of the National American Woman Suffrage Association, spoke to a packed house. Dressed in her well-known campaign costume, wine colored velvet, adorned with white point lace and amethysts and pearls at her neck, Miss Anthony appealed to Eliza, her friends, and the other attendees to carry the battle torch forward. Their generation, armed with college educations, business experiences, and a right to speak in public, and denied to those combatants before them, must fulfill the dream of an old woman.

As the three women left the reception, a sense of hope directed their way home. Eliza, with Adrienne still on her mind, shared with Edith and Charlotte one way a woman's right could make an impact. "Does anyone think for a minute, if women could vote, the Comstock Laws would exist? Those politicians would have gotten an earful from thousands of women, each with the power to unseat them from their chair in Congress."

"The discussion would never have made it to the floor. Perhaps we'd even have a representative to cut the proposal off at its knees," said Edith.

"And, my unmarried, sixteen-year-old patient this morning may never have marked April 9, 1902 as the birthday of her daughter, if she had the choice and access to use contraception."

Charlotte, who rarely confided in them, added, "And I may have been able to assist the prisoner who told me last week a guard raped her and begged me to abort the baby she knew was his."

Eliza and Edith gasped in unison. "Oh Charlotte, how dreadful for you, and for the woman facing such a terrible situation with no options," Eliza said.

Charlotte pushed her wire-rimmed glasses up her nose, "It is. Not that I know what I would do, even if it were legal. Instead, the only action I could take was placing a request for extra supervision of her cell. I pray she doesn't do something to herself, or the baby."

Instilled by Miss Anthony's speech, the lightness and buoyancy for a future of women achieving self-governance disappeared. Eliza reflected a moment more on Charlotte's revelation. "We've been called. We must continue Miss Anthony's fight–our fight–and ensure women win the vote. Then we can repeal the Comstock Laws, and other insidious ones like it to give women not only the right, but the choice to decide what may be best for them."

"Well put, Eliza," said Edith. "Now, cast off this serious conversation. Get home and enjoy dinner with your mother."

"You're not coming?"

"Estelle and Josephine are meeting Charlotte and me at Gimbel's. We thought it would be nice for you and your mother to have a quiet night together before Saturday."

Eliza beamed. She appreciated their thoughtfulness. On Saturday, Albie and Freddy would arrive to move their mother to Boston, leaving Eliza behind with her maiden aunts.

• • •

Moving the Edwards Wool Company offices to Boston created economic efficiencies which Charles and Nathan Putnam predicted five years ago. The Bay State beckoned with direct shipping routes from Liverpool and Glasgow, well-established mills north of the city along the Merrimack River, and ample and able workers. Albie opened the office in 1899. Freddy joined him the following year, declaring Boston "quite charming." Eliza suspected most of the charm he found came from the green eyes of one Beatrice, "Bea," Lowell, the daughter of one of Boston's oldest Brahmin families. If his courtship progressed, Laura might also assume mother-of-the groom duties. Eliza could only hope there would be a ring on Bea's finger soon. A Boston wedding would squash talk of one for Eliza in Philadelphia.

One frigid night back in February, as Eliza and her mother coaxed a fire from a cold parlor hearth for extra warmth, Laura cast another chill into the room. "What do you think of Mamie's suggestion?" Laura asked Eliza as they settled onto the divan, the flames in the hearth licking the upper reaches of the chimney flue.

When Albie and Mamie married, Eliza gained a sister-in-law who stepped into the family with ease. Having lost her own mother a year after the wedding, Mamie looked to Laura often for maternal advice. Her most recent letter, however, exceeded the bounds of *Shouldn't the baby be sleeping through the night by now?* and *How old was Albie when he took his first steps?* With their second child due in two months, Mamie put forth a more urgent plea: Would Laura consider moving to Boston to help her and Albie manage their growing family?

"I'm a bit surprised, to be honest," said Eliza. Mamie Edwards was not the first woman to have a second child follow eighteen months after her first. "With Albie's talk of their new home on Beacon Hill, I'm sure he could afford a baby nurse. A visit with them will be lovely, but a permanent move? Philadelphia has been...is your home. Our home."

"It is. But my baby," she picked up Eliza's hand, patting it softly, "is a remarkable young woman. A doctor, no less. My mothering days here are complete."

Complete? thought Eliza. Didn't her mother know how much the simple phrases such as she had just spoken meant to Eliza? Her mother's praise and encouragement shined the brightest rays of hope into Eliza's confidence on her darkest days.

"Oh Mother, I can navigate my way through the market and find the perfect cut of a pork loin thanks to your keen eye and instruction. You taught me how to calculate the interest due on my savings account. And I can summon an appropriate Bible verse from memory for conversation. But, I'll never stop needing you."

"I know you won't. But I am pleased Mamie asked me, her mother-in-law, to move in with them. Albie chose such a lovely girl. Her invitation means the world to me."

Time marches forward. As Eliza learned from Dr. Henry Gray, the heart continues to increase up to an advanced period of life. Her mother's fifty-four-year-old heart still had room to grow. Eliza would help open the door to that room and support her mother's choice, just as her mother supported hers five years ago.

• • •

The towers of wooden crates stacked as high as Eliza's waist. She wove her way through the maze to a clearing. With her feet propped on the footrest, her mother reclined on the parlor's divan. Around her, life poked through straw packing. Hand-painted vases and teacups, silver framed photos, and mirrors. Dresses, coats, hats, boots, and wraps. In her arms, Eliza balanced a pile of leather-bound books from the library. She placed them on top of an open crate, readying to snuggle them in for their northbound train trip. Beloved faces from her childhood stared up at her. They were leaving her too. It was time to share those favorites with Albie's children.

Tom Sawyer, Black Beauty, Mother Goose, Jo, Beth, Amy and Meg March, Captain Nemo, The Brothers Grimm. Alice. Eliza ran her finger over the red leather cover. The gold embossed oval framing a girl in a pinafore with long locks had worn away at the top edge. Alice was no longer hemmed in; freed, she journeyed through Wonderland. And how fantastical those adventures were! In a lost moment, Eliza thought of Alice's adaptation through the chapters. In the end, she asserts herself before the King and Queen of Hearts, finding her voice, and speaks up and out for herself. Eliza brought the book to her chest and hugged it tight like a soft pillow. "Mother, would you mind if I kept this one?"

Laura looked up from sorting paintbrushes, the ones still usable and the ones needing retirement. "Alice, Eliza, and Florence. The three of you spent hours lost in Wonderland."

"We did."

"Then keep it. Maybe someday you'll have a daughter to read it to?"

Here we go, thought Eliza. Twice in five months, Patrick Callaghan had joined the Pearson Edwards for dinner. At least twenty times since then, Eliza's mother dropped her not-so-subtle hints about Patrick's intentions.

"Maybe, Mother. Maybe someday I'll be rewarded with the most precious gift from God," said Eliza. "And I will not forsake my mother's teachings, for I know they are a garland to grace a head and a chain to adorn a neck."

"Proverbs 1:8-9," Laura grinned. Eliza mirrored her smile.

"Yes, you taught me well. But there's one reading I won't follow with your words."

Eliza pawed through the pile and withdrew *Grimms' Fairy Tales*. Reflecting back on her morning delivering teen-aged Adrienne, Eliza held it up in front of her mother, "I won't edit the fairy tales. A woman's life isn't all glass slippers, being awakened by a magical kiss, and happily ever-afters."

Eliza watched the air deflate from her mother's chest as her shoulders sagged. "But I will remember what Cinderella's real mother told her, 'Whenever you are otherwise in a predicament, then I'll send you help. Just stay good and pure.' Those words, I will keep close."

CHAPTER TWENTY-ONE

February 1903

A snow squall blew in through the main entrance doors of West Philadelphia Hospital, bringing mid-February into the waiting room on a Saturday morning. Darts of icy air sliced into would-be patients sprawled in wooden chairs. Family members pulled closer together. A boy tore in through the doors with the wind's kite tails. A girl of two-or-three-years old lay limp in his arms.

"Help! Please! Help my sister!"

Eliza dropped the stack of intake forms she was reviewing at the front desk and rushed to the boy's side.

"What happened? What is it?" Eliza said.

The boy gestured to the child's throat. "It's stuck."

Eliza pried the child from her brother and laid her on the floor. She tilted the girl's head back and opened the bluish lips. A whistling wheeze met her as she peered inside. Lodged against the pharynx, Eliza saw a green tangled ball of rubber. Sterile tweezers in the desk drawer may as well have been in Baltimore. The blue tint in the child's lips darkened and inched up her cheeks. Eliza wiped her fingers against her white coat before thrusting her thumb and forefinger into the girl's mouth. With a quick tug, Eliza pulled out the enemy and lifted the child up, thumping her back.

A wail spread through the room. The girl's cheeks colored from blue to purple to red as she screamed her fear out.

"Thank you, thank you. Oh, thank you," the older boy cried as he clung to Eliza's waist. He reached up to pat his sister's rump, "You're okay, Bini, it's okay."

Relief washed over Eliza. There were enough ways for the grim reaper to steal a child: pneumonia, influenza, tuberculosis, diarrhea from enteritis. Congenital anomalies. Remnants of a popped balloon in a windpipe should not be one of them.

"Sshhhh. Bini, hon. I know. That was scary. But your brother's right. You're okay," said Eliza.

Her palm rubbed the girl's back in slow circles, quieting her wails. Bini pushed herself off Eliza's shoulder, her thin arms stronger than the matchsticks they looked like.

"Down. Wanna get down."

Eliza lowered her to the ground but clasped the frail hand tight. She turned her attention to the older brother.

"You did a wonderful job..."

"Eric."

"Where's your mum, Eric? Or your papa?"

Eric shrugged and reached for Bini's hand. Eliza held it firm. Any procedure performed required documentation, even a five-minute emergency in the waiting room. She would have to rely on Eric to answer the questions on an intake form. He couldn't be over ten years old himself. There might be more blanks by the time she finished with him.

Behind Eliza, a man shut the entrance doors with a bang. His leather-gloved fingertips flicked a dusting of flakes from the shoulders of his gray wool overcoat. Both pieces of outerwear were virgin to the trials of long winter months. Tapping his black bowler hat against his thigh, more snow fell at his feet, melting and puddling on the green linoleum tiles.

"Blasted Pennsylvania," he said. "Orderly, clean up this mess. What are these ragamuffins doing here? Get them into an exam room or send them home. One or the other. They shouldn't be hanging around here. Inaction breeds disasters."

At last week's staff meeting, Eliza had learned of their new administrator, Dr. Douglas Whitaker. His slow, authoritative drawl announced he had arrived from Atlanta. Eliza shuffled the children into a nearby exam room with strict instructions to keep the door closed. She extracted a promise that they would stay put, so she could grab a bite to eat for them from the kitchen.

A boiled ham sandwich split between Eric and Bini worked its magic. Between bites, Eric answered Eliza's questions. Full name? Bianka and Eric Antkowich. Bianka's age? Three. Eric reported the balloon came from her birthday party a few weeks ago. And Eric? I'm nine, he said, sitting up straighter to proclaim his advanced years. Address? Around the corner. Eric had run fast for about two blocks, he guessed. Parents? Leonard and Greta. Where were they? Papa's working. Where is that? The factory. Mama yells at him every night to take off his stinkin' work clothes outside. He smells like a giant walking cigar. And Mama? Where was she? Must've taken the linens she irons out to deliver.

Eliza considered allowing the children to leave. Eric shouldn't be expected to supervise a curious, hungry three-year-old. The stark, black-rimmed clock on the wall above the door read ten forty-five. If she walked them home and spoke to the mother, she'd need at least twenty minutes, plus five more to bundle into her overcoat, muffler, and galoshes. In the corridor she could hear Dr. Whitaker imparting more instructions to the nursing staff, his voice clipped and sharp. Eliza imagined them shrinking with each of his barks. The hospital planned to introduce him at an eleven o'clock assembly.

"Eric, I need you to listen to me," said Eliza. "The way you took care of your sister will make your mama and papa proud. You are a smart, brave boy to bring Bini here. But, if your parents leave you alone to mind her again, you must watch her every minute. She's not as smart as you. She might put other dangerous things in her mouth or wander into the street, or worse. Maybe you can pretend you're a policeman walking his beat, checking on anyone or anything that looks out of place."

The boy saluted her, ready for his duty. "Yes, ma'am. I'll tie Bini to a chair if I have to, like Mama used to with me."

Dear Lord, thought Eliza. She wasn't sure whether she should be disturbed a child was tied to a chair or impressed with the ingenuity of the mother.

"That may not be necessary, just keep a close eye on her. All right, hold her hand every step of the way. Your mama is probably home and frantic, looking for you both."

From the staff closet Eliza took her knit muffler, wrapped it twice around Bini's neck, and tucked the ends inside the flapping thread-bare coat. She knelt to button Eric's jacket. At the exit, Bini lifted her mitten-less hand, closing her fingertips down to her palm and opening them in a toddler's wave of goodbye. Eliza smiled. The episode was fleeting, but memories of them would last. The demands of doctoring came in all shapes and sizes.

•   •   •

Hospital staff entered the operating room theater in an unspoken pecking order: soon-to-be retired administrator, Dr. Howe, and doctors, followed by Eliza and two other residents; behind them, nurses and orderlies spared from their duties. Eliza scanned the arced rows of seats. Nurses' white caps bobbed in the back like a regatta of sailboats. Below her, in the second row, third in from the aisle, she glimpsed Patrick's broad shoulders and black hair. Her lips lifted into a slight grin. He had paid heed to her advice that first impressions are lasting. His tousled hair smoothed into place by an extra heavy application of pompadour cream.

As the room settled into quiet anticipation, the door opened again to admit another staff member, the newest addition and the most senior. Dr. Whitaker walked to the center of the theater where Dr. Howe awaited him. Beads of deep-set dark brown eyes considered the personnel assembled before him. A thick mustache spread across his upper lip like a trimmed hedge, creeping to the far reaches of his cheeks. His starched high-collared shirt stood as stiff as the clipboard in his hands; his black suit and silk tie resembled an undertaker's. The new administrator stepped in front of Dr. Howe. Douglas Whitaker would make his own introduction.

"Good morning. For those who didn't read Dr. Howe's communication last week, I am Doctor Whitaker, Administrator of West Philadelphia Hospital. I've spent the past eight years at the esteemed Grady Hospital in Atlanta, Georgia, one of my city's newest hospitals. We've been rebuilding ever since your General Sherman marched through with torches in his hand and Southern blood on his sleeve."

As Dr. Whitaker continued to espouse his credentials and hint at other vestiges of hostilities from the War between the States, Eliza's eyelids grew heavy. Her shift had started at seven with a routine delivery, followed by the adrenaline-rushed emergency of Bianka versus the balloon. Now, with time to relax, fatigue enveloped her body. Her shoulders slumped as her head bobbed. When her chin hit her chest, she shook from the siren of sleep.

"...much to learn. I expect intake forms to be concise and complete. You'll follow orders without questions and treatments administered according to directives of your superiors."

Eliza caught these comments, thinking they were useless. Every staff member followed orders and administered care under their superiors' direction. Her patient forms and reports were always complete. She allowed her eyes to droop again. *I'm resting my eyes.*

"I am adjusting doctors' schedules and assignments."

Another jerk to awaken. Would re-assignments separate her and Patrick? He had served as her supervisor since she began her residency. Could Dr. Whitaker have heard rumors of their relationship? As much as she enjoyed Patrick's closeness during deliveries and patient rounds, she valued his teaching and wise words more. How he explained every nuance of a treatment plan. His guidance and encouragement. His sensitivity to difficult cases. Eliza's mind raced as she prayed, *Please, keep Patrick and me together.*

"Grady Hospital is similar in size to West Philadelphia. But I find the number of physicians here limiting. While I work to secure funding to hire more graduates from Jefferson or Pennsylvania, I will schedule separate female doctors or residents from the same shift. I've heard how too much time together can stimulate an alignment of womanly cycles. I won't have an entire shift of practicing doctors and nurses incapacitated on the same days each month."

Eliza and the other Woman's Med. graduates pinched each other as they had done in an operating room during their third year. Was Dr. Whitaker serious?

• • •

Four blocks from the hospital, Eliza rounded the corner. She looked over her shoulder toward the trolley stop. Most of the people hurried past her, bundled against the February cold. The snow squalls of the morning lingered into the darkening late afternoon. Despite the woolen scarves wrapped around heads and covering faces, Eliza didn't recognize any of them as hospital staff. She climbed aboard, searching for a slicked down head of black hair. At the rear of the car, Patrick removed the black bag from the seat next to him.

Eliza settled into the empty seat, yanking the tips of her gloves, finger by finger, "Who is this Dr. Whitaker? Is he from this century? Or maybe his ignorance and arrogance are a southern thing? Did you see the smug pride on his face when he mentioned the separate wing Grady Hospital is building for their Negro patients, just to divide them from white patients?"

Patrick picked up her gloveless fingers and stroked his thumb over the back of her hand. "Eliza. You're letting him fluster you into a tirade which won't end well. The Board will never allow him to enact any of his nonsense. The hospital has deep ties to Woman's Medical and a mission to serve all patients."

"Regardless. I think I'll borrow a few pages from Dean Marshall's history of Woman's Med. Some of those award-winning publications should set him straight. You can be my look-out when I sneak into his office and plant the irrefutable findings front and center on his desk."

"A wise man, even if he was an English parliamentarian, once said, actions speak louder than words. Show that witless doctor your abilities and presence of mind," said Patrick, "every day of the month."

"You're right, my wise man." Eliza leaned into his shoulder, "Which is one more reason I love you."

"And I, you. Now put aside Dr. Witless. There are far more interesting things to discuss, like today's date. Tell me, what's today?"

She thinks, February twelfth? It was hard to remember when she worked six ten-hour shifts a week. Days bled into another, into endless weeks and months of work. He released her hand and reached into his breast pocket, pulling forth an envelope. "Open it," he instructed.

A yellowed scrap of linen and a folded piece of stationery fell into her lap. She smoothed out the linen first. A family crest embroidered with green and white flourishes surrounded a knight, his shield displayed a wolf emerging from a forest. "Is this your family's?" she asked.

"Yes."

Eliza pointed to the woven script above the knight's silver helmet, *Fidus Et Audax*. "Latin for faithful and bold?"

"Yes," said Patrick. "Which is how I feel today, Valentine's Day, and every day."

He motioned to the paper. Scrawled over the sheet, Eliza read his words.

I watched the live-long day
For a messenger to bear
The words that I fain would say
To my little ladye fair.
And so, I sung to the wind
The tale that I longed to tell.
And hoped that the breeze might find
The maiden I loved so well,
And breathe it lightly around.
And she, I think, will divine
In the breeze's gentle sound
Who would be her Valentine?

"Patrick, I completely forgot while you wrote a poem for me? I'm useless."

"Useless?" he turned her coat collar down to nuzzle her neck. "And don't be so quick to give me credit. I spent my day off at the library. It took me several hours before I found this one, *Unuttered Words*, by an anonymous author. But these are mine, I promise to be faithful to you, Eliza. I ask you to hold this as my intention."

He pressed the linen into her hand. "Keep my family name close until I hope you'll add it to yours."

Add. A single word could change an entire sentence. Not replace, or take, but add to Eliza Edwards.

"Yes, I will."

She uttered faithful and bold words of her own.

CHAPTER TWENTY-TWO

September 1907

Eliza unfolded the morning edition of *The Philadelphia Inquirer*, savoring her Sunday off. Today she skipped church to take full advantage of the entire day to relax. After breakfast, she and Edith lingered with a second cup of coffee.

"Here's a good one," Eliza said as she scanned the front-page headlines. "*Two Plucky Women Fight Assailants: Miss Edith Ketosh Uses Hat Pin in Self Defense and Gowan City Girl Shoves Revolver Against Intruder's Head.* Well, there you go—a plucky Edith!"

Edith rose to look over Eliza's shoulder. "Another case of typhoid making the news," said Edith, reading the article headline adjacent to the one heralding the brave young women. "Clayton McMichael, son of the ex-Postmaster General, is on his way to Philadelphia from Maine in a private train car. He's being admitted to University Hospital today," she read. "I think I'll pop down there and see if I can interview him."

Upon reading Dr. George Soper's paper, *The Work of a Chronic Typhoid Germ Distributor,* in the June issue of the *Journal of the American Medical Association,* Edith developed a keen interest in the discovery of Mary Mallon as a carrier of the deadly typhoid bacillus. Learning that Dr. Soper had also called upon assistance from Dr. Josephine Baker to wrangle the uncooperative Mallon in for testing added another flair to the case.

When she wrote to Dr. Soper requesting an interview, she suggested a mid-September meeting. Upon hearing Edith's plans, Estelle announced she would accompany her. A woman should not be traveling to New York alone, nor meeting with a man whom no one knew beyond the newspaper headlines. A separate meeting with Dr. Baker, an inspector for the City's Department of Health, would round out their trip.

"That's an excellent idea. Your research will be valuable. Soon we'll be reading a paper by Dr. Edith Haskins in the Journal. You can bet, I'll be the first one to alert Dean Marshall to add your name, 'Plucky Edith Haskins,' to the list of accomplishments of a Woman's Med. alumna." Eliza tore the article from the page, giving it to Edith. "Shall we hold dinner for you?"

"No need. Patrick's coming today?"

Eliza beamed.

"Then don't wait. Enjoy. Give him my best."

Every Sunday he wasn't working, Patrick attended Mass at the Basilica of Saints Peter and Paul. After Mass, when he and Eliza had the same Sunday off, he crossed the street and joined the Pearson Edwards women for dinner.

Eliza gathered up the newspaper. Time to get the Smithfield ham into the oven and the corn shucked. She sighed, thinking she may never cure a ham or cream the corn the way Molly could. Much to the surprise of the family, four years ago, Molly announced her marriage to Lawrence Cleary. When Laura moved to Boston, the Pearson Edwards household held far fewer demands for a full-time cook and housekeeper. Molly subsequently accepted a position with her husband's employer and moved across the city. After four years, Eliza missed more than Molly's skills in the kitchen. She missed the mischievous twinkle in her feisty eyes and her short quips to keep them on their toes. At least she left her gingersnaps recipe with them.

・ ・ ・

Two weeks later, an open-air Dragon Touring Motor Car chugged down the street and rolled to a stop on its thin rubber tires. Side-hung lanterns and headlamps glistened. The steering wheel column rose high from the floorboard. The navy-blue body, accented with yellow trim, gave the auto the look of an exotic, tropical parrot.

"Here it comes!" Eliza stood on the sidewalk, waving to those inside the house to hurry to the curb. "Oh, wow!"

Lawrence Cleary jumped down from the black, tufted leather seat. A quick learner, he endorsed his employer's idea to add a touring car to his stable. He offered his services to transport Edith and Estelle to the Reading Terminal for the 2:05 train to New York City.

Eliza hoped to accompany them, too, but Dr. Whitaker vehemently denied her request for a five-day vacation. Every September brought sickly children to the wards, their faces swollen with measles and mumps and throats striated with strep. Eliza swore they became walking germ factories the moment they re-entered school buildings. An increase in injuries from harvesting accidents spiked, sending the more serious casualties to the city. And, maternity beds filled as the results of Christmas gifts from husbands to wives nine months ago arrived in swaddling clothes.

Instead, Eliza remained in Philadelphia, envious of the travelers as they embarked on a trip of firsts. The first from their household to ride in an automobile. No sitting in a carriage behind the barn smells of a horse, nor lugging their bags to the trolley stop, and weaving their way to the station. Once they arrived in New York, they would witness the RMS *Lusitania's* docking from its maiden voyage, a trans-Atlantic crossing from Liverpool, England. Eliza marveled at the facts Patrick shared with her about the magnificent ocean liner. At seven hundred and eighty-seven feet if drydocked, it would cover two-and-a-half city blocks. A mammoth, unsinkable vessel, it carried over three thousand passengers and crew and claimed the title of the world's largest passenger ship.

Eliza was even more interested in Edith and Estelle welcoming a *Lusitania* passenger off its gangplanks. After six years, her dear friend was coming home. Eliza fancied the pull of Aunt Maria's brooch steered Olga back into the waiting arms of her second family.

The veracity of the situation, however, arose from growing political upheavals in Russia. The war with Japan which ended two years prior led to worker strikes, peasant unease, and military skirmishes. Eliza worried about the Povitzkys' ties to Tsar Nicholas II. When she read accounts of the Tsar's dissolution of Parliament and an increase in strife, she grew more concerned. Anti-imperialists were targeting anyone related to the Tsar.

Eliza heard from Olga in August in reply to her multiple inquiries about the Povitzkys' safety. Olga's father secured first-class, one-way tickets on the *Lusitania* for Olga and her sister, Taniya, to travel to America. Olga's parents considered themselves too old for emigration, and Grigori, Olga's brother, had lost his battle with hemophilia. Despite Olga's dedication to research in hematology, she couldn't keep Grigori from his favorite pastime, charging across open fields on their Arabian steeds. The day he attempted a dangerous jump on a steeplechase course, the stallion tossed him to the ground. His internal injuries bled profusely as the life drained out of him.

Reeling from her heartbreak over Grigori's death, Olga also wrote to Eliza that for the first time, she questioned the value of her research. Six years of study produced no definitive answers or treatment options. She was ready for a fresh start again in America, gaining an assistant position at Woman's Med. alongside Rabid Rabi.

· · ·

Patrick toted two hard leather cases in each hand. He let out a low whistle as he walked down the steps, eyeing the car parked curbside. "She is a beauty. How fast can you get her moving?"

"They say with this four-cylinder, water-cooled engine, forty miles an hour, but I haven't tried her on an open stretch yet," said Lawrence.

"Decent sized engine, but will these valises fit?"

Patrick mumbled under his breath, "Men could have crammed everything into one bag. They're only going for five days."

"Women." Lawrence snorted his agreement.

"Make sure you're on time. We won't want you to miss Olga and Taniya. The docks will be dreadfully packed with news reporters and photographers," said Eliza as she gave final instructions to the travelers.

With their arms linked, Edith and Estelle looked like a double-yolk egg as they walked to the waiting car. Edith climbed in and held her hand out to guide Estelle into the seat behind Lawrence, nudging aside a valise to maneuver their feet into the narrow floor space. She called out the window to Eliza, "For heaven's sake. This isn't Olga's first trip. It will be much wiser for them to meet us at our hotel. I cannot make any promises that my meeting with Mr. Soper won't run late. He extended me the favor of the interview. I don't want to be rude and cut him short."

Eliza clapped her hands to acknowledge Edith's rationale.

"I'm excited to see Olga, that's all. Have a safe trip!"

Patrick sidled over to her on the doorstep and drew her in close. Laughing, he pecked her cheek, "She'll be here soon enough," he said.

She curved her body into the comfortable nook of Patrick at her side. A quiet solace descended and cloaked the couple. Eliza headed into the empty house. While Eliza missed her mother, she often confessed to herself, the distance offered some advantages. She didn't have to listen to remarks and hints about a prolonged engagement, as her mother wrote in her weekly epistles from Boston. Eliza buried those letters deep in her desk drawers.

Eliza paused. She and Patrick had been courting for three years. They had dined out often, attended medical lectures and the theatre, and visited her uncle's country estate, but they had never been unchaperoned in the house. A home held close a quiet familiarity. With tables to sit across from one another, eyes gazing and holding the other's. With sofas to sit upon, a thigh pressing against a thigh. With bedrooms, to tempt and taunt the flesh and heart.

There he stood in the foyer, looking at her, only her. He rolled his sleeves up above his elbows. His sinewy arms, covered in black hair, hung at his sides. The white rough-spun cotton shirt opened at his neck. Two top undone buttons allowed a creep of chest hair to peek over the neckline of his undershirt. His square jaw jutted out, his jugular pulsing. Eliza longed to place her trained fingers on his pulse, feeling his life. The stubble on his chin and cheeks sprouted a tint of red mixed in with the black and a stray gray, which would be a bushy beard if he let it grow. He took a step toward her, his eyes full of questions. Four more strides and he stopped next to her. His arms wrapped around her.

Eliza needed a distraction. "Patrick, dear, shall I make you a sandwich? There should be some roast left."

He propped his chin on her shoulder and teased her ear, "Forget the chicken. I'm hungry only for you."

Eliza tensed. He had figured it out. They were alone. Turning toward him, she tilted her head up to kiss him. His breath came hot upon her. Eliza absorbed his warmth into her own flesh. Able hands trained to care for a body in a different manner inched up hers. Feather-light fingers brushed the edge of her breasts, up and down, hesitant whether to move inward or upward. Eliza relaxed into his caresses. Her palms went to his face. The flushed heat burned. Was it her fingers, or his cheeks? Or both?

Her heart spoke louder than her voice. "I love you."

His hands moved down to encircle her waist. A guttural moan escaped his lips. "Eliza."

The flame intensified, shooting through her body. "Patrick, please. Yes..." She pressed tight against his chest and other body parts below his chest. Upstairs, buried among undergarments in her lingerie drawer, a pessary she had prescribed for herself awaited summoning. The brown wrapped package, intact and tight, concealed the contraceptive device. Eliza alone knew of its existence and proximity.

Their dance of intimacy became an awkward stutter of missteps. She remained adamant no one outside the family know of their courting during her residency. He insisted they delay marriage until his mother passed and he could marry a Protestant. As years passed, their desires waltzed in a never-ending circle. Eliza's confidence in her love for Patrick grew. She needn't wait for a ring and ceremony to proclaim an emotional and physical union. She was willing. He was able. Yet, bound by his Catholic teachings, Patrick refused her. Until the day he relented and ignored his Church's dictates prohibiting contraception, or she became Dr. Eliza Edwards Callaghan, their uneasy dance would make another trip around the dance floor.

He dropped his arms, extracting her from his embrace. "I'm going upstairs to lie down. I won't be long."

"Fine," she said, trying to mask her disappointment. As he ascended the stairs, Eliza huffed to herself. She knew what he'd be doing, and it did not include napping. Her head drooped as she stood alone in the foyer. The closed front door before her, an open staircase behind. Gazing upon the foyer table, she noted a yellowed tinge of the lace runner. When was the last time the table linens had been washed? She moved the crystal vase and candlesticks aside and gathered up the runner. Now was as good a time as any to give them a hard scrubbing, up and down the washboard, immersed in hot, sudsy water.

CHAPTER TWENTY-THREE

Five days after Edith and Estelle departed for New York, Eliza woke from a mid-morning nap after her night shift. Bags thumped into furniture before landing at the foot of the stairway. Four pairs of boots thudded on the hardwood floor. Voices mingled with bouts of laughter, disturbing the peace of the house. One voice with its thick accent laughed the loudest.

She rustled into her dressing gown and raced down the stairs.

The sparkle in Olga's eye gleamed as brightly as the day they had met ten years ago. Her bosom was plumper, shown off by the low neckline of her cream silk travel suit. Aunt Maria's brooch, fastened to a delicate gold chain, hung at the center of her chest. A smart taupe felt hat with a long white plume complemented the wide white sash at her thickened waist, a white piping edged the folded cuffs of her sleeves. Taniya, her younger sister, stood a step behind Olga. While she resembled her sister in appearance, Taniya's demeanor lacked any geniality. Her downward turned mouth accented the dullness in her eyes.

Eliza stretched for her friend to enfold her in a long-missed embrace, "It's so wonderful to have you home."

"Back like a bad penny." Olga winked at Eliza with a smirk.

"And Taniya, what a pleasure to meet you." Eliza extended her hand to the sullen looking sister. "I hope the trip wasn't too tiresome?"

Taniya replied, "Nice to meet you, Doctor Edwards. But I am quite tired, and my stomach still hasn't settled since we disembarked. Would you mind if I laid down for a bit?"

"I'm thoroughly exhausted, too, from all this traveling within a few days. I can show you to a room," said Estelle, reaching for her totes.

Edith intercepted her hand, "I've got them. Go ahead, I'll be right behind you. I want to organize my notes from the interview with Mr. Soper while they're still fresh in my head." She nodded to Eliza and Olga, "I'll leave you two to catch up."

Olga lifted her head and sniffed the air like a Russian wolfhound. "Be still my heart. Are those Molly's gingersnaps? What a dear to leave the recipe with you!"

"You give me too much credit. They may smell like Molly's, but they're not as yummy!" Eliza said.

After the three women were upstairs out of earshot and Eliza returned with a tray of cookies and lemon tea, Olga clapped her hands, "Thank goodness. Five days alone with her on the ship and I was ready to toss her overboard. She is a nuisance. I shouldn't say so about my sister, but all she has done is complain since Father announced he was sending us to America. She pouts and whines, cries, carries on, stamping her foot like our cousins, the spoiled tsarinas. Egad, I can't wait to drop her at Bryn Mawr tomorrow and let the college house mothers deal with her! They'll straighten her out right quick and show her how lucky she is to be here."

Olga exhaled a deep breath. "Now, Dr. Edwards. I'm ready to relax with the telling of your fairy tale. Start from the beginning. There's a lot more to the goings-on here in Philadelphia than what you've penned in letters. Dr. Patrick Callaghan? The mysterious, good-looking professor, with the dreamy brogue finally caught your eye, eh? When is the wedding? What's the delay? You needn't wait for me to come back and be your maid of honor. I'm older than the hills. I guess I could be an old maid of horror."

Eliza scooted over on the sofa, giving room for Olga. She tucked her legs beneath her and commenced with the grim tale of Eliza and Patrick.

"I suppose it started with our final Obstetrics exam when he spoke with me afterwards. Remember I told you how nervous I was? Fearing I might not graduate?"

"Yes, I do. I said you were ridiculous to doubt yourself like that."

"He was so kind, it seemed he addressed me as more than a student. I felt a connection then."

Recalling those first exchanges, Eliza heard anew the touching tone of his voice and how he emphasized the Irish prayer he said at the graduation luncheon–*For every problem life sends, a faithful friend to share.*

"When we started working together at West Philadelphia, his faith in my abilities was refreshing, especially after Dr. Whitaker joined the staff. Every day Patrick found ways to tell me to ignore Whitaker and focus on my duties."

Olga perked up. In a deep voice, she interjected, "Send the hens back to the hen house. Children and fathers need them by the family hearth, not in a hospital room."

"Ha—you read all my letters!" Eliza playfully punched Olga in the arm. "But if you're going to quote Whitaker, you must learn a Southern drawl. He uses it quite well to sweeten his caustic remarks."

"I'm not surprised Patrick's been supportive," said Olga. "By teaching at Woman's Med., he's surrounded by successful women in medicine. But what tipped him over from the category of teacher and supervisor to paramour?" She directed a slow wink, and a raised brow at Eliza.

"The day after I delivered the Silvestri baby. I didn't include all the details in my letters. It was very difficult to re-live that delivery and put it down in words. At first, I was furious with him. I couldn't believe he left me alone. I thought him a vile, wretched man. He showed no inclination to support me. He stood there dumb and mute, and a bit intoxicated. By the next morning, I decided I would request a transfer from his supervision. Then he arrives on my doorstep."

"The nerve! You slapped his face good and hard and sent him away–right? Ha, no, I'm guessing you didn't?"

"I couldn't. His plea to explain himself sounded genuine. Over breakfast, Patrick bared his soul. He admitted his mistake and weakness to me, not an easy task for a man. At that moment, I forgave him. I knew I loved him, too."

As Eliza finished the story of Patrick and his lost wife and daughter, Olga's eyes moistened. "It's heart-breaking. Watching my parents' grief when Grigori died nearly killed me. When a parent loses a child, whether the child is hours old or twenty-five years, rips a hole in your soul and rends the core of your being. Since Patrick has found you and has learned to love again, and you love him, why on earth are you waiting to marry and release your joy?"

"His mother."

Olga's brow climbed up her forehead.

"When I said we needed to wait on a public courtship until I finished my residency, Patrick honored my request and added one of his own. As much as he loves me, he says he can't marry without his mother's blessing, which he knows she'll withhold if we marry outside the Catholic Church without the proper sacraments. I'm not only Protestant, but an Episcopalian, which follows the Church of England."

Eliza sighed. "He gets very sentimental sometimes, like an Irish storyteller saying, 'he wants to scream his joy across the ocean from a green hill of Ireland and have his delight resound over the valleys about his love for me.' But his mother has lived through enough anguish. At sixty and with a tendency toward lung ailments, she has little time left. Why should he give her cause for more grief? I can't argue with him."

She nibbled a gingersnap, welcoming the tang of the spice and the sugar to bolster her energy to continue the saga.

"Although he hasn't seen his family since he was ten years old, he has kept strong ties to them. He writes home every other week. When his Da passed, his Ma went to live with Patrick's sister, Cathleen, packing with her the sorrows of loss and distance from her sons."

Eliza pulled the Callaghan handkerchief from her dress sleeve. She had told no one about Patrick's full story, his hopes, and his fears. She smoothed out the linen, revealing the family crest, the embroidery ragged, and the fabric yellowed from decades of folding and unfolding, crunched into a pocket, catching his tears. Once he gave it to Eliza, she kept it close, always in her sleeve or pocket, to feel his name, counting the months, then years, she would add it to hers.

"Patrick gave this to me. He's carried it with him since leaving Ireland. Mrs. Callaghan made him promise to remember his family and his faith. And he tries. Every day, he honors his mother's request."

Olga held out her hand, "May I?" Eliza pressed it in Olga's palm. "It's a ring–yes?"

"For now, yes." Eliza sipped the lemon tea. "At fifteen," she continued, "it fell to Patrick to write that his older brother had fallen in love with a German woman, a Lutheran, married her and left their Uncle's house. Patrick searched for him for months. He ran a Missing Family advertisement in the *Boston Pilot*, the Catholic newspaper, assuming they may have gone there, but he has heard no news of them. The letter his mother wrote back cut him. She blamed Patrick for not finding Owen. Since then, he has tried to make her happy and hold to his faith. When he married

Aileen, he received a proud and joyful note. He had righted Owen's wrong. He would be the one to bring the Callaghan name to America and raise his children in the Church. Then Aileen and Moira died, and he failed again in his mother's mind. So, if we wed now, he would send another disappointment back to Ireland."

Olga shook her head in a slow arc. "I don't know. Patrick seems selfish. I couldn't care less if I ever get hitched. But, for you, having a family is important. The longer you wait, the more difficult a pregnancy may be."

"You don't see him the way I do. I find it honorable he doesn't want to aggrieve his mother; it speaks volumes to the husband he'll be. Do you think I wish to marry a man who may forever hold regrets? Who could let those misgivings overcome his confidence and happiness? Or blame me and leave me? We'll wait. It won't be much longer, and after all my mother was thirty-one when I was born, and I turned out fine."

CHAPTER TWENTY-FOUR

May 1908

The infant's cry announced her arrival to the world. Her circle, for now, encompassed a modest, shared hospital room in West Philadelphia. The sole inhabitants were her mother, a nurse, and Dr. Eliza Edwards. As with every delivery, Eliza held the child close for a moment before placing the swaddled bundle into a waiting mother's arms. Before long, this baby girl's world would grow, creeping into unknown places like an ivy vine up the sides of a building. With her roots planted in the rich soil beneath her, she would reach forever upward. In those moments, Eliza imagined where this infant might travel, what she may see, who she may become.

She had become Dr. Eliza Pearson Edwards. And there was one person who deserved recognition more than anyone. Someone who had released old hopes to acknowledge a new dream. On this, the second Sunday in May, as Philadelphia commemorated a new celebration, Eliza sent a prayer of thanks to her mother. *Because of you, I stand here today, helping mothers. I hope they become the mother you are. I hope I am someday, too.*

Eliza placed a daughter into the outstretched arms of the woman on the bed. "A beautiful girl, Mrs. McDonnell. You'll be a wonderful mother. Love her and speak to her with your wisdom. Everything she needs right now will come from you."

The nurse cleaned Eliza's tools and returned them back into her bag. Eliza picked it up. Her shift had ended. She'd be home for dinner.

As she left the hospital, Eliza noticed a young woman lingering at the street corner. The haggard lines around her eyes belied her youth. A faded shirtwaist dress hung below the frayed hem of a cloth coat. The black-ribbed thick stockings showed holes like a child's face marked with pox. Greasy strands of hair framed her sallow face. Her brown eyes widened as Eliza neared her.

"Excuse me, Ma'am," the woman said, backing up a step. "Doctor Edwards?"

"Yes," said Eliza. She studied the woman. Generally, she remembered her patients, especially ones who were as young as this one.

"You delivered my cousin's baby last week. She raved about the wonderful lady doctor with the reddish hair."

"That's very kind. Who's your cousin?"

"Isabelle Grimaldi. She had a boy. Giovanni. Gino, they're calling him."

Eliza wouldn't forget the ten pound two ounces of the Grimaldi baby. Isabelle named him Giovanni, meaning a gift from God. He was bountiful, Eliza had joked to Patrick later that day.

"How are they? Everything all right?"

"They're fine," said the woman. She bent her head and picked at a thread on her coat.

"But my sister. Umm, I think she needs a doctor, a woman doctor." Her voice trembled. "Will you come see her?"

"Where is she?"

"She's at our rooming house in bed. There's blood."

Eliza touched the woman's shoulder to calm her shaking. "What happened? How much blood? Did someone hurt her? You need to tell me everything."

"I don't think so. She snuck out last night and came back early this morning and climbed into bed. I went to Mass and stayed to help clean after the service. When I got home, Sharon was still in bed. She was curled up tight like a ball, hugging her tummy. When she rolled over, that's when I saw the blood on the linens."

A single word entered Eliza's thoughts.

"Where was the blood? Under what part of her body?" Eliza asked.

"I guess around her backside. Please, can you come?"

Eliza gripped the handles of her bag. "Where do you live...? I'm sorry, what's your name, dear?"

"Christina. Christina D'Amato. We live on Tenth. It's not too far for you? Please? Please come."

Eliza's questioning of Christina during their walk confirmed Eliza's suspicion. Christina had watched her sister, Sharon, rise in the morning over the past two months, nauseated and complaining of sore breasts. Last week, as they walked to work, Sharon to the Palumbo School where she taught and Christina to her cleaning job, the women stopped on the sidewalk.

Christina shielded her sister from the stares of others as Sharon vomited into a trimmed hedge. When Christina suggested they go back to their lodging house, Sharon insisted she muster through her morning discomfort. Many women stood waiting for an open teaching position. Sharon couldn't afford to take a sick day. Her income supported them far better than Christina's scant cleaning wages.

As they neared the narrow doorway to the rooming house, Eliza slowed.

Two more questions needed answers.

"Christina, when was the last time you saw Sharon use sanitary napkins?"

Christina blushed. "Can't afford to buy napkins. We still use rags. Sharon and I always have our visitor at the same time. But now that you mention it, I'm the only one who's washed rags the last three times."

"You said you don't know where Sharon went?"

"She's been seeing a man but hasn't told me much. I think he teaches at the school, too. Or maybe he's the principal."

"Do you think she met him last night? Could he have hurt her?"

"No. When she's meeting him, she'll take a bath, fix her hair and iron a dress before she goes out. This morning she had on the same old day dress she left in."

Christina's last details left no doubt. Sharon D'Amato had visited an abortionist under the dark of night. Eliza hurried through the rooming house door and up the four flights of stairs behind Christina. At each landing of the staircase, questions exploded through her mind. *Could. Would. Should. Could she provide Sharon with the care she needed? Should she report a septic abortion as the law required and condemn Sharon and her abortionist? Could she tend to a woman who wanted to abort her baby? Would her treatment save Sharon's life?*

Christina's slight hand turned the doorknob. "Are you okay, Ma'am? Doctor Edwards?"

Eliza exhaled a heavy, breathless, "Give me a second, please." She needed a moment, not to catch her breath, but to catch hold of the answers she sought before the door opened.

As she entered, Eliza heard rapid, shallow breaths. Sharon lay in the twin bed, inches apart from Christina's in the room they shared. Her long dark hair fell around her wan face, matted in sweat, and bound in knots. Beneath her limp body, bed linens revealed deep burgundy splotches.

"I'm sorry, Mama," Sharon gasped. "So sorry. Please. I shouldn't have. Please. Christina. Don't tell the school. Please. Where's Mama? I want Mama."

"It's all right, Sharon. Rest now." Eliza stroked Sharon's forehead, brushing the hairs away and tucking them behind Sharon's ears.

Aspirin wouldn't help a woman hemorrhaging or fighting peritonitis, or both, in a life-threatening situation, but a glass of water to wash it down would give Eliza an excuse to ask Christina to leave the room.

"Christina, can you go downstairs and bring a basin and glass of cool water? We'll want to bring her fever down and I'll give her an aspirin."

When Christina left, Eliza drew a chair to the bedside.

"I'll take care of you," Eliza said, picking up Sharon's wrist. The feeble pulse ebbed like a late summer stream, slowed by dry riverbeds. Eliza rubbed her thumb back and forth over the pulse point, speaking to it, willing it to quicken.

Sharon moaned, squirming to find comfort, "It hurts. Please make it go away."

"I know you're in pain, dear. Will you let me examine you?"

Eliza pulled a syringe and a bottle of morphine from her bag. "Shhh, this will help."

As the morphine relaxed Sharon's muscles, Eliza pushed the matted hair aside. An innocence too frail to have endured the heartlessness of an abortionist's tools crossed over pale cheeks.

Sharon's eyes closed.

Eliza had one more question. She gently jostled Sharon, whispering her into consciousness. "Sharon, what happened? Who did this?"

Her long black eyelashes fought to flutter open. "I wasn't told her name. She expected me."

The clipped sentences sputtered. The rapid breaths faded. "She asked me the week of my last monthly and felt my belly."

Another shallow inhale, "Ordered me to take off my drawers and climb onto..."

Pinpoints of tears dripped down to her chin. "I should have left then."

Her closed eyes tightened as if the darkness would block her memory. "She took out a long rubber tubing from a drawer and pushed it up into..."

Her dehydrated body was bereft of any more tears. Tremors replaced the tears.

"She left it there and sent me home."

The lashes stopped fluttering. Her pulse ebbed to a trickle.

Eliza heard Christina's footsteps on the stairs as she neared the top floor. A glass of water for Christina's parched tongue and a wet cloth for her fevered forehead would be worthless.

"Sharon. The address. Do you remember the address?" Eliza implored.

The words passed her cracked lips with a final exhale, "South Front. Seven fifty-one."

· · ·

Outside the bedroom door, Eliza pressed her drooping shoulder against the thin wall, pushing back against the unfairness of Sharon's death. With a deep inhale, she prayed for another mother. A mother-not-to-be.

The immensity of death would always plague Eliza. When it came too soon, to a young woman like Sharon D'Amato, the injustice of unanswered questions could overwhelm her. Yet, she would not allow heartbreak to consume her like a raging fire, its flames grasping for air streams. Instead, she clung to Dean Marshall's counsel, "Rather than give sorrow words to raise you above your grief, give it actions."

Her black bag lay at her feet, her instruments inside untouched except for the syringe. Under her stethoscope, which had measured countless beats of the living, she would withdraw her folder of documents. On one of the blank forms, she would record the details of Sharon D'Amato. Age twenty-three. 901 South Tenth Street, Philadelphia, Pennsylvania. May 10, 1908 at 3:38 p.m. Cause of Death. The medical diagnosis was obvious: Peritonitis. The underlying sympathetic diagnosis often outweighed the scientific: Shame. Poverty. Fear. Unable to use contraception. Untrained abortionists. Dirty implements. Lack of follow-up care and instructions.

Eliza faced her grim task, thinking death certificates should include more lines to explain the cause.

• • •

On another day, Eliza would relish strolling through Little Italy. She would let the scents pervade her senses and crowd her mind. Aromas of tomatoes, oregano, red peppers, onions, and basil wafting from sidewalk cafés as if an entire vegetable garden grew in simmering pots in the back kitchen. From open windows along the street, chopped stringent garlic and yeasty bread loaves, hot and steaming out of a brick oven, would assault her nose and make her eyes water. Eliza blocked them all from her consciousness. Her quiet walk gave her a chance to consider what her healing actions may be to ensure other women wouldn't face the same tragedy as Sharon D'Amato. By the time she got home, the root of a plan had taken hold.

"I'm afraid it's a fact of life," Eliza told Olga when they were alone after Sunday dinner. "Women and men will have relations regardless if women could get contraception, or men used prophylactics."

"Which means unplanned pregnancies will happen."

"Yes, and for women like Sharon, they're bound to a hopeless situation."

As a teacher, if Sharon married, she would lose her job and the salary which supported her and Christina.

"What could she do? I'm not sure what I would have done in her shoes, but she made the choice she thought best for her. How many other Sharons are sneaking down shadowy side streets of Philadelphia with the same desperate decision on their minds?"

She wouldn't judge or condemn Sharon and others like her. But she would care for them.

"Will you report the abortionist? If Christina mentions your name to anyone, the police may come looking for you. Or the hospital. Dr. Whitaker would love a reason to fire a woman doctor," Olga said.

"I doubt Christina will say anything. Poor dear is too upset. Sharon didn't have a name, but I have the address."

"Will you tell Patrick?"

A valid question and one which also coursed through Eliza's mind. Sharon's death personalized Eliza's situation. The tragedy reinforced her stance with Patrick. If the day came when he finally gave way to their desires, she would insist on the use of contraceptives. Should he continue to cling to his papal directives, then she would deny him. There would be more naps taken and more laundry scrubbed. To Eliza, no contraception meant no intimacies, which meant no pregnancies. Without unplanned pregnancies, abortions could dwindle. And no abortions meant no deaths.

"I'll tell him only that I tended to her, not about my visit. He may call upon the Pope himself to come after me."

CHAPTER TWENTY-FIVE

In the eyes of an abortionist, Eliza may be considered a crusader and condemner. To ensure the door opened, Christina offered the perfect guise as a distraught eighteen-year-old woman accompanied by her older sister. Once inside, Eliza could assess the situation. From Sharon's limited details, Eliza assumed the abortionist had no medical training. The risk of losing a license or serving jail time was too high a price to pay. Given the immediate onset of the peritonitis, she doubted the tools used had been sterilized. The most heinous omission was sending Sharon home without care instructions or telling her of any worrisome symptoms to watch for.

The den of an abortionist would also provide fodder for telling a much-needed story on the horrors of dark alleys, wooden floorboards of wagons, and kitchen tables in cities and rural homesteads alike. Whether any newspaper ran the article she planned was questionable. But at least she could share the truth to bring a shred of empathy to the plight of many ashamed young women.

•   •   •

With Christina beside her, Eliza gave the hansom cab driver an address a block away from 751 South Front Street. As he slowed the horse, he warned them, "Are you sure this is the right place, Ma'am? You shouldn't be here this time of night."

"We'll be fine, sir, thank you," said Eliza as she paid the fare and motioned Christina to exit.

Knot-holed pine sheets covered many of the windows of brick buildings. Other windows gaped open with jagged shards stuck in the sills, reaching upward to the black steel web of fire escapes. Store aisles were empty; there was nothing to steal. The few streetlamps still on glowed dim. No one complained about repairing the lights. This part of the city craved darkness. Eliza and Christina turned the corner onto South Front, straining to locate a number over a doorway.

"This must be it," Christina gestured to Eliza, who paused before a faint light shining from a grime-streaked window. "The one before it is seven forty-nine and the one past is seven fifty-three. No other building has lights on."

Glancing up and down the deserted street, Eliza rapped on the door. A bloated and ruddy woman's face appeared at the ripped curtain's edge. The window panes framed her like a Wanted poster. "Who are you? Whadda you want?" she growled.

Christina inched forward, pushing her youthful face into view. "I have an appointment. Hank said you'd expect me."

"Don't know what you're talkin' bout. Don't know no Hank." The curtain dropped.

Eliza stepped in front of Christina. "Listen. I'm not sure why you're not expecting us, but I have fifty dollars and know you help girls who don't want to be pregnant. We're here and not leaving. We need this done tonight."

The door creaked ajar. "You said fifty dollars?"

"Yes," Eliza spoke up, lifting her purse for the woman to see its monogrammed clasp, the swirl of E's and P interwoven in a blur of status. Overpayment for service should entice the woman, appointment, or no appointment.

The door creaked open. The hardened face behind the curtain tossed and gestured them in.

Not a single piece of furniture graced the front room of the apartment. Eliza and Christina followed the woman into the kitchen where a wooden table covered with a discarded bedspread stood in the middle of the room. Kitchen tables should be a gathering spot, a place where humble families shared meals and conversations in comfort. Eliza cringed to think of lithe, innocent bodies lying upon it like a hunk of meat ready for carving.

She surveyed the room. A red and white baker's string dangled from an anemic bulb hung over the table. A gap yawned between the counters where a stove should stand. The dented metal sink pulled away from the wall where two screws had fallen out. Splatters of a rusty liquid dripped from a goose-neck faucet into the sink's stained basin. Four lengths of red rubber tubing snaked across a grungy, wooden countertop.

The woman toed a pile of once-white sheets torn into strips.

"Grab a handful," she said, pointing at Eliza. To Christina she said, "Do as I tell you; no questions and we'll be quicker than Jack Rabbit, maybe quicker than the bloke that did this to you," she smirked.

"Take off your drawers…"

Eliza interrupted the woman. "What is your medical experience, Miss, Missus…?"

"No names. Better that way. I've done plenty, that's my experience. Now dearie, do you want this done or not? Hop up on the table."

Christina grabbed Eliza's arm, her eyes filling with tears of fright and grief.

"Should she hop up like the sweet young Italian girl who was here last week? The poor precious dearie who died?" Eliza seethed.

The woman spun around. "Who are you? Who sent you? That scum, Detective Mercer?"

"We're not with the police. We don't intend to shut you down or report you. I am a doctor. I want to help the girls who come to you so another one doesn't suffer or lose her life like this girl's sister."

At the table's edge, Eliza smoothed her hand across the worn cloth, feeling for the women whose lives had forever changed here on this spot. She lifted her head to study the person responsible for those lives. "I won't tell anyone your name and I don't want you to know mine either. In case I refer someone, I cannot have my name associated with you. If a girl hemorrhages, you will instruct her to go to a hospital. She shouldn't lie in bed paralyzed with fear. And there are several easy steps to prevent infections. To start, you need to fix that sink for proper hand washing."

Eliza pulled a bar of soap and a brush from her bag. The first tools a surgeon must use. Eliza shuddered, thinking of her surgeon friend, Charlotte Fairbanks, and wondering if by now Charlotte had surrendered to other inmates' requests to take care of unforeseen situations.

"With hot water, lather your hands, then use the brush to clean under your fingernails. Hand washing should be the last step, so you don't touch anything else after you're finished. Where is the stove? You should sterilize every instrument with boiling water, or at least soak them in bleach. The rags you use..."

The woman waved her hand at Eliza and boomed, "Shut up. You have some nerve doctor lady. Preaching to me. They come to me because they don't have any other choice. You've got the medical experience to help these girls. But do you? Will you?"

Barbs of truth punctured Eliza's heart. Her hand felt for the wooden countertop to steady her sway as her knees went weak. A splinter snagged her palm. Before her stood a woman denied the teachings of science and sympathy. This loud-mouthed, gruff matron, with the hands of a longshoreman, cared for the most vulnerable groups of women while Eliza hid behind the decrees of state laws.

Eliza had rejected an invitation for a society debut which would have provided her with a simpler life. Instead, she heeded her calling. In her eleven years of studying and practicing medicine, one constant persisted. There would always be uncomfortable situations. Whether it was passing a chemistry class, witnessing a facial surgery, delivering a disabled child, or losing a patient, through each case her training instructed her that doctors don't have a choice. They must endure and show up.

Yet, today, in a back alley room, she had a choice. She could assist this taker-of-life to save others. But how many could she save? And were those few worth the risk of losing her medical license to never help another woman?

Eliza arranged the soap and brush on the table. While she couldn't help the girls who climbed onto this table, someone else could. A woman Eliza could trust to share the details of her visit to South Front Street. Someone who used a pen as capably as a paintbrush to tell a story. A woman who spent her life guiding others to attain the truths of their paths and dreams. A believer in women's rights.

The woman's stare bore into Eliza, daring her to answer.

"You're right," Eliza said. "I shouldn't be preaching to you. My intent is to help. I'm enlisting my aunt in Boston to write stories of your customers and bring them into a public discussion. These stories must be told. Can you, will you, let me interview these girls?"

Stony silence, hard and unmovable.

"Please," Eliza too stood stock still.

The woman turned away from Eliza, gathering the tubing to return them to the drawer.

Eliza touched the woman's arm. "I have to believe you don't want any of them to die. We can help them, together. You must want that."

The woman pushed the drawer closed, keeping her back to Eliza.

"Please. I beg you. No more dead girls."

The abortionist hung her head. "No names, right?"

Eliza nodded.

"And, doctor lady—you're gonna need more of them greenbacks."

• • •

After finishing six interviews, Eliza wrote to Florence. Other women of Florence's generation may have gasped, remarked that polite conversation, or any conversation, did not include abortion, and perhaps asked for smelling salts. But Florence replied without hesitation. Send them to me. Locked in societal cells, these women cannot protect themselves from situations of no choice. We must give them a voice.

From Eliza's interview notes, Florence titled the essays *Alone: A Woman's Fear*. "Whether they had blonde or red hair, blue or hazel eyes," Eliza told her, "each one became the raven-haired, brown-eyed Sharon, the one I could not save. Like Sharon, no one helped those women with their decisions. They rarely told anyone of their pregnancies. Most of them visited the abortionist by themselves as no one would risk breaking the law to accompany them. Each one, unmarried and married, returned to their homes to suffer in silence."

She sent Florence's essays out twenty times. Silence followed. Only one paper replied with a terse note, *It's illegal. No need to report*. Eliza wondered if anyone higher than the clerk who opened the mail read them.

"We'll hope this one will be different," Eliza said to the empty street corner. She banged the flap of the post box shut and patted the box's top three times. Maybe this time, someone would care. Florence had styled this version of the article inside the large brown envelope like a newspaper advice column. With the column, Eliza included a photo of pens, knitting needles, and wire coat hangers, captioned, *Tools of the Trade: The Homemaker's Guide to Abortions.*

The words fell on deaf ears, never to appear in print. Eliza knew that in the months and years to follow Mother's Day 1908, whenever she read an obituary notice for a woman in her late teens or twenties, she would think of Sharon. When the cause of death noted pneumonia, Eliza would question its truth. A young woman's death from a botched abortion would never appear in the pages of *The Philadelphia Inquirer*. The true story never told.

CHAPTER TWENTY-SIX

November 1911

"Mischievous boys who never grow up, swashbuckling pirates, and flying fairies. Or animated woodland creatures?"

"What?" said Patrick, his head buried in Jack London's newest tales of adventure, this time from the South Seas.

Eliza held up a leather-bound volume in each hand, selected from haphazard towers of books in the back corner of Lit Brothers' Department Store. "Help me choose. Peter and Wendy or Old Mother West Wind?"

Her annual tradition continued. Every November, she chose a children's book for Salvatore Silvestri. Inscribed on the inside front cover, she wrote the same message with her grandfather's pen. *For Salvatore. May God be at your side to guide you. Keep your family close. Always smile, laugh, and love. With kindest wishes on your birthday, Dr. Edwards.*

Tomorrow, Eliza and Patrick would join the Silvestris for Salvatore's tenth birthday. There would be many reasons to celebrate. He now belonged to a sacred population: the ten percent of mongoloid children who lived to the age of ten. They would give thanks that his compromised lungs had grown forceful enough to blow out a ring of candles. Thunderous claps would encourage his sure and steady steps, which replaced the jerking walk of his first years. Their words would praise him for the way he could wash and dress himself. Shouts of hurrahs would echo through the room when he counted to twenty, called for the brown dog, and distinguished between squares and circles. They would kiss his forehead, tap his nose, and tuck him into bed in his family's cramped Philadelphia apartment. Salvatore was home.

• • •

For the first ten years of his life, institutions served Salvatore well. On Saturdays, his parents visited him at the Sheltering Arms and then at the Elwyn Training School when he turned seven. The moment his mother entered the common room, he rushed to her and used the strength he stored throughout the week to wrap his arms around her waist. He was excitable during their visits, but the other days he obeyed the commands of his caretakers.

Despite his progress, Eliza worried. Reports surfaced about abuse and lapses in care. Most recently, she read of the case of a fifteen-year-old girl who died from heart failure. Yet, stated details were contradictory. The girl's father was unaware of an illness and not informed of any ailment. The school called her lazy, shiftless, quarrelsome, and incorrigible. Her father denied those descriptions. His daughter may have been feeble-minded, but she always had a sunny disposition when he visited. When they released her body to him, he engaged a local doctor to examine her. She had bruises around her neck with her skin rubbed raw in many places. He sued for neglect. The verdict found no evidence of wrongdoings. But to appease the father, the school dismissed one nurse.

Even more troublesome, Eliza tracked editorials and opinion pieces in the papers. Support for a vetoed bill was resurfacing. Dr. Martin Barr, the medical doctor at Elwyn, penned several of the articles in favor of "An Act for the Prevention of Idiocy." The bill's primary statement centered on fertility: *Given heredity plays an important part in the transmission of idiocy and imbecility; it shall be compulsory for state institutions entrusted with the care of idiots and imbecile children to examine their mental and physical conditions. If procreation of an inmate is deemed inadvisable, it shall be lawful for a surgeon to perform operations to prevent procreation.*

Eliza feared they would identify Salvatore as a subject. To supplement the state's funding, the administration accepted hushed payments from wealthier parents to ensure additional care for their children while ignoring boys like Salvatore. Eliza's concerns increased when she heard talk that children of "new immigrants" were being singled out for unauthorized procedures. Not wanting to alarm the Silvestris, Eliza instead appealed to Domenic's Christian duty. It was time to bring his son home to the safety of his family.

• • •

"I vote for Peter and Wendy," Patrick said. "Nothing like a bunch of buccaneers for a boy." He twirled his arm and poked Eliza in the ribs.

"For a boy, or for you?" Eliza said, pushing his finger away. "You won't have many chances to read to him before you leave. I think Old Mother West Wind is best. Look at these adorable pictures. Salvatore will love the animals. They're better suited for his five-year-old level."

"You're right. You usually are." Patrick winked at her and surveyed the other customers around them. No one was paying attention to the two people near the table piled with books. He kissed her cheek.

"I've got to steal a few extra ones and store them up."

The week before, Patrick told Eliza of the letter he received from his sister, Cathleen. Their mother had contracted consumption. She appeared to be failing fast. Cathleen thought she languished, suffering endless pain, waiting for Patrick to say goodbye. Could Patrick come home for Christmas?

CHAPTER TWENTY-SEVEN

March 1912

Set the date. Buy a dress. The telegram delivered to 1710 Race Street without a signee, only the telegraph office's origination, the village next to Parish Cahirciveen. Six words were all Eliza needed.

Sadness and delight competed for space in her heart. Was it wrong to feel conflicted? She should think only of Patrick. No matter her age or health, he had lost his mother. The finality of her death ended a chapter. He had lived that chapter, faithful and bold. It was time for the next one. He would marry Eliza to write their tale together. The script should be familiar. After seven years of courting, they had discussed their hopes and dreams. They knew each other's desires. Their story would start with a family. In twelve months, God willing, she and Patrick would prepare for their own wonder.

• • •

Eliza, Olga, Charlotte, and Edith lingered in the parlor with their after-dinner coffee. Eliza's aunts excused themselves earlier to retire. Josephine had ceased her visits to the Naval Asylum. Few veterans from the War Between the States remained and talk circulated that the Asylum would close. She had also scaled back her hours at Woman's Med. when Charlotte volunteered to help her one day a week. At the courthouse, Estelle refused to shorten her hours. She maintained her full forty hours a week schedule, determined to prove her skills stayed as sharp as when she had started twenty-five years prior.

Olga steered their conversation toward the evening's pressing topic, "Pink looks lovely on you, Eliza. There's a dilly at Wanamaker's. An exquisite dusty rose crepe de chine silk, short sleeves gathered at the shoulder. You can wear above-the-elbow white gloves for a nice formal touch."

She reached over to Eliza's bodice and traced a graceful looping arc with her fingers.

"The chest area has a sheer inset with a thin lace neckline, low enough for your pearls to hit the edge without interrupting the embroidery work around your breasts. Even your blessed Saint Patrick won't be able to keep his eyes off them."

Eight shades of red blushed across Eliza's cheeks.

"A diamond shape drops below the waist and frames a gentle whirled pattern. The front part of the skirt has three tiers, each finished with satin trim. The train is modest, which makes it easier for me to manage!" Olga laughed. "We'll top you off with a cream-colored veil with lace hems. Are you sure we can't reach Patrick in time to have him buy a piece of Irish lace? It would be a nice memento to honor the Callaghan name."

Eliza shrugged. When Olga started a fashion review, Eliza knew to sit and listen like an attentive pupil.

"No matter," Olga waved her hand, dismissing the detail.

"We'll ask Molly to find an Irish lace maker for us. We'll order a nosegay of lavender lilacs and lily of the valley fresh from an early May garden. I can see you now."

Olga stood and backed up from the divan. With her palms straight in front of her, she framed Eliza into a box.

"You'll be a stunning bride."

Olga had appointed herself wedding planner, claiming she had more experience than anyone else among the group. Eliza couldn't argue. In the past four years, Olga had planned her sister Taniya's wedding, and her own. No one ever imagined when she enrolled Taniya at Bryn Mawr College, a husband for Olga waited in the wings. Taniya continued to complain and fuss throughout her first term, prompting frequent visits by Olga. She discovered the easiest way to appease her were dinners at Philadelphia's finest restaurants. One evening, they sat next to Taniya's roommate, Susan McGuire, and her widowed father, Samuel. The foursome exchanged pleasantries between two tables. They became regulars sharing Friday evenings together. Soon thereafter, Olga and Samuel met on their own for Saturday dinners, followed by Sunday afternoon rides in Samuel's new automobile. By the end of Taniya's second term, Samuel asked Olga to marry him. Eliza, happy for her friend, stood up with Olga at a simple civil ceremony.

In two months, on May 18th, they would exchange positions. Olga would stand up beside the bride in the apse of St. Clement's, joined by the groom, Patrick Callaghan, best man, Lawrence Cleary, Reverend Abrams, and Father Dooley from St. Peter's and Paul's. A persuasive argument by Estelle, trained by years in Philadelphia courtrooms, convinced Reverend Abrams to allow Olga, a Russian Orthodox, and three Catholics, Patrick, Lawrence, and Father Dooley, at his Episcopal altar. An extra thick envelope in the collection box at St. Peter's and Paul's secured Father Dooley's attendance to bless the couple at an Episcopal altar.

"Any other news from Patrick about his visit to Dublin?" asked Edith.

"He's heading there soon. Trinity agreed to let him observe a week's worth of classes. He should have plenty of material for a comprehensive report," said Eliza.

Charlotte and Josephine kept Eliza apprised of inside discussions occurring at Woman's Med. As all-male schools opened their doors to women, enrollment in women's medical schools declined. By 1910, Woman's Med. remained the only all-women's medical school in the country. Financial difficulties became a constant discussion. Their graduates were more likely to take positions at maternity hospitals or enter public service and missionary work. These roles provided meager wages with scant excess for significant gifts to an alma mater. Other alumnae left their practice when they married and were without access to funds of their own for discretionary donations.

When Eliza learned several professors were researching options for proving that an all-women's model was viable and meaningful, she suggested Patrick research the move to co-education at the School of Medicine at Trinity College in Dublin. First-hand observations of their results would be valuable information.

• • •

The date was set, with ideas for a dress imagined. The reception menu and seating chart was complete. Eliza's wedding plans progressed on schedule. Olga, having already weighed in on Eliza's dress choice, turned to suggestions for her matron-of-honor attire to complement and never detract from the bride. Perhaps a smart mauve suit? Edith applied her attention to detail to the seating chart. She would ensure there would be lively conversations at each table and well balanced between Pearson Edwards family members, Woman's Med. staff and hospital colleagues, and Patrick's friends from McGillin's. Charlotte, with her surgeon's precision, conceived the timetable for the day, from the hour Eliza would dress, to the minute of the champagne toast.

One last detail remained. Eliza needed the groom to come home.

. . .

The warm weather, feeling like a gentle Georgia spring, must have moved Dr. Whitaker, thought Eliza. He rarely approved changes. But, after working overtime twice in the past week, Eliza requested an early dismissal, and he agreed after noting a lighter case load on the schedule.

A canvas worthy of the Philadelphia Museum of Art accompanied Eliza on her walk home. Logan Circle burst with color. Vibrant green stems of buttercups and yellow trout lilies spread their petals to a warm, late March sun. Sand cherry bushes, their blossoms on the cusp of bursting into delicate white-pink shrubbery, filled the air with their sugar-sweet scents. Red-breasted robins and goldfinches perched on tree limbs trilled their happiness to be back after their southern winter. Even the grinding noises of gravel hitting gravel from ongoing construction of a Champs-Élysées-styled boulevard to connect the Museum of Art and City Hall couldn't diminish Eliza's serene bliss. Two more weeks. Was she counting the days? Yes.

Josephine met her at the door with a smile and an envelope. "From Ireland. I expect it will be the last one before he leaves."

A thrill as gleeful as birdsong flowed through her body. His faithful letter writing traversed an ocean to keep her informed. Words that comforted and reassured. Her life would have a fairy tale ending. Her mother's worries of another unmarried Pearson Edwards woman would cease.

"Thank you. I'll share it tonight over dinner."

She would read the letter alone, then edit out any phrases meant for her eyes only when she shared it with the aunts and Edith. Extracting the pages, she unfolded them and guided her finger along the neat lines written by a pen in his hand. The thread of connection pulsed through her fingertip.

March 22, 1912

My Dearest Eliza,

I arrived in Queenstown this afternoon. After a week in Dublin, I found the countryside to the Celtic Sea a refreshing change. My countrymen have done a fine job with their railways. The Great Southern & Western connecting Dublin to Cork is top-rate. I secured a window seat for the four-hour trip. My blessings continued as we pulled out of the station. Sunshine, a rare weather phenomenon in Ireland, amplified its heat through the window. The train's steady humming lulled me to sleep. Lucky for me, I napped for only an hour, otherwise I would have missed the beauty of the passing lands. Never in my life have I seen so many acres upon acres of lush fields. County Kerry is beautiful, but this area of Ireland is grand. The expanse stretches to the horizon, with gradual rises and falls, interrupted only by intermittent clusters of short hedges and ragged stone boundary fences marking generations of clan lines.

Abundant clover floods the leas in peaceful green waves. Do you remember the tale I told you of St. Patrick? How his proclamation that the clover, or shamrock as we call it, symbolizes the Holy Trinity, and its abundance in Ireland means we are a blessed country? Seeing these lush fields makes me want to jump off the train and search for the luckiest of shamrocks and bring it home to you. I'd press that four-leafed clover close inside your chemise, tucked against your bare breast to keep the luck of the Irish with you always.

Eliza's eyes burned as a fire kindled below. Here was one paragraph she would edit for reading to the aunts and Edith. Olga, however, may enjoy the romantic musings.

Dotted among the green sea, white blots swayed and ambled. At first, I imagined I awoke in the American South. Did cotton grow in Ireland? No, they were sheep, their black-faced heads grazing on the cropped grasses which left only their winter woolly balls visible. Their plump bodies explain the Irish lamb stew found on pub menus. These quiet creatures look so content, ambling through the fields, I had the slightest pang of guilt, for I have often partaken dinners of delicious and aromatic stews.

Eliza licked her lips. Patrick had the Irishman's gift for storytelling. Or did the charm of the land and his Irish blood transport him back to his youth? His personalized details were as vivid as a figure walking across the pages of a great Irish novel with Patrick the principal character who belonged in that setting.

We had a quick line change to the Cork & Muskerry, which brought me to Queenstown, my departure point, which will bring me home to you. The station abuts the wharves where launches wait, taking passengers out to the mighty liners anchored in the great harbor of Cork, the second largest harbor in the world I am told. As the sun set, I turned to find my accommodations.

This task proved easy for one cannot miss St. Colman's Cathedral, rising above the roof lines, its multiple spires thrust upward, like arms raised to the heavens in exultation. The majesty of the building befits the glory of our Father. Espying St. Colman's was simple. Getting there was another matter. The intersecting streets deposit into the village center through a myriad of steep inclines. I fear there are many accidents of runaway buggies and autos at the foot of the hill.

I trekked up the aptly named West View. Stone dwellings flank the road. Connected in a row of ten or twelve homes, they're each painted in hues of a colorful palette. I walked alongside a rainbow which lifts the spirits and gives one hope as once more, the clouds rolled in.

Finally, I stood at the black studded doors. Please thank Molly again for the introduction to her aunt, Sister Mary Agnes. She expected me. After taking tea, she directed me to her sister's rooming house. They are both looking forward to dinner to hear my report of how their niece has fared in America.

I am grateful to have three weeks here before our sailing on April 11th. That should be ample time to organize my notes from Trinity for presentation to the Board. Will you review my paper when I get home? Your keen insight is invaluable. I am quite dismayed to learn that seven years after their co-education decision, their female students encounter many challenges, from taunting to enduring boos. Catcalls resounded in the middle of classes, with no squelching of the behavior by the class professor. Woman's Med. must continue its exceptional education of women with the support they receive from their peers in teaching and mentoring roles.

Excellent, thought Eliza. Confirmation that co-education may not be the best choice would benefit the cause of keeping Woman's Med. an all-women's institution.

I'm sure you have plenty of tasks awaiting me; all duties which I will eagerly undertake. Did Olga help you find a dress? Of course, she did, and it must be lovely, although you could arrive at St. Clement's altar in a gunny sack, and I would declare you beautiful. Tell Edith she needn't worry about my blokes. I gave strict instructions there will be no roll-throwing at each other or any other tousling of any kind. To be safe, however, she may want to alert the waiters to keep a close eye on the number of whiskey bottles delivered to their table. As for Charlotte, please ask her to not visit my apartment to set my alarm clock for the morning of May 18th. I don't expect to sleep a wink.

I must finish now. Miss O'Brien informed me of a strict schedule with supper at seven o'clock. A few other Titanic passengers have booked rooms here. I'm told that every night after dinner we raise a few pints to toast Ireland and send a few more off to America, who, like me, might never return to their dear homeland. Yes. Yes, I haven't forgotten your request. I'll be on the lookout for Mr. Astor and the scandalous young pregnant wife, although my second-class ticket may not allow mingling on the upper decks.

First thing in the morning, I shall post this letter with hopes you receive it before my arrival home on April 18.

Think of it, my love. One year from now, if we make good use of our honeymoon, we'll hold our child in our arms. I hope for a girl, as delightful, smart, and splendid as her mother.

Ever yours, Patrick.

We will make excellent use of our honeymoon. I promise, she breathed.

CHAPTER TWENTY-EIGHT

April 1912

"Will you be back for lunch?" Josephine asked.

Eliza jabbed the pin through the hat's straw side and re-adjusted the brim before the foyer mirror, "Maybe. I hope my fitting appointment at Wanamaker's is quick. They need to check the hem again. I should have time to pop home before my afternoon shift."

As she picked up her reticule, a shriek came from the front stoop.

"Oh, dear heavens!" Edith screamed.

Eliza's hat tumbled off as she rushed outside to find Edith in a heap at the foot of the stairs. The morning edition of *The Philadelphia Inquirer* splayed across the sidewalk, its pages fluttering, ready to blow away.

"Are you alright? Did you fall?" said Eliza.

Edith stood and retrieved the paper, folding it inward, hiding the front page from view. "I'm fine, let's go inside."

Puzzled, Eliza followed Edith into the house and to the dining room.

Edith called for Estelle and Josephine to join them. "Sit," she instructed Eliza.

"What on earth?" Eliza picked up her uncleared coffee cup—her mother's best Coalport china one—left behind, forgotten again.

Estelle spread the paper on the table. The stark black headline stared up at Eliza. Like a hot branding iron, letters leapt off the page, searing her eyes. Her lungs squeezed as if she still wore a corset, a knee in her back as Molly pulled its strings tight, sucking the air out of her. Coos from the other women, patting her shoulders faded into the walls. Her fingers wrapped around the cool porcelain went numb, sending it crashing to the floor. The golden arched fish handle severed from the cup, its graceful mouth now a gaping, hollow hole. Eliza gazed down at it, then with the toe of her shoe, ground it to a fine sand, feeling her heart splinter.

1500 PERSONS LOST WHEN GIANT *TITANIC* SINKS AFTER COLLIDING WITH ICEBERG OFF CAPE RACE

A tear cut down her cheek and fell onto the page. Eliza's trembling fingers outlined the block lettering. Ink smeared from the teardrop and stained her fingers. She turned them over, the black smudge as dark as the hole boring into her heart.

"We must think positive," implored Josephine. "See here."

She directed Eliza to the subhead, *Only 675 Known Saved...No Names Known Yet.* "He may be one of the 675."

Eliza shook her head furiously and screamed at Josephine, "Look," she stabbed at the sentence below: *Mostly Women and Children of Passengers in All Classes Picked up by Other Liners.*

"Patrick would make sure every woman and child boarded first. He's the most selfless man alive."

Alive. How could he be alive? She stood, knocking the chair over behind her. Picking up the paper, she shred it to pieces, denying the totality of its news. She surrendered to a torrent of tears, rushing as swift as a spring river. Ice water pulsed through her body, freezing her like a hulking iceberg, as if it sought to take another life.

• • •

A thunderous pounding sounded against the door. Olga left Eliza's bedside to level her wrath against the ignorant fool who dared to disturb the household at a time of grief. Yesterday, at the moment Samuel read the headlines to her, Olga rushed to Race Street. Eliza needed her. While she wouldn't ease Eliza's pain, she would sit with her, brush her forehead, listen, and wait. As Josephine suggested, they must have faith. It was all Eliza had. Hope and an unhemmed wedding dress hanging in a closet at Wanamaker's.

Olga found Molly's husband, Lawrence, on the stoop, waving his hand in the air with a grin spread over his face. "A telegram. My nephew's a delivery boy. He knew I would get here quicker in the car."

Olga snatched it from him.

Postal Telegraph–Commercial Cables.
TELEGRAM
Received at Philadelphia Station
April 17, 1912
To: Eliza Edwards, M.D.
Did not board the Titanic.
Will write soon.
Signed: Patrick Callaghan, M.D.

• • •

Twelve days later, as much as she wished to rip the letter open and deliver its contents into her quivering hands, she couldn't destroy any piece of the page, any part of him. A careful slit would preserve words written by Patrick. The hand-carved North Star decorated opener was always stored in the sideboard's drawer. Today, it wasn't. Instead, she skidded her thumbnail under the envelope's flap and inched it along the length.

April 21, 1912

Dearest Eliza,

I trust you received the telegram. I expect the dreadful news of this epic tragedy dominated your headlines as it has here and around the globe. There are no words to explain the depths of despair here in Queenstown. One hundred and twenty-three Irish passengers embarked from here, most of them in steerage class, emigrants like me seeking a future in America. Families descended on the last spot their sons, daughters, and siblings stood while they await word of survivors. I've ministered many of them for fainting spells and distressed stomachs. But I cannot relieve their pain. The only remedy will be to learn that their loved ones lived. We have learned twenty Irish survived, so we'll hold faith for the others.

Day and night, families pack into St. Colman's. Their prayers beseech a God who provides no answers. I too have knelt on its stone floor for many hours asking Our Lord, why? How could a ship, as immense as the Titanic, sink? Why did they carry only enough lifeboats for half its passengers? And <u>why, why,</u> wasn't I onboard? The only answer I've found is the divine intervention He has shone on me.

I rose early on April 11th. We expected to take the tenders to the anchored ship by eleven for the scheduled departure at one thirty. The morning, cool and misty like most Irish days, must have left an undetected film of ice or frost on the streets. I sat by the docks watching the comings and goings. Others joined me; the excitement was contagious. Songs broke out and pints from nearby pubs found their way into the square. We would sail on this magnificent vessel, greater than the Lusitania.

A chap in his mid-teens thrust a pint into my hand when there was a sharp change from lyrical voices to panicked screams. I looked over to the common area where the steep hills descend into the town center and finish as a cobweb of lanes and paths. Two carriages slipped on the icy cobblestones, flipped, and rolled over as they descended West View. Four giant draft horses on their sides pinned drivers and passengers beneath their tonnage. I have never heard a horse scream. I hope to never again. They drowned the whimpers from the people under them.

I raced to the tangle. It took me and six other men to move the horses. Most of them had broken legs and were helpless to raise themselves. I knew every second the passengers spent under those animals, the lesser the chance for survival. We pulled each of them out and I quickly assessed their conditions. Three women suffered broken limbs, and one a sprained ankle. Four of the men, including both drivers, presented signs of lacerations and internal bleeding. The most horrific sight, however, was a young boy cradled in his mother's lap, his neck twisted, his body lifeless. The mother sat in shock, muted, and dazed.

Eliza closed her eyes tight and bowed her head in silent prayer. How fortunate that Patrick was there to help.

By the time we transported them to the hospital, and I conferred on conditions and offered my initial assessments, dusk settled into the village. The tenders left, the Titanic raised its anchor from Queenstown Harbor and departed on its southwestern-bound route to New York.

I hoped to secure passage on the next scheduled New York sailing. While I waited, I visited the hospital each day to check on the accident victims. A lack of staff, resources, and knowledge of how to treat these severe injuries limit the care available. By the afternoon of April 15th, we heard the news.

Eliza, I am terrified to board a ship. Nightmares of sinking into the great black abyss of a frigid ocean, trapped in a steel coffin, assail my thoughts day and night. Yet, I have a greater fear—going against God's will. I believe He intervened and put me at the carriage crash. He brought me home to the land of my birth and family. By so doing, he saved me.

I must be bold, as my mother taught me, and forsake my own mortal needs. I cannot abandon my faith and the call of the Irish soil to my roots. Never would I have thought I'd pen words like this, but I owe you a direct truth. I won't be returning to Philadelphia. The county hospital offered me a position and I have accepted.

Could you, would you, come to Ireland? I fear I know your answer. How can I ask you to leave your family and country while I have stayed with mine?

I can only ask you to forgive me once again.

Love, Patrick

PART II

If I can stop one heart from breaking,
I shall not live in vain:
If I can ease one life the aching,
Or cool one pain,
Or help one fainting robin
Unto his nest again,
I shall not live in vain.
–Emily Dickinson

CHAPTER TWENTY-NINE

June 1912

Tinny beeps, blaring honks, and teapot whistles mingled with multi-tongued shouts from hansom drivers, each one battling for an advantage. Acrid black smoke from backfires mixed with the pungent steam of horse droppings. Summer rains exacerbated the road sludge as oil-slicked puddles pooled in gutters flecked with manure dotting circles of debris.

As the force of tires hit the pond of refuse, sprays of waste streamed upward and outward. Surrendered to thought, Eliza jumped from the curb's edge too late to dodge the splatter. The full side of her skirt hung in an oily mess of stain and stink. *Curses and damn Henry Ford and his Runabouts*, she fumed.

The severity of her thoughts and their meaning shocked Eliza. Henry Ford didn't deserve her condemnation. Patrick Callaghan did. If Patrick had returned from Ireland, she wouldn't be lost in a reverie of regrets. If Patrick walked next to her, he would stride along the curbside edge, sheltering her from the road's filth. If Patrick hadn't yielded to his fears, Eliza wouldn't have elicited a level of rage shaped by words foreign to her lips. *If, if, if. Why, why, why?* Every waking moment, and many more on the verge of slumber, these thoughts pounded through her heart like a locomotive charging full throttle toward a destination. Yet destinations meant an end. Eliza saw no conclusion to the track she was on, only an endless, empty line to nowhere.

Eliza bent to inspect her skirt. Should she go home to change or arrive at the Silvestris covered in road muck? She flicked off a few pieces of debris. Her wristwatch pointed to four forty-five, enough time for a quick visit before her evening shift.

She clutched a brown paper parcel to her chest and turned into the alley crowded with wooden planked row houses. Paint peels hung from the clapboards like decayed autumn leaves about to fall. She jostled her way through the throng of laborers and residents. English phrases mixed with thick Italian and Russian accents with Yiddish tossed in for conversations meant to remain private. She found Number Ten, stepping over discarded milk crates and dodging a foul ball from a stickball game.

Almond-shaped eyes level to the sill peeped through the second-floor apartment's front window. Thick waves of jet-black hair grown long over the small head obscured tiny ears. Eliza waved and smiled as the sparkle of recognition widened the searching eyes. The loving, pure face of Salvatore Silvestri warmed the bleakest heart.

"Hi there, Salvatore. I see you!" she called, pointing her finger at the boy's radiant grin. Eliza ignored the sticky June air and nestled closer to Salvatore on the shabby horsehair couch as she read aloud from *Old Mother West Wind*. The birthday gift from her and Patrick had become one of Salvatore's favorites. As predicted, Thornton Burgess' story captivated his imagination with the humorous animal antics. Salvatore, a city child, loved listening to nature come alive, painting word pictures of places where gurgling brooks and soft summer breezes traversed through meadows and briar patches, far from the noise, congestion, and smells of Philadelphia's streets. They reached chapter eight today, although Eliza suspected his sister, Louisa, finished the book with him before her visit. No matter. Like any other child, re-reading the passages thrilled him on the tenth reading as much as it did the first time.

"...soon all were in the bag but one, a willful little Breeze, who was not quite ready to go home; he wanted to play just a little longer," Eliza read. "He danced ahead of Old Mother West Wind. He kissed the sleepy daisies. He shook the nodding buttercups. He set all the little poplar leaves dancing, too, and he wouldn't come into the big bag."

She tapped the tip of his flattened nose, "Are you a willful little Breeze, Salvatore?"

"I's like to play long time, Doctor Ma'am. And dance. I wanna kiss da' flowers." His words halting after each one as he struggled to push them through his slow speech.

Salvatore scampered off the couch and with clumsy feet, spinning in circles, raising his arms up and down, he mimicked the branches of a poplar tree dancing in the breeze.

"See, I'm da little Breeze," he gasped.

A harsh voice rang out, "Shush now, Salvatore. You'll be wakin' the baby and look, you're already wheezing. Settle down."

Nina Silvestri emerged from the back room, a squirming bundle on her shoulder. Her wrinkled hand rubbed the pronounced rump. "Ay, either these babes come out heavier or my Louisa's titties are bigger than Harbison's milk cans."

Another grandchild for Nina. Louisa's Dorothy arrived merry and content as the spring day of her birth, bringing joyful rays to the Silvestri home darkened by the loss two months earlier of their patriarch, Domenic. Having Louisa, and her young husband, and now Dorothy, move in with her eased the emptiness of Nina's home.

"I'm pleased she's nursing so well, and Louisa is managing. But how are you feeling? Have you picked up the prescription for Ovariin I wrote for you? My mother and aunts swore it helped them through their mother-gone time."

Nina turned her back on Eliza and shifted Dorothy to her other shoulder without an answer. *Hell's bells.* Had the Rexall druggist refused to fill Nina's prescription? Eliza had heard from other patients that the pharmacist on Erie Avenue balled up and tossed prescriptions she wrote into a trash basket. He denied her validity as a doctor to sign one.

"I don't need those pills," Nina grunted. "Mrs. Lydia Pinkham's Remedy works wonders for me. I sleep as sound as this here babe."

I'm sure it does, Eliza snorted to herself. Lydia Pinkham's Vegetable Compound included twenty percent alcohol content, not any magical curative powers. Unless one considers the power of suggestion. Eliza recalled the advertisement in *Ladies' Home Journal* which proclaimed it restored the health of over 500,000 women who suffered from the worst forms of female complaints and touted it eased change of life symptoms, and that "wise women insist on Mrs. Pinkham's."

Nina Silvestri's old-fashioned wisdom may never yield to more modern ways. Convincing her a drug compounded by dissecting and pulverizing cow ovaries could stem menopausal symptoms sounded as foreign as warming a bed with an electrified blanket instead of using a hot water bottle, or a man's body.

Nina's brow softened, "The more important question Doctor Edwards, is, how are you? Any news from our Doctor Callaghan?"

"No news," Eliza said, her face drawn as tight as a knit muffler against a winter's wind. She pushed aside the days which came and went without a telegram or letter from Ireland. How she had spent hours pawing through mail piles. The questions she asked Molly and Lawrence, any word? Her subtle inquiries posed to the hospital administration and college. Their only correspondence was his resignation letters and his report on co-education.

Sensing Nina's dismay, she tried to brighten her answer with hope.

"But I expect he's finishing up tending to his patients from the accident. They should be on the mend. He's probably looking into the next sailing to New York, Philadelphia, or Baltimore. No need for him to get in touch before he squares his plans."

Deep in her heart, Eliza knew these reasons made no sense. A man with any intention of returning would write.

She rose and reached for her bag. "I must be off, or I'll be late for my shift. It's been wonderful to visit you all. Salvatore, can you please give this to your new niece?"

Eliza held out the parcel, the twine tied into a simple bow, one he could navigate by himself. Salvatore took the package with imploring eyes.

"Yes," Eliza nodded, "You can open it for her. Perhaps you and Louisa want to read to Dorothy after her nap?"

Salvatore peeled off the paper and smoothed it into a sheet for his mother to use later wrapping vegetables.

"Oooo, so pretty Doctor Ma'am."

He patted the book's cover, running his fingers across the embossed black, rose, and gold arbor framing the leather cover which invited readers to enter Frances Hodgson Burnett's, *Secret Garden*. Neither Salvatore nor Dorothy would understand the tragic beginning. What mattered the most at their ages and intellect was the basic act of reading aloud to them. In time, they would appreciate the happy, healing ending. Mary Lennox and Colin Craven found theirs. Eliza Edwards would find hers as well when Patrick wrote. When she became Dr. Eliza Edwards Callaghan. When she stopped feeling the tormented envy of watching mothers and children grow and thrive together. When she had what she was due, a husband in her bed and a child on the way.

Curses and damn you, Patrick Callaghan.

• • •

The shrill jingle vibrated from the foyer sideboard. Whereas Eliza and Edith listened to rings throughout their hospital and Board of

Health offices, Josephine and Estelle jumped at the foreign noise, still startled by the sound and wonder of the long-distance communication.

"Egad, that thing-a-ma-jig is loud. Who's ringing up at this hour?" said Estelle.

Edith raced ahead of Eliza to the black candlestick shaped metal column. She lifted the base in one hand and raised it to her chin.

Who is it? mouthed Eliza. Installed two years ago at Albie's insistence and expense, the few calls received at Race Street were usually from the family in Boston.

"Mother? Albie? Freddy?" Eliza whispered. Could it be, was it possible, Patrick? Returned to America?

Edith shook her head and held up a hand to silence Eliza's questions. Through the line crackle Eliza caught the sharp, curt words from the operator, "Collect call. Will you accept charges from Florence Pearson?"

"Yes. Thank you," said Edith without hesitation.

Florence? Their settlement house didn't have a phone. Was she at Albie's? Eliza snapped out her hand, motioning to Edith to pass the phone over to her. Again, Edith waved her off as if she were an irksome child, and spoke into the mouthpiece, "Yes, yes. That should be fine, we'll see you then." She clicked the earpiece onto its hook.

Eliza fussed, "Edith, why didn't you let me speak with Florence? What's wrong? Is it Mother?"

"She didn't want to run up the bill for Albie. Everything's fine. She's coming for a quick visit next Wednesday. That's all. Someone should give the spare bedroom a once-over."

While it wasn't a call from Patrick, a visit from Florence would brighten Eliza's gloom. But, why was she coming?

•   •   •

On Wednesday, Eliza begged St. Anne, the patron saint of laboring mothers as Patrick had taught her, to speed up the delivery of her patient. The poor woman had labored for ten hours and pushed for two to no avail. Although Eliza worried the woman was tiring, she also became impatient for a selfish reason–she would be late getting home to greet Florence off the train.

"One more with the next contraction. You can do it," Eliza encouraged, her gloved hands at the ready as the head emerged. "That's it. Okay, ease up, let him do the work now."

The infant dropped into her waiting catch. There he was. Another miracle. Breathing and squirming to proclaim his arrival. Eliza snipped and tied off the cord. "Well done, Mrs. Reynolds. It's a boy. The nurse will clean him up and bring him right over. You and I have a bit more to finish up and then I'll let your husband know."

She handed the baby over to the capable hands of the nurse. After a final check of the after-birth and that Mrs. Reynolds rested comfortably with her son at her breast, Eliza ducked out of the room, leaving her gloves, gown, and head covering in a heap on the floor.

When she got to home, the parlor lamps shone like lighthouse beacons signaling a safe haven amid the turmoil of her day. Inside Fearless Florence, her lifelong comforter awaited. Through the open window, voices drifted her way–a conversation about her, without her.

From Edith, clear and crisp, "As I mentioned in my letter, we're deeply concerned. Every night, she paws through the mail in a frantic search. She believes the trans-Atlantic postal service may have lost a letter. The other day she suggested, 'they lost a ship like the *Titanic* in the fog, who's to say they couldn't misplace a mail bag or two?'"

Eliza steamed. How dare they? Edith sitting there insinuating Eliza acted like a lunatic. She didn't paw the mail pile, she shuffled through it. And it was true. Mail bags were lost all the time.

Now Olga's voice drifted out to her. "Our Eliza is a smart, practical, positive woman. She's allowed an angry denial to overwhelm her. Eliza deserves better. Her patients deserve better."

Eliza placed her bag on the sidewalk without a sound. If she remained outside, the candid conversation inside would continue. She lowered herself to the granite stoop. Olga's harsh words struck her as hard as the stone she sat upon. Had she ever rushed out of a delivery room like she had today, placing her desire to hurry home above her patient's needs? No. She always took extra time to advise a woman after a birth, ensured the baby's vitals were normal, and took a few moments to celebrate with the family. Was she slipping in her duties, letting her distraught mind wander away into the hills and dales of Ireland?

"Eliza will listen to you," said Estelle. "Can you convince her to visit Boston? A change of scenery may help. She planned a six-week honeymoon. The hospital should see clear to allow her a week or two respite."

Her honeymoon. Their honeymoon. By now she and Patrick should be chasing each other through the Maine coast's frigid waves, enjoying sunrises over the watery horizon, and sending their best wishes to the emerald isle across the ocean. Instead, she stood here, and he stood there, both unwilling to cross that sea with waves of disillusionment washing over her. Estelle might be right. She would enjoy a trip, as long as her mother kept her remarks about her long-held hesitations about Patrick to a minimum.

Finally, Fearless Florence addressed her audience. Eliza leaned to her left, positioning her ear closer to the window.

"I've got the perfect ticket. A stunning new hotel is opening soon. We expect the Copley Plaza will be a city jewel, right down to the pearl-like lighting fixtures they've installed. The official date is in August, but they're serving tea in one room. There's talk John Singer Sargent painted the room's magnificent ceiling mural."

"Sounds lovely. But it may not be enough. Eliza's not as keen on art as you are," said Josephine.

A blank, frosty silence as dark and hollow as a coal mine shaft floated through the window.

"You didn't allow me to finish," Florence said. "We'll go to tea at the Copley the afternoon she arrives. Then we'll catch the Newport train the next morning. Albie leased a cottage for the summer. Freddy, his family, and Laura are joining them. It'll be a slew of fun with the kids. The Tennis Casino is around the corner and there are parties every night up and down Bellevue Avenue. There'll be no time to mope and wallow in self-pity. By the end of two weeks, I guarantee our Eliza will be back to her old sunny self, and to hell with Patrick Callaghan."

Over the past three years, Florence had increased her involvement in the suffrage movement. Throughout New England, she attended rallies, county fairs, in-home private gatherings, and any other spot she might find an audience. She honed her oration and persuasive skills to the point of the lawyers Estelle transcribed at the courthouse. Tonight, she voiced her mind about the rights of one woman and the means for her to take back her life. Eliza listened.

Time had passed. The time was now. Eliza hiked up her skirt, picked up her bag, and flung the front door wide with as much gusto as her brothers used to. The doorknob settled into the dent in the foyer wall. She entered the parlor ready with her own declaration. "This is some meeting of the minds you've all had. I'm glad you've figured out how to solve my lunacy and sadness," she huffed.

In the unison of a military line-up, four heads spun to the left where Eliza stood in the doorway. Comments rang out and crowded the room.

"Eliza, we didn't hear you come in."

"How long have you been there?"

"We didn't mean to upset you."

Eliza silenced them, "I appreciate your concerns. Florence, I hope your visit isn't just to talk sense into me." Her face softened as she looked at her favorite aunt.

"But, as usual, you're right. A vacation sounds like the smartest doctor's orders I've heard in a while."

CHAPTER THIRTY

July 1912

In the spectator area of The Casino tennis club, Eliza shifted in her rigid wooden folding chair, watching–or trying to watch–her brothers' doubles match against a talked-about newcomer team of Joe Alton and Harrison Shaw.

Thwack. The ball cleared the net and bounced once on the clay causing a puff of dust to rise and settle on the close-cropped lawn. The volley continued until the heft and force of a racket smash sent the ball sailing over Albie, landing within a hair's breadth of the baseline. "Game," said the Chair Umpire from his perch.

The opponent Shaw delivering the final strike smirked, clapped his partner's shoulder, and sauntered to his seat, calling across the net, "That's five. You'd think you Quakers from Penn would know the mighty Crimson will always prevail."

Nothing like a sore winner, Eliza thought, boredom forcing her eyelids and polite interest to slump.

The men resumed after a seven-minute intermission.

"Tired, dear?" Laura laid a solicitous hand on Eliza's.

Eliza looked out to the court. Even after two hours of play, the lawn remained as smooth as billiard table velvet. Two players positioned themselves on either side of the net, one closer and the other at the baseline. Clad in their tennis whites, they stood as solid and stoic as the white columns of the Vanderbilt's Marble House.

"Swinging a racket now and then is okay, but it's boring to watch, don't you think?" Eliza didn't bother to stifle a yawn. "Back and forth, back and forth, like the pendulum in the grandfather clock."

Her head tilted from side to side, mimicking the pendulum. Her straw hat, adorned with pale yellow roses and ringed with a navy brim, bobbed with her sway. A single rose petal shook loose and fluttered to her lap.

Thwack. Over. *He loves me. Thwack.* Back. *He loves me not. Thwack.* Over. *He's coming back. Thwack.* Back. *He's not.* Whenever she found herself blank of thought, her mind returned to Patrick. *Please let the men from Harvard triumph soon and end my misery.*

She turned to her mother, "Let me know when it's over. Jack London's latest is far more interesting. I hope to finish it this afternoon and post it off to Edith. She'll find it fascinating. London took the history of the black plague and blended it with suppositions of devastation of ten thousand years of culture and civilization from a single, invisible germ."

"Sounds positively dreadful," said Laura.

Eliza reached into her doctor's bag. She brought the satchel with her on every outing. It served as a catchall for her personal items and a carrier of her basic medical equipment. Hair and hat pins, a dulled black lacquered ballpoint pen stuffed into a notebook, and reading materials, like *The London Magazine* lay scattered at the bottom of the bag. The May and June issues featured installments of London's *The Scarlet Plague.*

"Listen to this description. Who knew Jack London, a writer of wolf stories, could describe a medical condition with such accuracy?" Eliza's voice came alive reading, *"'The heart began to beat faster and the heat of the body to increase. Then came the scarlet rash, spreading like wildfire over the face and body...The heels became numb first, then the legs, and hips, and when the numbness reached as high as his heart, he died.'"*

Eliza had kept to herself in Newport for three days before she heeded the prescription Florence advised. She relented and agreed to an outing, but only to attend the tennis match. Laura Edwards leaned over her daughter's gloved forearm as she flipped the pages. She grabbed Eliza's finger, moving down the page to end the recitation.

"Eliza, please. Pay attention to the game. It means a great deal to your brothers you came today. If nothing else, put away that dreadful magazine and soak up this glorious sunshine and fresh air. They can cure. Breathe deep. Release those ills from your heart."

"You needn't scold me, Mother. I'm not a child and I certainly know more about curing ills than you do," said Eliza. She resumed her reading as the players on the court readied for another game within the set.

A yell screeched from the far side of the court and roused her from the magazine.

"Damnation and bloody hell!"

"Mr. Shaw!" admonished Albie. "I remind you my mother and sister are in the grandstand."

The women, concerned with the commotion on the court, stood from their chairs. Eliza squinted, trying to assess the situation from her spot in the grandstand. She heard Albie call out again, "Great Scott! What happened?"

A faint moan escaped from the screeching man as he tried to put weight on his strained leg. He extended his knee for a forward step. Scanning the grandstand, his partner shouted up to the few spectators, "We need a doctor."

A voice which had called her name for years, whether it was when they played hide-and-seek as children or when he begged for a cessation of her questions, rose into the stands. "Eliza," said Freddy. "We need your help."

Help. Few words prompted such swift action from a doctor. She grabbed her bag, leaving the magazine splayed open on the table. In her other hand, she lifted the short train of a creamy linen skirt above her ankles to hasten her stride to the far side of the court. The opponent Shaw appeared in distress, his face ashen and slick from perspiration. Slumped into a referee's chair, his right leg angled out to his side. Albie held the man's wire-rimmed glasses.

Freddy managed quick introductions. "Harrison, my sister, Dr. Eliza Edwards. Eliza, Harrison Shaw."

"Pleased to meet you Mr. Shaw, although I suspect we both wish it were under better circumstances. Can you tell me where the pain is?"

Albie interjected, "I played net and saw him dive for Freddy's return. He over-extended his leg. He grabbed the top of his back thigh as he went down."

Eliza peeled off her gloves and picked up his hand, cradling it as she placed her fore and middle fingers on the inside of his wrist. His pulse ran quick.

"I'm all right, if you chaps can get me to Joe's car, it's an easy jaunt to the hospital," Harrison said.

"Well, I don't think the hospital is necessary. Sounds like an injury to the biceps femoris muscle, a pulled hamstring. To be sure, let's move him to the bench so he can lie flat. I'll complete a quick exam," Eliza said.

Before he could protest, Albie and Freddy hoisted Harrison and moved him to the low bench which ran alongside the court. Eliza commanded him to lie face down, motioning for Albie to place a towel under his head.

"Really, Miss Edwards, I'm fine. A hospital doctor can check it out. Newport's finest probably came from Harvard. I suppose I wouldn't even mind a Yale Eli."

A heat rose along the back of her neck and crept around into her cheeks. Lest he think she was blushing, she fired back.

"Dr. Edwards," Eliza retorted. "Mr. Shaw, I have an accredited medical degree and have been practicing medicine for eleven years. I am more than qualified to give you a proper assessment of your injury, maybe more so than any Newport physician, even a Harvard man, who, since it's Wednesday, will be four highballs into his golf round by now. Lie still. This will only take a few moments."

Stunned into silence and prone on the bench, Eliza caught him wincing as the light-weight flannel of his pants pressed against his leg, the fabric a thin film between his skin and her soothing touch. Her hands maneuvered beneath his leg and moved down to his shin. With her hands under his shin, she bent his knee. "A pulled hamstring for sure. There is a depression where the string is torn. When I bend your knee, Mr. Shaw, how did that feel? Better or worse?"

"Better, much better," said Harrison.

CHAPTER THIRTY-ONE

August 1912

"Pleeeeeeeeeeeeeease Auntie E? I was very good at church yesterday. I didn't ask Papa any questions, and I didn't scream when Ricky pinched me, and I didn't pinch him back. I shoulda though, don't you think?"

Eliza smiled down at her niece, Bessie, and suppressed a chuckle. Ricky deserved a pinch now and then, the imp always tormenting his sister. The girl blew a breath upward to push aside the red-gold lock of hair that had escaped from a pink satin bow. Eliza gathered the loose strands and re-clipped the bow. The current plea from Bessie centered on her discovery in Muenchinger's Confectionery and Toys, a tin tea set painted with scenes from the nursery rhyme, *Mary Had a Little Lamb*. Bessie held up the service tray for closer inspection. Her chubby finger outlined the painting.

"See the little lambs? I wish I had a lamb. Papa says there are lots and lots of lambs in Scotland who give us their wool that's as white as snow. Aren't they such nice little lambs to share their wool? Do you think someday I might go with Papa and pet their fleecy backs?"

Bessie's comments and questions fell like the rush of a waterfall. Curiosity at a young age would help her niece explore many paths. *Atta girl. Good for you, Bessie.*

• • •

Eliza's spirits had lightened thanks to carefree days she spent with her nieces and nephews in Newport's magical allure. She couldn't find a single minute to mope. On sunny mornings, she shepherded the children onto the open-air electric trolley traveling the Beach Line to Gooseberry Beach. They built sandcastles and collected shells in the protected cove. When they ventured into the surf, Eliza supervised their every move, more vigilant than any nanny would be. She released her feet from her tight-laced boots and let the cool, moist sand cover her toes as her heels sank further into the shore with each wave's return to the sea.

In the afternoons, Albie skippered a forty-foot rented sloop for a sail through Narragansett Bay. Salty spray misted across her face with soothing powers as calming as any medicinal spa. Sometimes she sat as the fourth chair at bridge luncheons with her mother and sisters-in-law, Mamie and Bea, chatting with new friends. At first, Newport was a refuge, a hideaway where the sad ending of the tragedy of Eliza and Patrick was unspoken. As the days went on, she felt more secure in her decision to take a vacation. If Patrick returned, he could find her in Newport. In fact, force him to come to Newport. Make it more difficult for him. He had turned her life upside down. Now it was her turn.

Florence joined them for a week's stay in late July. She invited Eliza to accompany her to a tea hosted by the grand dame of Newport. In her suffrage work, Florence had met Mrs. Alva Vanderbilt Belmont. Upon hearing there would be a fundraiser at Alva's "spare cottage" which she obtained after her divorce from William K. Vanderbilt, Florence jumped at the chance to attend, bringing Eliza with her.

Outside on the rolling green lawn, the famed Marble House's gardens bloomed in bursts of glory, with roses in every shade of red from orange to pink, cream and yellow, banked by bushy hydrangeas with balls of purple and blue. Anything seemed possible to Eliza, including women's right to vote, when a living rainbow exploded around you. The teacup she held further affirmed the possibility. Alva commissioned a complete collection of china cups and saucers emblazoned with Votes for Women to commemorate the luncheon. The phrase glazed into the china gave a sense of permanence to the cause. The luncheon was liberating on many levels.

Evenings brought mirth and laughter, watching vaudeville acts and theatrical productions staged at the Casino Theatre. Other evenings, Eliza dressed in flowing gowns from Bea's closet, the latest Parisian fashions, to attend a concert or dinner party at one of the Newport Four Hundred's palaces and fortresses. Carved from marble, brick, and stone, the estates vied for the ultimate in grandeur and magnificence. The Berwinds of Philadelphia, friends of her mother, invited Eliza to her first Newport soiree at their cottage, The Elms. Hardly what Eliza considered a cottage, its tan exterior and filigree graced the front door with sculptures on every corner. As she entered beneath the portico, she lifted her sights to see Greek-inspired friezes, frolicking on the rooftop's edges.

Freddy and Bea were determined to lift Eliza from her sorrows. When Bea commenced her confinement period with her third pregnancy, she suggested Eliza stand in and accompany Freddy to the events offered by the invitations that stuffed their mailbox. The evening at The Elms would be the perfect outing to wear one of Bea's favorite gowns. The beaded Empire-waisted, muted Kelly-green silk fell to the floor with swirls of lace overlay and black velvet trim at the hem and bodice. Carnival glass beads and knotted chenille fringe at the cinched waist completed the gown's adornments. Bea added opera-length black gloves, bejeweled satin pumps, and a teal-colored metal mesh bag with a gold chain to drape from Eliza's shoulder.

"You're a regal beauty," exclaimed Bea. "The green is so becoming on you, with your red highlights. It's too bad women have to pin their hair up. Yours would be stunning, long and loose."

Eliza thanked her sister-in-law and stepped backward from the cheval mirror. For the first time in over eleven years, she allowed herself to abandon her serious, doctoring self and for the first time since the *Titanic* sank, she smiled a full-hearted grin.

The colorful opulence inside The Elms enfolded her as if she had drunk from the glass bottle in *Alice's Adventures in Wonderland* and had shrunk small enough to walk through a queen's jewelry box. Emerald greens, ruby reds, and sapphire blues embellished each room. Twinkling crystals hung from chandeliers like tiaras strung together with platinum thread. Gilded surfaces adorned the furniture, ceilings, and wall moldings. Perhaps King Midas had been the first guest to the house. A Newport Season played out like royal fairy tales.

When a server passed a silver tray of Waterford champagne flutes, Eliza took one and downed it in two draughts. The bubbles tickled her tongue. She might have a second.

• • •

On cloudy days such as today, when the fog rolled in, the children begged for a trip to Muenchinger's Confectionery. At the fingerprint-smudged glass cases, they pointed to and named their choices of chocolate cream and jellied gum drops and French burst almonds. A savvy proprietor, Gustav Muenchinger, also stocked his store shelves and tables with toys, books, crayons, and paints. Patrons exited to Thames Street with sacks bulging with candies or other trifles.

"If I buy this for you, do you promise to serve me tea this afternoon?" Eliza asked her niece.

A male voice spoke from behind them, "Afternoon tea sounds lovely. Do you serve scones or tea cakes, Miss? I prefer scones myself. Have you tried any with dried cranberries? They're my favorite. If you're serving scones with cranberries and clotted cream on top, may I be so bold as to ask to join your party?"

The forward invitation startled Eliza. Who would eavesdrop on a conversation between a little girl and her aunt and admit to his indiscretion? Eliza glanced down, catching sight of a cane's rubber tip. An elderly gentleman having a bit of fun. No harm done; most likely he was a neighbor who knew Bessie. As she raised her head to address the frail gentleman and extend a warm welcome to join them for tea, a sturdier figure came into view, an athletic build toned from hours spent on a tennis court. Harrison Shaw held the grip of a brown hickory cane in one hand and a tin of watercolor paints in the other.

"Mr. Shaw. I'm pleased to see you up and about. It appears you heeded my advice. Ice, rest and elevation for your leg."

"Ah, Dr. Edwards, yes. Thank you. I'm delighted to report I've been the perfect patient. I followed your prescription to a T and added a few of my own: ice, scotch, and a shot of whiskey before bed."

Eliza couldn't help but grin at his own mockery. "I suppose those remedies have their own curative powers, although you may be hard-pressed to find a doctor willing to write that prescription."

Bessie tugged on Eliza's skirt. "Auntie, have you had a crabbyberry? I have tried strawberries and raspberries and blueberries, but I don't think I've ever tried a crabbyberry. Can we ask Bridget to make us scones with crabbyberries?"

Harrison rapped the cane on the floor and roared with laughter, "Crabbyberries! How precious. You're precious, and what is your name, my dear?"

"Mr. Shaw, this is my niece, Bessie. My brother, Fredrick's daughter. Bessie, say hello to Mr. Shaw. He played tennis with your Papa and Uncle Albie."

"Hello, Mr. Shaw. How do you play tennis with a cane?" quizzed Bessie.

"Also, observant. Unfortunately, I can't play tennis right now. I hurt my leg playing against your Papa. But, your aunt, the doctor, she fixed me up so I can get back on the courts again soon."

"That's good. Auntie E. is a good doctor. My brother, Ricky, had an awful ache in his ear and only Auntie stopped his crying. She takes good care of my Mama, too. My Mama's going to have another baby. I want a sister. Ricky is a pest."

"All right, Bessie. We mustn't detain Mr. Shaw with stories of Ricky's earaches and such. I hope you're back to the Casino soon, Mr. Shaw. You're a fine player. I'm sure my brothers would enjoy a re-match."

"As do I, and I hope you'll be there to watch again. Enjoy your tea, ladies. And try the crabbyberries. They are delicious."

Eliza paused in front of the store's window. Beyond Thames Street, Newport's Bowen Wharf bustled. A deckhand untied a tether and hopped onto the deck of a sleek, forest green hulled sloop. Another crew member hoisted the headsail, its tan canvas flapping until it caught a puff of air over the starboard side. Liberated from the dock, the sloop pulled away, bracing to meet the waters outside the Bay.

She turned to Harrison, "Why don't you join us? Bessie's tea set serves four."

Bessie clapped her hands, "Yes, please come, Mr. Shaw. Can you bring some crabbyberries?"

Eliza watched as Harrison bent to pick up Bessie's hand and brush a light kiss across the back.

"I would be delighted, Princess Bessie," he said as he bowed, play-acting for the benefit of a six-year-old.

Turning to Eliza, he said, "At what time shall I present myself? It's the Barclay cottage on Ledge Road, yes?"

"That's correct," said Eliza. "Four o'clock should be fine."

With a tip of his Panama hat, Harrison strode to the sales counter. Eliza noted the cane hanging from his bent elbow, unused. Apparently, pleasant conversations had curative powers, too.

•　•　•

Afternoon tea led to Harrison joining the Edwards for dinner and an evening of card play two nights later. Eliza leaned into the conversations as Harrison shared more about his interests and talents ranging from legal work to tennis playing to painting. Harrison Gordon Shaw, never Harry, completed his studies at Harvard College and Harvard Law School, where he met Joe Alton on the lawn tennis team. Together, their indefatigable doubles play brought championship winnings home to Cambridge. At Joe's invitation, Harrison left his uninspiring position with an insurance agency to spend the summer in Newport with the Altons. Besides their home on Beacon Hill, the Altons had completed construction of their Newport cottage. Harrison told Eliza how his eyes would glaze over, listening to the excruciating details of the ten bedrooms, each with an adjoining water closet, and the wrap-around porch facing southwest to capture the gentle summer ocean breezes. Well-aware of Harrison's prowess with a paintbrush and a tennis racquet, Joe mentioned his mother's hunt for original paintings of their ocean vista. In exchange for a few wall-hangings, Harrison could lay claim to one of the ten bedrooms for the season. His purchase of the watercolors paint set at Muenchinger's was for practice before moving into oils.

Beyond the paintings, however, Joe also mentioned tennis. With Harrison's help, they would ensure the names Alton and Shaw were engraved on silver trophy cups at The Casino, Newport's tennis club and home to the US Lawn Tennis championship.

"So, here I am. The most fortunate man in Boston, enjoying a delightful season in Newport, attending socials, tennis matches, concerts, golf, and fancies," said Harrison, finishing his travelogue as he laid down a winning hand of rummy. "From bourgeoisie beginnings in Quincy, Massachusetts–the birthplace of presidents, you know–to the summer dominion of Boston, New York, and Philadelphia moguls."

Intrigued that a man would leave his position, even an uninspiring one, for a summer of leisure, Eliza asked, "What's next?"

Across the card table, Albie answered for Harrison. "We've been discussing Massachusetts business laws. Harrison's knowledge and ties to his Harvard classmates in Boston and Washington run deep as excellent resources and contacts. We're hoping he'll accept an inside counsel position with us to free me up for other management dealings."

"And, I'm considering it," Harrison said, winking across the table at Eliza with soft velvet brown eyes behind his wire-rimmed glasses. "Although if I continue to take your money over a few hands of Gin Rummy, you may have nothing left to pay me with, Mr. Edwards."

Confident, a good sense of humor, well-mannered, and many talents. Harrison Shaw, a modern-day Renaissance Man, thought Eliza. She knocked on the inlaid mahogany card table.

"Really, Eliza, all ready? We've hardly had four rounds," said Harrison.

"Yes," she said. "Just ask my brothers. When I'm certain of something, I make my decision known."

•　　•　　•

One evening, as Harrison and Eliza finished a brandy on the terrace, he suggested they stroll outside for a better view of the night sky's gem. Tonight, the moon smoldered full and low in the sky, an iridescent opal, its blues, greens, and purples played across its milky face.

"Does the moon look this lovely in Philadelphia?" he said, stopping at the wrought-iron gate of the path's end. The tangle of privet hedge boxed them in close, offering a frame of the sea beyond. Her arm remained in the crook of his, the white of her glove gleamed against the black sleeve of his dinner suit. The late-August night hinted at cooler autumn evenings. Eliza snuggled her shawl closer around her shoulders as the damp air skimmed her cheek.

"I'm embarrassed to admit, I've buried my head in studies and work for so long, I can't recall taking notice of it before, in Philadelphia, or here. There is a quiet peace to it. Thank you for opening my eyes."

"Your eyes are as lovely as the moon, too. Let's go out," he said. "The shine on the water is spectacular. But the privet blocks a view of its magnificence." Harrison lifted the gate's latch and stepped out to the rocky swath of ground, less than eight feet from the cliff's edge. He reached for her.

An imminent danger waited before them. A single wobbly rock, one misstep, and they would plummet to the jagged shore below where heaving waves collided onto themselves.

A lone seagull cried into the wind as it returned to land, searching for shelter as night fell around them. Overhead, the stars appeared, sending their shine across the sea like silver nuggets. Eliza took his hand and followed him toward the ledge.

The stars' reflection illuminated the scene, giving them an unobstructed view of the ocean as it churned and thrusted itself against the coastline. Harrison encircled her waist. Eliza relinquished her body to his pull. He brought his lips to her ear and whispered, "My mother used to say seeing the moon over your shoulder is good luck. I think she was right. I am very fortunate we've met. Not only are you the most beautiful woman I have ever known, but your passion for your work is inspiring. You are a rare gem."

He moved his lips from her ear to her cheek to her lips. He kissed her.

Eliza let her fingers linger on the spot as she locked her eyes upon the darkened line of the horizon.

Staring at the churning sea and hearing Harrison's profession of admiration, stirred remembrances of the scandalous book, *The Awakening*. In what seemed like a lifetime ago, she and Olga had read Kate Chopin's book together in dark, secret nights. The story about a woman's growing awareness of her own emotional and sexual needs, adultery, and promiscuity was a devilish diversion from the drudgery of medical texts and lab reports. Whispers crossed their room in hushed voices. Eliza couldn't imagine her mother's fury if she heard the words read aloud under her roof.

The heroine, Edna Pontellier, trapped in marriage, sought an identity beyond wife and mother. The story sparked chats between Eliza and Olga. Their conclusions arrived at the same point: becoming a doctor, married or not, would provide meaning in their lives.

A particular passage had haunted Eliza: *The voice of the sea is seductive, never ceasing, whispering, clamoring, murmuring, inviting the soul to wander in abysses of solitude.* The sea's invitation was persuasive. A woman, like Edna Pontellier, submitted to its power, yielding her soul to the black abyss; the air sucked from her lungs as she sank to the graveyard of broken shells and shipwrecked hulls. But a self-assured woman would dive into the waves. She would ask them to wash her clean of anguish and loneliness. She would emerge focused on a new destiny: companionship and perhaps, in time, children, and love.

Eliza felt inside her sleeve and pulled out a scrap of linen, its embroidered stitches fraying. Her fingers caressed the thread-bare piece for a moment before dropping it to the ground. She watched it tumble across the gravel until it snagged on a twig. She reached for Harrison's arm to brace herself as she toed the square free at the same time a gust swept it into the air. Like a blown dandelion, it floated over the precipice's edge and into the roiling sea. The piece needed to meet its destiny in the waves. To Ireland.

"The view is glorious," Eliza said. "But I need to retire soon. I didn't sleep much last night. Bea woke me thinking her labor had started. I'm concerned about her high blood pressure. Thank goodness we've moved beyond bleeding and purging to treat Pregnancy Induced Hypertension. I can monitor her bed rest and handle an injection of magnesium sulfate if needed."

His wide-eyed gaze stopped her monologue.

"Oh dear," she fretted. "I shouldn't ramble on about a medical issue which you must find boring, and perhaps, inappropriate."

"Not in the least. In fact, I hope you won't consider my honesty off-putting, but that day at The Casino, I didn't have any faith in you, a woman, being able to assess my injury. You changed my mind with your accurate diagnosis and prescribing proper care. You are a talented doctor. Your dedication to your sister-in-law is commendable. You must bring her great comfort during this difficult time."

"I suppose I am. Her condition is one reason I've extended my stay here in Newport. My supervisor in Philadelphia approved a leave of absence for me. I'll be joining Bea and Freddy in Boston to monitor her until she delivers."

"One reason? What may be the other reasons keeping you here?" he asked, the corners of his mouth curving upward.

More time spent with Harrison Shaw, the charming lawyer, tennis player, and painter from Boston, counted as another reason. But she was not ready to tell him, yet. Eliza turned from the cliff, reaching for his arm to guide her away from the ledge.

He patted her hand and slid it down to his waist. With his hand on the small of her back, wrapped together like hinged halves of the shells on the rocky shore, he opened the gate and steered her onto the path. Moonbeams illuminated their way. Their footprints, side by side, dotted the dew-covered grass.

CHAPTER THIRTY-TWO

September 1912

Dearest Olga,

Finally, a few minutes to write! My third nephew, Gerard Allen Edwards, has kept us busy. After the scare of Bea's PIH, she is recovering well. The staff at Boston Lying-In were most gracious and allowed me to supervise the delivery and her postpartum care. Bessie has appointed herself my assistant and fusses over her mother and baby brother to her heart's delight. My mother visits daily and Freddy has hired a nurse, leaving me free to take on other duties.

More exciting news—I've secured a job at Boston Lying-In. During Bea's stay, I met Helen Turner, who graduated from Woman's Med. three years after us. I recall Charlotte tutoring her, which has served Helen well. She is now the preferred surgeon for ovariotomies. Helen suggested I apply for a position opening in January. An obstetrician is retiring when she marries. I'm sorry to learn she is leaving because she is marrying, but her loss is my gain. I have been idle for too long!

In the meantime, I've explored Boston. No wonder my brothers chose it for the company's expansion. The influx of more families from Eastern Europe looking for employment provides skilled workers for the mill north of Boston, while an abundance of universities graduate smart, hard-working men for managerial roles. Wellesley, Radcliffe, and Wheaton College are also in Boston's backyard, and I've convinced Albie to consider some of those graduates for a few managerial roles, too. Believe it or not, big brother has heeded the advice of his little sis and is quite pleased with the women's work ethic and aplomb in the office.

Beyond the business, living in Boston is like Philadelphia in many ways. History steeped in our American Revolution creates an attitude of personal freedom. Albie's and Freddy's lovely homes, close to each other on Chestnut Street, resemble Race Street with red-bricked fronts, black shutters, and cobble-stoned roads and walkways. The Public Garden is two blocks away, and remind me of Logan Circle, although much larger. I enjoy morning walks along the paths, edged by thick green grass and ribbons of flower beds. The serene setting is a glorious way to clear one's head. In the afternoon, I take the children for picnics under the shade of the stately oaks and rides on the famous Swan Boats in the lagoon.

One Saturday, soon after arriving in Boston, Harrison escorted Eliza on her first Swan Boat ride. With his hand holding hers, Eliza leaned into his shoulder, her head cocked to the side, a hair's breadth away from him. The rim of her hat tickled his ear under his straw boater. Overhead, a kite escaped from its young owner and floated on the breeze, its yellow and blue tail ribbons waving like butterfly wings. The child stood at the lagoon's edge, watching his prize drift across the pond. Eliza pointed it out to Harrison, "The little boy must be sad, but doesn't the kite look happy to be free? Not a care in the world, floating off to unknown places where untold adventures await."

Behind them on the boat, the graceful neck of the swan curved forward to eavesdrop into the low coos of its passengers.

You're probably sitting there across from Samuel, huffing and puffing and declaring, 'Why doesn't she get on with it? Who cares about picnics and boat rides? What's going on with Harrison Shaw?' I won't keep you in suspense any longer.

Mr. Shaw and I have continued to see each other. Albie hired him as inside counsel, and both he and Freddy praise his work. In the few spare hours they've afforded him, Harrison squires me about Boston. During a Swan Boat ride, Harrison explained the history of these peculiar boats. The proprietor's idea came from the opera Lohengrin, which tells the German tale of Princess Elsa. Her love interest crosses a river in a boat drawn by a swan to defend her innocence. Too bad the story of the current proprietor, the man's widow, isn't as endearing. She must prove her ability to run her establishment each year by securing testimonies from other local business owners as to her abilities because she is a woman. I guess our trials never end, no matter our vocation or experience.

The owner's proof of her worth was a triumph enjoyed by visitors and residents of Boston alike. Eliza hoped her new position wouldn't include the same obstacles, for she knew there were men like Dr. Whitaker in every hospital. But, after nine years, she had validated her abilities before him. She dreaded starting over again with another supervisor. When she mentioned her doubts to Harrison, she took comfort in his response. *I will march over there myself and talk to any imbecile who dares to deny your abilities.* While she would never allow a man to speak on her behalf, she appreciated his support.

Harrison and I have dined at both Durgin Park and the Union Oyster House, the two oldest restaurants in the country where it feels like you're transported to the early 1800s with exposed beamed, low-hanging ceilings, tables crammed together, and Windsor-backed chairs wedged into corners. They make delicious clam chowder. I could enjoy no other type now. I'm a convert to the New England style! Meaty chunks of clams, cubes of salt pork, and potatoes swim in thick cream with onions and parsley snips. I order only a cupful to save room for dessert at the Parker House, where they serve a scrumptious Boston Cream Pie. Thank goodness we walk back to Freddy's house and climb the South Slope sidewalks of Beacon Hill after these lavish dinners; otherwise, I would need a whole other wardrobe to accommodate a thickening waistline!

Speaking of dresses. The words you're about to read may make you think I'm mad in the head. I assure you; I have all my faculties.

There is one dress I left behind in Philadelphia, which I hope will fit. My wedding gown...I'm marrying Harrison in the chapel of his church, Boston's Trinity Episcopal. I've chosen the opportune date of October 12th.

Can you come? Will you bring the dress to me to ensure its safe delivery? Will you stand up next to me?

A picture of Olga in her sitting room, reading the letter to Samuel, formed in Eliza's mind. She saw Olga's reaction develop like a dramatic play. From boredom over chowder and pie details, to delight about Eliza's new position, to interest in the Swan Boats' history, to shock over her engagement. Would Olga close the final act with her trademark comedic jab to lighten the scene, "Thank God we're done with the nonsense of Patrick Callaghan"? Or would she crumple the letter, disgusted, and toss it into Samuel's spittoon?

•   •   •

Three days before the wedding, Olga arrived at Eliza's new Beacon Hill townhouse with a dusty rose crepe de chine gown wrapped in tissue and packed into a box longer than Olga was tall. Together they unpacked the silky folds and readied it for Eliza's fitting, six months after her last appointment in Philadelphia. Eliza circled slowly, looking over her shoulder into her bedroom full-length mirror at the cascade of buttons down her back and the two-foot train flared out behind her. "What do you think?" she asked.

"That, my friend, is a loaded question," said Olga. "Do you really want me to answer?"

She had avoided an expected lecture from Olga all day. At this moment, she had no desire, intention, nor time to listen to any rebukes from her dearest friend. Time was fleeting. Like hourglass sand dribbling into a mound of nothingness, Eliza's life had disappeared into an abyss waiting for a woman in Ireland to die. Hoping and waiting for that woman's son to marry her, father their children, and settle into years of comfort, respect, and companionship. Eliza would wait no longer.

"The dress," Eliza replied without missing a beat. She thrust her arms forward. "Are the short-sleeves and the color appropriate for an October wedding? Maybe we should pop over to Filene's."

Olga tugged at the sleeves' lace edges before moving her hands onto Eliza's shoulders. Eliza felt Olga's stare penetrate her blue eyes, diving deep for a genuine response. "It's fine," said Olga. "It's a perfect fit. Your cream-colored gloves, instead of your white ones, deepen and complement the pink in the dress. We'll pin golden, sienna, and navy dahlias to your hat; that'll make it very seasonal. But I'd rather give you my opinion on a different issue."

I'm sure you would, thought Eliza. She expected Olga's remarks would differ from her mother's. Laura's endless praise and encouragement had wearied Eliza. She had already said yes. Harrison gained Laura's endorsement each occasion he called on Eliza, showing every inch of propriety possible. Even Bessie's opinion counted; she declared his recommendation for crabbyberries in scones the best idea since clotted cream. When Albie and Freddy hired him, Eliza held her brothers' approval in high regard. His announcement that they could marry at Trinity Episcopal Church catapulted him into the winner's circle.

"Would you unbutton me, please?" Eliza turned her back to Olga. Thirty buttons should take her five minutes to undo. Olga's history, known for dropping countless histology slides, meant the task could take her ten minutes. At least she wouldn't see Olga's disappointment while she listened to it in her voice.

"Five years ago, I asked you the same question. Are you sure, Eliza? Is Harrison the one? How can you know after three months?"

Eliza fired back, "How well did you know Samuel? You courted for less than a year before you went to City Hall. You haven't even met Harrison. We're compatible, he has many interests, he's intelligent, a hard worker, he appears to support my career, my mother is happy. What more do I need?"

"Love?"

"Love! Where did that get me? I'm thirty-three years old. I'm finished holding out for love. Contentment, agreeability and God-willing, motherhood. That's enough."

"I'm done," said Olga.

•   •   •

The Paul Revere suite at the Copley Plaza Hotel shimmered. From candlesticks and wall sconces shaped like the famed lanterns, to vases and an iced champagne bucket, to dove-gray satin bed linens, silver accented every surface in the rooms to honor its namesake's profession. Eliza stood in the suite's bedroom, counting the seconds as Harrison's fingers flew down the column of buttons on the back of her dress. He handily beat Olga's time.

"I'll be just a minute," she said, picking up her overnight case and headed for the powder room.

He raised his champagne flute toward her, "I'll be here."

Eliza examined the woman's face in the mirror hung over the sink. Over a decade of medical school and practice, she had seen every part of an unclothed human body, female and male. Her fingers had touched them. She had studied them, probed them, tended to their aches and pains. But tonight, Eliza would abandon her practical teaching. Her experience moved from professional to personal. The mirror reflected Mrs. Harrison Shaw.

She returned to the bedroom in a creamy silk and lace negligee covered by a matching robe tied with a pale pink satin bow under her bust. Harrison sat under the bed's top sheet, resting against the headboard. At the footboard, he had folded the duvet into a neat accordion stack. His white sleeveless undershirt revealed his tennis-playing toned pectorals and biceps. He held a tumbler of scotch in one hand while his other rummaged through the contents of the brown leather toiletry case on the bedside table. Each item had its place nestled into purple velvet: two ivory handled brushes, shaving brush, a black Bakelite handled straight razor, nail file, tweezers, whalebone toothbrush, a glass vial of toothpicks, and a palm-sized tin. From the tin, Harrison fumbled with a Genuine Transparent Ramses Rubber Prophylactic.

Eliza went to his side of the bed and covered his hand with hers. "No need," she said and closed the toiletry case with a sharp snap.

In this room named for Paul Revere, she'd be taking her own ride through Boston tonight.

CHAPTER THIRTY-THREE

November 1912

The elite of Boston and Newport insisted respectable honeymoons include a Grand Tour of Europe. London, Paris, and Rome extended exquisite scenery of mountains and vales, museums displaying the world's masterpieces of art, restaurants with expansive menus, and palatial accommodations at each stop for honeymooning interludes. Her mother and sisters-in-law twittered about selecting original pieces befitting a Beacon Hill townhouse, an extravagant but much appreciated wedding gift from Albie and Freddy. Bea turned down pages of *Harper's* and *Vogue*, marking ideas of stylish Parisian fashions to fill Eliza's armoire. Between Harrison's increased salary with the Edwards Wool Company and years of Eliza saving, they could take full advantage of a European honeymoon.

Harrison campaigned for the trip, checking for the next sailings from Boston. But not Eliza. She had no intention of setting foot on a ship for a trans-Atlantic crossing. Train travel with stops in New York, Washington, Williamsburg, Raleigh, and Savannah, provided many options for amusement and sight-seeing. And they could spend Thanksgiving in Philadelphia.

• • •

Eliza leaned on the top of her valise to push it closed. She snapped the locks tight and handed it to Harrison.

"What's in here? Bricks from the College as remembrance blocks?" Harrison said with a wink as he feigned a struggle to carry the packed suitcase.

"I thought all those tennis matches and rounds of golf made you strong enough for anything," Eliza teased. "I put most of my books in the pile to ship, but my grandfather's *Gray's Anatomy* is a treasure. I'd never forgive myself if I lost it."

Catch-ups jammed their extended stop as tight as Eliza's valises. A spike in the frequency of Josephine's vertigo spells in September prompted Eliza to insist Josephine not make the trip for the wedding. Not wanting to leave Josephine unsupervised, Estelle stayed home, too. When Eliza and Harrison arrived in Philadelphia, the aunts clamored for every detail, from the flowers she carried–white stephanotis mixed with pink orchids–to which readings her brothers read at the service–1 Corinthians, *Love is patient, love is kind*, and 1 Peter, *Above all, love each other deeply, because love covers over a multitude of sins.*

Over dinner one evening, Edith shared the success her Board of Health office had in creating a new position at the Elwyn Training School. From Edith's persistent push for more oversight, a recent graduate from Woman's Med. joined the school. The resident would work alongside Doctor Barr to document any further instances of abuse or attempts at unauthorized surgeries. Eliza looked forward to visiting with Nina Silvestri to tell her the news. Although Salvatore lived at home with his family, Nina expressed her concerns to Eliza that other students were not as fortunate. Woman's Med. graduates achieved another quiet triumph on behalf of their community.

"Are you sure you don't mind stopping by the Silvestris?" Eliza said.

"Not at all. We have time. I've heard so much about them; I want to meet this young chap who captured your heart. He sounds like a marvel, thanks, I suspect, to the way you've stayed involved with him and counseled his parents."

Harrison held out his hands to draw her in for a kiss. She leaned into him, "Thank you. I am proud of him. My little wonder boy."

Eliza tucked a wrapped parcel into her tote. She had chosen a raffia string to complement the inked woodland creatures which frolicked across blue paper. How fortunate Thornton Burgess continued to write his delightful stories. She hoped Salvatore would enjoy this year's present, *Mother West Wind's Animal Friends*, as much as he liked his first copy in the series.

A year ago, she and Patrick were choosing between Peter and Wendy and Old Mother West Wind. Today, she stood next to another choice. Harrison Gordon Shaw. Her husband. Would this decision meet with the same level of success as Old Mother West Wind?

• • •

They reached Savannah early enough in the day to enjoy a walk-through Forsyth Park. Eliza fell in love. Who needed to visit London when Savannah's many squares rivaled English gardens? Beneath Spanish-moss draped oak trees, mysteries skulked hidden in the city's streets. Union General William T. Sherman had spared the city from his burn and pillage orders during his march to the sea from Atlanta for good reason. Gracious stone-fronted townhouses and twenty-two parks provided benches for rest and greenery during each season, complete with flowing fountains. The residents, typifying Southern charm, extended a warm hospitality to visitors, including marauding Yankees.

During their fourth night, as mid-December cooled the air, Eliza and Harrison tarried over an intimate dinner at the restaurant which adjoined their lodgings at the 17Hundred90's Inn. Their eight-week honeymoon was ending. Eliza meant to savor each minute before heading home to Boston in time for Christmas. She discovered the many restaurants' lavish menus offered dishes which titillated their taste buds. This evening's selection boasted the region's finest seafood starting with Oysters Rockefeller, six open-faced oysters topped with spinach, parmesan cheese, and a fiery Cajun cream sauce, then finished with Seafood Neptune, a delectable blend of wild Georgia shrimp and sea scallops, crab cakes drizzled with hollandaise sauce, and autumnal root vegetables on the side.

To top off the bottle of Bordeaux he drank with dinner, Harrison ordered a Campari for Eliza and a cognac for himself. A pianist in the corner of the dining room played familiar sing-alongs from tunes on phonographs across the country. A tinkling of keys started American Quartet's newest favorite, *Everybody Two-Step*. Eliza's Italian boot tapped beneath the white skirted table. Such frivolity. She had never kept the beat to music with Patrick. Harrison felt her foot move and stood up. He spun around on his heel in front of her, the tails of his dinner jacket swinging in a wide arc as the song rounded into its second refrain of the chorus,

> *...Let's two-step and dance in old Havana style*
> *Just act like you were made of rubber, chile*
> *Slide along the floor and slide your feet a little bit*
> *MMM, MMM,...MMM...that's it!*
> *Everybody two step and grab a girly-girl,*
> *Everybody two-step and do the twirly-twirl...*

He bowed before her as he slurred, "Come my girly-girl, let's do a two-step. I shall twirly-twirl you about the room."

The brazen, loud declaration and his tug on her hand sent the four men seated to their left into a roar of laughter and applause. Eliza's neck and cheeks reddened and wilted under a pulp of inner weight. During their travels down the Eastern seaboard, Eliza witnessed glimpses of the insidious effect liquor produced in him. Yet she remained silent, thinking each time the boisterous outburst marked singular lapses of a man on holiday, enjoying his honeymoon before returning to the stress and demands of working for her brothers. Tonight, she would not hold her tongue.

"Harrison, sit down. You're making fools of us."

"C'mon. The music is infectious, and you look so beautiful I want to show you off. There's a light in your face brighter than the glinting moonlight on Newport waves."

Eliza shook her head and blushed again, the earlier red of embarrassment fading. Her glow had nothing to do with the candles on their table, nor the Campari in her glass. Their wedding night consummated eight weeks ago had produced one of her ultimate desires. At thirty-three years old, Eliza Edwards Shaw would become a mother.

"I said no. I'm tired and would like to retire. We've a long trip tomorrow and the train leaves early."

Harrison shoved his chair into the table. The glass of Campari trembled and toppled. Dark red liqueur bled onto the white starched tablecloth. He strode over to the group of four men who had applauded his bold move.

"What say you, gentlemen? Know a spot to find a nightcap in this fine city?"

The most inebriated man rose and clamped his hand on Harrison's shoulder. His Southern drawl bid Harrison into their circle, "Ah, to be sure I do. My son tends bar over at the Pink House. He pours the finest whiskey this side of Appalachia. We're heading there ourselves. Join us...if the missus allows."

Harrison glowered at Eliza.

"Lead the way, my good man."

Eliza stared down at the reddened tablecloth. The stain darkened as the liqueur soaked into a maroon scar. The blemish crept toward the blue enameled cigarette case, a gift from Eliza, which Harrison had left on the table. She retrieved the case before the Campari licked its edges. Gold mounts bracketed the interlaced waves of guilloché engraved into the case's outer sides. A sapphire stone served as its thumbpiece. Imported from St. Petersburg, the gift resembled a flattened Fabergé egg. Turning it over and over, she caressed the smooth enamel, as if another Russian treasure lay in her hand.

Oh, Olga, what have I done?

CHAPTER THIRTY-FOUR

July 1913

The electric fan's wings rotated in a mesmerizing circle. Eliza, transfixed on the motion, willed them to move faster. The breath of breeze hitting her face was as light as a cheek puff. She'd rather have a hurricane force gale; despite the destruction it may bring. Harrison brought the chaise outside to their back patio and positioned it beneath the kitchen windowsill where the fan stood pointing outward. Eliza reclined; the yards of her white maternity dress folded around her like the bolts of cotton fabric they were cut from. Harrison sat across from her this Saturday morning. His cigarette smoke hit the stagnant air and remained trapped in the tight space.

Over the past twelve years, Eliza examined expectant mothers at every stage of their pregnancies. Her hands passed over their bellies, palpating for the life growing inside each month. Now she rubbed her own protruding belly with one hand and fanned herself with the other. The joint efforts of electric and manual fans were no match for the cigarette-laced, heavy July air which suffocated the breaths she struggled to take.

"Oh, here comes one," Eliza said as she pulled the front of her dress taut across the mound. "I'm afraid there's a tumbling act in a vaudeville show in the future with these somersaults."

"If that's his destiny, so be it," said Harrison, a chuckle in his voice as he rose from the chair. "After he finishes Harvard. Then we'll pack up and go on the road with him."

"Or her," Eliza reminded him.

He moved to her side and together they stroked their child. They watched and felt the baby turn-over, seeking a more comfortable position in the crowded corner of Eliza's womb. *That's right, little one,* thought Eliza. *Snuggle in for a couple more weeks until you are safe and content in the best position of all. My arms.*

Harrison bent to kiss the top of her head. Eliza lifted her chin and raised her hand to encircle his neck, pulling him down to her. His lips found hers for a gentle brush before he straightened.

"Where's your mother? I thought she was coming over this morning."

"Out shopping, again. This child will need an armoire larger than yours and mine combined. I've told her hand-me-downs from the nephews and nieces are fine, but Mother won't hear of it," Eliza said.

Upon their arrival in Boston at the end of their honeymoon, Eliza confided in her mother of her suspicion of her pregnancy. Not since her graduation day had she recalled a brighter glow in her mother's face. Eliza knew Laura adored Albie's and Freddy's children, but there was a special, unspoken bond between a mother, her daughter, and her child. A line of motherhood, as strong and vital as the umbilical cord, flowed unbroken between them.

"Do you think she'll be much longer? I don't want to leave you alone."

Eliza looked toward the black satchel on the flagstones. "You do recall, I've delivered a fair number of babies? I can deliver by myself, like a pioneer woman in a buckboard. Go along. I know you need to warm-up before a match."

She watched him leave, his tennis bag slung over his shoulder. His wiry body from the back was slender and straight like a cucumber. Eliza peered down at her watermelon bulk. She wiggled her hidden toes to make sure they were still there.

. . .

The click of the wrought-iron gate woke Eliza from her doze. Annoyed by the sound, she squirmed in the chaise. Uninterrupted sleep had become as rare as a robin in the Boston Common in January. With a grunt, she swung her legs over the edge and pushed up to sit. Waking always woke her bladder. Or her bladder caused her to awaken. Either way, the constant need to urinate became tiresome. She reached into her bag as her mother walked onto the patio, her arms laden with Filene's boxes.

"Did you leave anything for the rest of Boston's new babies?" Eliza asked, withdrawing her stethoscope.

Laura sat in the chair next to Eliza, "Only the layette pieces not as beautiful as these."

As Laura held up each item for approval, Eliza grinned as she fit the earpieces in her ears and positioned the bell part on the hardest spot of her belly she located with her fingers. She gestured for the fashion show to halt. Monitoring the second hand of her wristwatch, she counted, listening for the muffled beat...*one hundred and twenty-five, one hundred and twenty-six, one hundred and twenty-seven.*

"Everything all right?" Laura said when Eliza returned the stethoscope to her bag.

"Right on the button."

Laura exhaled, "Wonderful. But I hope you've toned down this obsession."

Her obsession, her mother deemed it, was only a medical professional assessing the well-being of a baby, even if she checked the fetal heartbeat almost every waking hour. Trained experiences shaped her concerns over complications which may arise. She hadn't told her mother about the day two months ago she phoned Harrison at work to bring her to Boston Lying-In. She had sensed no movement in three hours and while her heart rate raced and pounded in her chest, the baby's had dropped to ninety beats per minute. Within twenty minutes, all was back to normal, and the hospital sent her home with instructions to stop her worrying.

"I'm not obsessed, Mother. Just cautious."

"Overly cautious, I think. You must worry less," said Laura. "Your stress isn't good for the baby. We don't want her to arrive anxious from day one. This time, your training is not helping. *For with much wisdom comes much sorrow; the more knowledge, the more grief*—Ecclesiastes 1:18."

Eliza rolled her eyes and looked to the heavens; Bible quotes wouldn't quell her fears. "Can you help me up, please? I need the toilet. Again."

•   •   •

Two weeks later and five days earlier than expected, Eliza joined the ranks of her patients. While she hoped Olga, Charlotte, or Edith would deliver her, she understood their commitments in Philadelphia. Olga's husband, Samuel, was failing, his senility worsening. The prison appointed Charlotte chief surgeon for all inmates, male and female. And the phones rang hourly at Edith's Board of Health office, where she fielded urgent demands for placements in the state's tuberculosis sanitariums. None of them could afford time off to travel to Boston for a date that might fall anytime within a three-week window. Eliza requested a female graduate of the Boston University of Medicine, but hospitals created their schedules and assignments according to their needs, not when a patient began her labor.

Dr. Henry Davies stood at the base of Eliza's hospital bed as the final pushing phase began. She summoned forth every utterance she remembered from delivery rooms in West Philadelphia. From the wails of Nina Silvestri's "Aaaaiiiiiiis," to the screams of Adrienne's "Dear Mother of God," to every other curse and saint she had heard called out and called upon.

"Mrs. Shaw," said Dr. Davies, "I think it's time you take the chloroform. No need to be a hero or martyr."

Eliza winced and bit down on the rag between her teeth as another contraction rolled back, ready to crash forward. She yanked the rag from her mouth. "No."

"You don't strike me as a Bible-thumper. No need to atone for Eve's sins. It'll make you feel much better, and it will help me perform my job here."

With one of the spare ounces of energy she had left, she waved him off. How could she ever deliver another woman now that she was a maternity patient herself and not feel the entire experience? From the first butterfly flutter at sixteen weeks, to the sleepless nights and worry-filled days, to the strange desire for melon slices at breakfast, lunch, and dinner, to the tempest now roiling inside her womb, she embraced each nuance and nuisance of pregnancy. When she returned to practice, she could treat her patients with the truest form of not just sympathy, but empathy as well. With the contraction completed, Eliza panted, "Please, is she crowning yet? Check the cord. Where is it?"

"Please calm yourself. I'm delivering this baby, Mrs. Shaw. Not you."

Another surge built. She pressed down from the tip of her cranium to the nail on her pinky toe. Beads of sweat streamed down the side of her face. She squeezed her eyes shut and prayed, and prayed, and prayed. There was nothing else she could do.

On August 7, 1913, at 8:03 pm, Eliza Edwards Shaw's prayers were answered. The most perfect being in her world, William "Will" Harrison Shaw, six pounds and eight ounces, twenty inches, her child, lay in her arms.

CHAPTER THIRTY-FIVE

May 1915

A white cotton sock, balled into a tight wad, shot into the sky. Freed from the prison of socks and shoes, stubby toes wiggled and dug into the soft spring earth. A cry of delight rang through the air. The toddler watched a breeze pick up the sock and carry it over the lagoon before it landed among lily pad flowers. He grunted and pushed himself up. With ten months of experience, he walked toward the pond.

Eliza sat by the water's edge in the Public Garden, staring over the carriage parked next to her. The mid-afternoon sun glinted off the chrome handle and blinded her sight. Her mind, however, had darkened a week ago. Headlines blazed again with tragic news of a ship's sinking. German U-boats torpedoed the *RMS Lusitania*, sending it and twelve hundred crew and passengers to murky depths off the southern coast of Ireland. Rescuers brought the survivors to the nearest port in County Cork: Queenstown, last known address of Patrick Callaghan. Three years passed since his letter. Nearly three years also passed since she had used her doctoring skills. Now she was Mrs. Shaw or Mama.

A shrill shout startled Eliza from her gloomy thoughts. She shielded her eyes, looking for the voice. An elderly woman on the gravel path pointed to the lagoon. A boy waded forward up to his knees toward a wayward sock.

"Will!" Eliza screamed, jumped from the bench, and ran to the pond. She scooped him up, his arms and legs flailing and shaking water drops, quacking like a captured duckling. This wasn't the first time she had held him in a vise grip. By the grace of God, he hadn't figured out how to wrangle free, yet. As soon as Will learned to walk, he discovered he preferred moving to sitting. Flowers and leaves awaited picking. Balls and cats needed chasing. Kites, and apparently socks, could fly away for escapades.

Eliza's unexpected shriek woke the baby. At seven months, Edward "Teddy" Shaw had pulled himself up to sit and check out the world beyond blankets and stuffed animals. His brother's activity always provided a source of amusement.

The writhing Will kicked his legs against Eliza's hips. "Down. Down."

"If I put you down, you must stay right next to Teddy's carriage and not move an inch. You are not a duckling. No going in the pond. Where are your shoes?"

She checked the carriage before reaching for the wayward shoes. Teddy grabbed the carriage's edges and rocked himself back and forth.

"Oh, no you don't. This is not the day you stand up."

God help her when Teddy shadowed his brother in antics and actions. This was the reason most women had babies in their late teens or twenties. She would never keep up with them. She was outnumbered and out of energy. Energy levels, however, had been the least of her worries when she became pregnant. At thirty-three, Eliza knew the medical risks for herself and her baby. When Will showed signs of normal physical and mental development, her fears eased enough to consider another quick pregnancy to give him a sibling. Fourteen months later, they celebrated Teddy's arrival. Her sons, when they weren't trying to swim in a lagoon or escape from a carriage, brought her the love and joy which had been missing from her life. Thankful for two healthy children, she wouldn't tempt the Fates and try for a third. Before Teddy rolled over, Eliza prescribed herself a contraceptive. She used the pessary on the nights she didn't refuse her husband.

Will squatted at his mother's feet and quacked.

Clever boy. Will already inherited the quick wit of his father and knew how to use it, like Harrison, when he wanted to charm her.

• • •

A bang echoed through the foyer as the doorknob smashed into the wall. As a girl, Eliza would rush to the sound of heavy doors swinging open, excited to greet her brothers. When Albie and Freddy came home, they brought masked affections for their sister. They wouldn't admit they enjoyed spending time with her, rolling their eyes and feigning interest in recaps of life at home with the aunts. But she knew. She knew they loved her and to this day, watched over her and cared for her as a father would. Albie, who led the Edwards Wool Company, financed her trip to Newport to escape the reminders of Patrick. He helped her and Harrison secure the townhouse blocks away from his own. Freddy maintained a routine dropping by every Tuesday for a tussle with Will and another stuffed animal for Teddy.

The grandfather clock in the drawing room chimed seven times, an early night for Harrison. Eliza hoped it was a two-Scotch dinner. Two-Scotch dinners meant a better chance that a jovial, witty, and charming Harrison might stride through the door. She needed the genial Harrison for the discussion she wanted to have with him, not the irritable Harrison, or the five-Scotch, belligerent Harrison.

Eliza tried to understand his logic the first few times she expressed her dismay over his intoxicated, ugly entrances. He reminded her of the words Freddy read at their wedding, "Love covers over a multitude of sins." Wives must forgive and overlook lapses caused by the influence of alcohol. The most successful business deals, he bellowed, happened over beefsteak dinners, not stuffy offices and as many rounds of drinks as it took to secure ink on a paper. As war in Europe escalated, the demand for woolen uniforms continued to rise. British factories scaled back their production and lost workers to trenches and graves in France. But mills in New England churned out and shipped hundreds of thousands of uniforms as quick as they found ships to transport them. When the *Lusitania* sank, newspapers predicted it wouldn't be much longer before the United States' War Department would place uniform orders, too. Contracts landed daily on Harrison's desk. He intended to sign as many as possible to ensure his percentage would secure his right to a seat at those beefsteak dinners, membership at The Country Club golf course and the Longwood Tennis club, and his own cottage in Newport.

With limited hours together, tonight would be Eliza's rare chance to speak with him. On workdays, he left before she dressed herself and her sons. Weeknights brought card games and dinners with government and business associates. Eliza preferred to not think of the evenings when he came home after eleven o'clock with hints of cheap perfume on his coat. With late spring, canvas tarps came off the courts at Longwood for endless tennis matches on Saturdays and Sundays. Saturday nights included social commitments with the same circle of associates and their wives when the men continued their talk of business and war and the women shared upcoming summer plans for Cape Cod, Newport, and Bar Harbor. Sundays spent with her family were not the place for a conversation between a married couple.

Despite the hour, the severity of the door bang signaled at least a three-Scotch night. Most nights like this she retreated to the spare bedroom.

"You're home early," Eliza said as he neared the trolley table of liquor bottles.

"Representative Gifford took the seven o'clock train to Washington. I've a qualifying match tomorrow morning. I need a good ten hours tonight."

As he turned to start up the stairs, tumbler in hand, Eliza rose from her chair.

"Should be a nice day tomorrow, perhaps I'll leave the boys with Mother and come watch."

"You know Will is a runner. Your Mother can't keep tabs on him anymore, best you stay home."

Eliza bristled at his words. She stayed home for two-and-a-half years, to be exact, by her choice. She wouldn't be told when to stay home. "Would you give me five minutes?" she asked.

•   •   •

Buried memories of Patrick and her work in Philadelphia surfaced during her afternoon daydream in the park. Patrick may never return, but there was a way to return to her other passion, medical work. The Denison House, where Florence taught painting, needed to expand its medical clinic operation. In the past year, before navies seized steamers and established blockades, immigrants from southern and eastern Europe teemed onto ships and into ports like Boston as they fled the encroaching reaches of the German army.

Beyond seeing up to ten patients a day, Denison added evening clinics for laborers to come after work for treatment of minor injuries. Further reports of home visits to some patients revealed that housing intended for one family sheltered four to eight. The cramped quarters created fetid conditions of squalor, which led Denison's governing board to deem the health and integrity of the children who lived there at risk. Mothers required training in cleanliness, prenatal, and baby care. Florence suggested Eliza lead classes on Mondays and Wednesdays.

Eliza mulled the idea over for three days. Will and Teddy grew before her eyes. Faster than a cat pouncing on mice in a tenement alley, they would be off to school for most of their day and she would be home, alone, in a large, empty house. Unlike most women, she never developed an interest in painting, needlework, or flower arranging. She enjoyed reading, but there were only so many minutes she might hide behind the fictional lives of characters on a page. Further, expectations for Mrs. Harrison Shaw kept her tied to her mother's versions of a fairy-tale ending while Dr. Eliza Edwards had walked away from the pages and lived a true life.

The instructional position was available now. Not in three years when Will started school. Her sons needed a mother's care. She scoffed at Harrison's suggestion they hire a baby nurse when Teddy came along on the heels of Will. An outsider would not tend to her sons. She would manage, thank you very much. How could she tell him she wanted to abandon them to satisfy her own desires?

Florence pointed out six hours a week was hardly abandonment, and an outsider wouldn't watch the children. She would schedule the classes for the afternoons. Eliza's mother would babysit, assisted by Bessie to chase down Will during his escapes. The boys would be fine with their grandmother and cousin, and Dr. Edwards would be an ideal choice as an instructor. A doctor and a mother were the rarest gem.

"The position sounds perfect," Eliza said to Florence. "But I'm not sure how Harrison will react. In Newport, he admired my passion and how I cared for Bea. He was supportive of my initial plan to join Boston Lying-In until I got pregnant. But now that I'm the mother, he's asserted this is my profession and I should be attentive to caring for the needs of my family."

Florence waved her hand, brushing Eliza's words from the air between them, "Tommy rot. When have you ever let anyone, or anything triumph over your passion? Everything you want–and I mean everything–children and work, is on the other side of your concerns. Jump over the worry fence and tell–don't ask–Harrison, you intend to take the job."

• • •

From the stairs, Harrison turned on his heel at Eliza's request. She sat on the sofa, her cream linen dress falling midway to her shins. Her face, a perfect oval with expressive eyes, radiated a homey warmth. Two babies and the advanced age of thirty-six years had not diminished her beauty.

"Do you need me to extend the credit account at Gilchrist's? We have the Forbes next week if you need a new dress," said Harrison.

Did he think the dresses she wore to take care of babies would be her choice for a dinner party at an exclusive Louisburg Square address? Eliza steeled herself. His mind centered on domestic affairs and societal expectations, looking presentable on his arm. The fear fence loomed in front of her like a white steeplechase hurdle. She called forth the strength she had summoned years ago when she spoke to her mother about Woman's Medical.

"I haven't forgotten the dinner. You needn't worry about my gown. I'm informing you that Mother and Bessie will be here tomorrow afternoon in the off chance you come home early. They'll be minding the boys. I'll be at Denison House with Florence. There's a volunteer position available–a medical position. I have an interview at four."

"Will you now? How noble of you, Eliza. Seeing to the rats who live in filthy slums rather than care for your own children, leaving them with an old woman and a little girl."

His point made, he turned back to the staircase.

"Harrison. It's six hours a week teaching classes. I won't be visiting patients in their homes. My mother is not frail and senile, and Bessie is almost nine. She'll love reading to them and helping

Will learn his letters and numbers. Denison needs my experience and I need to do more than stroll through gardens pushing carriages. I'm telling you, not asking for your permission."

He shrugged, calling over his shoulder, "Do whatever you want. Just make sure you don't neglect my children or sicken them from the filth you may bring home."

She dismissed his absurd directives and landed on the other side of the fence, triumphant.

CHAPTER THIRTY-SIX

October 1916

Every so often stars aligned as they did this week in late October. As Eliza waved goodbye to Harrison, Olga arrived on a parallel track at Boston's South Station. The trains swapped out a husband and brought in a friend.

In Harrison's briefcase, file folders of contracts bulged with terms and conditions for the Edwards Wool Company to supply uniforms to British and French forces. Battles near the Somme River and in Verdun had raged for months. The death toll extended into hundreds of thousands. Representatives for both countries beseeched the United States War Department to assist in any form it could muster, even if it were uniforms to replace those buried with their wearers.

Olga's valise contained a handful of slim, sixteen-page pamphlets to aid American citizens with a different war which persisted in grand townhouses and tenement apartments alike: a woman's right to decide whether or not to become pregnant. Recently, hushed whispers spread among various women's groups of a guidebook detailing birth control options within a woman's grasp. The *Family Limitations* pamphlet was only available from a family-planning clinic in Brooklyn. Olga's visit to Boston included a lay-over in Brooklyn to obtain a copy. It was the most covert and least likely means of violating the Comstock Laws, which prohibited mailing Obscene Literature and Articles of Immoral Use.

•   •   •

Eliza shook her hands to stimulate blood to her cramped fingers. Two stacks of papers, one in English and one in Russian, covered the dining room table. Emboldened by Fearless Florence's suffrage work, Eliza dedicated her efforts for women's rights where she would make the greatest impact, through education on ways to prevent an unwanted pregnancy. Sharing tips copied from the *Family Limitations* pamphlet was the first step.

"This should be enough," Eliza said.

"Dah–yes." Olga slipped into a heavy Russian accent, summoned forward from memory. Eliza needed a translator for the special mothers' class she planned today at Denison House in the South Cove.

In recent years, Boston's Irish and Italian families moved out of South Cove, across the Fort Point channel to South Boston and to the north side of the city, taking their Catholicism with them. Eliza had no desire to rankle the priests of Patrick Callaghan's faith who preached using contraception subverted the natural course of conception. To them, contraception was a pagan belief leading to higher rates of prostitution, promiscuity, sterility, and insanity.

She refused to bow to accusations of being a pagan or heretic, like the women in Salem over two hundred years ago. Instead, she planned to inform women who didn't answer to a Catholic church. They were the newer immigrants of Boston: Jews who hailed from Syria and Russia, Greeks and Armenians, and an increasing Chinese population. The immigrant women of South Cove were also the poorest. They were the ones who begged for her help while they delivered a sixth, seventh, or eighth child. These mothers struggled to feed and clothe the children they already had. If they learned how to prevent a pregnancy, they wouldn't have to try to nurse them through fevers, which shook their feeble bodies and left them crippled or lifeless, and in need of a coffin they couldn't afford.

If mothers controlled their bodies, they controlled their future and their children's. They would achieve a new height in women's rights, even without the vote. The suffragist, Elizabeth Cady Stanton, didn't have contraception in mind when she stated: *Nothing adds such dignity to character as the recognition of one's self-sovereignty.* But, in that phrase, Eliza found a quiet direction for her mission.

Male doctors abhorred birth control and opposed what they called the vulgarity of many of the methods. Further, their conservative manner kept them from speaking plainly with a female patient, let alone show her how to use a douche, or fit her with an appropriate-sized pessary. But a woman doctor who used them herself, could, someone like Dr. Eliza Edwards Shaw. She would begin with the Russian mothers. Class began at two o'clock sharp.

"Here's my mother to watch the boys," Eliza said, moving a pile of pamphlets into her bag when she heard the front door open.

"Will you grab the rest?" she asked Olga.

• • •

"I think it went well. Did you hear any chatter?" Eliza said as she walked among the wooden chairs. A few of her hand-copied tip sheets remained on chairs, others were tucked under blankets in baby baskets or into skirt pockets. Eliza put the rest inside brown wrapping and stowed them in her doctor's bag. There would be more chances to distribute them to the women she met.

"Once the tittering stopped," Olga said. "They seemed interested in each method. Mrs. Davydov wants to try a calendar. She's been tracking along in her head but keeps getting the days mixed up. Is Day One the first day her menses starts, or when it stops?"

"Excellent point. Can you speak with her tomorrow and tell her? Maybe we can get a hold of pocket calendars, too."

Any aid which might help, Eliza would explore, right down to free calendars available from local druggists.

"They'd be a good start, but there's their home life to consider," Olga continued. "Most husbands won't wear a condom and withdrawals are too much effort on his part. Douching may be impossible for women in line with twenty other families for a turn in a bathtub, if her building even has a tub. Plus, I find the Lysol soap used with the douches is vile, with the burning it leaves and its horrid cresol scent."

"Perhaps we should show them another use of their clothespins," said Eliza, thinking back to Olga's trick for getting through pathology lab.

"Ha! There'd be a lot of empty clotheslines in Boston! The pessaries are the best options. Their husbands won't be any the wiser. But they must figure out how to find a private spot to insert it. Imagine the queues outside water closets. Snaked down and around a hallway every evening before bedtime. There's the cost, too."

Eliza's cheeks bloomed at Olga's suggestion of the pessary, or womb veil. Without Harrison's knowledge, she chose one after Teddy's birth. She figured with the course she was on having two children within three years, she might bear ten more before her mother-gone stage. The $1.50 purchase at Liggett's drugstore didn't deter Eliza. A woman from the South Cove, however, couldn't ask her day-laborer husband for half a day's wages to purchase an item to give her control over their marital relations. Eliza's eyes narrowed, lost in a trance of thought. With a quick snap of her fingers, she gestured to Olga to wait.

"Perhaps we could collect an extra dime from each donor at the next suffrage meeting. We'd be raising funds to support women with a personal liberty. They'd recognize the benefits of educating and helping our poorest mothers."

"You always have a plan, don't you? But what about you? Harrison is getting worse. You should stop being so ignorant, I hate seeing you unhappy," Olga said.

Olga's words hammered against the walls. "You don't understand, Olga. There is no simple choice. I wish I could figure out a plan which would be best for me and my boys. But for now, his frequent Washington trips help," said Eliza.

"Divorce is becoming more acceptable. Look at Alva Vanderbilt. She's fine. Discarding disagreeable husbands is as easy as taking out the trash, which is where ones like Harrison belong."

Eliza bristled at her closest friend's blunt statements. Hearing his faults from someone else made them open and real. "I've never heard you speak like this before."

Olga bent down to pick up a stray tip sheet. She turned it over to read out-loud to Eliza the last sentence, "Only ignorance and indifference will cause one to be careless in this most important matter."

She pushed the sheet with the teachings for women to take control of their lives into Eliza's hand. "I've been quiet for too long. During the drawn-out Patrick ordeal, I said nothing. I should have said something, and I'm sorry. With Harrison, I asked you if you were sure and you ignored me. Now I hear of his drinking and insensitivity, which is destroying you. I want you to have what I had with Samuel. Your boys, too. They deserve a role model who loves and respects his wife and makes her happy."

Eliza tucked the last sheet into her bag with the rest and atop the envelope of other papers she kept close, including her favorite poem,

For there is no friend like a sister in calm or stormy weather;
To cheer one on the tedious way,
To fetch one if one goes astray,
To lift one if one totters down,
To strengthen whilst one stands.

Christina Rossetti wrote astute words. Olga Povitzky McGuire spoke them. Eliza Edwards Shaw knew they were true.

CHAPTER THIRTY-SEVEN

July 1918

Harrison grasped the glass and raised it in an upward arced motion. The amber liquid sloshed inside the crystal tumbler. A single ice cube clinked against the sides. How many times had he instructed Eliza best not to dilute the Scotch with too many cubes?

"A toast to the end."

Eliza marked her page in *My Ántonia*. The electric bulb under the lamp's globe found the thin strands of gray blended into her darkened auburn hair.

"Harrison, what a dreadful statement at a moment like this."

He picked up the cigarette case on the table and pressed the thumbpiece. Crammed inside lay nine white soldiers. The Chesterfield ad may claim *They satisfy*, but for Harrison Shaw, complete satisfaction came from a Turkish tobacco in one hand and a glass of aged malt Scotch in the other.

"I meant the Scotch. This is my last bottle. The way these damn Prohibitionists are gathering steam, it might be our last. I guess shipping off to France has a silver lining. Barrels and barrels of rich Bordeaux. The French may not be the best soldiers, but they aren't fools."

Tomorrow morning, Harrison Shaw, age thirty-four, married, and father of two young sons, would report to Boston's Naval Yard as a Field Secretary with the American Expeditionary Forces.

He and thousands of other men would march up the gangplanks of the *USS America*, bound for Europe to defeat the barbarous Huns of Germany. Crowded shoulder to shoulder, each soldier would wear a uniform and pack a blanket in his duffle bag, both manufactured in the Lowell mills of the Edwards Wool Company.

Thus, six years after the *Titanic* crashed into an iceberg, Eliza found herself on the verge of another disaster. A third man in her life would board a Europe-bound ship. Aunt Josephine with her old-fashioned superstitions, *God bless her soul*, would have reminded her bad luck comes in threes. At the cusp of her birth, Eliza's father sailed to England and returned to the family in a wooden box, never to know his daughter. On the threshold of marriage, Patrick Callaghan left for Ireland, never to return and meet her at the end of a wedding aisle. Today, Harrison would head to France. Would the evils in Europe claim number three?

Would it be more likely a superstition came true because one desired it? Had life with Harrison become so miserable she dared to imagine him never returning? And then there was Will and Teddy. Should they grow up fatherless like Eliza and her brothers? Not because their father's heart failed, but because hers had.

"I wish you would reconsider," said Eliza. "You're not a soldier and you're older than the conscription age. And you're a father. Your sons need you."

"I won't discuss this again. I have told you. General Wood reiterated that the War Department needs more men. Soon enough, the Selective Service will raise the age to anyone under forty-five. If I go now, there's a better chance of a non-combat position. Further, I can't claim an exemption any longer for states-side work. We've inked all the available contracts and retained a large share of manufacturing rights as long as the demand holds for uniforms and blankets."

He surveyed the liquor trolley table. From the array of brown, amber, and clear liquids, he selected the brandy decanter to pour a fresh glass of the night-cap comfort choice.

"We'll be extremely comfortable. Most of all, how can I have Will and Teddy see me sailing in Newport while our mill workers and my fellow countrymen sit in trenches across France? Soldiers in mud and water up to their thighs, bayonets, and guns in their hands, and me with a tennis racket in mine? My sons deserve a father who believes in his country and honors what it asks of him."

•　•　•

Four legs stuck ramrod straight out on the back seat of Albie's car, too short to bend at the seat's edge. The hem of blue and white striped gabardine shorts and the tops of white socks exposed bony knees.

"Will, Teddy, look. There's Daddy's ship." Eliza patted knees on either side of her and directed her sons' attention out the car's open window.

Four brown-tie shoes stilled their clockwise and counterclockwise rotation.

Will, weeks before his fifth birthday, resembled Harrison. Medium brown hair, a slender nose, and brown eyes which focused hawk-like whenever he espied a new adventure. He loved to run. His sturdy legs were strong and ready for tennis courts and any other sporting activity his father tossed his way.

Teddy held a copy of the newest Thornton Burgess book in his chubby three-year-old hands. His long eyelashes fluttered over blue eyes as he stared down at the smiling squirrel on the book's cover. His red hair combed and slicked with a dab of his father's hair oil to wrestle down the cowlick.

"Yes, boys," Harrison called over his shoulder, "The USS America. A well-chosen name for a ship, don't you think?"

The gun-metal hulk with two centered steam stacks floated, tethered to the piers of the Charlestown Navy Yard, across the mouth of the Charles River from Boston. In the streets leading to the Yard, a mass of tan swarmed as if dust from the Great Plains blew eastward carrying bits of the heartland. Those pieces of America's heart carried duffle bags slung from shoulders. Pictures of sweethearts, mothers, wives, and children traveled with them, tucked into pockets for safe keeping. Broad-brimmed hats dipped low over brows, shading their eyes from the blazing July sun. The men pushed forward, straining to reach the *America's* gangplank, fortified by the irony that their transport ship was the former German passenger liner, *Amerika*. US authorities seized it when war broke out in Europe. Omens for victory abounded with their departure planned for days after the Fourth of July celebration and from the birthplace of the American Revolution.

Albie slowed the car, "That's as close as I can get. You'll have to walk from here. Troop training starts now."

"That'll be fine, thank you. Everyone out. We'll have our goodbyes here," commanded Harrison as he opened the rear door.

Will jumped off the seat and went to his father's side, standing in his shadow. Harrison reached for Eliza's hand. She turned toward Teddy, who nestled into her lap, burrowing his head into her chest. His nose bumped against the card pinned to her breast, imprinted with BELGIAN BABIES, adorned with red, black, and gold ribbons. The florets tied to the ribbons tickled the tip of his nose, and he giggled. Eliza nudged him to quiet.

"Teddy, come along dear. Time to say bye-bye to Daddy."

"Let him stay. He's too young to understand, anyway."

Harrison turned to his older son, "I'm counting on you to pick up my slack and cheer on Big Babe for me. He had a wallop of a homer yesterday. Make sure our Red Sox keep first place, okay? Maybe your uncles will take you to a game before you head off to Newport. What do you say, Albie?"

"I think we can manage a game or two," Albie winked at his nephew.

"And Will," Harrison said, "I'll need you to buck up and take care of your mother and brother while Daddy is away on his grand adventure. Will you do that for me?"

Will stood in awe of his father, dressed for the first time in his Army uniform. The nap of the wool brushed free of wrinkles. The stand-up collar buttoned tight. A bar pinned above the left breast pocket signified a Field Secretary rank. Will raised his fingers to his brow and saluted, "Yes, sir."

"Atta, boy," Harrison returned the salute.

He dropped his voice to speak to Eliza, "While I'm gone, you need to stop this work with Florence. Those tenements are getting more dangerous every day. Yesterday's *Globe* wrote of strikes by cigar makers and garment and jewelry workers. Someone needs to deal with these unions soon. With decent men joined up, what's left is a bunch of no-goods, hanging around the street corners, or lolling in the bars and rolling home stinkin' drunk."

Eliza almost said *like you?* but smothered her argumentative words. The man was going off to war.

"There are plenty of hospitals for their women. They should know how to care for their babies. I don't want you mingling with them and their filth."

His caustic remarks chafed. She enjoyed teaching her mother and baby classes. They gave her another purpose beyond Will and Teddy. Since the war department called up more doctors, Eliza added more responsibilities. In the evenings, she tended to adults with a wide variety of complaints, from applying antiseptic to infected rat bites to confirming that a stomachache and weight gain was a pregnancy.

"These are your last words to me? Condemning my work?" said Eliza.

Before he could counter, she rose on her toes and brushed his cheek with her lips in a gesture expected of a woman sending her man into battle. For now, her sons needed to see an act of civility between their parents. It may be the last time they saw them together.

CHAPTER THIRTY-EIGHT

September 1918

The *Globe's* front page resembled a telephone directory with lists
of surnames and hometowns. But no one wanted to find names of
New England men in this listing–*the United States Army List of
Casualties: Killed in Action, Wounded Severely, Wounded,
Missing in Action.*

Eliza read the page aloud to her mother and Florence each
evening as a somber end to their day. After the reading, they
prayed for those lost and that tomorrow would pass without
Western Union delivering a telegram for Mrs. Harrison Shaw
which would open with, *The Secretary of War Desires to Express
His Deep Regrets.* At each rap on her door, Eliza held her breath,
waiting for the prophecy of threes to materialize.

Most nights, Florence teared as a familiar name connected to
the settlement houses fell from Eliza's lips. A father, a brother, or
a son. A black shawl and veiled hat became Florence's daily attire
in deference to the families she would visit the next day. Two
managers from the Edwards Wool Company appeared a week
ago, brothers who insisted on assignment to the same troop which
put them on the same battlefield at the same time.

"None tonight?" Eliza asked.

"Thanks be to God, no," said Florence, her gritted teeth relaxed.

Eliza scanned the headlines, "Here's some wonderful news. *Americans Capture 20,000.* They must be succeeding with those types of numbers, don't you think?"

Laura reclined on the green velvet divan. Her wrinkled hands clasped in her lap, her eyelids fluttering, her head bobbing with slight jerks. She shook herself from her dozing, "I should say so. On this encouraging note, I'm going to bed. I'm getting too old to chase those bundles of energy you call your sons through the Public Garden."

"I'll ask Albie tomorrow if Bertie can spare an afternoon," Eliza said. "The kids would love a romp with their big cousin."

Eliza turned the broad-sheet pages. Filene's Store advertised fall hats and coats in its children's department, priced from $7.50 to $45. A child's coat for forty-five dollars should have mink collars at that price! Will would be a size six this winter; he seemed to outgrow every stitch of clothing in a matter of weeks. She made a mental note to take him to Filene's on Saturday and have Teddy try on Will's outgrown tweeds. Before she knew it, they'd both be in long trousers, they were growing up too fast for her liking.

The page-one column subtitled, *Gives Allies Much Better Base for Future Operations*, ran onto page twelve. A bold-print title buried below the war story caught her attention. *Sees No Cause for Alarm.* What else could alarm at this point?

1,000 Cases of Spanish Influenza in Camp Devens Now. The reporter who traveled to the camp in Ayer, Massachusetts, interviewed the camp's division surgeon, Lieutenant Colonel McCornack. *There is no cause for alarm. We are getting our share of a disease that is making the rounds. It is nothing more than the grippe, unpleasant, but in no way serious if due care is exercised.*

Eliza's training and intuition told her Doctor McCornack misstated the facts. A thousand cases were not a trivial outbreak. A new battle raged fifty miles away, in Boston's backyard.

· · ·

The next morning, Eliza phoned Camp Devens to speak with Dr. McCornack. Two days later, she stood at the ward's entrance, steadfast as any soldier awaiting orders. The mask over her opened mouth hid her astonishment, but her eyes betrayed her. Round and unbelieving, they moved across the room, over and down, multiplying columns and rows of beds. In a ward meant for sixty patients, two hundred were jammed in. Cots and stretchers occupied every available spot. Bloody sputum and mucus drips stained the white starched sheets beneath the men's heads. Manic, fevered bodies begged nurses for water. Moans drifted through the wards, interrupted by hoarse, hacking coughs.

Eliza shuddered as each cough rose from the depths of clogged chests. At this battle front, no trenches, nor barbed wire blocked the enemy. The Spanish influenza attacked the ward, its casualties marked with bluish complexions, punctuated with purple blisters. The blue pallor showed a lack of oxygen in the blood as the heart and lungs failed. Death would come within hours to snatch another victim. The deceased list of hundreds named Killed in Action would grow by one.

Four nurses flitted from bed to bed, each attending to fifty cases. Caps sat askew as they pushed aside loose hairs with the back of their arms to keep their germ-streaked hands away from wearied and saddened faces. The odor of camphor oil hung heavily, competing with vapors from the Vicks ointment rubbed on chests to ease congestion. Combined, the odors clouded the air, adding to the oppression.

Next to Eliza, Dr. Victor Vaughan, Surgeon General of the U.S. Army, gestured in a sweeping motion. His sturdy frame sagged with the weight of the cases in front of them. The ends of his mustache drooped in an arc, echoing his frown. "Dr. Edwards–or is it Mrs. Shaw?"

"Dr. Edwards is fine, sir. Thank you."

His voice, defeated and low, acknowledged the scene. "We've reached a crisis state. The strain we are dealing with is invincible. Our biochemists have yet to identify an effective vaccine. We tried flushing their systems with fluids, but the risk of edema is too high for lungs already over-taxed. We focus on supportive care."

"Well, thank heavens for the nursing staff," she said.

Eliza surveyed the two women closest to the entrance. One sponged the peach-fuzzed face of a soldier, the other spooned warm broth into blue-tinted lips of another. Strong, brave women tending to near-corpses. "Are they capable? They look quite young."

Vaughan held a clipboard in his gnarled fingers, arthritic from years of tedious surgical work. "We've sent over 9,000 American nurses to France this year. Our regular staff is working fourteen-hour shifts. We needed help from the nursing schools. The girls here are managing, but it's a tragedy their first on-the-job experience is working in these death wards."

Nurses handled patient comfort and diagnoses appeared to be as simple as looking at a man's blue face. Would they require more physicians?

"How can I help?" she said.

"Our professional duties are minimal and much the same as the nurses who need supervision for the best approach to palliative care. I'm sad to say the most demanding task for doctors is to pronounce the deceased and sign toe tags. We wrote sixty-three of them yesterday."

So be it. Eliza hefted her medical bag to her hip, a constant companion for seventeen years. "Where shall I change, sir?"

•　•　•

Besides breaking to use the ladies' room twice and to nibble on two Lorna Doones a nurse shared with her, Eliza's day blurred into a catatonic haze. She could scarcely remember a single name of the men she attended, nor the eight whose names she penned onto death certificates and toe tags. Since leaving West Philadelphia, she could recall at least twenty-five women and most of their babies, too. If she remembered the soldiers' names, would they live? Did blocking their names erase their existence?

Eliza checked her watch while she sat outside Dr. Vaughan's office. 6:50 p.m. The summer sky remained bright outside with the Daylight-Saving Law passed in March. Yet, the narrow windows denied the sunlight. Darkness prevailed.

Starting in her heart, fatigue claimed her body. A throb in her temples spread to a twitch in her fingers. Eliza knew exhaustion on a first-name basis. Over her career, it visited her often, made itself at home and settled into her bones. But this debilitation consumed her unlike any other time. Her life classified fatigue into physical or emotional. Exam study, double shifts at the hospital, and looking after two energetic sons required physical exertion. The heartbreak of losing Patrick, cradling a dying patient's hand, dealing with Harrison's volatility, or concern over her children's health drove emotional exhaustion. Here, she fought a simultaneous battle. Hour after hour she tended to patients. She lifted their limbs, walked the rows in an endless loop like Will's train set, and carried trays of water and salves. Her arms and legs numbed. Men died; not one, not two, but eight over the course of nine hours. The enormity of it drained every fiber of her verve. A helpless anguish seized control.

Eliza rubbed her throbbing forehead with hands reddened from constant scrubbing as she disinfected any exposed part of her body. The journey back to Boston would take two hours as night crept over the single lane highway. Inexperience as a driver worried her that she might injure herself or hit someone else. If she dared the drive, she would arrive past the boys' bedtime. Her mother would have her hands full. Teddy would ask for one more chapter of *The Adventures of Happy Jack*. Will would build another wall for his fortress with his Lincoln Logs, pleading, Five more minutes?

"Dr. Edwards?" Dr. Vaughan opened the office door and stepped into the dimly lit hallway.

She jumped to her feet. "Yes, sir. I wanted to check in with you before you left. Have you drawn up this week's schedule? If you'll have me, I'd like to add my name for as long as you need help."

"I'll be happy to enlist your services. You did a fine job today with the right measure of firmness with the nurses and accuracy with your documents. I didn't notice you falter once."

Dr. Vaughan paused. "I daresay our wards resemble or come close to scenes after a battle. You managed remarkably well for someone who has limited work beyond a maternity ward. Your family, though. Your husband's in France and you have young children? You know the contagion risk is high."

She ignored his remark about her experience and focused on his validation. With her confidence raised, she felt assured she was making the right decision.

"Yes, my husband is in France. They've re-assigned him as an ambulance driver. I guess we're both on the front lines of the medical corps." Eliza attempted to lighten the conversation.

Harrison's latest letter informing her of his re-assignment surprised her. His poor eyesight kept him in tents to manage the officers' communications. It appeared he sought more action and volunteered with the Red Cross. They must be in dire straits to allow him to drive injured men.

"If there's a spare cot in the nurses' room, I would prefer to stay here rather than go back and forth every day, and as you mentioned, risk spreading the contagion to my family. My mother and aunt will watch my children. I want to ring them though, if I may, and stay over tonight. My driving skills are far inferior to my medical ones. If I leave early tomorrow morning to make arrangements, I can be back here by the afternoon."

"Wise decision," he said. "I don't trust my driving either on these winding roads, let alone at night. You're welcome to use my phone. There's a diner down the street which serves a half-decent egg salad on rye. I'll see you tomorrow, and thank you, Dr. Edwards." He trudged down the hallway to another round.

• • •

The chief medical officer's work area resembled a low-level manager's at the Wool Company. Towering stacks of requisition forms covered an unadorned wooden desk in its center. A memo pad with half of its sheets torn away sat on top of the piles. In neat lettering, a staff assistant had written fifteen soldiers' names, a dash and a different name next to it. In the morning, Dr. Vaughan would send fifteen telegrams to a wife or mother. Their names personalized the death more than seeing a corpse under a blanket, waiting for Eliza's gloved fingers to close his eyelids.

By the phone was a piece of stationery embossed with the U.S. War Office emblem. The Surgeon General's scrawl covered half the sheet. Eliza looked down at the phone's base. The inked message on the crisp white sheet caught her eye. She didn't want to read it, she shouldn't read it, but she couldn't avert her eyes. The words were inches from the dial set. She wouldn't touch it nor disturb its placement on the desk. A phrase like ones from

Jack London's *The Scarlet Plague* froze her, sending a chill through her veins despite the warm, stuffy office air.

We must humbly admit our dense ignorance...

...If the epidemic continues its mathematical rate of acceleration, civilization could easily disappear from the face of the earth...

Maybe she offered her services too quickly. She was a wife, a daughter, a niece, a sister, and an aunt, but mostly, a mother. If the end of civilization loomed, shouldn't she be with those she loved and cared for the most?

Jack London's *Plague* was a work of fiction. The Spanish influenza was not.

Lt. Colonel McCornack is wrong, Eliza thought. There was cause for alarm and it was terrifying.

CHAPTER THIRTY-NINE

Eliza knocked on her own front door. Above the door frame, three double windows aligned on top of each other, their glossy black shutters secured against the red brick with black metal scrolls. Beyond the blue damask drapes of the first window stood two bureaus, the four-poster marital bed, and her writing desk. Eliza noted to collect her stationery and grandfather's pen to take with her. She owed letters to Olga, Charlotte, and Edith. Above her bedroom, twin beds crowded the nursery. White cotton eyelet drapes fluttered inward over the electric train set, Harrison's gift to Will for his fifth birthday. The window of the attic room above where Harrison escaped to paint was shut tight.

The door cracked ajar. Her mother's blue-gray eyes scowled over her spectacles and around the door's edge. She clutched her silk dressing gown, pushing aside her undone white hair. "What on earth? Did you forget your key?" Laura said in a harsh tone, chastising Eliza as if she were a girl who had forgotten her gloves for church.

Laura pulled the door open, but Eliza stepped back. "Sorry, I didn't mean to wake you. I hoped to catch you before the boys woke up."

"For heaven's sake, come in. I'll put tea on."

A cup of brisk tea with a spot of honey would settle her nerves, but she didn't have time to linger over tea. The conditions unfolding at Camp Devens would soon move to Boston. In her desk, she had folded and tucked away the yellowed copy of Anandi's letter into a cubby hole drawer. Anandi's words from years ago guided her through challenges in the past; she needed them again now.

"I..." Eliza hesitated. "I can't get any closer. I may carry the contagion. The influenza is far worse than the papers are reporting, and it will spread. I need you to listen to me and do as I ask. My sons' lives and yours depend on it."

Eliza gave her instructions swift and terse. Her mother and Florence must take Will and Teddy, leave Boston this morning, and go to Albie's cottage in Newport. The isolated spot in the off-season would be the safest place to quarantine. She hoped Albie and Freddy would heed her advice and send their families, too.

"Can you also pack up a few things for me? A couple of changes of clothes–my oldest day dresses, my stationery, and pen. I'll wait here," Eliza said.

"Eliza, you're overreacting. Why you went there is beyond me. I'm not packing anyone's suitcase," Laura opened the door wider. "Your boys will be up. Come in and see to their breakfast."

Eliza yanked the door from her mother's grip, pulling it toward her. With a shield reinstated between them, she spoke through the inches between door and frame. If scaring her was the only way to make Laura acknowledge the severity of the situation, Eliza would not mince her words. "Yesterday, I wrote eight death certificates. That's more than what I used to write in a month. This germ is deadlier than anything we've ever seen. If you won't accept my medical opinion, know that the U.S. Surgeon General himself is declaring it a catastrophe of epic proportions. I'm frightened. And you should be, too."

Through the slit of space, Eliza watched her mother falter as she grabbed hold of the chair next to the foyer table and fell into its worn cushion.

Her voice quaked, "Run over to Albie's and ask him to drive us. You can follow when you're sure you're not contagious. What is that? A day or two?"

Looking above, she noticed Harrison's attic room. She recalled their conversation from the night before his departure. How could he, an able man, go to Newport with a racquet in his hands when others carried guns in theirs? He spoke the truth. A war waged. His country needed him in France. Here in Massachusetts, there was another war. How could she, a trained medical professional, flee to Newport with a bag of candies in her hand? Like Harrison, she would give her sons a parent who believed in her country and honored what was asked of her.

"I'll tell Albie while you pack, but I won't be coming until Dr. Vaughan can spare me. Even then, I'll stay in the carriage house to make sure I'm not contagious. There are few doctors or nurses available with so many serving in Europe. I have to help. It's my duty as a doctor."

"Your duty as a mother is more important," Laura countered. She slammed the door.

Eliza slumped to the stoop and curled into a tight ball against the quiet of the early autumn morning. Her eyes moistened like the dew clinging to the bottom of her skirt. Inside, her sons would stir awake. Will would throw off his covers and flick the switch on his train set, sending the engine chugging forward in its endless circle. Teddy would search beneath his bed for his stuffed dog, Woofie, that always ended up on the wrong side of the covers.

"Mother," Eliza called through the closed door loud enough for her mother to hear. "Please make sure Teddy brings his Woofie."

Twenty feet from the car parked in front of her house, Eliza stood on the sidewalk. She found one of Harrison's handkerchiefs in the car and tied it over her nose and mouth. Neighbors passed her with puzzled looks. She kept her head down. After what felt like three hours, but which was closer to thirty minutes, Albie exited her home bearing the last two suitcases. Behind him, Laura clung to her grandsons' hands and descended the steps.

Will saw her first. "Mommy!" he wrenched free from his grandmother's hand. "Look, it's Mommy. We're going to play cops and robbers! Where's my kerchief? I wanna be the bad guy to stick up the bank."

"Mama," cried Teddy, bumping Woofie down the steps as he squashed one long ear in his chubby fist.

Hearts didn't break in half. They exploded into pieces, sending their shards coursing out from its aorta to stab and cut every inch of a body. As Eliza watched Albie race to catch the whir of Will coming toward her, she shattered. With only her eyes visible to them, would they reveal her full emotional expression? Would they know? Beneath the handkerchief masking her lips, she mouthed to the boys Albie wrangled into the car, *Mommy loves you, Will. Mommy loves you, Teddy.*

•   •   •

After she collected herself, she staggered inside to phone Edith in Philadelphia to warn her and Estelle of the looming threat. Edith should recognize the implications, yet she too declared Eliza an alarmist and dismissed her warnings. Edith trusted her supervisor at the Board of Health who assured her the limited cases in the area were at nearby military camps, like Devens, and did not expect them to spread.

Two weeks later, Eliza learned with near-unbearable dismay that Edith and Estelle joined hundreds of thousands of Philadelphians for a Liberty Loan parade, a display of patriotism to celebrate news the war would be over soon. Throngs swarmed along Broad Street, cheering wildly in the open air. The scourge struck with the ferocity of a firestorm twenty-four hours after the parade, the length of the incubation period. Panic descended on the city as the epidemic metastasized. Within four days, death crepes hung on front doors up and down every street. The stench of decaying bodies wafted out open windows, saturating the air with motes of death. Undertakers stacked bodies three and four deep as they awaited shipments of more caskets, often never arriving. Gravediggers fell ill, forcing the Board of Health to arm prisoners and Catholic priests with shovels to meet the demand for quick burials. In Massachusetts, upon reading the morning paper's account of the dire situation in Philadelphia, Eliza dropped her forehead into helpless hands and sobbed.

Upon completing nine days straight at the base, Dr. Vaughan insisted Eliza take a day off and go home to Boston to rest in a bed more comfortable than an Army cot. Eliza agreed to a twenty-four-hour leave. The moment she walked inside, before heading to bed, she called Albie in Newport. There had been no news from Race Street in over a week, and her mother was increasingly anxious to hear from Estelle. With few operators well enough to work, Bell Telephone instituted restrictions on any calls except emergencies. The hell with Bell Telephone, Eliza fumed to herself. She sent telegrams to both Race Street and Olga. She hadn't heard from Olga in days either. A night's rest did little to drown out grisly nightmares of toe tags swarming around her like a cloud of angry bees. The jingle of the phone downstairs broke through her haze. She flew down the stairs and grabbed the phone's earpiece in time to accept the charges for a collect call. Olga!

"Oh, thank goodness. I've been worried sick; you're okay?" Eliza's voice warbled.

"By the grace of God, I'm okay. I'm so sorry for my delay. Taniya and her daughter were down for three days. They'll pull through, but I couldn't leave them."

"Poor Taniya! This is just dreadful. I'm glad they're doing better. What about Edith, Estelle? Have you been able to reach them?"

"They've cut back the streetcars. Too many drivers are sick or have passed, but I caught a trolley this morning. I'm here now."

Olga described the scene she discovered at the house. Finding the front door locked, she entered through the kitchen door. A stillness seldom found in a household of women greeted her. A pot of chicken broth simmered low on the stove top, evaporated down to mere dregs. She knew. In Edith's bedroom, she found rumpled linens strewn across an empty bed. The door to Estelle's adjoining room was open.

Olga paused. "Estelle and Edith are both gone. I think it was quick. Most of the time, it is."

Woman's Medical trained its doctors on how to inform family members on the loss of a loved one. Eliza appreciated Olga's directness, but it didn't soften her grief of losing an aunt and a friend.

"Lizzy, there's one more thing. I'll leave it to you if you want to tell your mother," Olga hesitated.

"If I want to tell my mother?"

"If you want to tell your mother," said Olga, "Estelle was loved. She wasn't alone at the end. She died in the arms of her love."

CHAPTER FORTY

November 1918

The window sash flew up, framing faces beaming with excitement. Will Shaw angled his head sideways to listen for the sounds two blocks away. He stretched his arm behind him, helping Teddy climb upon the desk chair he pulled close to the wall. An incessant tooting of horns mingled with the clang of spoons against tin pie plates. A mix of cheering voices, male and female, young and old, joined the musical ruckus. Another impromptu parade broke out to celebrate the Armistice signing. Today was as boisterous as the prior two. Boston, the country, and the world needed to revel in its victory and exhale a deep, long-held breath. There was so much to celebrate: defeated Huns and a Kaiser's abdication. U.S. troops would come home, including Lt. Harrison Shaw.

"Will! Teddy! Get away from the window before you fall," Eliza commanded, alarmed to find her sons leaning over the open window's edge. They survived the Spanish influenza; she wasn't about to lose them to a careless accident.

"Aww, Mama, can't we please go?" said Will, climbing off the chair and tugging Teddy down with him.

"There's not much to see, just a bunch of men acting like Barnum's circus clowns. You can listen from the courtyard. Run downstairs and ask Aunt Florence to take you outside. Maybe she'll dig out some pie plates to make your own drums."

Despite the steady decline in cases, Eliza worried that crowds continued to pose a risk for infection. She wouldn't chance her children attending a public gathering for a few more weeks, nor rely on the ridiculous lengths other mothers had gone to at the height of the epidemic, stuffing salt up children's noses and hanging goose grease poultices of garlic around their necks. She also advised Olga to avoid train travel. The cost would be dear, and the trip would take twice as long, but a hired car would be a safer choice to bring her to Boston in time for Thanksgiving to fill Harrison's seat. She had been part of the extended Edwards family far longer than Harrison, and for Eliza, more welcome. Olga's sunny humor could brighten the darkest days. Harrison was unpredictable.

• • •

The lamps' glow reflected against the cream paneled wainscoting in the parlor. Heat from the gas fireplace softened the nip from the late November night. A mate of mahogany chairs, their seats and backs covered in a forest green brocade, resembled Mary Lennox's thicket of hedges in *The Secret Garden*. Olga stretched for the cigarette case on the pedestal table next to them and shook loose one of Harrison's Chesterfields. She fitted it into her holder and flicked a lighter to the tip. As she inhaled a long drag and released a puff of smoke, she squirmed deeper into the chair. Eliza agreed with the sentiment, loosened the rose-colored sash at the waist of her modest beige dress, and kicked off her shoes. She sat on the matching seat facing Olga, extended her legs out, lifted her heels off the ground, and twirled her ankles.

"Your mother is right. Those boys are like a couple of Mexican jumping beans," Olga said.

A smile spread across Eliza's face. She adored those cute, active beans. Will had started kindergarten. He knew his alphabet, and with Eliza's help he read shorter tales from Mother Goose. Teddy could count to five, pausing at four to announce, "Fouah–that's me!" Eliza thought, when had the son of a proper Philadelphian picked up a Boston accent? She was proud and thankful for her strong, healthy, and intelligent boys. She prayed they were gentle and kind, too, like Salvatore.

Poor, darling Salvatore Silvestri, her wonder child who defeated the odds and would forever hold a special spot in her heart. Born with compromised lungs, the influenza stole him weeks before his birthday. Would he have lived to seventeen, if not for her intervening at his birth? Would he have celebrated his tenth birthday at home after she helped the Silvestris remove him from the Elwyn School? Did a new book every year give him dreams, hope, and laughs? Had a most basic human need–love–strengthened his heart for years longer than anyone expected? She believed her actions made a difference, even if no research would ever prove it.

"They are a handful, but I wouldn't trade them for all the tea in China. After their Newport exile, the Armistice hoopla overwhelmed them. They're counting on their Daddy coming home soon. I haven't told them it'll be a while yet."

• • •

The last news received from Harrison was in September for Teddy's fourth birthday.

My dear little boy,

Four years old! My, what a big boy you are getting to be! I asked Mommy to buy you a little express wagon. Did she pick out a red one? You can fill it with packages and make believe that you are a salesman and sell some to Will.

I hope that you have had a happy summer, and have been a very good, helpful little boy, and that Will has, too. Daddy misses you, and he takes you with him every day–not really, but in his heart and thoughts. Daddy sends you and Will his very best love and these funny crisscross marks are Kisses. X X X X–one for every year you've brought me happiness to be your Daddy.

His words were as much for Eliza as for Teddy. He loved his sons; she must know that truth. She did. Which was why her boys wouldn't grow up haunted by a persistent question in their minds. *Why didn't you want to be my Papa?*

•   •   •

Harrison's next note arrived days after the Armistice. A clipped telegram which Eliza repeated now to Olga:

War over. More work ahead. May be six months. P.S. Send cigarettes. French ones horrid. Gas mask needed to smoke them. HGS.

"I can't fathom why an ambulance driver needs to stay on for six months," Eliza said. "They would move the injured to the troop ships first."

Olga shrugged. "They could have re-assigned him and he can't divulge information about a new position. Armies, bah, always so secretive. Let's hear Charlotte's letter. She's never stingy with her words."

Eliza shuffled through a pile of mail on the table to find the thin envelope postmarked from Luzancy, France. In typical Dr. Fairbanks fashion, she addressed it in her crisp handwriting to Dr. Eliza Edwards Shaw. Among classmates they would always be Doctor first. The arc of their careers had been different, but Eliza could only admire Charlotte's fortitude. As chief surgeon at the Philadelphia County Prison, inmates and guards alike regarded Dr. Fairbanks as a skilled professional, blind to the dress she wore under her surgical gown. To them, she was a physician who saved lives whether they were serving a two-month bit, a life sentence, or sat on death row. But Charlotte aspired to a higher calling–one which didn't lock her skills away, hidden from public view.

Her prison experience using primitive tools readied her to join nine other doctors who established the Medical Women's National Association in 1915. By July 1918, with no backing of the war service committee, they partnered with the Red Cross to form American Women's Hospitals. Their first location was near Paris and within the war zone. Initially they focused on medical and emergency relief for civilians and refugees. But as battles raged into the fall, the AWH became a *Hospital Mixte*, also treating urgent military cases. Dr. Fairbanks served as the chief surgeon, joined by a dentist, the Chief of Staff, and five other general practitioners. All of them were women.

Eliza perched a pair of Harrison's spare wire-rimmed glasses on her nose. She withdrew the pages from the envelope and began her best attempt at mimicking Charlotte's native Vermont accent.

"November 5, 1918. Dear El-oy-za,"

Olga burst into laughter, a cheerful sound which had laid buried in her throat. "Ha, ha, ha. Well done. But you'll drive me coconuts if I must listen to the entire letter in her accent. I tolerate it from Charlotte because she's Charlotte, and I love her, accent, and all. But good God, not from you!"

"Don't worry, I couldn't pull it off. Instead, make do with thinking of Charlotte."

With her palms parallel in front of her, Eliza framed an air box, horizontal, then vertical. "Now sporting the latest in Army fashions for our doctors, Charlotte Fairbanks. Note her smart khaki uniform, shirt and tie beneath the belted jacket and a skirt which stops above Army-issued boots. And we are grateful for the little things in life–she has traded in those dreadful, bowler-type hats she likes for a sharply creased cap. But Lord save the person who mistakes it for a nurse's cap."

Olga grinned. Eliza resumed reading.

Dear Eliza,

Charlotte had crossed out the first line, leaving a noticeable indentation on the thin paper. Eliza tried to decipher the struck words but could read only a few. *Tell you, unfortunate.* Puzzled, she continued with the visible lines.

By the time you receive this, I pray you are celebrating this ghastly war's end. We expect it is imminent. Nightly air raids in Paris have ceased and the Huns are in retreat. The silence is comforting after being awakened by the ear-splitting clamor of the Alerte with its Banshee wail of sirens, followed by the deafening booming explosions which signal we would be busy again in the morning.

Arrived last week in Luzancy, about fifty miles east of Paris. The villagers have suffered. Besides the typical war traumas, we've been treating pneumonia, tuberculosis, and influenza cases caused by the unsanitary conditions left by the retreating Germans and a scarcity of food.

You were wise to evacuate your family from Boston. I haven't heard from you since then and how you fared at Devens. The care of humanity has rested in many able hands. I pray you, your boys, mother and Florence have remained safe and well. Blessings to all of you, whatever your news may hold.

Eliza looked to Olga, "We need to get a note off to her. She'll want to know about Edith."

Olga brought her handkerchief to her eyes.

With lighter news, the nickname bestowed on me, Docteur Coupe Coupe, brings some levity to my day. Can you imagine Dr. Rodman's reaction if he learned his surgical student is called Doctor Cut Cut? I don't think he'd see the humor in it. Yet, my most recent case would please him. The Army sends a few soldiers when they're overwhelmed. Three weeks ago, I attended to a farm boy with a mangled hand. He was an absolute mess, with the bones crushed or fractured. Most surgeons would have amputated. I spent four hours putting the fragments back together. The nurses and I monitored him until they moved him to a hospital in Paris. Yesterday, I spoke with the ambulance driver who delivered him. He told me the famous Parisian surgeon, Dr. Tuffier, marveled at my work and reported the boy's hand well-mended and he will have full use of it when he gets home. I'm so glad I helped him become whole, at least in a physical sense.

"What, no count of the number of stitches? No recording of how much morphine she used? Docteur Coupe Coupe is slipping with her detail," said Olga.

Eliza's countenance grew soft again as her face lit with the mirth Olga always brought to a conversation.

I love this corner of France. Once the rains wash away the grime of gunpowder residue, we find the most beautiful flowers still in bloom. The sweet townspeople have endured the ravages of war in the front yards of their stone homes and the back acres of their farms. We are thankful for accepting us, eight women doctors, into their community. They trust us and our abilities despite a lack of resources. No one hesitated when the French government asked us to remain after the signing of an armistice. We must not fail them.

With friendship and kindness,
Charlotte

The newsy letter opened with a puzzle and contained a few highlights of Charlotte's work, but it strayed from other letters Eliza had received as if Charlotte was trying to deflect or divert attention. Since when did Charlotte comment about flowers blooming? Most of her letters included detailed descriptions of surgeries, a blow-by-blow of patients' backgrounds, and a run-down of the staff assigned to assist her. Charlotte heaped praise upon the nurses who assisted her, for any doctor knows without their aid, a doctor can't perform her job. Names, ages, and physical descriptions brought a nurse to life in Charlotte's notes. This one lacked her usual litany.

CHAPTER FORTY-ONE

June 1919

The Boston Public Garden and Common burst with hues of summer. As if on cue to commemorate the unfolding event, rows of yellow, purple, and white irises rose phoenix-like from their winter dormancy. On this day, the blooms' colors earned their mark as the suffrage movement's symbols for faith and hope. At the corner, across from the gold-domed State House, women of every description swayed in unison. Seventy years prior in Seneca Falls, New York, a dedicated purpose propelled Elizabeth Cady Stanton and Lucretia Mott forward with a singular mission: Votes for Women. Today, June twenty-fifth, three weeks after the House of Representatives passed the bill, the Massachusetts House assembled to vote on ratification of the 19th Amendment. White parasols fought off the mid-afternoon sun while yellow placards fanned against the heavy air, reminding the women to *Keep Cool* and *Raise a Breeze for Suffrage.*

Eliza felt herself wilting in the heat. Olga stood by her side, while Eliza's mother reclined on a stool they carried over from the house. At her feet, Eliza's niece, Bessie, sat on trampled grass, cross-legged, despite her grandmother's tsk-tsk at the inappropriate position for a girl in public. In her hand, Bessie held a notebook and polished black lacquered pen, a gift from Eliza on her twelfth birthday. With a pen like her grandfather's, Eliza hoped Bessie would develop a confidence to write stories about women, by a woman, just as medicine had inspired Eliza to care for women, as a woman.

"How much longer?"

"The first skill you must learn to be a journalist, Miss Bessie Edwards, is patience," said Olga. "A good story is worth the wait."

"This moment is far more than a story," added Eliza. "It's history in the making."

Eliza motioned toward the men climbing the State House steps. "They're back from lunch recess; it won't take long to finish the roll call. Should we move closer? I can't wait to see Florence's expression when she comes out."

"I can't believe they allowed her inside. You'd think the police detail would have the agitators' names. She'll stir up a ruckus if those men don't vote in favor," said Olga.

Laura lowered her eyes and sighed. "Please, Olga, I'd rather not relive that embarrassment," she said.

Bessie perked up. "What agitators? What embarrassment?"

"It wasn't embarrassing, Mother. It was inspiring." Eliza tapped Bessie's notebook.

"Another important part of journalism is background research. Take some notes. It'll bring your story to life when you document the present enlightened by the past."

Bessie flipped her pad to a fresh page and poised her pen, ready to listen and learn.

"About four months ago," Eliza began, "your great-Aunt Florence and two dozen other members of the National Women's Party gathered at this same spot to picket President Wilson's arrival in Boston. Do you remember his visit?"

"Yes, we could hear the cheers when we were in the schoolyard after lunch. I read in the evening paper there were a half million people."

"That's right. Most of the city cheered his success at the Peace Conference in Versailles. But Aunt Florence and other suffragists protested with jeers. They condemned him for championing the rights of Europeans, while American women remain stifled without the right to vote."

"I never thought of that. My teacher never brought it up in our civics class. Come to think of it, I don't think we've discussed the 19th Amendment ratification process at all."

Laura tsk-tsked again, "Well, they should. You are living through momentous history."

"Yes, they should indeed." Eliza made a mental note to speak with the principal at Will and Bessie's school. What were they teaching in civics class?

She continued with the details of the day's event back in February, explaining to Bessie how the women were cited for holding a meeting without a permit, rounded up by the police, and tossed into the House of Detention for Women.

"Your Uncle Albie offered to pay the five-dollar fine, but Florence refused. She felt they must send a message. A right to assemble should extend to women, the same way it allows men. They remained in jail for eight days."

"Eight days!!" exclaimed Bessie. "That's awful."

"It was dreadful, but thankfully I could visit to see for myself they weren't treated like other women arrested eighteen months ago after peacefully picketing in front of the White House. Those women were chained, beaten, and stabbed. Baton-wielding policemen dragged them to a jail in Lorton, Virginia. They resumed their protest inside the jail by staging a hunger-strike. Their strike ended when the guards force-fed them raw eggs."

Bessie dropped her pen to the grass as she drew her hand to her mouth, gagging at Eliza's conclusion of recounting the suffragists' Night of Terror.

At the noise of a skirmish at the State House's doors, Eliza halted her story. A throng of reporters rushed down the steps to sprint to their offices, vying to break the news. Behind them five women, their yellow sashes pinned tight to their shoulders, declaring their dedication to the cause, strode into the crowds, heads held high, fists in the air. Florence Pearson grinned like the Cheshire Cat. The Commonwealth of Massachusetts, following on the heels of Pennsylvania the previous day, confirmed the 19th Amendment to the Constitution.

Loud and clear, Eliza heard her aunt's voice ring out amidst the crowd, "Hurrah! Eight down! Twenty-eight to go!"

Once the three-fourths majority prevailed, women across the forty-eight states of America could proclaim: *The rights of citizens of the United States to vote shall not be denied or abridged by the United States or by any State on account of sex.*

Eliza echoed Florence's "Hurrah!" She grabbed Bessie's hands and spun her around. "Here's the rest of your story, Bessie. Florence and women like her have campaigned for years, leading to this triumphant day."

"There she is!" Bessie called out, breaking free from Eliza's spin, "Aunt Florence! Over here!" Bessie jumped up and down, waving her placard.

Florence elbowed her way through the crowd. Calloused hands of immigrant workers and smooth, jeweled fingers of Beacon Hill matrons patted her arms. A few hugged her. Each one beamed with appreciation and shouts of "Well done, sisters!"

Bessie grabbed her notebook and pen and galloped to Florence's side like a filly set loose from a paddock. Florence enveloped her and smiled over her head to Eliza, Olga, and Laura. Bessie extracted herself from the embrace, took a step back, then leaned forward to pose her questions.

"Miss Pearson," Bessie cleared her throat. "The Commonwealth of Massachusetts is one of the first states to ratify the 19th Amendment. As a leader of the state's National Women's Party, would you care to comment?"

"Why, thank you, Miss Edwards. Yes, it is a grand day for the women of Massachusetts and across our dear United States. Like Paul Revere's lanterns of 1775, Massachusetts continues to shine."

"Hold on, I can't write this fast. I want to get it all down," said Bessie.

Although she fancied Bessie's enthusiasm, Eliza's thoughts sagged, *What a shame Estelle isn't here to teach Bessie a few shorthand tips.*

"Okay, I'm caught up, go on," Bessie urged.

Florence slowed her speech, allowing Bessie time to compose each sentence. "Massachusetts continues to shine as a beacon of liberty. I am honored to live in a state which claims the birthplace of its pioneering and revolutionary daughters, Lucy Stone and Susan B. Anthony. Today, we carry the torch of liberty onward in the name of progress. We send our prayers and fortitude out to our fellow citizens in the next twenty-eight states that they, too, will have speedy and positive ratifications."

With a bow to her audience, Florence opened her arms wide, "Now, excuse me, I need to celebrate with my favorite women. Who wants to join me at Brigham's for a dish of peppermint ice cream?"

Bessie tucked her journal under her arm and her pen behind her ear. Her hand shot up. Every celebration in the eyes of a twelve-year-old deserved a trip to Boston's beloved confectionary shop for a scoop of ice cream, plopped into a frozen silver pedestal dish with a ladle of rich hot fudge sauce oozing onto the matching silver plate.

CHAPTER FORTY-TWO

July 1919

"Everybody two-step and do the twirly-twirl..."

The July heat clung to the silent shadows of the night. Up and down the streets of Beacon Hill, open windows beckoned cooler breezes to pass over Boston Harbor and travel up the Hill. A melodious, albeit slurred, baritone voice, trained in a church choir, broke the silence, and reverberated against the brick walls of the homes.

"Everybody two-step and grab a girly-girl..."

Harrison Shaw dropped his duffle bag to the gas-lit sidewalk and stumbled up the steps of his home. The blue and white fleur-de-lis drapes fell out over the sill. His merry melody continued as he crooned to the fluttering drapes.

Drawn to the window, Eliza, dressed only in a sleeveless white lace chemise, leaned out checking for the sight of any other man on the street. No, not a soul except for her sot of a husband, returned from France with no prior notice.

"Lord almighty, Harrison," she hissed out the window, her eyes widening like the full moon above them.

"What are you...when did you...where...why didn't you?"

"Enough with the questions. Open the door," Harrison shot back. The cheerful song in his voice dropped to a growl.

Leaving his duffle on the sidewalk, he staggered up the stairs to the foyer. Eliza pulled the baggage inside, closed the door, and made up the bed in the spare bedroom.

•　　•　　•

In the morning, after a joyous reunion with Will and Teddy, Eliza and Harrison faced each other on the mahogany side chairs. She sat straight and rigid, forcing every vertebra against the chair's hardness, hands folded in her lap, her legs covered by her dressing gown, and crossed at her ankles. He slouched with his shoulder blades resting upon the chair back, his hands wrapped around a cup of coffee, his legs splayed in front of him like a rakish colt. The distance between them spread as vast as the Atlantic Ocean that had separated them for the past twelve months.

"May I now ask my questions?" Eliza said, curt but soft.

"As they say in the trenches, fire away."

He answered her questions with short quips.

"Why didn't you send word when you left France?"

"Last minute ship assignment."

"When did you get into Boston?"

"Tuesday morning."

"Two days ago? Where have you been since then?"

"Billy Wellman's."

"Who's Billy Wellman?"

"Who's Wellman? Only the most celebrated American daredevil and fighter pilot of the Escadrille N. 86 of the Lafayette Flying Corps. I've been writing his story."

"Why didn't you come home first?"

"Billy's got a swell cache of liquor."

"Honestly, Harrison, it's not worth discussing anything with you in this state. Go back to bed. I'm scheduled for my visits to Denison today. Since you didn't have the desire or courtesy to tell me your plans, I can't rearrange my schedule now. You should sleep it off while I'm gone."

He placed the coffee cup down with a clunk. Splatters leapt up and over the rim onto a stack of Women's Victory Liberty pamphlets. "For Christ's sake, Eliza. I'm not a child. You needn't tell me how long to sleep."

Eliza rose from her chair and headed to the kitchen. As she brushed past him, she uttered in a seething whisper, "Don't act like a child and I won't treat you like one."

• • •

From her writing desk she gathered her stationery, pen, and a bundle of letters from Charlotte. She could catch up on her correspondence before going to Denison. Moving to the bed, she opened her palm to spill two aspirin tablets onto the bedside table. Harrison's snores grew louder. A reek from Billy Wellman's swell cache of liquor escaped through his open mouth. Gin-soaked wafts of breath hung in the stale air, as pungent as the juniper bushes edging their back courtyard. Eliza closed her palm tight around the tablets, shook her fist into the air of Harrison's snores, and tip-toed from the room.

In the kitchen, she brewed another pot of coffee and poured a bowl of cold Grape Nuts for a late breakfast. As she chewed the hard barley, the methodical rhythm cleared her mind. Eliza untied the twine around Charlotte's letters and selected the thinnest envelope. Dated November 6, 1918, it arrived two days after the first one from Luzancy. Another letter so soon had surprised Eliza. The letter took moments to read with short and simple sentences, while the words' implication was long and complicated.

Dear Eliza,
As one of my dearest friends, I feel compelled to tell you one other piece of news. I am sorry I didn't include it in yesterday's

letter. Last week, I faced the regrettable situation of writing up a nurse. I dreaded placing the black mark on her record. However, I must report behavior unbecoming of any member of the Army Corps. I had to ask the name of the man with whom I found her engaged in intimate relations. I didn't see his face, only a shock of light brown hair with a cowlick sticking up, his wire-rimmed glasses on the table, and his Red Cross armband. The nurse confirmed my guess when she said he was a lawyer from Boston. It was Harrison. Without revealing I knew him, I've since learned of his reputation across the villages and hospital wards of France. It appears he single-handedly drove the Army's issuance of prophylactics into short supply.

I am deeply troubled to write you with this information, but I think you should know. The war will end soon, and you must prepare for his return. I wish I could have told you in person and hold your hand to discuss the matter with you face to face. I trust Edith and Olga will help you figure out how to deal with this unfortunate situation.

Ever your friend, Charlotte

Eliza re-read the words, although even eight months later, she knew them by heart. The first few times she read the letter; Charlotte's revelation pierced her with tiny pricks until they melded together into a single long gash. Over the months, however, hints of other indiscretions bubbled up, and the gash mended as if Charlotte's skilled hands moved over her, helping her to heal, and to see. She recalled the many nights Harrison came home after midnight with traces of cheap perfume on his jacket. The winks he gave to a certain raven-haired Italian maid at the Forbes. All the tennis matches he insisted she needn't come and watch. Their wedding night. She had paused by his open toiletry case when she came to his bedside. Did the tin of Ramses look brand new, or was it dented in the corner as if he had purchased it several months before? Were there three condoms in the tin? Or was it empty after he pulled one out?

Evidence presented itself, building a case like a scene in Estelle's courtroom. But Eliza had been too busy with babies. Had she let the denial of truth, like Patrick leaving her, rule her inaction once again? Or did she simply not care enough to confront him? A case stalled, never moving beyond a first step of discovery.

Outside the window, the sun cast an ominous blood red haze as it climbed the summer morning sky. Another one of Josephine's superstitions clambered forward from Eliza's memory. *Red skies at night, sailors delight. Red skies at morning, sailors take warning.*

• • •

Eliza hurried through her afternoon at Denison House and finished early. An extra hour before she was due home offered a chance to clear her head. Yet did she rush through the Baby Hygiene appointments? Did she note eight ounces or twelve ounces in baby Rima Keilani's weight chart? The four-ounce differential mattered. If Rima gained only eight ounces, then she had not hit her target weight at her two-month check-up. Eliza should instruct Mrs. Keilani on how to sign up for the reduced cost milk station. She would check on Rima again tomorrow and not wait for next week's appointment.

Pushing aside her concern about Rima, Eliza lingered on her walk home through the Public Garden. The swan boat's paddle wheel turned in a slow churn, sending concentric ripples to lap the pond's edges. She watched each ripple touch the deep brown dirt at her feet, muddied like the situation which awaited her at home. What happened to the days when she laid her head on Harrison's shoulder and watched a free-flying kite float off into the sky?

She chose a bench close to the pond to sit and contemplate the best way to frame her conversation with Harrison. Words swirled in her mind, stirred by a seven-year cloud of decisions and events she could not undo. Their meeting started with an instance of pain. Should she expect that an encounter triggered by pain would end with the same?

The ripple ended as the swan boat docked. A stillness descended over the pond. The water reflected the overhanging branches of the nearby trees. Eliza stared into the mirror. A sense of clarity and resolution came to her. She would not tolerate Harrison's behavior any longer.

• • •

With Charlotte's letter as evidence, there was no question Eliza possessed the legal arguments for a decree against Harrison. The hardest choice would be to choose on which grounds to proceed for divorce.

Adultery? Yes. Gross and confirmed habits of intoxication caused by the voluntary and excessive use of liquor? Yes, and yes. Impotence? Doubtful given the escapades Charlotte mentioned and Eliza's other suspicions, but unconfirmed as she had avoided their bed since his return. Cruel and abusive treatment? Thankfully, no. Although his verbal assaults in Eliza's opinion cut deep, a court would never consider them abusive. And Harrison had never struck her as he struggled to maintain the moniker of a gentleman.

Utter desertion for three consecutive years? She couldn't count a year in France, so no. Neglect to provide suitable maintenance. No. With Harrison employed by the Edwards Wool Company, his income provided a comfortable life. Her sons didn't want for anything.

As time passed, she lost confidence in pursuing a case. She would catch Harrison on the floor with Will whooping and hollering as the Lionel trains circled the boys' bedroom, bursting through blockades they made with Lincoln Logs. Other times, he packed a blanket and picnic hamper and took Teddy with him to the banks of the Charles River, where they spread out for an afternoon of coloring and painting sailboats and bridges. In the evenings, he stretched out on one of their narrow beds and read aloud sports scores and the daily comic serial of Mutt and Jeff. The warm words in his birthday note to Teddy exposed a gentler side, a father who was present even when he was thousands of miles away.

But, on other nights, a phone call to say good night to his sons replaced frivolity and tenderness. His speech already slurred, she heard Billy in the background urging him to hurry. The night was young. She cringed to imagine the times Harrison spent out with Wellman, the celebrated flying ace. As his wingman, Harrison may have his arms draped around a cheap tart found in a North Street brothel, a quick walk from their home, yet miles from any semblance of respectability. The recent strike by most of Boston's police officers brought the tarts out in full view, flaunting and taunting with their wares of undone hair, low-cut blouses, and high-cut skirts.

The worst nights descended into fits of alcohol-induced rages, as if Harrison meant to drink his store before the 18th Amendment went into effect in January. When the whiskey poured from the decanter before five o'clock, Eliza shuttled her sons off to Albie's or Freddy's house for the night, safe within the circle of their cousins. Alone, she faced Harrison with a series of questions: *please don't, why won't you? can't you?*

She knew answers would never come; there were no treatments for an undefined illness with unknown causes. Abstinence, the only cure, seemed unlikely given Harrison's success with sourcing rum-runners and speakeasys since the day he disembarked from the troop ship.

Alcoholism was chronic, progressive, and often fatal. She feared for the coming years of Harrison's life, and for her sons. Unlike an airborne influenza, what if alcoholism was in-born?

Time and time again, Mendel's theories proved true. Did a gene lurk inside her boys that was no different from the one which gave Will his father's brown eyes or Teddy his cowlick?

Each day and night, Harrison's behavior swung between fatherly attention and grounds for divorce. Eliza's mind crowded with noise and chaos like rides at Paragon Park, the amusement park south of Boston and a family favorite for summer outings. Each ride called her with tinkling, tinny music clamoring for her to place a ticket in the grubby and eager outstretched hand of the ride operator.

Carousels spun in endless loops. Painted ponies with frozen smiles and hollow wooden heads and bodies pumped up and down to the rhythm of a mechanical xylophone's plinking. She could remain fixed in her marriage like a carousel pony, a pole through her center as her life revolved around her, expressionless and empty, or she could board a scarier ride with highs and lows and twists and turns as terrifying as the Giant Roller Coaster, her hands thrown into the air yielding control to the sudden drops ahead on rickety tracks. Was there another option? One more like the giant Ferris wheel with its even ascents and descents to give her time to prepare for what may come next?

• • •

"Albie, I need your help," said Eliza.

"It's about time. I can rustle up a wop from the North End to take that boozehound husband of yours to the middle of the harbor for an eternal swim."

"Please don't use that language."

"What—wop or boozehound?"

"Both."

"Okay, okay. So, what can I do to help?"

Across from her brother over lunch at the Union Oyster House, Eliza laid out her plan. Would Albie recommend Harrison to serve as a personal secretary to Congressman Charles Gifford? Harrison's work prior to his enlistment brought him to Gifford's offices many times to finalize contracts. Harrison would move to Washington. Eliza and the children would remain in Boston. During congressional recesses, he could take the boys to Cape Cod where Gifford summered, if she felt assured to trust them to his care. He could still be part of their lives as their father.

Four hundred miles between them would create an acceptable pretense of a separation without the disgrace of a divorce settlement splayed across the *Globe's* pages and ample fodder for embarrassing her mother more than Florence's imprisonment. Sending him to Washington would also build a buffer from any further evidence of Harrison's wayward actions and limit his poor example of manhood in front of his sons. Harrison would support them but be denied any inkling of dating or marrying another woman. Let him have his tarts on the side. Everyone else in Washington did.

"What about you, Lizzy?" Albie asked. "Will this make you happy? Can you live knowing you wouldn't be able to see, or marry, another man, either?"

She had rejected her debut with its intent of finding her a husband. During seven years of medical school and her internship, she had traded suitors for studies. Waiting for Patrick Callaghan's mother to die filled another seven years. Six years ago, she wed a man whom she should have never accompanied to the edge of a cliff.

"I've lived this life for twenty years. For my sons, what's a few more?"

CHAPTER FORTY-THREE

October 1919

In the solace of a Sunday afternoon, sitting in Eliza's parlor reading the newspapers before dinner at Albie's house, Laura settled her section into her lap and cleared her throat. "Eliza, do you remember Maria's comment to you about male doctors?"

Remember? The dying words from her aunt propelled her into the life she lived today.

"I do, Mother," said Eliza, with a catch in her voice, "She feared they wouldn't understand her grief."

"She was a wise woman, my sister, and now I understand. I would be more comfortable with someone like you who knows how it feels."

She rose from her chair and unbuttoned the front of her older-styled shirtwaist.

"Mother, what are you doing…?" Eliza began.

Laura shimmied her shoulders out of the sleeves and stood before her daughter with the dress bodice pooled at her waist. Her arthritic fingers faltered and shook as they fumbled with the white laces of her brassiere. Her voice matched her fingers, wavering and hesitant, "I didn't want a man touching me here."

Eliza pushed her mother's trembling fingers down to her side. With precision and deftness, Eliza finished the unlacing, a lump of her own forming in her throat.

"Which one?" She searched Laura's eyes and found the dark fear.

• • •

Eliza heard the black Model T barreling down Hancock Avenue. Turning onto Mount Vernon Street, the left tires lifted off the asphalt by a fraction of an inch, the acrid scent of burnt rubber puffed up from the side of the street. The car came to a stop in front of Eliza's house.

From the front door, Olga barked, "Heavens, Charlotte! Do you always drive like a bat out of hell?"

"I have taken out a hedge or garage now and then," Charlotte admitted as she climbed the steps.

"How's Mrs. Edwards faring? When I spoke with Eliza last week, the prognosis sounded bleak. I'm not sure I can help."

Olga glanced at Eliza, descending the stairs with a bed tray, and placed her hand on Charlotte's arm as they crossed into the foyer, "Not good."

The day Eliza felt the lime-sized betrayer in her mother's right breast paralyzed her. At that size, the lump was powerful and gripping, squeezing her mother's desire to fight and overcome its toxic hold.

"Charlotte! You're here." The tray in Eliza's hands told the story. A deep purple autumn aster wilted over the edge of a crystal bud vase. A piece of untouched toast lay on the center of a spring green plate. Tea in a cup with a golden arched fish handle had gone cold. Eliza's eyes and shoulders drooped as low as the flower head.

"Thank you so much for coming." She hugged her stiff, ever-formal surgeon friend. "I can't tell you how grateful I am that you'll be performing the surgery. Can you believe the idiotic doctors at Mass General wanted to perform a radical mastectomy on the spot, taking both breasts? They had no intention of telling my mother!"

Charlotte scoffed, "Dr. Halsted may have succeeded on a scientific level when he introduced the procedure, but neither he, nor his followers, address the after-effects with their patients. They don't think to advise how to fill an empty brassiere, or why a woman would want to. They wrap them up mummy-style from midriff to neck and send them home."

"A patient's state of mind and the post-operative instructions they're given should always be considered. It can make a tremendous difference in recovery," said Olga.

"You're right," added Eliza. While her mother spent time after the operation in the hospital, Eliza would prepare for recuperative time at home, starting with a shopping trip. Extra dressings and salves, a new night gown and quilted bed jacket, lavender sachets in a crystal bowl, the sweet gentle story, *Rainbow Valley*, another installment in the Anne of Green Gables books.

And syringes and morphine.

•   •   •

Charlotte performed the surgery the next day at Massachusetts General. By departing from Halsted's accepted practice of removing both breasts and the entire underlying chest muscles and lymph nodes, Charlotte minimized the trauma, the potential for arm paralysis, and extensive scarring by taking only Laura's right breast. There would be no cure, only the hope of easing Laura's fears by cutting out the intruder which held mass and was palpable, unlike the other poisoned cells, silent and deadly, waiting to strike a defenseless, resigned opponent.

Days and nights passed as Eliza served as doctor and nurse. Sitting next to her, Eliza brushed Laura's forehead with a touch as soft as a kitten's paw. When Laura drifted into an unconscious state, Eliza still held her hand, unable and unwilling to release their connection.

When she labored for breath and her fingertips tinted blue, Eliza plunged the syringe into the bottle of morphine. She alone among the family could administer the sweet drops of relief. Not her older brothers with their expertise of managing a thriving business. Nor Aunt Florence with her dedication to women's rights. Only Eliza. Only Dr. Eliza Edwards Shaw could help. Of the thousands of patients she cared for over the years, here, in this moment, did her degree become its most valuable. Greater than a daughter's concern, she had the desire, right, and acumen to ensure her mother's last moments would be as painless as possible.

On Laura's lucid days, they discovered an intimacy latent for decades. One afternoon, they discussed the court case of Mrs. Tolber from years ago, when the elderly defendant had uttered, "Sometimes it pays to be a woman." Eliza remembered Estelle with her solemn expressions. Her gold-rimmed glasses perched on her hooked nose; eyes focused on every task asked of her. Estelle, working in a man's domain, day after day, sitting in a courtroom, transcribing arguments of others to bring truths to the world.

Eliza said, "Did you suspect anything?"

"Suspect what? That there are advantages to being a woman, even concerning financial affairs?"

"No," said Eliza. "The courtroom reminds me of Aunt Estelle and what it means to be a woman. What it meant to Estelle, living an untraditional life with her secret. Did you ever suspect her relationship with Edith was more than a friendship?"

"I suppose I did, but never thought to discuss it. If Estelle wanted us to know, I think she would have told us." Laura closed her eyes, shaking her head. "But I'm not certain. I wish she had. It makes me sad she assumed we might judge her. She was our sister. I wanted her to be happy, to feel complete."

Eliza caressed her mother's hand and fingered the wedding band, which spun on a frail, wrinkled ring finger.

"She found her completeness with Edith. I'm happy they found each other and could find their way to live in their love," said Eliza. Seven years ago, Olga pointed out love should be the cornerstone of a relationship. She had been right. Without it the ties which bound loosened like undone apron strings, letting the protective pieces fall to the ground.

• • •

On the days Laura felt well enough to eat but unable to hold a fork, she would wait for Eliza's steady hand. Yet each day, the light in Laura's eyes waned a fraction more. Her speech slowed, the effort too great to form thoughts in her mind and press them over her tongue. Eliza read aloud from her long-loved favorites and *Rainbow Valley*, the recent book she purchased. She closed *Wuthering Heights* and sighed. The circuitous story of Catherine and Hareton ended with a happily ever after.

"I loved Patrick, Mother. I still love him. Maybe I should have gone to Ireland," Eliza admitted to the heavy air of the sickroom. Could her mother hear through the morphine haze?

"I shouldn't have married Harrison. It was a mistake driven by spite and despair, not love and respect. You showed me, Mother, how a devoted love can last a lifetime."

Laura opened her eyes and forced words forward. "Will and Teddy. They are your life. You are a mother."

A mother's words, maybe her final ones, spoken with wisdom, imbued with love. Eliza bowed her head. Her heart grew again with joy when Will and Teddy entered her life, giving her the honor of being called Mommy.

Moonbeams and a low lamp lit the room. The covers over Laura's body rose and fell as slow as a feather floating on a light breeze. Eliza leaned in close. With her own words, she whispered into her mother's ear.

"Enough. Papa has been waiting a long time for you. We'll be okay. I'll be okay. I am okay."

•   •   •

Next to it, an overturned dirt pile of earth awaited its duty. Eliza's gloved hand went to the pearls draped around her neck. She fingered the beads, feeling each round, smooth surface and recalling her mother's words on her graduation day. *"And pure white ones signify new beginnings. I think they're the perfect choice for the doctor who stands before me. A woman driven to gain great wisdom and who is ready for her next beginning. I couldn't be prouder of you."*

Today would not be a day of endings, it would be a day of a new beginning. A day to reflect, but also to dream. She opened her Bible to a marked page.

"From Proverbs 31. *Who can find a virtuous woman? For her price is far above rubies. Strength and honor are her clothing; and she shall rejoice in time to come. She opened her mouth with wisdom; and in her tongue is the law of kindness. Many daughters have done virtuously, but she excels beyond them all. Let her own works praise her in the gates."*

Eliza replaced the ribbon marker. Looking out to the faces assembled before her, she saw Laura Pearson Edwards in each of them. The serious stare of Albie, who had shouldered the Company's business with Laura's guidance. A whisper of a smile on Freddy's face, perhaps recalling her firm directives of giving him permission for his Alaska trip. Starry lights in the eyes of grandchildren she adored. Florence's prominent forehead which resembled her sister's and would carry on a Pearson presence in their lives. Olga and Charlotte, strong and honorable women whom Laura embraced like daughters. At her breast, Olga wore the cameo Laura had given her upon their graduation.

"Today, we will not mourn. We will rejoice and praise. My mother sparkled more than a ruby, more than any gem. She was a voice of humanity and wisdom. She was a woman whom we can't place a value upon except to know we will feel her absence, and her presence, every day. With her love, we will move forward." She steered her eyes over to Will, Teddy, Bessie, and her nephews.

"New adventures and challenges lie ahead for you. Know that she will always be by your side, proud and grateful that you called her Granny."

CHAPTER FORTY-FOUR

August 1920

A quick, even in-and-out pant of the saw vibrated in Eliza's ears. In the air of the cramped workspace, earthy, fermented odors knocked her back to the pathology lab at Woman's Med. Scrunching her nose at the scent and the memory, she turned to Olga as they entered the sign-maker's shop. "Is there any chance you still have a clothespin in your pocket?" she asked.

Olga leaned down to brush the fine sawdust particles from the hem of her dress. "Ha. I'm afraid I don't. My secret worked well, though, didn't it?"

Twenty-three years ago, Eliza and Olga became partners, studying and toiling their way through medical school with its highs and lows and tugs on every emotion in between. Today, they stood at the opening of a new chapter, awaiting to take forward strides of a new type of woman. Peals of success rang across the country from Nashville on August 18 when state legislators adopted the Nineteenth Amendment, making Tennessee the thirty-sixth state to deliver a majority. Eight days later, the United States Constitution formally ratified a woman's right to vote. Opportunities expanded. Doors would open. Eliza Edwards Shaw, M.D. and Olga Povitzky McGuire, M.D. embraced the calls from the suffrage movement's leaders. The talents and efforts of women would not be denied or ignored.

Behind them, a burly man in coveralls approached them with a notepad in hand and a pencil nub stuck behind his right ear. "Excuse me, ladies. Let's pop into my office. I can't hear myself think in the shop, let alone make sure I hear directions correctly."

"Thank you," said Eliza, following the wood carving shop owner out of the doorway and into a box-sized office where he deposited himself onto a stack of crates. He propped one knee over the other and balanced the notepad on his thigh.

"All right, Doctor Ma'am...," said Olga.

Eliza's lips settled into a slight grin. Salvatore Silvestri bestowed the endearing title Doctor Ma'am upon her.

"...decision time. First names or not?"

"I know, I know, but I'm still not sure. Eliza and Olga on a sign will reassure women they've found the right office," Eliza said.

Olga countered, "Yes, but if their husbands see the sign, will they pay our fees? Will they allow their wives to even make an appointment? Discretion may work in our favor."

From the shop floor, noises escalated as a symphony of scratches scraped against oak pieces, readying the slabs for chisels. The shop owner interrupted Eliza and Olga's discussion, "Ma'am, I'd like to get your order placed today if you want the sign by September 8th as we discussed. You also need to decide if you want the chain or spaces to screw it directly to the building's exterior wall."

"Can you remind me of the total costs?" Eliza asked.

"Four dollars for oak, and that includes ten letters. Five cents per letter after that, and fifty cents for the chain. The black lacquer paint is another fifty cents."

Eliza watched Olga tally and multiply in her head, her eyes raised to the ceiling as her head ticked with each silent summation.

"I still don't agree with the chain. Bolted onto the wall will make it much more difficult for a man to steal it. You know it happens. Men," Olga said, looking at the wood carver with an apologetic pause, "can't stand the competition for patient fees when it comes from a woman."

"But the sign, jutting out from the wall makes a statement, don't you think? Hello there, see us? We're here, open for business," said Eliza. "And, if we hang it high enough out of reach, it should be safe."

"What'll it be then?" the wood carver asked. "My spelling's not too good, so say each letter in order."

Eliza looked to Olga for a final confirmation. Olga nodded.

"Add the chain and pole. For the carving, it should read: E period, P period, E-D-W-A-R-D-S comma, M period D period on the first line. O period, P period, M-C-G-U-I-R-E comma, M period D period beneath."

"Not Shaw?" Olga said.

"No, I decided last night. My license is listed as Edwards. The Shaw name means nothing to me, nor my degree or training. If Harrison wants to throw a fit, let him."

"Got it," said the wood carver. He turned his pad around for them to check his transcription. "I've got to hand it to you, ladies. Sounds like you've thought through every detail. If you pay as much attention to your patients, I'm sure your business will thrive. What you're doing takes guts, and I'd like to help. I'll throw in the two MD's at no charge." He winked at them both and rose to head back into his shop. The office sign for Dr. Edwards and Dr. McGuire was due to deliver in eight days.

• • •

August drew to a close and summer vacations faded as quickly as the weather turned from stifling days to chillier evenings. On the last Saturday of the month, the Public Garden and Boston Common teemed with families, hoping to cram in final hours of pleasure before school and work ushered them inside. Eliza and her sons spread the plaid wool picnic blanket out to claim their square of grass among the other families. Will espied a stick ball game and dashed off before Eliza could impart all her instructions. "Stay with that group right there where I can watch." Will waved his hand over his shoulder, his other clamped his cap tight on his head. *Seven years old, going on seventeen*, thought Eliza.

Teddy left the blanket, crawling across the lush lawn. With his head focused on the greenery beneath him, he looked like a bloodhound, plodding on a methodical hunt. "Teddy, what are you looking for, sweetie?" asked Eliza.

"I wanna find a four-leaf clover. They're supposed to be good luck. That's what Bessie told me Bridget says."

"I've heard that, too. From an old friend who's Irish, just like Bridget. Let me know if you find one."

Eliza drew her legs to her side and leaned on one hand, watching Teddy continue his scour of grass, weeds, and clover. Her mind left Boston and disembarked on the shores of Ireland. *Patrick,* she sighed to herself. Callous and impulsive. That's what she'd been when she nudged Patrick's handkerchief off the Cliff Walk in Newport. She should have at least tried to send it back to him, wherever that may be now. Shaking memories from her mind, she glanced back to check on Will. He stood at third base. Seeing her attention, he waved again in victory. She held her hands high for him to see her clapping.

"Woo-hoo!" Teddy plucked a stem from the dirt and held his success over his head.

"You didn't?" Eliza called.

"I did! Look!" Teddy stood, his knees grass-stained, his socks down at his ankles. He rushed over to her and opened her hand, laying his prize on her palm. "It's for you, Mommy. I want you to have good luck in your new job."

Eliza tousled his russet hair. "Oh, Teddy dear, thank you." With her index finger, she lightly traced the four leaves. She would focus on the good luck symbol from Ireland, not the wilted love bound up in an embroidered handkerchief, drifting aimlessly on the sea.

After church the next day, Eliza stopped by Olga's apartment at 41 Irving Street, on the back side of Beacon Hill. Olga left a week ago for a visit with her sister in Philadelphia, leaving Eliza in charge of final furniture arrangements to transform Olga's front sitting room and smaller, second bedroom into their office and examination room. Throughout the summer, Eliza and Olga handpicked each furniture piece. Unlike most sterile atmospheres, the office of Edwards and McGuire promised comfort and care. Putting patients at ease would help in building a relationship from the first appointment.

Floral paintings in yellows, blues, and pinks by the artist Florence Pearson decorated the walls. Interspersed with the paintings, a charcoal of a curved hand, singular and stark, invited visitors to enter and take a seat. Florence gave Eliza the drawing by her student, Kahlil Gibran, to celebrate the practice's opening. Bessie contributed her own gift to complement the drawing. After practicing calligraphy for hours, she copied a phrase from a collection of poems Kahlil was working on and shared with Florence:

Say not, 'I have found the path of the soul.'

Say rather, 'I have met the soul walking upon my path.'

For the soul walks not upon a line, neither does it grow like a reed.

The soul unfolds itself, like a lotus of countless petals.

Two framed proclamations bracketed the charcoal drawing, declaring the graduation and accreditation of Eliza Pearson Edwards and Olga Povitzky from the Woman's Medical College of Pennsylvania, May 19, 1901. On a low bookcase, Eliza shelved an assortment of children's books from her own library, including her well-worn *Alice's Adventures in Wonderland*, and a few from her sons' *Animal Stories* collection by Thornton Burgess. They would entertain children who accompanied their mothers. Eliza purchased the polished mahogany book stand from an antique shop on Charles Street. On an angle in the room's corner, it stood four feet high to offer easy access to the book displayed on its slanted top. Her brothers commissioned a bronze plate, which Freddy screwed into the front edge of the stand. Inscribed with the words, *Until the day's dawn, and the shadows flee away*, from Song of Solomon 2:17, it replicated the dedication in her grandfather's copy of *Gray's Anatomy*.

When she wasn't looking up information, Eliza kept *Gray's* open to Chapter 17 where she first discovered the details of a female system. From those pages, she took bold steps upon an unknown path, searching for a light within the shadows. She found her guiding beam one morning in October 1897, when she summoned her intellect, abilities, and empathy to cross over the threshold of Room 204 at Women's Med. There she met the good-humored, engaging Olga Povitzky, an endless spring of light in her life...and Dr. Patrick Callaghan, a shining star in her sky.

Albie and Freddy carried her grandfather's desk up the flight of stone steps and positioned it between the windows. In neat stacks on the desk, Eliza arranged prescription sheets and a receipt pad of Medical Services Rendered, awaiting patients' details and figures. She opened her black bag to retrieve her grandfather's pen and Daniel Dangerfield's letter opener and placed them in the grooved holder of the desk's middle drawer. *Guidance of others.* No matter who they were, no matter their circumstances, Eliza would continue the mission she began at this same desk twenty-three years ago when she posed a question to Aunt Florence. *Could there be more in her life?*

From the bag, she also pulled out a letter from nearby Massachusetts General Hospital denying admitting privileges for the private practice of Edwards and McGuire. This morning's scripture reading rang true to her fury over receiving the letter, *Prove me, O LORD, and try me, test my heart and mind*, from Psalm 26:2. The administration at Mass General tested her and

Olga to no end. Yet, the women's vindication would be unwavering. Eliza would set the Hospital straight as to why their degrees and experience were worthy of admitting privileges. She'd already written the appeal in her head, but still might need to evoke her grandfather's tacit diplomacy and Florence's calls for women's rights when she picked up her pen.

• • •

A scramble of footsteps clambered down the stairs. Will bent his knees, crouched low, spread his arms before him, and launched himself over the last three steps. He landed on the rug runner and slid into the wall. Unfazed by an encounter with hard plaster, he yelled to his brother who remained at the top, "Let's go, Teddy! C'mon!"

Teddy trudged down behind Will, dragging his stuffed dog by one leg. The seam attaching the dog's ear to its head sported seven different colored threads. Laura never found the right shade of brown to match the original stitching of her grandson's beloved friend. She stopped looking, deciding a rainbow of color gave the worn dog added whimsy. Since her death, Teddy rubbed the threads saying, "Granny did this."

"Aw shucks, you can't bring Woofie with you. You'll look like a baby. I don't want a baby walking with me to school," implored Will.

"I don't wanna go to school. Can't I stay home and go to story hour with Auntie Florence?" Teddy whimpered.

Eliza waited at the base of the staircase. Her doctor's bag, its leather cracked and worn, sat on the chair by the door. "School will be fun," she said. "Come now, Mommy's got to get to work. Leave Woofie on the chair. Look, I'll turn it around so he can watch out the window for you. Florence will keep an eye on him. After school, she'll take you both to the library."

She reached for Teddy's hand as he positioned the dog onto the chair. "I wish Daddy was here," he said.

Eliza gently squeezed his hand. "We'll write Daddy a letter tonight. Maybe you'd like to color a picture of a sailboat for him? You could use lots of blue, lighter for the sky, and mix in a touch of green for the ocean. Daddy will think of your blue eyes and an outing with you on the Charles River. Okay?"

"Okay. Do you have your four-leaf clover, Mommy?"

"Yes, I do. Right here." Eliza patted her left chest. She would keep Teddy's best wishes for her, and the luck of the Irish, pressed close to her heart in the tucked spot inside her brassiere where Patrick Callaghan wanted to place one. Her tap on the tip of Teddy's pug nose with her index finger came from rote memory of when Florence had done the same with her. Teddy smiled up at her and dropped her hand, racing ahead to catch up to Will.

•　　•　　•

Eliza set her bag down on the sidewalk and gazed up at the gleaming black sign, swinging gently on a metal rod over the entranceway to 41 Irving Street. The lettering, E. P. Edwards, M.D. and O. P. McGuire, M.D., may not say Eliza Pearson to those that passed by, but Eliza knew its meaning and purpose.

"Are you thinking of going in?" A woman's voice hovered over Eliza's shoulder.

Eliza turned to find a woman in her mid-thirties standing next to her. The woman wore a calf-length, black skirt, and camel colored jacket, trimmed with black piping. Eliza noted the loose, wide sash that didn't hide a bloated waist. The woman gestured to the swaying sign.

"I hope this is the right office," the woman said, "I'm looking for Doctor Eliza Edwards. Bea Edwards from my bridge group recommended her."

She dropped her voice as two men stepped into the street to pass them. "My monthlies are unbearable. I've tried to ignore them and certainly wouldn't discuss it with our family practitioner." A wince crossed over the woman's face. She moved her hand to the small of her back, massaging a spot with her fingertips. "I'm not sure who would be more uncomfortable with the conversation, me or him. I'd prefer to speak to a woman doctor. You too?"

Eliza's silent appraisal took only a moment. Over thirty. Bloated stomach, back pain, difficult menstruation. Fibroids, most likely.

"I know exactly how you feel. In fact, I am Dr. Edwards." Her voice carried from deep within, confident and comforting as she extended her hand to the woman. "I'm sure I can help. Why don't we step inside for a private discussion?"

At the top of the stairs, Eliza inserted the brass skeleton key into the keyhole. She heard a click and felt the metal cogs align into a mesh of certainty. Glancing over her shoulder, she crossed the threshold and beckoned the patient to follow her in.

THE END

AUTHOR'S NOTE

Inspired by a love of social history, the time of my grandparents' lives has always fascinated me, especially my paternal grandmother who lived from 1879 to 1957. Think of the global events she witnessed as a young woman: the dawn of a new century, a World War, the *Titanic* and *Lusitania* sinkings, an influenza pandemic, and ratification of the 19th Amendment. From these events, I formed the initial storyline for Eliza. With a desire to learn more about Elizabeth Peirce Elliott Robinson, who died before my birth, I fell into the rabbit hole of genealogy research. I knew from off-handed remarks that her grandfather was a Judge Peirce in Philadelphia and the family hailed from the city's society circles. Unfortunately, I never asked my father questions before he passed to learn more. How and why did my grandmother move from Philadelphia to the Boston area? Why did she not marry until she was thirty-two? (An advanced age for a first-time bride in 1912.) Why did she endure a twenty-year separation and refuse to divorce my grandfather until her sons graduated from college? Having no answers, I created them instead.

Two nuggets about Judge William Shannon Peirce propelled me forward. From *Rittenhouse Square, Past and Present*, Charles J. Cohen wrote of his friendship with Judge Peirce, noting: *He would take great delight in discussing various phrases of the Old Testament with which he was very familiar. His daughters were women of character and intellectual attainments.* In fact, according to census reports and the family plot in Laurel Hill Cemetery, Philadelphia, I pieced together the Judge and his wife, Elizabeth, had seven daughters and one son who lived to adulthood. One daughter was named Florence. And, while still to be confirmed, I sourced a Florence Peirce, who while working at Denison House, discovered Kahlil Gibran's drawing talent. The unusual name, the spelling of Peirce, and years aligned to make it possible that Florence was one of the Judge's daughters.

The second piece of information comes from *FamousAmericans.net*. Most of the entry discusses Judge Peirce as an advocate of emancipation. As co-counsel with the Anti-Slave Society, he defended Daniel Dangerfield, a runaway slave from Virginia, who, although found not guilty and set free, fled to Canada through the Underground Railroad. Given my graduation from an all-women's college, the last line of the entry, however, ignited the spark for my story: *He took an active part in founding the Woman's Medical College in Philadelphia.* A young woman surrounded and influenced by a widowed mother and maiden aunts of high intellect and character, and a grandfather who embraced equal rights, would embark on a journey to become a New Woman of the early 1900s.

Eliza and Edith are composite characters created from diaries, letters, and reference materials I accessed through Drexel University College of Medicine's archives. The Woman's Medical College (WMC) of Pennsylvania was the first accredited medical school in the country for women, established in 1850, and the last to remain open as an all-women's institution until it admitted a few men in 1970 and changed its name to the Medical College of Pennsylvania (MCP). In 2001, Drexel purchased MCP but ran it as a separate non-profit corporation until it finally merged completely into the Drexel University system in 2014.

I am forever grateful to Matt Herbison for assembling a cart teeming with materials from the late 1890s and early 1900s for my research during the day I spent buried in Drexel's archives, including grade reports, expenses, a Bone Box, and the leather-bound journals of the Board of Trustees' meeting minutes from 1852-1855, inked and signed by William S. Peirce, Esq., Secretary.

Many readers may find it unbelievable Eliza could enter Woman's Med. straight from high school. The entrance requirements, however, until the 1890s admitted eighteen-year-olds who provided recommendations and passed the arduous Entrance Exam. Since I could not find the exact year the admittance rule changed to requiring an undergraduate degree, I allowed Eliza to enter in 1897.

I based three characters on real graduates of Woman's Med. One of the first search returns for WMC is the story of Anandibai Gopal Joshi. When I read her application letter, I knew these women's stories needed to be told. I took some author license to place Anandi at WMC in 1897 to align with my timeline, instead of 1886, when she graduated. Her tragic story is true. I also adjusted the graduation of Charlotte Fairbanks, M.D. from 1902 to 1901. Her remarkable educational achievements included degrees from Smith, Yale, and Bryn Mawr before attending WMC. She joined a team of women doctors who went to France as part of the American Women's Hospital, eventually named surgeon in charge and received the Medal Reconnaissance from the French government and awarded French citizenship. While she did not work at the Women's Prison, other WMC graduates did and reported similar experiences to those I assigned to Charlotte. Olga Povitzky, M.D. emigrated from Marijampole, Russia (Lithuania) and graduated in 1901. The phrase about the Darwin lecture and monkey business is attributed to her. Hence her spunky character. She did not return to Russia, but remained in the US, working for the NYC Department of Health for forty-one years, also served with the Women's Overseas Hospitals, and was active in the suffrage movement. She designed a culture bottle which Salk later used while developing the polio vaccine.

I tried to stay authentic to the novel's setting, including terms and references which would be unacceptable today–Negress, wop and the use of the term, mongolism. Down syndrome became standard terminology in 1965. The horrors and abuses detailed about the Elwyn Training School are true. I lifted Dean Marshall's introductory address identifying women as a slave to society from one of her speeches. I based the facial surgery scene and the WMC students' reactions from the experiences of Dr. Mary Bennett Ritter as documented in her autobiography, *More Than Gold in California*. The newspaper headlines and articles I used are verbatim, thanks to the indispensable resource for a historical fiction writer: *NewspaperArchives.com*.

The *Unlocked Path* is a work of fiction, although through extensive research, I hope I've created a story which educates and offers glimpses into the lives of the pioneering women who entered the medical profession when only five percent of doctors were women. They paved the path, brick by brick, for all who followed. We, their patients, are thankful for the doctors today who approach their practice with a careful application of sympathy and science.

- Janis Robinson Daly, August 25, 2022

READING GROUP GUIDE

1. The Female Medical College of Pennsylvania opened in 1850 (changed to Woman's Medical in 1867) to become the first medical school to award accredited degrees to women. Over the next forty years, the Seven Sisters schools (Mount Holyoke, Wellesley, Bryn Mawr, Barnard, Smith, Vassar, Radcliffe) and many other colleges opened their doors to provide women with access to higher learning. By the 1960s there were 281 women's colleges. Because of societal and financial demands, by 2018, most had closed their doors or merged into co-educational institutions. The Woman's Medical College (WMC) merged with Drexel University in 2001. Today, approximately thirty-one active women's colleges remain. Are single-sex schools still relevant today? What can women gain from a woman-exclusive learning experience?

2. When Eliza and her classmates graduated from WMC in 1901, only five percent of doctors were female. Nearly 120 years later, women comprise 36% of all U.S. physicians with an expectation that number will continue to rise as 2019 marked the first time the majority of U.S. medical school students (50.5%) were women.[1] In Pediatrics and OB/GYN, the numbers of women surpass men. Beyond those traditionally female fields, have you been treated by a woman physician? For women readers, do you seek a woman physician?

3. Eliza's Aunt Maria claims male doctors could never understand her motherly grief. Laura Edwards, Eliza's

mother, admits her modesty of baring her breasts to a man other than her husband postponed a breast examination. Teenage mother, Adrienne, declares she won't have a man (Dr. Callaghan) care for her while in labor and exposure of her private parts to his eyes. At WMC, Eliza and her classmates trained within the frameworks of sympathy and science. Do women bring a more sympathetic approach to medical practice, regardless of the field? If you have been attended to by doctors of both genders, have you found a difference in their bedside manner?

4. From *Gray's Anatomy* to *Alice in Wonderland* to *The Awakening*, books and their stories influence Eliza's journey. Are there books from your childhood which informed your decisions in life or that you turn to for comfort?

5. Eliza and Florence share special times, reading *Alice in Wonderland*. Eliza wishes to instill a love of shared reading with her patients, starting by giving books to Salvatore Silvestri. Do you have a memory of someone reading to you? Which children's book is your go-to as a favorite to read with children or gift to them?

6. Inspired by her Aunt Florence, Eliza marches forward into the 20th Century as a New Woman. She embraces her need for independence and self-fulfillment. By attending medical college and pursuing her profession as a doctor, she challenges the feminine ideal of the times. The concept of a New Woman first appeared in Henrik Ibsen's 1879 stage production of *The Dollhouse*, where the main character, Nora, asserts: "I must first try to educate myself. In that you are not the man to help me. I must set to work alone...I must try to gain experience...I must be thrown entirely

upon myself if I am to come to an understanding as to what I am and what the things around me are." In 2017, the Fearless Girl statue appeared on Wall Street as a symbol to empower women to speak up and strive for justice and equality in boardrooms. Since then, women expanded its meaning to include resilience, self-confidence, and hope for change. How is a New Woman of the early 20th Century and Fearless Girl of the early 21st Century the same in their concepts? How are they different? How far have women come in the past one hundred years in advancements for independence and self-fulfillment?

7. The author chose a span of twenty-three years for the novel's setting. Her grandparents, who were born in the late 1800s and passed as late as 1989, lived through an incredible period of history, including the early years of their life, 1897-1920. The invention of the telephone and automobile crept into the households of the masses. War sent them, their brothers, and husbands overseas to fight for world democracy. Suffragists won their battle for the passage of the 19th Amendment. A global pandemic descended on their families, stole lives and instilled fear of the unknown menace of germs. The *Titanic* sank, shattering beliefs the mighty and strong were unsinkable. Did you learn anything new about this time period?

8. Identify a slice of twenty-three years in your life, your parents', or grandparents'. What were the significant inventions and global events of that slice of history?

9. Eliza and her friends lament the existence of the Comstock Laws, which prohibited the dissemination of birth control. The laws denied access to any form of birth control, including to married women who needed their husband's

consent to secure a device for therapeutic needs. Eliza asserts, "Does anyone think for a minute, if women could vote, the Comstock Laws would exist? Those politicians would have gotten an earful from thousands of women, each with the power to unseat them from their chair in Congress." Today, women can vote, can run for and secure seats in Congress, and serve on the Supreme Court. Yet, discussions about women's rights for choice continue. What can we learn from the past on this issue to guide thoughtful current discussions?

10. Meeting Anandi and reading her application letter moves Eliza and motivates her decision to attend medical college. Anandi's words also launched the author's further research into WMC and directed the writing of *The Unlocked Path*. Is there one person, or one piece of writing, that impacted and directed your career and subsequent life choice?

[1] *Nation's physician workforce evolves.* Association of American Medical Colleges, 2019.

ACKNOWLEDGEMENTS

As a debut author, I have so many friends, family members and associates who helped my dream of writing a novel come true. First, to my Wheaton sisters. You embody the meaning of college friends forever. With you, I know I'm not alone. You are my Wolfpack. To my writing mentor and award-winning author, Ashley Sweeney, Wheaton '79, thank you for choosing me to pay-it-forward, helping a sister navigate the demands of writing, editing, and publishing. I am awed by your kindness and mastery of this craft called writing.

To my editors. For reading my disastrous first draft, thank you to my brother, Mark Robinson. You attacked that tedious version, one glass of wine at a time, and used the red pens I gave you without hesitation. Ellen Notbohm, thank you, thank you. You challenged me to further probe Eliza's motivations and emotional responses, while identifying plot holes which needed filling, and pointing out historical inaccuracies. Thanks to another Wheaton grad, Lisa Goodrich, '89, for final copy-editing and your encouraging words as you completed each section. And, to make sure every (I hope!) stubborn typo disappeared, thank you to the keen proofreading eye of Susan Phillips.

Beta readers Susan, Barb, Bonnie, Karyn, and Mariellen. What can I say? Your feedback directed my deletions and emphasized spots to enhance as I embarked on this journey. Dennis, Chelsa, Jeff, Ted, and Karen–I am so fortunate to have met you through writing conferences and groups. As other aspiring authors, you understand the need for honest, critical feedback. I wish you all the best and hope I can return the favor. Judge Dennis Blackmon and Dr. Theodore Spevack, I also appreciate your professional expertise in reviewing the courtroom scene and the medical descriptions.

A very special thanks to Eliza Lo Chin, M.D., Executive Director of the American Medical Women's Association (AMWA), who offered to read and critique as a woman in the medical profession. The AMWA, formerly known as the Medical Women's National Association, is referenced with Charlotte's involvement with the American Women's Hospital. To write a novel with no medical background, Dr. Chin's review ensured my medical scenes were correct and Eliza's actions and reactions were in character. Dr. Chin also connected me with Mollie Marr to read with her professional eye as a behavioral neuroscience student and co-producer of AMWA's film, *At Home and Over There: American Women Physicians in World War I* available at www.amwa-doc.org. For the women in medicine now, I follow many of you through #womeninmedicine on Instagram. Thank you to those who granted permission for me to mold your sentiments into emotional responses for Eliza.

Also, on social media, thank you to my followers. You patiently reacted to my posts for years, waiting for publication news. And, to those who assisted as my Little Free Libraries elves—thank you for spreading my name recognition before pages ever hit a printing press. Hopefully, I am giving you a book you can recommend to others.

To the groups and associations which have supported me every step. The members of NCL BookEnds, my book club of over twenty years, who inquire at every meeting "What's up with Eliza?" From offbeat book selections—hello Zane!—to some of my unusual, book themed appetizers, you've always been my guinea pigs. For the talented members of the Women's Fiction Writers Association, thank you to fellow workshop participants and discussion groups where we learn from each other and provide resources to improve our craft. For the esteemed historical fiction authors who took the time from their incredibly busy schedules to read a debut novelist's manuscript and provide a blurb, thank you from the bottom of my heart. Your endorsement means the world to me: Tracy Enerson Wood, Juliette Fay, Sally Cabot Gunning, and Kerry Chaput. I love your books; I'm honored you like mine.

To Reagan Rothe and Black Rose Writing, thank you for believing Eliza's story warranted a five-star rating, and needed to venture out into the world of readers. Darcie Rowan, your enthusiasm for *The Unlocked Path* lifted me from uncertainty to confidence that together we would do great things. We would, we are, and we will.

Finally, to my family. For my grandfather, Eliot H. Robinson, Sr., a Renaissance Man–lawyer, painter, tennis player, secretary to a congressman, author, and ambulance driver. Another grandparent I never knew, but through whom I hope I inherited a flair at least for literary accomplishments, including his ghost-writing *Go Get 'Em* for flying ace, William Wellman. Family lore tells *Wings*, produced by Wellman and the winner of the first Academy Award for Best Picture in 1927/1928, was adapted from *Go Get 'Em*. If anyone wants to turn *The Unlocked Path* into a film or mini-series, please contact me.

Thanks to an Ancestry DNA test, I reconnected with my first cousin, Carolyn "Robin" Robinson Griswold. I am forever grateful Carolyn put aside whatever differences our estranged fathers had and warmly welcomed me to her home for a visit. She recalled spending time as a young girl with "Nana," going to Brigham's. Even more touching was when Carolyn shared family photos, along with a few other items. The most endearing item brought me to tears, a birthday note our grandfather wrote to my dad. I replicated that note, word-for-word when Harrison writes to Teddy. It's clearly written by an absent father who missed and loved his son. The inspiration for Salvatore Silvestri comes from Carolyn's half-brother and my cousin, Frankie, who was born with Down syndrome. I never knew Frankie. I wish I had.

Most of all, thank you to the men in my life. Each of them has supported me on this path during years and years of writing, editing, and seeking publication. My other brother, John, and my sons, Peirce and Brendan, you feign interest in women's historical fiction, and unprompted, always ask how the story's going. And for Jim. My best friend for forty-one years. You never complained when I woke you at 3 a.m. when I needed to jot down an idea. You encouraged me to go away for solo fact-finding research and writing weekends. You binged through Netflix and Hulu series alone while I wrote. And you gave me one of the most thoughtful gifts ever, noise-canceling headphones, so I could write in the next room while you watched war movies and laughed at videos on Barstool Sports. You always make me laugh. I love you.

RESOURCES

For more information on the Woman's Medical College of Pennsylvania and early women in medicine, I recommend:

A New and Untried Course, Steven Peitzman, M.D.

"Send Us a Lady Physician" Women Doctors in America 1835-1920, edited by Ruth J. Abram

Women Physicians in American Medicine, Regina Markell Morantz-Sanchez

Restoring the Balance: Women Physicians and the Profession of Medicine, 1850-1995, Ellen S. Moore

Out of the Dead House–Nineteenth Century Women Physicians and the Writing of Medicine, Susan Wells

The PBS original documentary:
https://www.pbs.org/video/daring-women-doctors-physicians-in-the-19th-century-vcbv7v/

American Medical Women's Association's exhibitions:
https://www.amwa-doc.org/wwi-exhibition/

Other invaluable resources and inspiration:

The Awakening, Kate Chopin
The Prophet, Kahlil Gibran
Alice's Adventures in Wonderland, Lewis Carroll

The Worst of Times–Illegal Abortion, Patricia C. Miller

Back Rooms, An Oral History of the Illegal Abortion Era, Ellen Messer and Kathryn E. May, PYS.D.

Well-Behaved Women Seldom Make History, Laurel Thatcher Ulrich

Family Limitations, Margaret Sanger

Massachusetts in the Woman Suffrage Movement, Barbara F. Berenson

The PBS original documentary:
https://www.pbs.org/wgbh/americaneexperience/films/influenza

ABOUT THE AUTHOR

Intrigued by the discovery that an ancestor was a founder of the Woman's Medical College of Pennsylvania, Janis Robinson Daly found her next career direction: unearthing the stories of women whose lives have remained in the shadows. Her debut novel, *The Unlocked Path*, balances authenticity and rich historical detail with deep emotional connections to create engaging fictional characters. A graduate of Wheaton College, MA, with a B.A. in Psychology, Daly explores female-centric issues and the power of supportive relationships developed among women. Daly, her husband, and rescue pup reside in Massachusetts on Cape Cod.

To learn more about Janis Robinson Daly, including her reviews of historical fiction, book club tips, and information on other forthcoming novels, connect with her at www.janisrdaly.com or scan the QR code below.

NOTE FROM THE AUTHOR

If you enjoyed *The Unlocked Path*, I would greatly appreciate it if you would post an online review. Even a starred rating and a quick sentence or two helps other readers discover my work.

Thank you!
Janis Robinson Daly

We hope you enjoyed reading this title from:

Subscribe to our mailing list – *The Rosevine* – and receive **FREE** books, daily deals, and stay current with news about upcoming
releases and our hottest authors.
Scan the QR code below to sign up.

Already a subscriber? Please accept a sincere thank you for being a fan of Black Rose Writing authors.

View other Black Rose Writing titles at
and use promo code
PRINT to receive a **20% discount** when purchasing.

CPSIA information can be obtained
at www.ICGtesting.com
Printed in the USA
BVHW070935160822
644715BV00006B/177